NOTHING ELSE
REMAINS

By Robert Scragg

What Falls Between the Cracks
Nothing Else Remains
All That is Buried

NOTHING ELSE
REMAINS

ROBERT SCRAGG

Allison & Busby Limited
11 Wardour Mews
London W1F 8AN
allisonandbusby.com

First published in Great Britain by Allison & Busby in 2019.
This paperback edition published by Allison & Busby in 2019.

A CIP catalogue record for this book is available from
the British Library.

10 9 8 7 6 5 4 3 2 1

ISBN 978-0-7490-2319-5

Typeset in 10.5/15.5 pt Adobe Garamond Pro by
Allison & Busby Ltd

The paper used for this Allison & Busby publication
has been produced from trees that have been legally sourced
from well-managed and credibly certified forests.

Printed and bound by
CPI Group (UK) Ltd, Croydon, CR0 4YY

To my wife Nicola,
for making me want to be a better man

CHAPTER ONE

He walked into the bank like he owned the place, past the queuing mums, pushchairs weighted down with shopping bags, the suits checking their watches, counting down lunch hours. Over to the personal banking desk, matching the man behind it smile for smile. Fresh out of college by the looks of it. Early twenties at a push. Hair scraped back from a shiny forehead, and last traces of acne like a faded join-the-dots. Daniel, according to his name badge.

He slid a passport and bank card across the desk, batted back small talk where he could. He could actually pinpoint the moment that Daniel clocked the balance in his account, eyes popping with a mix of surprise and envy. Fended off the valiant attempt to book him an appointment with one of their investment bankers.

He could practically smell the sweaty palms that pushed the signature slip his way. He scrawled his name across the dotted line, slid it across, and leant back in his chair.

'Anything else you need from me?'

'No, Mr Jackson, that should do it,' said Daniel.

Gordon Jackson scraped back his chair, retreated before Daniel could offer a clammy handshake, exited through the main door and out onto George Lane. The glare of the sun hit him like a paparazzo's flash, and he winced as he crossed the road, popping his top button and wiggling the knot of his tie down an inch. Summer had been late coming to London this year, but it meant business.

Quick push of the key fob in his pocket, and the lights winked on a Volvo parked opposite the branch. He slipped a laptop case out from under the passenger seat, fingers dancing over the keys, connecting to the weak Wi-Fi from a next-door Costa Coffee. One username and password later, he allowed himself a brief smile as he saw the balance in the account. A dozen keystrokes later, and it was off through the ether to a new home.

He powered down the laptop, stashed it back under the seat. Took out his wallet, removing the cards one by one. Driver's licence, MasterCard, Visa. Dropped them into a plastic sandwich bag, to be burnt when he got back to the house. And just like that, Gordon Jackson ceased to exist. The man left in his place checked his mirrors, signalled to pull out, and disappeared into the midday traffic.

Careful. Always careful.

Max Brennan peered at his watch for what felt like the twentieth time in as many minutes, eyes following the lazy sweep of the second hand. Almost an hour late. No call. No message. He checked his phone again. Nothing. No sooner had he put it back on the table, it started to vibrate, creeping towards his coffee cup.

He snatched at it, feeling guilty at the disappointment he felt when he saw Jen's name, not his dad's.

'Hey babe, how did it go?'

'Could have been better,' he said.

'You didn't end up arguing, did you?'

'Not yet, but there's a pretty good chance we will if he ever turns up. To hell with him, I'm coming back. See you when I get home.'

Max clicked to end the call, then instantly felt bad for taking it out on Jen. He fired off an apologetic 'Sorry for being snappy' text, adding an extra 'x' on the end for good measure. It wasn't the waitress's fault his dad hadn't showed either, and he dropped a handful of coins in the tip jar on his way out. *Screw him, his loss.* Disappointment turned to frustration, frustration to anger. He'd been stood up by a few girls before, but never by a parent, and decided on a new destination before he even reached the car.

He slid into his Audi, cursing under his breath as his knee cracked against the steering column. It was half an hour's drive to his dad's street from here. Max made it in just shy of twenty-three minutes, running two debatable amber lights, and incurring the wrath of an old lady in a white Nissan that he'd cut off, who shocked him with her impressive arsenal of hand gestures. Woodside was as suburban as its name suggested. No 'Street' or 'Avenue' tagged on the end; just the one name, like the Adele or Madonna of town planning. Trees lined both sides of the road like a guard of honour. Canopies of green, flecked with the first burnt orange of autumn. A stone's throw away from Woodford Golf Club, all the houses were a variation on the same template; two-tone white cladding and exposed brick. The kind of street that made you feel underdressed when you came to visit.

Max rang the bell, following up with a knock even before the chimes had faded away. He could feel his fuse burning shorter with every second. No sign of life. He knocked again, leaning over to peer through the front window.

'If you're looking for Gordon, you're two days too late.'

Max spun around to see an elderly man in a white cotton shirt and dark green corduroy trousers, shuffling along the path of the house next door.

'What do you mean, two days too late?'

'He was here on Wednesday morning. Least I'm pretty sure it was him, loading boxes into a car, and he's not been back since. I'm assuming he's moved, although I never saw a for sale sign. Didn't really know him well enough to ask, mind you.'

'He sold his house?'

'Either that, or he's just had one hell of a big clear-out.' The old man wheezed a dry laugh at his own joke. 'Sorry, I'm just kidding around, but yes, I'm pretty sure he has. Saw a young lady here twice last week, driving a car with some logo plastered on the side. Beacon something or other.'

'Beacon Estates?'

Max had seen their slogan plastered on billboards and winced at their cheesy radio ads, promising to sell your property in record time, or you don't pay a penny.

'They're the ones,' said the old man, his smile making a web of creases spread outwards from his mouth, like ripples in a pond. 'And I'm sorry, how rude of me. I'm Gerry. Gerry Whyte. And you are?'

'I'm Max. Brennan.'

'You and Gordon work together, or are you just a friend?'

Max let out a big sigh, like a balloon deflating. 'I'm his son.'

'His son?' said Whyte, bushy eyebrows bouncing up like caterpillars on a trampoline. 'I didn't even know he had any family.'

'Funny,' said Max, 'neither did he till three weeks ago.'

Jake Porter loved his job, or at least the ten per cent of it that felt like it made a difference; the buzz of making an arrest, of breaking a suspect's crappy alibi into pieces. The rest of it had far too much paperwork and waiting around for things to happen for his liking. That was the part they never showed you in *CSI* or *Line of Duty* type dramas on TV. The last three hours of his life fell into this latter category.

Andrew Patchett had disappeared into the Holiday Inn at Wembley Park almost three hours ago, according to a tip-off. The barman confirmed he'd served him around that time, and that he'd had a young lady with him. Porter scanned the rows of windows, wondering which one Patchett might be looking out of. It wasn't the prettiest of hotels and, without the green Holiday Inn branding, could have been just another high rise in any inner city. The seventies had a lot to answer for when it came to architecture.

Patchett was the last man standing of any significance in a corrupt organisation Porter had brought to its knees earlier in the year. It still stung Porter that the key figure behind it all, Alexander Locke, had been killed by a stray gunshot before he got a chance to arrest him. His second in command, a beast of a man called James Bolton, had met a similar fate. Not that Porter felt sorry for them. More that they'd never been called to account for their crimes. Patchett felt like a last chance to do something worthwhile. He'd been swept up in the arrests that followed Locke's death, but incredibly had managed to post bail thanks to an overpriced lawyer on retainer for Locke's company. He'd been released two days after Locke's death, and hadn't been seen since. Truth be told, the case against him was on the light side, mainly circumstantial. Patchett, being the fool that he was, turned to shooting his mouth off down his local that he was moving up in the world, filling the gap left by Locke and Bolton. Thankfully for Porter, his boasts about having some of his former employer's stash of drugs had been within earshot of Paddy Tiernan, a burnt-out ex-junkie who regularly played both sides, and called in with the tip. A search team hit a storage unit Patchett kept this morning and found three kilos of uncut cocaine. It was hardly on a par with Pacino in *Scarface,* but it was enough to bring him back in.

He heard a squeak of leather and turned to see Nick Styles bringing his knees up towards his chest, lacing fingers around the top of his shins. Porter winced at the quick-fire *crack-crack* when they popped. Even with the seat pushed back, Styles and his six-foot-four frame still looked cramped.

'You'll give yourself arthritis if you keep doing that,' Porter said, looking back towards the hotel entrance.

'Yeah, yeah, and chewing gum clogs up your insides, and the wind changing direction makes your face stay that way. Thanks, Dad.'

Even though they weren't that far apart age-wise, Porter only two years ahead at thirty-eight, he sometimes did feel like more of an adult. Styles had a comeback for everything, but he also knew when to switch from class clown to all business; most of the time anyway.

'Bet you don't give Emma as much backchat at home.'

Styles chuckled. 'She slaps me back down if I try. I store all mine up for you instead, boss.'

'Lucky me, eh?' said Porter.

He froze as the hotel door swished open, but relaxed again when an elderly couple shuffled out, arm in arm and stepping in sync like a three-legged race. A soft muted click told him Styles was checking the time on his phone again, and Porter resolved to give it another half hour tops. He might not have anyone apart from Demetrious the cat waiting at home, but Styles had Emma. He had a life to go back to.

'What if he's holed up here till tomorrow?' Styles asked.

'Don't worry, I'll let you get your beauty sleep. Half an hour and we'll call in reinforcements.'

'I'm not complaining, guv, I . . .'

'I know, I know. It's fine. I've got stuff to do as well,' he lied. A microwave dinner and an evening on the sofa was as exciting as it would get, but he didn't want Styles to feel obliged to hang around for a beer or, worse still, invite him to join him and Emma for dinner. Not that he wasn't grateful, and he did accept occasionally, but pride stopped him from saying yes every time. He was nobody's charity case. Not even Styles's.

Porter screwed his eyes closed. Felt the low bass drum of a headache starting to beat. What he'd give for eight hours' solid sleep. There was a time when he had to be forcibly evicted from bed on his days off. That was before it all happened. Before he lost Holly. Correction – not lost, she was forcibly taken from him. Nowadays he was content to call four hours a success. He dug his thumb and forefinger into the corners of his eyes, rubbing small circles. Trying and failing to massage away the gritty feeling, like grains of sand trapped under his lids.

'Here we go.'

Porter snapped his eyes open again, blinking away the fireflies, to see Andrew Patchett scurrying out of the hotel. Patchett stopped a few yards away and looked around, head tilted up a touch, as if he was sniffing the air. He seemed satisfied that nobody was waiting for him, and looked down at his own jacket, patting at his pockets. Porter didn't wait around to what he was looking for. He and Styles were out of their car and had covered half of the hundred or so yards to the entrance before Patchett looked up again.

'All units move in.' Porter spoke in a low voice so as not to alert Patchett that the net was closing.

Patchett was a runner by nature. He'd run when they'd taken down Locke and his crew, or had tried to anyway. Porter was ready for him to try the same again. Two officers in the hotel bar, posing as a couple, were coming up behind Patchett now. Another pair were just rounding the corner of the hotel in case he bolted for the safety of the shopping outlet. Patchett saw Porter, recognition in his exaggerated smile. He shot a quick glance left and right, then whirled around, back into the hotel, nearly colliding with the officer behind him.

Patchett lifted both arms, waving his hands at no one in particular.

'Surrender, or jazz hands. You decide,' he said, with somewhere between a smile and a snarl.

'You're a regular laugh a minute,' said Porter, clocking the pair of officers who'd come from around the corner to help pen Patchett in. 'Next stop *Britain's Got Talent*!'

'Officer Porter, what a coincidence, I was just coming to turn myself in.'

Porter didn't bother to correct him on the rank. No sense rising to the bait. Give men like Patchett the slightest sense that you were niggled, they'd press it home. Patchett was forty-five but looked at least ten years older. Bald, with lines etched into his face, giving him a mouth that looked like it was on hinges, and he had the type

14

of rough edges to his voice that only years of dedicated smoking can create.

'Thought we'd save you the bus fare,' said Porter. 'Found your little nest egg this morning, Andrew.'

The smile stayed on Patchett's face, and his tone was light enough, but Porter saw the hate in his eyes. 'Don't know what you mean, Officer.'

'Right you are, mate,' said Porter, the last word spat out with as much sarcasm as he could muster.

'Wouldn't want to be your mate, Officer Porter. Saw what happens to your mates, like that pretty lady.' Patchett pretended to shudder. 'Heard she's still getting wheeled around.'

The lady in question was Detective Sergeant Eve Simmons. She'd had her head slammed against a wall by James Bolton and had come too close to not waking up for Porter's liking. Porter's fingers curled into fists but stayed by his side.

'It's Detective Inspector Porter, and you're under arrest, Mr Patchett, for breaching the terms of your bail.'

Porter nodded to the young constable behind Patchett, Gus Tessier, half-French, half-Ghanaian, and a tank of a man, who grabbed one wrist, then a second, snapping cuffs into place and reading Patchett his rights. Porter stepped closer, until he was only a few feet away.

'You should have turned over a new leaf while you had the chance, Patchett. Got a nice job in a pub, or a bookies.' Another step closer and he was only twelve inches from Patchett's face, albeit looking down at it thanks to a six-inch height advantage, but the smaller man just stared at him, looking mildly amused.

'Might apply to be the carer for that lady copper of yours. You know, wheel her around, empty the shit from her bag, that type

15

of thing. No telling how grateful she might be.' Patchett leant to the side, spitting on the ground, missing Porter's shoe by less than an inch.

Porter's hand shot up, grabbing Patchett, and Patchett's lips squished up like a kid pulling a funny face. Hands pulled at him from all sides, dragging him away, back towards the car park, his fingers rasping off Patchett's stubble as they slid off the smaller man's cheeks.

'Come on, guv.' Styles spoke low and urgent. 'He's not worth it.' Styles put an arm across Porter's back, steering him off to one side.

'You want to listen to your boy there. Wouldn't want to do anything you regret.'

Patchett's face split into an impossibly wide smile, flashing rows of greying teeth, and Porter knew he'd given Patchett exactly the reaction he was looking for. Porter's cheeks burnt as if he'd been sitting too close to a radiator, and he sucked in a deep breath, kicking himself for letting Patchett get under his skin.

The pair of officers behind Patchett grabbed an elbow each and marched him towards one of the unmarked vehicles waiting in the car park. Patchett twisted his head around to look at Porter as he passed.

'That's assault, strictly speaking, Officer. Might let you off with it. Might not. I'll let you know.'

'Looked like resisting arrest to me, guv,' said Tessier, steering Patchett at a fair rate of knots.

'Eh?' Patchett started to twist, doing his best to shrug Tessier's hand away, but the constable's fingers dug into Patchett's arm hard enough to make him gasp out loud. 'Watch it, lad. That's police brutality right there as well. Rotten to the core, the lot of ya. Gerroffme.'

Porter kicked out at a cigarette butt, shoe scraping against the tarmac. He shrugged Styles's hand away.

'It's OK. I'm fine.'

Styles said nothing, just raised both eyebrows and stared, waiting him out.

'I'm fine,' Porter said again, with a little more grit this time, feeling anything but. This was the first time he'd ever laid hands on a suspect like that, and it left a bad taste in his mouth. It's not like he'd hit the guy, but that wasn't the point. He'd let emotions cloud his judgement, and for what? It wasn't even as if there was anything between him and Simmons to get worked up about. There'd been a hint that something *could* happen, if he wanted it to. More than once as well. But each time, it had seemed like even thinking about being with someone else felt as good as cheating on Holly. Even now, more than two years after her death, she was everywhere. From the choice of colours on the walls of their flat, to the only two designer-label shirts in his entire wardrobe. She was still the screensaver on his mobile, for God's sake.

Sod it. Simmons was, is still, one of them, and that's as good as family. If you can't stick up for your family who can you stick up for?

'Shit.' Styles swore under his breath.

Porter looked at him, frowning. He realised Styles was looking beyond him, and he whipped his head around. Shit indeed. Two kids, teenagers by the looks of it, stood on the opposite side of Wembley Hill Road. They could have been clones of one another. Hoodies baggy enough to fit Snow White and all seven dwarves in, and jeans with the backside hanging down by their knees. Trainers so white they looked Tippexed.

Porter spotted what had caught Styles's eye. Teen One's mobile phone was held up at eye level, pointing straight at Porter. Teen

Two's shoulders jiggled, arms crossed, as he laughed at whatever crap joke his pal had just cracked. Porter trotted towards the road, but before he'd even reached the kerb, Teen One lowered his phone and headed off up the road towards Wembley Park Tube station, with Teen Two in tow.

'Whoa, hang on there, lads. Can I have a word?' Porter called after them.

'Yeah, bruv,' Teen One shouted over the noise of the traffic that zipped past from both directions. 'I got a word for you . . .' But his voice mingled with the growl of a bus engine.

Porter wasn't sure if he'd heard right. Styles was up by his shoulder now, and Porter turned to him.

'Did he just say I was trendy?'

'Trending,' said Styles. 'As in online.'

Porter closed his eyes and swore softly. Patchett. The kid had seen the lot. Recorded it as well. Worse still, in ten minutes, half of London would have seen it too. Porter toyed with dodging the traffic, chasing after them, asking them to take the clip down, but he couldn't exactly force them to, and they had a healthy head start already. He turned to Styles, putting on his best *who gives a shit* face.

'It's fine. I barely touched him anyway. What's the worst that can happen?'

The electric motor of the garage door grumbled until the edge met the floor with a solid *clunk*. The man who used to be Gordon Jackson climbed out of the red Renault Clio he now drove, having sold the Volvo to a local dealer for cash. He slung the strap of the laptop case across his chest, and went through the adjoining utility room, and out onto the back yard. His clothes were different, too;

suit swapped for faded jeans and a dark blue waterproof jacket. Hair that was once immaculate had been ruffled somewhere along the line, as if he'd been walking into a strong wind.

He unlocked the shed with a key from his pocket and closed the door carefully behind him. It was beyond tidy in there. White shapes on the walls outlined where every tool belonged, like a series of mini crime scenes. He laid the laptop case on the bench and knelt down, sliding a small stack of cardboard boxes out from under the work surface. He felt, rather than saw, the edge of a floorboard at the back, the length of his forearm, nails scratching at the edge as he eased it out. A second board followed, and he put his hand into the new gap, fingers running over the lumpy earth below like he was reading Braille. They closed around something that crinkled and he pulled out a plastic sandwich bag, empty except for a black USB stick.

The laptop whirred into life and he plugged the memory stick into the side. A few quick clicks later and the only file on it, an Excel workbook, opened up. One long column of numbers. He scanned through them, running through a list in his head long since committed to memory, and clicked on the numbers that corresponded to Gordon Jackson. Two more clicks and the cell changed from white to green, like all those above it. Ran the numbers in the next cell down against the list in his head for a new name: Harold Mayes.

The corners of his mouth twitched, a hint of a smile swimming to the surface then sinking without a trace. It only took him a minute to reset the scene. Memory stick, floorboards and boxes were slid back into place. He bounced to his feet, closing his eyes, taking in a deep breath as if filling his lungs would help bring his latest incarnation to life. He held for a three count, opened his eyes and nodded to himself. And with that, Harold Mayes strode out of the shed and back towards the house.

Max lay with his head in Jen's lap, feet dangling over the edge of the mocha-coloured sofa. She wound her finger through a loop of his hair, curling it in a tight little brown ringlet around her index finger.

'Why even bother to arrange to meet up? That's what I can't understand. Fair enough, it was me looking for him. Me who found him. Made the first move. But he didn't have to even acknowledge I existed if he didn't want to.'

'Call him,' said Jen. 'Put him on the spot and just ask him straight.'

'That's twice he's skipped town and left me. Twice. The fact I wasn't born the first time round is just circumstantial. Give me one good reason why I should give him the benefit of the doubt.'

'He's your dad, Max, and you can't count the first time; he didn't even know.'

'Biologically, yeah, but that's as far as it goes. If it's all the same, I'd rather just let it go. I lasted over thirty years without him, so I'm sure I'll cope. Part of me wishes I'd never found him in the first place.'

He swung his legs around and sat up, rotating his neck through a slow three-sixty, feeling something grind inside. He headed into the kitchen, smiling as he saw the picture on the fridge. A stick figure in a dress, a line of smaller figures stretched out behind it. Jen was a teacher at a local primary school, and a steady stream of artwork followed her home every week. She kept them all in a couple of shoe boxes upstairs, joking that if any of the kids became the next Damien Hirst, she could stick them on eBay.

'Stir-fry OK for you?' he called out.

'Sounds good.'

She padded into the kitchen after him, bare feet shushing against the tiles, and pulled a half-empty bottle of Pinot Grigio from the fridge. Max came up behind her as she poured them each a glass, snaking his arms around her waist.

'I know I can be a moody little shit at times, but you know I'm worth the hassle,' he murmured, lips brushing against her ear.

'Mm-hmm, you'll do till Colin Farrell comes to his senses,' she said, wriggling around to face him. 'You know I'm behind you whatever you want to do, don't you?'

'I do,' he said, nodding slowly, pulling her close so that her head slotted neatly into the groove of his neck. Two pieces of a jigsaw. They stood like that for a few seconds, until Jen broke the silence.

'Can't smell the stir-fry yet.'

'Cheeky!'

She danced out of reach as he tried, and failed, to land a playful smack on her backside. To hell with his dad. He had all he needed right here in this kitchen.

The man watched Harold Mayes, the real Harold, making his way through the fruit and veg aisle. He made a show of rummaging in a tray of apples, watching from the corner of his eye, as Harold stopped by the Galia melons, giving one a quick squeeze to test its ripeness. He looked the other way as Harold came towards him, pretending to check through the items in his own basket even though they were just window dressing. Props to help him blend in.

A steady stream of shoppers criss-crossed the aisle between them. Most of them looked as if they were on autopilot, eyes glazed from a day in the office, leaning on their trolleys like they were a Zimmer frame. Eat, sleep, shave, repeat. He had been like that once upon a time, but he'd never go back now. He cruised the aisles, a shark circling a shoal, looking on as Harold walked over to a self-service checkout. No need to panic or speed up as he watched Harold scan his items from three back in the queue. No need to worry as Harold headed out into the twilight. He already knew where Harold lived. He'd already been inside. Tonight was just part of the preparation. Part of the ritual. Study. Learn. Plan. He collected his change from the tray under the checkout, and headed out into the night.

CHAPTER TWO

The sound seeped slowly into Max's consciousness, easing him out of that halfway house between dream and reality. Jen's head was buried in her pillow, as if she'd fallen into bed from a height. The noise coming from her was less a snore and more of a whisper, as if she had a slow puncture somewhere.

Max eased his legs out from under the duvet so as not to disturb her, although he suspected only something on the Richter scale would make a difference. Ten minutes later, hamstrings shouting in protest, he was up and out, pounding his regular route around the nearby park.

When he arrived back home half an hour later, Jen had migrated as far as the sofa, watching the morning news through the haze coming off her peppermint tea. She puckered her lips, nodding as he peeled his top off.

'I'll give you twenty cash money right now if the shorts go too.'

'Add a few more zeroes and we might have a deal,' he said with a grin.

She stuck her tongue out and he headed upstairs, knowing full well she'd probably follow him up before long and sneak a peek for free. He stepped into the shower and twisted the dial to the far left. Even though he knew it was coming, he still gasped out loud as the icy needles of water pounded down. The guys he trained with swore by it. Something about improving the body's recovery rate, but part of him still wondered if it was just a wind-up. He'd google it later.

He was showered, dried and changed into faded jeans and a black V-neck T-shirt before Jen came up. She leant in for a light peck on the lips as she glided past.

'I'm going to grab a quick shower, but make sure you don't work too late tonight. I might have a little surprise for you.'

'If it's anything lacy or frilly, I'll be back before lunch,' he said, raising an eyebrow in his best homage to Roger Moore.

'Ha, you should be so lucky.' She laughed. 'No clues, though. You'll just have to wait till tonight.'

Max shot her his best pout, but she ignored him, and started undoing the belt on her dressing gown, humming the David Rose stripper tune. As she turned away from him, the robe became a puddle of fabric at her feet and she looked over her shoulder as she walked into the bathroom.

Max alternated between watching her go and glancing at the clock. A second shower would almost certainly make him late for work. Then again, some things were worth getting into trouble for.

The kitchen clock showed a few minutes past 8 p.m. as Max's keys slid across the grey granite worktop.

'Jen?'

No response. He called her name again, cocking his head to one side, listening to the silence. Nothing. She'd mentioned a

24

surprise. He hoped he'd guessed right, and she was waiting upstairs in an outfit that left little to the imagination, but after standing still for a half-dozen heartbeats, he gave up and opened the fridge to see what leapt out. His stomach gurgled its disappointment at the mostly empty shelves. Jen had promised to hit the supermarket on her way home, but he wasn't sure he could wait.

He picked up his phone and scrolled through until he found her number. Straight to voicemail without ringing. Probably elbow deep in the frozen food aisle. To wait or not to wait? A chorus of grumbling and rumbling from his gut made the decision for him, and he went through to the study to see what offers Domino's had online this week. Before his finger could hit the power button, he heard the hum of the internal fan and hard drive already ticking over. Max flopped into the swivel chair, shook the mouse, and the screen came to life, browser window open on the Beacon Estates home page.

Why the hell would Jen be looking at their page?

The answer was blindingly obvious; his dad. She must have tried to reach him through the estate agents. He pushed the chair away from the desk with a grunt. What the hell was she playing at? He was done with his dad. He'd been pretty clear on that. He stared at the screen until the rest of the room blurred around the edges. Suddenly it was no bad thing she was late. It'd give him time to calm down. He pulled himself back towards the desk and went to the Domino's website. Jen didn't like meaty toppings, so he ordered a large pepperoni and went into the lounge to wait for his food, and Jen, preferably in that order.

CHAPTER THREE

Max woke with a start, TV remote falling from his lap and landing in the pizza box by his feet. He checked his watch; almost 7 a.m. He yawned, wiped a speck of crusty sleep from his eye, peeled himself from the sofa and shuffled towards the stairs. He flicked the light on as he walked into the bedroom and took a few seconds to process the empty bed, neatly tucked in at the edges.

'Jen?' He called out her name, not sure whether to expect a response. Nothing. He grabbed the handset from the bedside table, dialling her number from memory.

Hi, this is Jen. Listen out for the beep, you know what to do.

Hearing her voice burnt off what was left of the fog in his mind. The beep came and went. After a few seconds of silence, his brain kicked back into gear.

'Hi, babe, it's me. Call me when you get this. Just wondering where you are.'

He ended the call and went back downstairs, taking them two at a time, and grabbed his mobile from the sofa. He tried Ally next, her best friend. She might have popped in for a gossip on the way home, had a glass or two, and decided against driving.

Surely she would have called, no matter what though. Texted me at least.

He launched straight in with no preamble. 'Hi, Ally, it's Max. Did you see Jen last night by any chance?'

'Max?' She sounded half asleep. 'What time is it?'

'A little before seven. Was she at yours last night?'

'No,' she said, stifling a yawn. 'I've not spoken to her since the day before yesterday. Why? What's wrong?'

'She didn't come home last night,' he said. 'She's not answering her phone either.'

'Have you tried her parents' house?' said Ally, sounding more awake now.

'They're next on my list. Sorry to bother you so early.'

'No, no, don't be daft,' she said. 'Let me know when you track her down, OK?'

Max promised that he'd call her when Jen turned up, and dialled Jen's mum and dad next. No danger of waking anyone up there. Bill and Tina Hart were both early risers, and sure enough, Bill picked up on the second ring.

'Hi, Bill, it's Max. I don't suppose Jen's at your house, is she?'

'No, why would she be here at this time?'

Max gave a loud sigh. 'She's not here, Bill. Didn't come home last night and isn't answering her phone.'

'Have you two had an argument or something?'

'No, no, it's nothing like that. She just . . . it's just not like her to disappear like that. Look, I'm going to make a few more calls. Will you let me know if you hear from her?'

'Course I will,' Bill said, then lowered his voice. 'I'll not say anything to Tina yet. You know how she worries.'

Max signed off and slumped back into the sofa. There was little chance of anyone being at the school, seeing as it was smack bang in the middle of summer holidays. What if she'd been in an accident? He googled the number for St Stephen's accident and emergency department, and sat through a few minutes of classical hold music, only to be told there had been nobody admitted by the name of Jennifer Hart.

He tugged at his bottom lip, leg bouncing a nervous beat as he tried to figure out what to do next. There was one person he could try. Might be jumping the gun a little, but she'd never done anything like this before, and his mind was racing in a dozen different directions, none of them good. What the hell, it couldn't hurt. He scooped his phone back up, scrolled through his contacts. Even as he tapped the name, he told himself he was overreacting, even as something slithering in his stomach told him he might not be.

Porter had never been a fan of social media. He had no desire to post pictures of his food for the world to see, no need for a connection to a hundred friends that he never saw. He had given into peer pressure from his sister and set up a Facebook profile, but in six months had amassed a total of twelve friends and zero status updates.

He'd never liked the whole concept of it from the start, but today his opinion had hit a new low. A clip of him grabbing Patchett had been on Twitter before he'd even made it back to the station yesterday, and he was fairly sure that's why he'd been summoned. He hadn't seen it himself, but Styles had given him the heads-up after seeing a trio of younger officers huddled around an iPhone downstairs.

The door to Superintendent Roger Milburn's office was half open already, but he knocked anyway.

'In you come.' Milburn's voice, the very definition of authority.

He had one of those voices that filled whatever room he was in, a bit like Brian Blessed. Good for press conferences, but he'd never mastered dialling it down a notch for smaller venues, like his own office. Porter walked over to the desk, waiting for an invitation to sit that didn't come. Milburn smiled, one of those politician's ones that crinkled the face in all the right places, but the eyes couldn't be colder if he'd just chewed a snowball. Put that together with his perfectly capped teeth, straight off a dentist's promotional poster, and it put Porter in mind of a great white.

Right now, he'd take his chances with an actual shark rather than be here. He and Milburn had clashed over the Alexander Locke case. Porter's former boss at the time, Superintendent George Campbell, had been kicked off the force in disgrace over corruption charges soon after. Porter and Campbell had had their fair share of clashes, but Milburn had made it clear he tarred Porter with the same brush, suspected him of cutting corners and thought him liable to become the team problem child given half the chance.

'You wanted to see me, sir?'

'Yes, Porter,' said Milburn, rummaging in his jacket pocket. 'Yes, I did.'

He produced a phone, tapped out a rhythm on it, and slid it across the desk. The kid who'd shot it had been at least fifty yards away, so when he'd zoomed in, things blurred a little around the edges, but even then there was no doubt as to what and who he was watching. Milburn had left the sound on, and the kid chattered away to his mate throughout.

'Whoa, check it, bruv. Shit's going down,' a voice said, Porter presumed the cameraman; young, brash, with more than a hint of excitement at the possibility of violence.

'Six on one,' a second voice said. 'That ain't a fair fight.'

'Bloke coming out might be tooled up.'

'Hope so,' came the second voice. 'Might be able to flog this for a few quid to Sky News if he takes a few of them down.'

Porter clenched his jaw at how casually they hoped for it. Watching it back now felt wrong, all out of context with only an arrogant little wannabe gangster narrating. He saw himself square up to Patchett. Watched as his hand shot up. Saw himself being hustled away by Styles. Without Patchett's taunts, it was only half a story, but even he had to admit it didn't look great. The clip finished, freezing on a grainy still of Patchett being pushed towards the car.

'Well?' Milburn sounded like a schoolteacher. 'What have you got to say for yourself?'

'I know how it looks, sir, but—'

'It looks like shit, Porter,' Milburn cut across him. 'It looks like an early Christmas present for his solicitor.'

'With all due respect, sir, there was provocation on his part. This man was part of an organisation that almost killed Simmons. He—'

Milburn held up a palm to silence him. 'And he'll have his day in court for that, but lowering ourselves to their level isn't acceptable. Not ever.'

Porter felt his cheeks flush, partly anger at Milburn, partly at himself for causing the situation in the first place. A dozen retorts swam around his head, but he knew Milburn would swat them all away, quoting conduct rules, chapter and verse. He made do with clenching his fists below the desk level, where Milburn couldn't see, until his joints ached.

'We've barely fought our way back from the whole Campbell debacle, and I will not' – Milburn stabbed the desk with his finger to emphasise his point – 'have anyone else drag us back down there.'

Porter imagined how it would feel to grab Milburn the same way he'd done with Patchett. To be up close, in his face, spell it out to him as if he was a five-year-old child.

I'm not Campbell, his voice raged inside his head. *I stopped Campbell. I exposed him for what he was. You swept the whole bloody mess under the carpet. Not me. I. Am. Not. Campbell.*

Porter's anger simmered below the surface, hot, molten, but Milburn seemed oblivious. The superintendent sat back in his chair, one arm across his chest, the other raised up, a finger tapping against his lips in a shushing gesture. Porter met his stare, holding it as the silence dragged out.

'So here's what we're going to do,' said Milburn finally. 'You're off the case, not that there's much left of it anyway. You'll hand over to Clayton and Schofield.'

Porter opened his mouth to protest, but Milburn beat him to it.

'This isn't up for discussion, Porter. You'll do it, and do it today.'

Porter sat back, arms crossed. With Patchett back in custody, Milburn was right, it was almost a done deal, but that wasn't the point; it was his case. After what he went through to bring down

31

Locke and his mini-empire, he deserved to see it through. Milburn wasn't finished.

'As you know, I've been leading on the inquiry into Superintendent Campbell's conduct, reviewing people's files to see who else was involved with him. Spotted in there that you'd lost your wife a while back. That can't have been easy.' Milburn's face softened for a second. 'Apparently, you turned down the offer of sessions with a counsellor after it happened.'

The reference to Holly, even without using her name, was like a slap across the cheek, and Porter sat in stunned silence. Where the hell was Milburn going with this?

'I appreciate that can't have been easy, especially with nobody ever being arrested for it.'

Holly had been on her way back from a parents' evening at the school she worked at, when a car had lost control and mounted the pavement. Hit and run. She'd lasted three days in A&E, the longest three of Porter's life. He blinked as an image of her flashed to mind. Her face a mixed palette of bruises, purple and black. Eyes closed, arms by her side. Even now it made his breath catch, swallowing hard before a lump could form.

'I'm not saying that's the cause of this' – Milburn gestured towards the phone – 'but whatever's going on inside here,' he said, pointing to his own head, 'it needs putting right. I can't have my officers snapping like that. I know you took what happened to Simmons personally as well, so you're to make an appointment this week to see Occupational Health, and to attend as many sessions as they see fit.'

'Sir, that's really not necessary,' Porter protested.

'That's for them to decide, not you. Damage limitation, Porter, for the force and for you.' The order in which Milburn prioritised his two points wasn't lost on Porter. Protect the good name of the police force first, its officers second. 'The press has picked up on it and been hounding us for a comment. If Patchett tries to sue, this will help in mitigation and, who knows, it might actually do you some good. Call her today, that's an order.'

Porter felt the pressure building in his head. Going against a direct order from Milburn was as good as saying he was done. Milburn pulled his phone back across the desk, shaking his head as he looked at the image still on the screen.

'That's all, Porter. You can go now.'

Porter stood up, not trusting himself to say anything else for fear he'd tell Milburn what he really thought of him right now. He left the office without another word and headed downstairs for some fresh air. His job was hard enough without being shackled like this. Forced to give up his case, and waste God knows how many hours with a stranger trying to pick through his thoughts and tell him that he wasn't over Holly. That talking about it would help. That he needed to move on.

The idea of being over her scared him almost as much as the prospect of talking to anyone about it. The thought that she could be relegated to a footnote. Besides, things like that were private. Not to be shared. He didn't need to sit in a stuffy room and tell a counsellor that he thought about her every day, dreamt about her most nights, to know he hadn't put it behind him.

He stepped out into a morning heat that felt oppressive, heavy, like a heavy blanket draped over the city. Rush hour was over, but traffic still zipped past at a fair pace on the Marylebone flyover off to his right. He hustled over the road towards Edgware Road

Tube station, glancing at the pub next door, The Green. A couple of die-hard regulars stood outside, cigarettes in hand, putting the world to rights over the first drink of the day. Porter angled off to the right, past the station, the right-hand side of it an explosion of green amongst the otherwise grey buildings. He'd read somewhere that the wall, consisting of over ten thousand plants, was meant to trap pollution. Whether it did or didn't, it was just nice to have a flash of colour amongst the grey buildings.

Five minutes. Just enough time to get Milburn out of his system, then he'd head back inside. The superintendent could force him to go to the sessions, but he couldn't make him say anything in them. He slowed his walk to an amble. Closed his eyes. Breathed in deep as he walked past the curtain of green on the wall. So tired. Not just a lack of sleep, but tired of people like Milburn. Tired of the sort of bullshit that stopped him doing his job. Of people who hadn't set foot from out behind a desk for years and had forgotten what it was like to be a detective, rather than a politician.

Porter wondered, not for the first time, whether he had the strength to do it all; do his job, stand up to the bureaucracy, come to terms with a world that didn't include Holly. If he wasn't a detective, what else could he be? His phone buzzed deep in a jacket pocket, and he rolled his eyes. Milburn, probably, asking if he'd called the shrink yet. But when he pulled it out, the name on screen raised a smile. Anything not work-related would be welcome right now.

'Morning, stranger. Long time no speak.'

He listened to the voice on the other end of the line, and the smile was gone inside five seconds.

* * *

The room Jen was in could be a broom cupboard or an airplane hangar for all she knew. The complete absence of light made figuring out any dimensions impossible. Darkness so absolute, all-encompassing. Would it run through her hands like wet sand if she tried to grab a fistful? She'd welcome the chance to find out, but her hands were fixed firmly in place, probably with whatever covered her mouth. Tape, maybe?

How long had she been here? More to the point, where the hell was *here*? All she could hear was her own breathing, ragged and rapid through snotty nostrils. She tried to control it, to slow it down. Her heartbeat thudded in tandem with her pulsing headache.

She swung her head left and right, looking for something she could latch on to, anything to break the monotony of inky blackness. Time oozed by like treacle. Minutes? Hours? Who knew? She closed her eyes again. Breathed in for five. Out for five. When she opened them again, she nearly dismissed what she saw as having screwed her eyes too tight, but she blinked a few times to make certain. Sure enough, a horizontal line of light seemed to hover in front of her. Other lines, fainter, but definitely there, ran vertically up from either end. A doorway?

A metallic rasp, a key in a lock, perhaps, and the darkness was burnt away as the door opened. Jen turned her head, wincing as the light flooded in. She opened her eyes; the shape of the doorway had burnt into her retinas, reappearing with every blink. She heard footsteps, a scraping like nails on a blackboard – chair legs, maybe? She kept her head bowed down, away from the glare that stung her eyes.

A click, and overhead a strip light spluttered into life. The footsteps stopped. Her breathing sped up again, tape sucking in against her lips, nostrils flared.

'Hello, Jennifer,' said a man's voice. Vaguely familiar. No accent that she could place. 'You and I have quite a bit to talk about.'

She chanced a glance towards him, eyes still recovering. A blurred shape moved in front of her, towards her. Fingers scrabbled at the edge of the tape on her mouth. Ripping it off in one smooth action, like a Band-Aid. Jen heard the scream. Listened to it for a few seconds before she realised it was coming from her. The worst part was that the man made no move to stop her. That meant he either knew nobody could hear her, or he just didn't care. Either way, she wasn't walking away from this, whatever *this* was.

'When was the last time you spoke to her then?' Porter asked, turning on his heel and heading back towards the station.

'Yesterday morning, before I left for work,' said Max.

'And you're sure she's not just crashed out at a friend's house?'

'She would have called. You know what she's like. She would have told me.'

Max was putting on a brave front, but Porter could tell he was worried, talking a little too fast, stumbling over his words, only slightly, but Porter had dealt with more worried relatives than he cared to remember over the years. Besides, Max was right – it was out of character for Jen, and Max wasn't one to worry without reason. Porter had known him since school, Max being a couple of years below him, and boxed with him at the local gym. They still met for the occasional beer, and the less than occasional sparring session.

Like Porter, Max had joined the army straight out of university, serving five years to Porter's nine. Porter had swapped one uniform for another when he joined the Metropolitan

Police's Homicide and Serious Crime Command, whereas Max had hung his up altogether. He was a staff photographer now for the *Daily Express*.

'To be honest I feel daft even bothering you with it,' Max went on, 'but I've tried her folks, her mates, even the hospital, and I'm out of ideas.'

'She still driving the Honda?'

'Mm-hmm. She might have even just broken down somewhere, and her phone's died; something stupid like that.'

'OK, I'll have a word with some of the lads on patrol this morning if you text me the reg plate. Ask them to keep an eye out.'

Porter heard a sigh on the other end of the line. 'Thanks, mate. I owe you one. Beers on me soon, yeah?'

'No worries,' Porter said, walking back past the Tube station. 'I'll call you if I hear anything.'

He disconnected the call, and before he'd managed to cross the road, Max's text with Jen's registration number came through. The little voice in his head whispered that this didn't feel right. He'd known Jen for some time now. They'd all gone out for drinks a few times when Holly was still around, and she was as sensible-girl-next-door as they came. Max's scenario of a broken-down car didn't feel right, but then again, nobody liked to consider anything too bad right off the bat.

Porter knew from bitter experience that life didn't always have a happy ending. He'd stood on too many doors, delivering bad news to unsuspecting families. Work had made him more realist than optimist. Bad things happened to good people all the time. There wasn't a damn thing you could do about it. Holly had been as gentle a soul as he'd ever met, but when a car had mounted the pavement, sending her spiralling over the bonnet, it had counted for nothing. Porter still remembered getting the call. The way his head spun, as if he'd just stepped off a ride at the fairground. Stomach feeling like it had been hollowed out with an ice cream scoop.

If he could find Jen, settle Max's nerves, stop him from feeling even a hundredth of what he'd felt himself, it would trump all the other crap he had to deal with today.

'It'll be fine. She'll be fine,' he muttered to himself as he trotted back up the stairs towards the front door to the station. He almost believed it himself. Almost.

Max was full of restless energy, insides churning as if they were in a blender. He called in a favour from Callum Carr, a friend from the office, to cover for him for a few hours while he headed out to drive around a few of Jen's usual haunts. She had mentioned needing to pop into the school for a few hours yesterday, but the car park was deserted when he drove past. Where the hell could she have gotten to? An image of the monitor from last night flashed to mind, the yellow lighthouse of the Beacon Estates logo shooting out a beam of golden light at the top of the page.

Max pulled over, typed the name into the browser on his phone and clicked to call the office number.

'Good morning, Beacon Estates, Amy speaking. How can I help you?' She sounded young, with sing-song sickly sweet enthusiasm that seeped down the line.

'Hi, Amy, my name's Max, Max Brennan. This might sound a little odd, but I'm wondering if my girlfriend called you folks up yesterday. Jennifer Hart? I think she may have called about a property that you guys just sold for my father, Gordon Jackson. Does that ring any bells?'

'You're in luck, Mr Brennan,' she said. 'It was me that spoke with Ms Hart yesterday. What was it I can help you with?'

'I just need to know what she called about. Nobody's seen her since yesterday, and I'm a little worried, so anything you can tell me would be a big help.'

The perky tone was dialled back a notch when she spoke again. 'Oh, right, I erm, well I didn't actually see her. I only spoke to her on the phone, so . . .' The last syllable stretched out, warding off any follow-up.

'Why did she call in the first place, though?'

'She wanted your father's forwarding address. Said he'd written it down for you, but you'd lost the Post-it he'd written it on, or something. Of course, I couldn't just give that out, client confidentiality and all that, but I said I'd pass on a message.'

'And?' said Max, unable to keep the frustration out of his voice. 'What was the message?'

'Just to say she'd lost his mobile number,' she said, with an undisguised undertone of *yeah, right*, 'and to ask if she could meet him for a coffee. She gave me her number to pass on to him.'

Silence. Max pictured her at her desk, fingers splayed out as she painted her nails, a hundred more important things to do than talk to some bloke firing questions at her that didn't involve buying or selling property.

'And did he?' Max asked.

'Did he what?'

'Meet her for a coffee?'

Jesus, she probably thinks you're a stalker, he thought.

'I have no idea, sorry, Mr Brennan. I left your dad a voicemail, but I didn't speak to him, or your girlfriend, after that.'

'What time was that?'

'Around twelve-ish. Maggie, one of the other girls, had just gone out for lunch, and Ms Hart's call was one of the first I took. Rang off the hook for the next hour till Maggie came back.'

Max thanked her and left her his number in case she heard from either Jen or his dad. His next call was to a number he'd nearly deleted a few days back. Straight to voicemail, and he listened to his dad's greeting apologising for not taking the call. A few days ago, even up until this morning, he didn't care if he never heard his dad's voice again. Listening to it now, he wondered if he and Jen had met up. Where had she gone afterwards? Did his dad know where she'd gone? Where she was?

Max's message was short, and to the point.

'It's me. Max. I need to speak to you. Call me when you get this.'

A dozen questions, and the one man he'd sworn to turn his back on now looked likely to be the only one with any answers.

When Porter made it back into the station, he did a double take. Most of the people in the office, Styles included, had gathered at the far end, but he couldn't make out anything past a general murmur of group chatter. He ignored them and slumped into his chair. It creaked as he leant back, like a door in a haunted house, and he saw Styles clock him over his shoulder.

Nick Styles towered above the others. At six foot four, he made some of the others look as if they were standing in a trench next to him. He beckoned Porter over with a jerk of his head. Porter nodded an acknowledgement, but leant back, closed his eyes for a few seconds. How long had it been since he'd taken any time off? Real time away, not just a few days, or a long weekend. Holly's funeral, and the week afterwards, but barely anything since. Seemed almost pointless. When she died, he was like a boat that slipped its mooring in that respect. The only thing that made sense was his job. It kept him sane, focused.

These last six months had taken more out of him than he cared to let on, even to Styles. Evie Simmons almost dying on the job had felt like Holly all over again. The prospect of someone close to him dying, and him powerless to do a damn thing about it. Not that anything had happened between the two of them, other than a single drunken kiss.

'Someone to see you, guv.' Styles's voice snapped him out of his moment of self-pity.

Porter pushed himself out of his chair, swearing under his breath as his knee cracked against his desk drawer. He bent down to rub it as he wandered over to see what all the fuss was about. As he stood, the line of people parted like a big reveal in a West End show.

Evie Simmons's smile seemed to double in size when she saw him approaching. It spread across her face like a ripple on a pond, reaching all the way to the edges. Porter slowed, feeling a smile of his own surface. He hoped it didn't look as goofy as it felt. Simmons had sustained a life-threatening head injury in the Alexander Locke case. James Bolton, Locke's right-hand man, had slammed her head into a wall, triggering a blood clot that almost killed her. She'd flatlined twice; once in the ambulance, and again as surgeons battled to stop the bleeding on her brain.

It had been five months since he'd seen her, and her hair was longer than he remembered. She usually wore it up for work, but it spilt down in a dark wave over her shoulders. She looked small, almost child-like, as she turned to face him, knuckles white where she leant forwards on her hospital-issue crutches.

'Morning, guv,' she said, as a few of the crowd peeled off back to their desks.

'Morning,' Porter replied, doing his best to ignore the smirk on Styles's face. 'You're not back yet, are you? Didn't think we'd be seeing you for another month or so?'

She shook her head. 'Just a social visit. Well, mainly social. The super wants to have a chat about a phased return, but yep, hoping to be back next week actually; well, a few half days to start with. Drives me mad sat round Mum and Dad's house all day.'

'I'll pity the poor bloke who tries to cross you while you're wielding those,' said Styles, nodding towards her crutches.

She flicked the end of one of them towards his legs, giggled as he skittered out of the way. This was definitely a better version of her than Porter had seen when she was discharged from hospital earlier in the year. He'd toyed a few times with getting in touch via her father, just to see how she was coming on, to let her know he cared enough to ask. The guilt of those missed opportunities sat heavy, front and centre in his chest now.

'I'll, um, just leave you two to catch up,' said Styles. 'These naughty criminals don't just lock themselves up you know. Good to see you though, Evie. Get back in here soon, yeah?'

She flashed another of her full beam smiles at him. 'You don't get rid of me that easily.'

Styles wandered past Porter, back towards his desk, leaving just the two of them.

'How long do you have to use the crutches, then?' he said.

'Get rid of them this week, hopefully.'

'I meant to give your dad a call, you know, see how you were doing, but, you know . . .'

'It's fine,' she said. 'I'm fine. Just looking forward to getting back now.'

Even with the murmur of background noise, people getting on with their day, Porter felt as if all eyes were on them. On him. It was like that moment in a club, last dance finished, house lights on, scrabbling for words.

Porter snapped out of it first. 'Yeah.' He nodded. 'Yeah, I bet.'

He didn't know where to pick up from whatever connection they'd started to make, back before her accident. Didn't know whether there was even still anywhere to pick up from. He opened his mouth, not entirely sure which of a dozen lame lines might come out first.

'Listen, Evie, I—'

'Simmons!' Milburn's unmistakable voice, cranked up to near-max volume. 'Ready when you are.'

He looked over her shoulder, saw Milburn's head and one shoulder hovering through the doorway to his office.

'I'd better get this over with,' she said, pivoting on her right-hand crutch. She stopped after a few steps, turning back to him. 'Shouldn't be more than an hour. If you're around when I'm done, maybe we could grab a cuppa. You still owe me one, remember?'

Porter smiled. 'I haven't forgotten. Yeah, that'd be good.'

He watched her go, bobbing up and down with every swing of her crutches, remembering a drunken kiss outside a bar almost six months ago. Had she thought of it since then? Was that what made her smile like she was in a toothpaste ad?

Oh, yeah, because of course she's not had anything more important to think about, has she? Like five months of treatment and rehab for starters. Have a word with yourself, Jake.

Styles's eyebrows were practically vibrating up and down as Porter headed back to his desk.

'So . . .' he said, drawing it out as if it had half a dozen vowels at the end.

Before Porter could fire anything back, the phone on his desk rang.

'Saved by the bell,' said Styles, narrowing his eyes.

Porter ignored him and scooped up the handset, wondering who had come to his rescue.

'Detective Porter, Sameera Misra. I'm a counsellor with the Occupational Health Unit. Superintendent Milburn asked me to give you a call to set up an appointment.'

Did he indeed, thought Porter. Says a lot when Milburn didn't even trust him to make the call.

'Yeah, he and I spoke about that earlier this morning. I'm a little tied up at the moment, but maybe we could set something up for next week?'

Whatever slot she gave him for the following week, he'd find a reason to be somewhere else. He could be doing a hell of a lot more by sweeping up the dregs of the Alexander Locke case than fidgeting in some counsellor's leather chair watching the seconds tick off the clock.

'Really?' Misra's tone sounded borderline amused. 'Superintendent Milburn said he'd stood you down from a case, and that you'd be free today. You're in luck as it happens, I've got an opening in an hour.'

Porter slumped into his seat, eyes closed. Deep breath. He felt about as lucky as a turkey at Christmas, but this was like quicksand; the more he struggled, the more Milburn would smother him, stop him from doing his job.

'Fine. Where do I find you?'

He'd turn up, sit in the chair, nod in the right places, tell her what she wanted to hear, and hopefully be back out in half an hour tops. He agreed to meet her up on the second floor in an hour's time, and let the handset drop the last inch, clattering back into place.

'You look less than chirpy, guv. Care to share?'

'Nope, right now, actually I don't.'

Styles leant back in his own chair, holding both palms up, and turned his attention back to his monitor. Styles was the one person he did open up to, albeit once in a blue moon, and usually over a few drinks, but Porter felt ruffled by the twin pronged attack from Milburn and the well-meaning OHU counsellor. He had time to kill, and no case to work. Milburn's door was still closed. Maybe he'd finish with Simmons before Porter's appointment. Maybe there'd be time for that coffee. Somewhere away from the station, where they could talk properly. All those *maybe*s felt like they were in cahoots with Milburn, conspiring against him.

He opened his mouth to apologise to Styles but closed it as another thought hit him. What if the real problem, when you stripped away all of the politics and procedure, was that talking about everything, Holly included, might actually help him come to terms with it all? To move on. To accept that she was gone for good. If normality was accepting a world without her, he wasn't sure he wanted any part of it.

Can't let go of her. Can't keep going like this. Restless nights. That ever-present gritty feeling behind his eyes. Something had to give.

Just hope it's not me.

* * *

Milburn reminded her of her Uncle Alfie. Ramrod straight like he had a broom handle down his back. Using a dozen words when two would do. In love with the sound of his own voice. Eve Simmons rubbed at a twitching muscle in her thigh. Felt like a grasshopper was bouncing inside. Milburn droned on, saying the right things, how they'd welcome her back, that there'd always be a place for her, that they needed more of her spirit and dedication. Whether he'd stick to the party line when she caught her crutches against his shin in the corridor was another matter.

Coming back in was harder than she'd thought. Sitting at home, it was all she could think about. Now she was here, she felt like an outsider. Plenty of warm hellos, but just as many lingering stares. Unasked questions. Could she come back from her injury? Would she have their backs if it happened again, or would she freeze up? She'd asked herself these more times than she cared to remember and wasn't convinced by the answers.

She smiled and nodded at the right places. Yes, she was looking forward to getting back to work, even though the thought of it terrified her. She still saw flashes in her dreams of what had happened. She hadn't actually seen much at the time, but her brain filled in the blanks. Shadows rearing up around her, black as coal, heavy, like a wet blanket. Pain like she'd never thought possible. Not real, of course. Only a nightmare, but enough that she still felt the echoes of it every time she woke up in a cold sweat.

Milburn said his piece, started checking his watch, and she was glad to hobble back out into the open-plan area. She scanned the rows of desks, looking for Porter. Nick Styles was there, but the desk beside him was empty. Porter was a source of confusion for her. She had practically offered herself to him on a night out earlier this year, before someone saw fit to stave her head in against a wall, of course. She was usually good at picking up signals, working out whether someone was interested or not. Her gut told her he was, but it was as if he wasn't aware of that himself.

She had hoped he would have been in touch while she had been off. Check in and see how she was doing. No strings, no expectations. But he'd kept his distance. Was she damaged goods now? She knew about his wife, how she'd been killed in an accident. Office gossip said he hadn't so much as looked at another woman since, but that was a few years ago now. Couldn't grieve for ever, surely? She loped over to where Styles sat, long strides on her crutches as if it was the same as stretching her legs after sitting so long.

'Porter still around?' she asked.

He looked up at her, with what? Pity? Curiosity? Hard to say, but it irritated her all the same. 'He had to pop upstairs into a meeting.'

'Meeting?'

'Yeah.'

'Anything interesting?'

'Dunno, he didn't say.'

Like pulling teeth. Didn't say because it was none of her business, or didn't say because it was just an excuse to pass on the coffee? These last four or five months had eroded her confidence like a melting glacier. Same bar, same situation today, and she doubted she would make any kind of move on him. Wasn't sure how she'd handle the knock-back. That's what was coming if she did, surely. If he was interested, he would have been in touch these last five months. Would have waited around for her today, or at least left word for her.

First day back at work would be challenge enough. One step at a time.

The angry rattle of Max's mobile against the glass coffee table made him jump like a slap across the face. He sat up, wincing as he swung through the sunlight that scythed through a gap in the curtains. The anchor on Sky News was wrapping up the headlines, handing over to an unnaturally cheery weathergirl. Pins and needles fizzed along his right arm. He reached for the phone with his left hand, shaking life back into the other.

'Hello?' Not a number he recognised.

'Mr Brennan? It's Amy, from Beacon Estates. We spoke earlier about your father?'

'Yes, of course, hi.' Max sat bolt upright. 'Has he been in touch?'

'I hope you don't mind, but I took the liberty of calling him. He says he can meet you here at three-thirty if you're free, at our office.'

Max checked his watch. Five hours to kill. 'Yep, I'll be there. See you then.'

He hung up and looked at the screen after the call had cleared, checking for missed calls or texts. Nothing. Jen's face stared back at him from the screen. His background shot was the two of them on a night out in Vegas, Bellagio Fountains dancing behind them. Good times. Max forced himself back to the here and now, flicked into his contacts, and tapped Porter's number.

Hey, it's Jake. Leave a message, and I'll get back to you as soon as I can.

Max's message was short and sweet, telling Porter where he was headed, and asking him to call back, news or no news. He slipped the phone into his pocket as he stood and was halfway to the door before he turned back. He scribbled a hasty, hopeful note to Jen, left it propped up against that morning's coffee cup on the kitchen bench, and headed out to finally meet his father.

'He's just been under a lot of pressure, Em,' said Styles, looking over his shoulder to make sure Porter hadn't come back yet.

'So have you, Nick, but he's the last person you'd take it out on,' Emma Styles replied. 'I bet you've not told him yet either, have you?'

Styles sighed louder than he'd meant to. 'It's not exactly a good time.'

'It never is,' she snapped back.

'I will,' he said, keeping his voice low. Open-plan offices didn't make for the most private conversations. He debated calling her back from his mobile and heading outside. 'Just not today. I'll explain when I see you, but Milburn's already torn him a new one. I'll take him out for a beer one night this week.'

'It's not like it's all bad news,' Emma said. 'He's going to be godfather to Styles junior, assuming he accepts of course.'

'He'll say yes.'

'You're not having a change of heart, are you?'

'What? No. Why would I ask someone else?'

'I mean about the job, silly.'

Styles paused, only a few seconds. Hopefully not too long. 'No, of course not,' he said. 'It's just that I haven't even heard if it's definite yet. No point in saying anything till it is.'

She didn't reply at first. He gripped the phone. His old boss had said the job was his if he wanted it, back in the Specialist, Organised & Economic Crime Command, promising him DI within two years. After everything that had happened in the Alexander Locke case, Simmons nearly dying, Porter getting shot at, in Emma's mind it was only a matter of time before Styles was the one in the line of fire. Truth be told, Styles still wasn't sure he wanted the move. He'd worked hard to get where he was, and the thought of taking even the tiniest step backwards brought out his stubborn side.

He felt boxed in, painted into a corner. Emma was a bundle of nerves at the best of times, but now she was pregnant, everything was a risk in her eyes. Getting bumped around on crowded Tube trains, worrying about someone's bag swinging into her stomach. Whether eating too many Snickers bars could give the baby a nut allergy from birth. Styles's job was just another uncertainty.

Finally, Emma spoke. 'As long as you're still sure, then.' Another stretched-out silence.

'I'd better go, Em. Got a witness to interview in a few minutes.' The lie came easily. Easier than where the conversation was headed.

'Love you,' she said, voice almost a whisper.

'You too.'

He ended the call and huffed out a loud sigh. She'd asked him the same night she'd told him she was pregnant. Would he take a sideways step, somewhere less in harm's way, for the baby's sake? She wasn't alone. His family had waded in on her side, his mum and grandma to be precise, both forces to be reckoned with. A week visiting Grandma Clara in Barbados over the summer had made him a captive audience for her and Emma to whittle away at his resistance, and his mum had picked up the slack as soon as they'd gotten back to London.

What could he say, except he'd see what he could do, but for him, this would feel like a backwards move. He'd be letting Porter down as well. Not that his partner would ever say as much, but they'd been through a lot in the three years they'd worked together. Porter was a man who you knew would do right by you, even if he'd been a little distant lately. Would their friendship survive the move if he did make it? Their usual banter came in fits and starts these days. Had since the Locke case came to a head. The old Porter was still there – he just switched places with a moodier version of himself more often than Styles liked.

Having said that, Styles wondered how he'd cope if he lost Emma. How would he feel? He tried to imagine it but felt too morbid and gave up. Up ahead, Milburn's door opened. Simmons hauled herself out, glancing towards where Styles sat, looking for Porter no doubt. He saw her smile shrink back when she realised he wasn't there. They exchanged nods at a distance, and she hobbled towards him.

Could just as easily have been me.

He was going to piss someone off either way. His wife, or his partner.

Eenie, meenie, minie, mo.

Walking into the room reminded Porter of trudging into the headmaster's office. Not so much the decor, but the feeling of being forced into a room by the threat of what might happen if you didn't. Sameera Misra stepped back from the doorway as he passed. She had one of those faces that dared you to guess her age, a contradiction of features. Laughter lines rippling out from her eyes, but barely a wrinkle on her forehead. Grey streaks in her hair that made the neighbouring darker patches look inked in by comparison. She couldn't be more than a few inches over five feet and flashed him a dazzling smile as she introduced herself, holding out a hand that he shook briefly as he moved past her.

The room was like a staged setting in a showroom, generic art print on the wall, chairs that looked basic, but probably took two hours to assemble. Porter walked over to the window and looked out over Edgware Road, people scurrying past like ants. The door clicked shut behind him, but he waited a beat before turning back to face her.

'Please, Detective, have a seat.' She gestured towards the seat closest to the window.

He sat down, started to fold his arms but thought better of it, and rested his hands on his knees instead. Best not to appear too defensive, even though that's exactly how he felt. She took her seat opposite him, still with a hint of a smile, hands clasped together on her lap.

'So, Detective Porter, thanks for coming on such short notice. Am I OK to call you Jake?'

He shrugged. 'Yep, that's fine.'

'Great, thanks. So, Jake, I don't know if you're familiar with what we do here, but everything we talk about is confidential. This might sound like a cliché, but what you get out of these sessions is entirely up to you.'

That's exactly what it sounded like, but Porter swallowed a half-dozen comebacks, choosing instead to nod and tilt his head as if he was listening, hanging on her every word.

'Why don't we start by telling me a bit about yourself?'

Porter shrugged again. 'I joined up after I left the army. Been on the job eight years now, DI for the last three of them.'

Her smile was the kind teachers give a child: patient, encouraging. 'I know that part already. I mean about you personally, away from work. What about family, friends, hobbies, that type of thing?'

Porter paused a beat, saw no danger in giving a quick *This Is Your Life* style bio. 'Both parents still around. One sister. Two nephews. Been married once, no kids of my own.'

'And your wife, she passed away a few years ago?'

Porter nodded, tight-lipped. 'Uh-huh.'

'I understand nobody was arrested in connection with her death?'

'Right again.'

'Superintendent Milburn is concerned that you didn't speak to anyone at the time. That what happened recently with Andrew Patchett, it's somehow linked to your wife, to what happened to Eve Simmons. That maybe you're not coping with things as well as you think you are.'

'I'm coping just fine, thanks.' He heard the edge in his own voice, abrasive like sandpaper, but didn't try and disguise it.

'Sorry, maybe that's the wrong way to put it. Could it be that you lost control with a suspect, because you've been more affected by your loss than you're aware of?'

'You're the expert, Doc, you tell me.'

She shook her head. 'I'm not a doctor, Jake. And I'm not trying to make you feel uncomfortable. Your job, what you do, every day, it's one pressurised situation after another. It's OK to feel that pressure. My role is to help people make sense of it, to not be defined by it.'

Porter's left knee started an impatient bounce. 'What do you want me to say? That I miss my wife? Of course I do. That someone should pay for what happened to her? Of course they should, but things don't always work out like that, do they.'

She shook her head. 'No, they don't, but sometimes, not getting the outcome we think is right affects us in ways we're not aware of, or in control of.'

Porter sat forwards. 'I grabbed hold of Patchett's face because he was being disrespectful to a fellow officer. One who was almost killed by someone just like Patchett. He walked away without a mark on him. More than can be said for her. Should I have done it? Probably not, but it doesn't make me a bad copper. We have each other's backs out there,' he said, pointing at the window. 'She wasn't there to stick up for herself because of the likes of him, and that's all I was doing, sticking up for her.'

'No one's saying you're not a good policeman, Jake. Far from it. These sessions are more about you as a person, how the job you do affects you and those around you. How we can help make sure the job doesn't chew you up and spit you out.'

Porter opened his mouth to reply, when his phone went off. Max. Perfect timing. At this stage, he would have answered the call even if it was someone trying to help him claim his PPI back. He remembered with a flash of guilt that he hadn't asked anyone to look out for Jen's car yet. That could be his first job when he got back downstairs.

'Sorry, I have to take this.' He stood up before she could say anything. 'I'll call you to finish up another time.' He went out into the corridor. She'd probably be straight on the phone to Milburn.

'Hey, sorry I missed your last call. Got your message though. How was Beacon?'

Max sounded out of breath when he spoke. Porter's eyes widened as he listened.

'Shit. Don't move, Max, I'm on my way.'

Max had made good time, parking up opposite the Beacon Estates office a full fifteen minutes before his dad was due to arrive. He toyed with waiting in the car, but for all he knew, his dad could already be inside. The signage was the same green and gold as the logo, splashed above the entrance. An array of properties for sale, like rows of tiles, covered most of the front window. Bold red 'Sold!' stamps made for an almost perfect diagonal line across the grid, like a giant game of noughts and crosses.

Inside, the plain white walls were peppered with enough identical-looking ads to double as wallpaper. Clearly they'd never heard the saying 'less is more'. The lone member of staff sat behind a desk that looked fresh from an IKEA catalogue, phone sandwiched between her ear and shoulder as she pecked away at a keyboard with long nails. She held up a finger, mouthing that she'd only be a minute. Max recognised her from her voice as Amy, the girl who'd called him earlier, and nodded an acknowledgement. After some more furious tapping of nails on keys, she said goodbye to whoever was on the other end and turned her attention to Max.

'Hi there, how can I help?'

'Hi, my name's Max Brennan. We spoke on the phone earlier.'

'Ah yes, of course. Your dad isn't here yet,' she said, stating the glaringly obvious. 'Feel free to have a seat. Can I get you a drink while you wait? Tea? Coffee? Water?'

'I'm fine, thanks,' said Max, making himself comfortable on one of the tan fabric chairs either side of the water cooler, and settled in to wait. People ghosted past the window, mostly hidden by the sales display, and he tensed every time one went from right to left, towards the door. The irony that the first meeting with his dad would now be here wasn't lost on him. Here, in a place where people bought and sold pieces of their lives. Where they came to sever ties with their home, a fundamental piece of their life, and move on to greener pastures.

He wondered, for the thousandth time since he'd found out about Gordon Jackson, what his dad had thought and felt as he'd left town back then. Had it at least been a painful decision, or was it more like shrugging off a dirty shirt after work for something clean from your wardrobe? No matter what he'd said to Jen about no more second chances, dozens of questions crawled around his mind, nipping like ants at a picnic. What kind of man was he?

The sum total of his knowledge so far was limited to the handful of letters they'd exchanged over the last three weeks. Max couldn't remember the last time he'd received a handwritten letter, let alone written one. They were few and far between in this day and age, but somehow the thought of trying to reconnect by email had seemed too impersonal and putting pen to paper had just felt right.

Six weeks ago, his mum had sat him down and bared her soul, sharing what she had referred to as the only skeleton in her closet. Her cancer scare six months back had set in motion the chain of events that brought him to Beacon today. A lump in her right breast, that thankfully turned out to be nothing worse than a cyst, had given her the worst scare of her life. After the emotional high of getting the all clear, the next four months passed like nothing had happened, until she invited Max round for dinner, spoilt him with his some of his favourite food, then finally told him he truth about his father.

The first time Max could remember asking about his dad, he'd only been four. She'd told him that Daddy used to shout lots, so he'd gone to live in another town, but little else. The older he got, the more he'd wanted to know. When he was seventeen, his mother told him how his dad had left not long after she fell pregnant, accusing her of trying to trap him. That was where her story finished. What she hadn't told him until this year was what happened next. A week later he had come back, tail between his legs, saying they could make it work. That he'd stand by her. Anger and pride made her spit out four words that meant Max was raised by one parent instead of two.

I had an abortion.

The words that had spun his life off on a tangent, like a train changing lines at a junction. She'd said them with conviction at the time, because that's exactly what she intended to do. She'd been young and scared; too scared to go through with it, as it turned out. The fear of going to the appointment alone turned out to be greater than the fear of her parents' reaction. She had expected more judgement than support, from her own father in particular, who had never been Gordon's biggest fan, but he'd insisted Gordon had a right to know. A chance to do the right thing.

By the time she plucked up the courage to tell him the truth, he'd disappeared, with no forwarding address. Max already knew how the story played out from there. She had never married. Never shown any interest in anyone, and channelled all her energy into raising Max. There was one more revelation, though, one he hadn't seen coming. A plain cream envelope, the possible answer to his questions. She'd hired a private investigator to track down Gordon, and it had been up to him to decide if he could do what she hadn't been able to over thirty years ago; tell Gordon he was a father. Maybe even meet him after all this time.

That they would meet here, now, under these circumstances, wasn't how Max had seen things playing out. Jen was all that mattered now, though. Whether he could forgive his dad for standing him up a few days back wasn't a question for now.

He glanced at his watch. Gordon was over an hour late. Traffic crawled past the window like cars on a production line, people bustled past, and the door stayed firmly shut. Amy stood up from behind her desk, making a show of stacking some papers in a neat pile, looking a little embarrassed as she spoke.

'I'm really sorry, Mr Brennan, but I need to close up early today.'

Max felt the beginnings of a headache lurking behind his eyes. Unbelievable. Stood up twice in a week. He toyed with asking Amy to call his dad again, but why should he get yet another chance to come good? There wouldn't be a third. He'd find Jen on his own.

'Don't worry about it. If he does get in touch, you've got my number.' He had one hand on the door when something else occurred to him. 'What about the buyer? Can you tell me who bought it from him? They might have another number or a forwarding address.'

'I can tell you, but I don't think it'll help you much,' she said with a shrug. 'The buyer was us.'

'Sorry, you've lost me there,' said Max. 'Do you mean you bought it yourself?'

'I mean Beacon. We bought it.' Max only managed a grunt.

She clearly took it as a need for more information, and the words babbled out, as she checked her watch.

'We offer a seven-day purchase scheme for anyone who needs a fast sale. The offer is below market value, obviously, between ten and twenty per cent depending on the case, then we flip it round and sell at the going rate.'

'Really?' Max's eyes widened. 'You can do it that fast? Took me three months to buy mine.'

'It's not for everyone. Obviously, they get less for their property this way, but you'd be surprised how many go for it.'

'And my father was happy to take a hit like that?'

'I assume so, but you'd have to ask him that yourself. Now, if you'll excuse me, I really must lock up.'

If it was that simple I wouldn't be stood wasting my time with you, Max thought, but let it go, heading outside to work out his next move. He toyed briefly with the idea of hanging around the shop, but if Gordon was going to show he'd have been there by now, or at least have called to say he was running late. Max watched as Amy joined, then disappeared into the ebb and flow of pedestrians. Enough about his dad, he had to focus on Jen. Still no calls or texts on his phone, from Jen or anyone else for that matter. He tried Porter again, with the same voicemail promising a call back, but left no message this time.

Jen's face smiled back at him from his phone screen, but this time, instead of making him smile, it was like someone had reached in, squeezing his insides. Where the hell was she?

Max was as good as on autopilot on the drive home. Part of him wanted to keep moving, head to her friends', her parents', anywhere she might be. If there was even the slightest chance she could be waiting at home for him, though, he had to check, had to see for himself. Besides, there had been a steady stream of enquiries from those he'd contacted, asking for news. If she'd turned up at any of their houses, they'd have let him know by now. Home was a two-bed semi on Hamilton Road, just outside Harrow. The houses were tightly packed, wedged up against one another, wearing cladding on the front like face masks. As he made the turn onto his street, his gut did a roller-coaster-like flip at the sight of the empty driveway and the curtains still drawn, just the way he'd left them.

Max turned off the ignition and just sat for a full minute, the ticking engine marking time. The headache hadn't progressed beyond a six out of ten, but things were starting to catch up to him as the reality of the situation sank in. Getting out of the car and walking to the door felt more of an effort than it should have been. A loud gurgling from under his T-shirt reminded him that he'd hardly eaten all day. Not that he had much of an appetite, but maybe forcing a sandwich down would give his energy levels a boost.

He slung his jacket over the carved wooden bannister and trudged into the kitchen. He stared at the contents of the fridge, pulling out a packet of Swiss cheese and half a red onion. Two slices of each shoved in between a pair of doorstep-size slices of crusty bread wasn't exactly his finest work, but it'd do for now. He didn't bother with a plate, eating where he stood, back propped against the cool granite worktop.

He'd just sunk his teeth into the second half when a dull thud registered from somewhere out back. Max went over to the window and stretched forwards, hands on the edge of the sink, craning his neck left and right. The bin lay on its side, contents spilling out onto the patio.

'Jesus,' Max muttered as he opened the back door. 'If I ever get my hands on that bloody cat . . .'

He left the sentence hanging, knowing full well the worst he'd do would be to shout at it. He walked over to the bin, leaving it where it lay as he picked up the scattered rubbish. A half-eaten banana in a coat of mottled brown and yellow skin. Bean sprouts he'd picked out of a stir-fry. He lifted the bin back up, pushed it flush with the wall and headed back inside, grabbing his sandwich from beside the sink and staring back out at the garden as he took another mouthful.

It had been a tangled mess until Jen moved in and brought some order to the chaos. Pansy-lined paths, half a dozen rose bushes and a small army of terracotta-coloured pots, exploding with colour. A line of trees twice his height at the far end gave them privacy from neighbours.

Max stared out, through his own reflection, scanning for any signs of the cat, but the only things moving were tree branches dancing in the wind. Was it the breeze, or was something making its way through the foliage? He narrowed his eyes, squinting at a dark patch near the far left corner, so focused that he didn't see the transparent arm reflected in the window, moving up past his left shoulder until it was across his neck.

He started to turn towards it, more reflex than conscious decision, body a few steps ahead of brain, but still too late to stop the arm looping under his chin, tight against his throat, pulling him backwards. Max dropped his chin to his chest. He remembered that much from self-defence training in his army days; protect your airway. He pushed back against whoever was behind him, feeling something slap against his forehead hard. A sickly sweet smell sent his head spinning. Coarse cloth slid over his eyebrows. The smell grew stronger. Chloroform? If he hadn't tucked his chin down, it would be clamped over his nose and mouth. Whatever it was, the kitchen was starting to blur around the edges.

Max fought the urge to suck in a full breath, chest tightening as he grabbed the crook of his attacker's elbow and pulled, winning back half an inch. He threaded his other hand inside the arm holding the cloth. Pushed up and away, forcing the rag away from his face. The chokehold slackened, just a touch, and yanked backwards, squeezing against Max's jaw now. Max went with it, adding his weight to it, driving them both into the kitchen unit behind.

A muffled grunt from behind, and the arm across Max's neck dropped down across his chest, fingers scrabbling at his jumper. Max took a half step forwards and to his right, dropped his shoulder and turned at the hips, momentum pulling his attacker from behind him. A figure in dark blue jeans and black sweatshirt swung into view, black balaclava hiding their face. They still had hold of Max's jumper, and the two toppled to the floor, landing chest to chest, and Max heard a loud grunt as his full weight drove the breath from the man's lungs.

Brown eyes stared up at him from behind the mask, teeth gritted with pain or effort. Max reached over with one hand for the hem of the balaclava. Their heads were less than a foot apart, and he almost didn't see the headbutt coming. The man's chin caught on Max's forearm, deflecting the blow onto his cheek, still with enough force to make Max rear up and back. The shift in weight was enough, and the man rolled his weight onto his right hip, whipping an elbow around against the side of Max's face, landing on the same cheek, and Max rolled sideways into a cupboard door.

The man scooted his hips back, away from Max, flipped over onto his knees, scrabbling away a few feet, then pushed himself up and stumbled out through the back door. By the time Max followed him out, the only thing moving in the garden were tree branches, bobbing in the breeze.

'And you're absolutely sure that everything was locked up when you got home?' Porter asked. 'Couldn't have been that you forgot to lock the door on your way out?'

Max sat opposite him, pack of frozen peas crunching against his cheek every time he moved. Max was the same age, a slightly leaner, taller version of Porter, but he'd always been able to handle himself, so it was no surprise to Porter that he'd fought off whoever had attacked him. The strain of the last twenty-four hours was showing, though. A sandpaper coating of stubble on his chin and shadows under his eyes gave him a look that bordered on hungover.

'Absolutely positive,' said Max. 'I had to unlock the front door to get in, and the back door to go and sort the bins out. He must have already been inside.'

'Not necessarily,' said Porter. 'He could just as easily have been waiting outside for you to open the back door. He could have been the one who pulled the bin over in the first place.'

'Does it really matter? All I can think about right now is finding Jen.'

'Of course it matters,' said Porter, leaning forwards in his seat. 'Have you considered that there might be a connection between the two?'

Max gave him the kind of look that suggested he'd just said the world was flat, and opened his mouth to speak, but Porter held up a hand to stop him.

'I'm just thinking out loud here, but Jen goes missing and you being attacked in your home are both pretty significant events in anyone's book. The odds of two things like that happening to one couple is slim to say the least.'

Porter sat back again, arms folded, seeing confusion on Max's face as he tried to make sense of what Porter had suggested.

'So where's the link, then?' Max said finally.

Porter shrugged. 'I get paid to look at all the angles, even ones that might not make much sense. Force of habit. There might not even be one. Probably isn't, but that's the way my mind works. Eliminate all the possibilities you can, and what you're left with usually makes sense.'

Max pulled the frozen peas away from his face, staring at the bag as if all the answers he wanted would be right there, next to the nutritional information. When he turned it over and pushed the other side back against his cheek, its contents rubbed together with a crisp crunch that reminded Porter of footsteps on snow.

'You said you were at the Beacon office today. Who else knew where you were, and when you'd be home? Who was there when you went? Who did you speak to on your way there, or after you left?'

'Nobody. The answer to all of those is nobody, except for the girl at Beacon. So where does that leave us?'

Porter heard the frustration in Max's voice. Wished he could reach across, pat his friend on the shoulder and tell him not to worry, but he couldn't bring himself to lie. Everything about this felt bad. If this had been a break-in, why was nothing taken? Maybe Max and Jen had just had a fight, and his pal was embarrassed to own up? But if that was the case, her family or friends would know, and Styles had called the list of numbers that Max had given him, striking out every single one.

'Did you notice anyone following you today, either before you got there or after you left?'

'Why would anyone follow me?' Max asked, eyebrows raised at an *are you mad* kind of angle.

'Forget it,' Porter said. 'Like I said, just trying to jog your memory for anything that might help.' He stood up, motioning towards a young female officer by the back door. 'This is DC Farida Benayoun. She'll take you to A&E to get checked out. I'll see you there. Just got a few things I need to take care of at the station.'

Max let out a long sigh. 'Sorry for snapping at you, it's just . . .' His fingers tightened around the peas, making him wince at the extra pressure.

'You've got enough on your mind without worrying about hurting my feelings.'

That got the first smile of the day from Max. Porter quit while he was ahead, and left Max with Benayoun. He pulled his phone out as he walked towards his car. Max might not have been able to answer Porter's questions, but he knew someone who could help out with at least a few of them.

It wouldn't be the first time a hunch has been wrong, he thought, *but it never hurts to check these things out.*

The black balaclava skidded across the kitchen bench, and the man winced in pain as he prodded the base of his back. He'd hit the kitchen counter pretty hard. Hadn't really felt it at the time, but he sure as hell felt it by the time he had slid into his car a few streets from Max's house. He moved into the hallway, head twisted around to look in the full-length mirror. A horizontal red stripe was tattooed across his back where the edge of the counter had dug in. He let the hem of his T-shirt fall back down and walked into the kitchen again, questions swirling around his mind like water draining down a plughole.

What was his next move? He knew, of course, what it should be. He should do what he did best. Disappear. No wasted thoughts about Max. Pack up what few possessions he cared about and head for the safety of the south coast. The house there was just what he needed right now. Closest neighbours over a mile away. Rest up. Forget about this . . . what would you even call it? A blip? Yes, that'd do.

That was exactly what he should do, but he knew his inner perfectionist wouldn't let him. He had to know. Where had he gone wrong? If he walked away now, what's to say he wouldn't make the exact same mistake next week, next month, next year?

He walked over to the fridge, pulled out a smoothie that claimed to have more fruit and veg in than most allotments. Looked more like someone had sifted algae from a pond and slapped a cheery label on it. He cracked the seal as he walked to the door that led to the utility room, swiping the balaclava from the bench as he passed. He paused, put the bottle down and rolled the balaclava down his face until it covered everything bar his mouth. He tipped the bottle up and drank the lot, watching the green liquid coating the inside oozing down the sides.

Enough stalling. Down to business. He pulled the last inch of his mask down, pulled a set of keys from his pocket and unlocked the utility door. Jen Hart was slumped forwards, curtain of hair covering her face. Maybe he didn't need to speak to Max after all. Maybe she had held out on him the first time around. Doubtful, but after today he had to consider anything as possible. He'd know soon enough. He could be very persuasive when he needed to be. Exactly what form that persuasion took would depend on how talkative she was when he woke her up. He smiled to himself, stepped back out of the room and locked the door behind him. She'd keep.

CHAPTER FOUR

October 1979

It was the first day of his life as he knew it. The first he could remember, anyway. First but not the worst. Those days were still to come. It was the smell he remembered more than anything. Like a *Tom and Jerry* cartoon, where scents waft out from the kitchen, except this one wasn't anything to rave about. Undiluted bleach, tendrils sneaking up his nose, taking root, making his eyes water as sure as if he'd rubbed chopped onions in them. He remembered wondering if somebody had been sick. Maybe the smell was part of the clean-up. A full-frontal assault on the senses, strong enough to blur his vision and make him breathe through his mouth.

Muffled voices filtered through the dark oak door to his left. A woman's voice, the lady who'd brought him here. Mrs Johnson. She had arms thicker than his thigh, and fingers like stuffed sausage casings that looked ripe enough to burst. All smiles and sing-song voice. He was going to like it here, she'd said. Larchfield was full of

68

other boys and girls with no mum or dad, and he was sure to make lots of new friends.

A second voice, lower, more of a rumble, like thunder clouds in the distance. He jumped as the door creaked open, a tall willowy man framed in the doorway. Mrs Johnson had told him about Mr Archer, about how he'd take care of him now. About how he takes care of all the boys and girls like they were his own.

Mrs Johnson squeezed past him, back out to where the boy sat. She tried to bend at the waist to ruffle his hair, fingertips only skimming the strands that stuck up thanks to the limited tilt her ample belly would allow and waddled off down the corridor. The boy watched her disappear around the corner, then looked back at the still-open door. Mr Archer stood off to one side, beckoning the boy into his office. The boy studied Mr Archer's face. Its mouth turned up at the corners in what he supposed was meant to be a smile. When he pictured it in his mind years later though, the smile only ever graced the mouth. Never the eyes.

CHAPTER FIVE

Max was fidgeting on a hard plastic chair when Porter walked into the waiting room. DC Benayoun had her back to the room, stabbing an angry finger at an unresponsive vending machine.

'How's the patient?' Porter dropped into the chair beside Max.

'Really?' said Max. 'You had two hours and that's the best cliché you can manage?'

'Even I can't be witty twenty-four-seven,' said Porter. 'Seriously, though, what have they said?'

'Not much really.' Max sounded dog-tired as he spoke. 'Nothing broken, just a bit banged up. You get your things taken care of?'

'You could say that.' Porter nodded. 'I know you think I'm full of daft ideas, but I took the liberty of checking the CCTV footage from around the Beacon office this afternoon. Had the pleasure of watching you stroll out.'

'OK . . .' said Max, stretching the word out, somewhere between an acknowledgement and a question.

'I also asked for some traffic camera shots along the route you took home. Might be nothing more than a coincidence, but there was a car a few back from you, black Lexus, that passed through all the major junctions you did. Rings any bells?'

'I don't usually check for a tail, Jake. It's not like I'm MI5.'

'OK, OK,' said Porter. 'I don't get paid to settle for coincidence, though. It's registered to a Harold Mayes. Home address around a forty-five-minute drive from yours. As I said, might be nothing, but there were two of those junctions you took on amber, and he stepped on the gas both times to get through rather than sit and wait. I'm sending a car over to his. Might even swing by myself. Worst case they'll speak to him about his dodgy driving. Best case . . . I'm not even sure what the best case looks like right now, but that's all we've got.'

The man cupped a hand around the cigarette perched on his lips, sucked on the filter as the lighter flame licked at the tip. He leant against the wall at the back of the house, staring up at the night sky. Orion's Belt, high and to his right, was the only thing he recognised amongst a handful of stars, flickering like cheap Christmas tree lights.

A soft meow from within the clump of fir trees at the far end of the garden, and a black shadow slid out, prowling towards him. He disappeared inside, and came back out with a Tupperware container, milk sloshing against the edges. He was pretty sure it didn't live here. There was no litter tray for starters. Maybe it belonged to the lady across the road. He'd seen her trying to coax it in yesterday.

'Take what you can get, wherever you can get it,' he said to the cat. 'Man after my own heart.'

The cat ran a tongue around its mouth, arching its back in appreciation. *Of the milk, or the comment?* he wondered. *Maybe both?*

He snapped his head around at a noise. A voice. Faint, but definitely a man's voice. He cocked his head to one side. Held his breath. Listened.

'Mr Mayes?'

The voice sounded like it was coming from the front of the house. A faint chime echoed from inside. He took a step back towards the house but froze at the sound of footsteps. It sounded like they were coming from the path along the side of the house, getting louder, heavier. Nosy neighbours? A glow from underneath the gate. A torch? Who knocks on a neighbour armed with a torch?

He had been careful, obsessing over detail, but with a car in the driveway and lights on, albeit behind closed curtains, there was no hope of bluffing an empty house. A glance back at the house, at the door that led back into the kitchen. Decision made, he kept his eyes fixed on the gate as he edged slowly backwards until he melted into the treeline.

The voice was louder now, right beside the gate by the sounds of it. He cursed himself for not checking earlier whether it was locked.

'Mr Mayes?' A woman's voice, but who?

He heard the creak. Saw torchlight flickering through the branches, lighting up the patio. He narrowed his eyes, leaning to his right, peering through a gap in the pine needles. A shadowy figure stepped into the pool of light from the kitchen window. A woman in a dark suit. Young. Mid-twenties, maybe. Hair so dark it looked like it was still in shadow. Alone.

'Mr Mayes?' More authority this time. 'This is DC Benayoun

with the Met Police. Is anyone there?' The officer spoke softly, presumably into a radio. 'Back door's wide open. Kitchen light on, but no sign. I'm going to take a look inside.'

The man watched as the officer took a step towards the door, paused, listening to a response he assumed.

'Understood. Standing by.'

How many others were here with her? Were they here for him, or for Harold? The girl was inside, but that would do them no good. He'd taken precautions. She'd seen his face once, briefly when she got in his car, and even then, he'd been wearing sunglasses and a cap. The laptop was still powered up on the kitchen table, but if there was even one more officer out front, the odds started to slide away from him. Not that he was afraid of getting physical, but he was nothing if not a man of measured decisions.

He reached down, patting his pockets, relaxed a little when he felt his car key and mobile. Another phone was next to the laptop, but nothing on there could be traced back to him personally. The laptop itself might as well be brand new out of a box. Only one file open on it. Strings of numbers, no context, that might as well be in a foreign language for all the good it'd do them.

Either way, it was a moot point. He wasn't about to risk going back inside. More torchlight along the side of the house. A man joined the woman, exchanged a few whispers, and gestured her inside. Only when both had disappeared inside did he risk moving. He turned slowly so as not to disturb the branches around him, backing into a clear space no bigger than a phone box by a rear wall only a few inches taller than him.

The cat strolled into the clearing, watching as the man pulled himself up and over at a snail's pace. It continued to stare at the brickwork even after the man disappeared. Only for a few seconds,

73

though, before it got bored and padded over to the kitchen door to see if the new occupants had anything they'd like to share with him.

Porter edged forwards, one hand on DC Benayoun's shoulder as they stepped into the kitchen.

'This is the police,' said Benayoun. 'Anyone inside the house, please make yourselves known.'

Porter spotted the laptop first, screen facing away, then the glass by the sink. He moved towards the laptop to see if it was powered up, when he heard it. A noise. Something, or someone, coming from behind the door in the far wall. He tapped Benayoun on the back, pointing at the door. They moved quietly over to it, and Porter stepped to one side before trying the handle. Locked. There it was the sound again, louder this time, muffled by the door, like someone shouting from a distance.

Porter called out a warning for anyone inside to clear the doorway and aimed a kick just below the handle. The frame splintered but didn't break. A second kick did the trick, door exploding inwards. Light spilt from the kitchen through to the utility. The usual collection of washer, dryer and tired-looking cupboards, probably from a previous kitchen. Half in, half out of the shadow, Jen Hart's shoulders bounced up and down as she sobbed into her cloth gag.

'Ssshhh, Jen. It's OK. You're safe now. It's OK.'

For the second time today, he was baffled. Why had the officers turned up looking for Harold? Was it Harold they were actually after, or was there a link to him? If it was the latter, how the hell had they made that link? He was as certain as he could be that he'd taken all necessary precautions in Harold's house. There'd be no trace of him, no documents they could use. Fingerprints on the glass, maybe, but they weren't on record anywhere. He had accessed online banking pages on the laptop to complete a transfer, but the money would have made at least two more leaps before they got anywhere near it.

He hadn't finished with the girl, though, or Harold for that matter, but both were a write-off now. He wandered over to the reclining chair in the living room. His room. His flat. His name on the deeds, although he couldn't remember the last time anyone had spoken it out loud. An amber inch of Glenmorangie swirled lazily around the glass as he settled into the seat, fingers clamped around the rim like a claw grabbing a toy at a fairground.

He closed his eyes, listening to the rain spit at the window. What if he took some time off? Just walked away for a few weeks, a month, even. Wasn't like he had anyone to answer to. What was stopping him? He thought back to Max, to the policemen who'd forced him to walk away from Harold Mayes. Seconds that had oozed past as he watched from behind the trees, chest tight to the point of aching. Being forced off course was a slap across the face he couldn't walk away from, at least not without knowing why.

The girl hadn't been easy to understand at times, all snotty-nosed with fear. What she'd told him was sketchy at best. She lived with Gordon's son, Max. How had he missed that? His preparation had always been meticulous, flawless. Didn't do for anyone to be poking around, enquiring as to the wellbeing of those on his list. If he'd known about Max, Gordon would have been forgotten about a long time ago.

Professional curiosity needed satisfying, if indeed there was such a thing in his line of work. He nodded to himself, mind made up. Tipped the glass up, draining it in one swallow. Back to the drawing board.

* * *

75

Porter felt like an intruder. Max was like a guard dog, perched on the edge of Jen's hospital bed, a hand on hers, thumb tracing a circle on the back of her hand as she talked. He'd interviewed dozens of victims, but never anyone he knew personally. This was different, and he wondered whether he should have waited for Styles and let him take point. She had a private room at least, but her eyes flicked to the closed door with every set of footsteps that passed.

'I never saw his face. He always wore a balaclava. All I could see were his eyes and mouth.' Her voice was frayed around the edges, husky from crying.

'Just relax, Jen,' said Porter, softening his own voice. 'Focus on what you did manage to see. Spit it all out and let me worry about sifting through it. You never know what might come in useful. Start with the phone call.'

She nodded, wiping the back of her free hand across her nose. 'I called Beacon. They passed on my number. He called and told me he'd meet me outside there for eleven.' She paused, looking over at Max. 'I just thought, if I could just . . .' Words stuck in her throat, and she squeezed her eyes tight as a handful of fresh tears broke loose.

Max shook his head. 'It's OK. Jen, it's OK. I know you were only trying to help.'

She nodded, eyes still closed. 'He pulled up in a black car. I don't remember what type. He asked if we could talk over a coffee, so I got in. He said something about picking up a parcel from a friend first. We only drove for a few minutes. It looked like the back door to a shop or something.'

She paused, took a sip of water. Her tone had flattened out now, like she was reading from a script, one that had happened to someone else.

76

'He disappeared inside for ages. I only went in to see if everything was alright. Someone grabbed me from behind, put something over my face. The next thing I remember is waking up in that room.'

'Then what, Jen?'

'He just kept asking me questions. Lots of questions.' She paused again, confusion wrinkling her forehead, staring into space like she was back in the room.

'He wanted to know why I'd called the agency. Who I was. Why I was looking for Gordon. Who you were.' She nodded towards Max. 'I just wanted to know what he wanted, what I had to say for him to let me go.'

She swallowed hard, and Porter wasn't sure how much more to push her. Her eyes filled up again, like clouds ready to burst.

'Who was he, Max? What did I do wrong? Why did he . . .' The rest was snuffed out by sobs. Max shuffled closer, and Porter wished he could tiptoe out and leave them like that, but he still couldn't quite wrap his head around what was going on, and Jen was his best bet right now. The only sounds were Jen sniffling, and a voice outside on the PA system that was about as clear as the ones you hear at a train station. The three of them sat like that for what seemed like an age, until Porter's phone buzzed to break the silence. He pulled it out of his jacket, holding it up in apology to Max, and headed out into the corridor. The number was the generic station switchboard, but by the time he'd clicked to accept, whoever it was had rung off.

He turned at the sound of the door opening behind him, to see Max following him out into the hallway.

'She's exhausted,' he said. 'Any chance we can let her try and get some sleep and finish this up tomorrow?'

Porter wanted to tell him no. That time was of the essence. But Max looked like he hadn't slept for a week. His cheek was a puffed-out pink blotch from earlier, eyes bloodshot, and he looked like he'd been out on an all-night session. Porter nodded, against his better judgement.

'You should get some sleep yourself. I know the last thing you want to do right now is leave her, especially after what she's been through, but trust me, you're no good to her if you're fit to drop yourself.'

'How the hell do you expect me to sleep after today?' No matter how exhausted Max looked, he still had some gas in the tank judging by his tone of voice.

'You'd be surprised,' said Porter. 'She's safe now, Max. She's safe, and she'll be out for the count soon enough. She won't even know you're gone, and you can be back here holding her hand before she wakes up in the morning.'

Max shook his head. 'The nurse said I can stay the night. I'll get some sleep in the chair by the bed. If I was home, I'd only be lying there wondering if she's OK.' He took a few steps towards Porter, rubbing fingers in his eyes, hands trailing down his face and rasping off his stubble. 'I know there's not a mark on her, but who knows what she's been through. She was missing for almost two days, and there was nothing I could do. The least I can do is stay here with her now.'

'OK, OK,' said Porter, conceding, both hands held up. 'To be honest, I'd probably do the same, but if you change your mind I can easily justify sticking someone on the door to keep an eye while you head home.'

Max gave him a tired smile. Porter fancied he saw his friend sway a few inches to one side, as if he was about to collapse, but

Max righted himself before Porter had a chance to step in. A series of rumbling clicks made him turn around, and Porter sidestepped as a bed wheeled past him. A young woman, almost as pale as the white walls, oxygen mask misting with every breath, lying with eyes closed, arms by her side.

Porter did a double take as she was pushed past. Dark hair framing features so delicate they could be porcelain. The same nose, slight upturn at the end. It was as if he'd stepped back almost three years, to the night of Holly's accident. Something in his stomach uncoiled, a phantom of the nausea from that night. Then she was past him, hidden from sight by the white polo shirt of the hospital porter pushing the bed. He was vaguely aware of Max talking but kept staring until he felt a hand on his shoulder.

'Are you OK?' For all Max was exhausted, he was more concerned about everyone else but himself.

Porter felt like he'd clamped his lips around a hairdryer, and he licked them as he turned back to Max. 'Yeah, of course, I'm fine.' Down the hall, the bed rounded the corner, and out of sight. 'Tell you what, if you won't go home, how about you let me buy you a coffee before I head off?'

The cafe was probably the least clinical place in the hospital, but still a far cry from Starbucks. It was almost deserted, save for an elderly couple sitting at the table nearest the door. No mistaking who was visiting who; her in a pink fluffy dressing gown, him in cords and a tweed jacket. Porter paid for two coffees and joined Max at a table on the far side.

'It's OK, Jake,' said Max, as Porter pushed one of the cups towards him. 'You can say it. He might be my dad, but he took her. God knows why, but he took her.'

Max's voice was low when he spoke, but Porter knew him well

enough to hear the anger simmering below the surface.

'Too many questions, not enough answers,' said Porter. 'We don't even know for sure that it was him.'

'The agent arranged the meeting. You heard her in there,' he said, pointing back towards the ward. 'She spoke to him before she got in the car. This wasn't some random nut job that happened to be driving by. You don't need to play devil's advocate because of who he is.'

'True,' said Porter, popping the lid off his coffee. 'But she also said he asked questions about you, and some about Gordon by name. Who asks about themselves like that?' He tore open a packet of sugar and tipped it into his cup. Max said nothing. Porter wished he knew the answer himself. Every question spawned two more, like cells multiplying in a Petri dish.

'Go on, go to her. Get some sleep and let me do my thing. I'll call by and see you both tomorrow.'

Porter clicked the lid back on and stood up. Max followed suit. They walked back towards the ward until the corridor split off towards the main entrance.

'Thanks, Jake,' said Max, clapping a hand against Porter's arm.

'What for? I've not done anything yet.'

Porter turned and headed out to the car park. Drizzle tickled his face as he walked outside. He stopped, closing his eyes, tilting his head up. Leaving the hospital was like slipping off a heavy backpack. He had never been a fan, not even before Holly. The squeak of rubber soles on hard floors was like nails on a blackboard.

He checked his phone as he walked over to his car. He had muted it on his way into Jen's room, and hadn't even felt it vibrate. Voicemail from the station. Styles.

'Boss, I'm clocking off for the night, but if you get this at a decent hour give me a bell. Few interesting bits to tell you from the Mayes house.'

Porter checked his watch. Quarter to eleven. Whatever it was could keep till morning.

CHAPTER SIX

March 1983

He had always been small for his age. A natural target for anyone higher up the pecking order. The schoolyard was a microcosm of the animal kingdom. Survival of the fittest. Runts of the litter fending for themselves, while everyone else pledges allegiance to the alpha male. There were three others from Larchfield at St Agnes School. Two in the year above him, plus another a year up again. Most days he was left alone, save for the occasional taunt about having no parents. He drifted through the days, invisible, hiding out in the library when he could.

He was a loner by nature. A loner, but not lonely. It wasn't that he lacked social skills, but, when it came to the company of others, he could take it or leave it. Why bother when most people, given half a chance, would let you down. Mrs Johnson had. She'd been back twice a year since she first brought him to Larchfield, but even that stopped when he was thirteen. The last time he saw her, she had left a sheaf of papers on the coffee table and gone to the bathroom. Curiosity got the better of him, and he learnt the truth about how he'd ended up at Larchfield.

He had been told his mum died after a brief illness. That much was true. What had been left out was that the illness was self-inflicted. Planted deep inside her by a needle. Life was all about choices. She'd made hers, however misguided. He had to live with the consequences, more than could be said for her.

CHAPTER SEVEN

Sleep didn't come easy to Max, and when it did it was plagued with dreams he could have done without. He woke with a start around two, after reliving the struggle in his kitchen, except this time, the hand that came around his throat had held a knife. No matter how tight he screwed his eyes closed, how slow and deep he breathed, he couldn't drift back off. The hours crawled by, until a warm glow crept around the folds of curtain a little after six.

He looked over to where Jen lay asleep. So peaceful now, compared to last night. He wondered what she'd seen, what she'd had to endure. Had her sleep been as troubled as his, or had she managed a degree of rest, courtesy of the hospital pharmacy?

Max pushed up from his chair, hands reaching above his head, interlocked fingers, yawning so wide that his jaw clicked. Jen stirred, turning away from him onto her side. Part of him wished she could sleep through all of this madness, wake up with everything back to the way it was a few days ago. He padded around the bed, gently moving a lock of hair from her face before she managed to inhale it.

He picked up his trainers and opened the door at a glacial pace so as not to wake her. The hospital cafe's Americano hadn't been great last night, but it was that or nothing. Last night's conversation with Jake replayed in his mind as he ambled his way through the maze of corridors. On one hand, what he'd said made sense. If it was Gordon who'd taken Jen, why would he ask questions about himself? Equally as puzzling was the idea of it not being him. That someone else had turned up in his place. Who would do that, and why?

Max's head felt jammed with a hundred questions, like the M25 at rush hour. The cafe looked closed, cover still pulled over the till, so he made do with the vending machine. He wandered over to a window in the far wall. The sun had barely broken free from the horizon and hung low between two tower blocks. Whatever the hell was going on, his father was involved somehow. To what extent, and to what end, he had no idea, but he swore to himself that he'd find out.

The main entrance to Paddington Green station was still draped in shadow when Porter arrived. Milburn didn't usually arrive before eight so he had an hour's grace. Last night's dream had been a variation on a theme. He and Max switching places, him sitting holding Holly's hand as she lay asleep in a hospital bed, tubes and wires snaking over her chest. He felt surprisingly alert despite the restless night, but he knew from experience that it wouldn't last.

He'd spent the drive in working through the possible angles from yesterday. Max had always been fiercely independent, even back when he was a kid. Including his call to Porter about Jen, he could count on one hand the number of times Max had reached out for help. Porter knew he should have forced the pace last night, kept questioning Jen while things were fresh. If it had been anyone else that's exactly what he would have done. There was no way he was about to hand the case over to anyone else, but he was doing nobody any favours, least of all Max or Jen, if he couldn't stay objective.

He nodded an acknowledgement to the desk sergeant as he strode past, punching in the entry code to access the interior offices. Styles was already at his desk, hunched over his keyboard. He looked up as Porter approached.

'Morning, Boy Wonder,' said Porter.

'Well, well, well, if it isn't Sherlock Holmes himself,' Styles fired back.

'Even when you're being cheeky, it's nice to see you acknowledge my superiority as a detective,' said Porter with a smile.

'I was aiming for that half-arsed respect, you know, the kind you give your grandparents so they keep you in the will.'

'Well, you needn't worry there, you're not in mine to begin with.'

Nothing like a few friendly insults to start the day. Porter realised he was still smiling. That didn't happen often enough these days.

'Saw your call last night, by the way, but it was a bit late by the time I left the hospital. Much to report?'

'Well, whoever took her, it wasn't Harold Mayes,' said Styles, very matter of fact.

'You sound pretty sure of that,' said Porter. 'I'm assuming that's based on more than just a hunch?'

'That's based on a search of the house turning up the body of one Harold Mayes in a chest freezer. My hunch is that he didn't climb in there just to hide from us.'

Styles toggled between windows on his PC, and Porter got his first glimpse of Harold Mayes. He lay on his right side, face turned away and tucked downwards. Knees up against the chest, arm draped over his leg. His clothes and hair were dusted white with frost. All tucked up like a puppet in a kid's toy box.

'Touché,' said Porter. 'I'm inclined to go with your gut on this one.'

'No firm time of death yet thanks to the conditions we found him in. Should know more this afternoon, though.'

'What about Gordon Jackson? Any sign of him?'

Styles shook his head. 'We do have the laptop, though. I had a quick look myself, and it's clean to the point it's almost fresh from the store.'

'Almost?' Porter interrupted.

'Patience, Sherlock, patience. If you let me finish, there are a few files on there. Excel spreadsheets. Password protected, though, so couldn't open them. They're small, only thirty kilobytes or so, but still worth a look. I've sent them to Morgan to work on.'

Ross Morgan was their resident IT guru. Any hint that you shared in interest in the technology itself and he'd talk at you for hours. Felt like a foreign language to Porter, but the guy knew his stuff.

'He says to give him an hour and he should have it cracked.'

Porter nodded. 'Let's use the time to make a start on Mr Jackson's background, then. Any previous form, forwarding address, finances, inside leg measurement, the lot.'

Styles cracked a knuckle and spun to face his keyboard. 'Your wish is my command.'

* * *

Four hours and two coffees later, Porter was still sitting clicking through frames of traffic camera footage, when Styles wheeled himself across. Harold Mayes's black Lexus was centre frame, waiting at traffic lights. Porter squinted at the screen, moving closer as if that would bring it into sharper focus. The driver was there in plain sight, but thanks to a baseball cap pulled low, only his chin was visible.

'How you getting on?' said Porter, without taking his eyes from the screen.

'OK – Gordon Jackson, born Maidstone, Kent. Last known residence Woodside, just outside Woodford. Date of birth has him just short of his fifty-first birthday. No forwarding address left with the estate agent, just phone number and email. No priors. He had an account with Barclays until Monday. He closed it down, transferred the lot somewhere else; we're working on that as we speak. Drives a Volvo that I've put a flag on. He's got an Amex card as well, but that's not been used for over a fortnight. We'll be the first to know when he does, though. Works for a hedge fund called Marlin, based in the City. I've left a message with their HR director's PA to call me back.'

Porter turned to face him. 'Right, that's a good start. I was hoping he might have popped up in convoy with Mayes,' he said, turning back, pointing to the screen.

'Oh, there's one more thing,' said Styles. 'Inside leg measurement is thirty-four inches.'

This time Porter laughed. When was the last time he'd done that? Too long.

Ross Morgan was one of those people who could go a whole day or more without actually speaking to another human, and not bat an eyelid. His desk was a curved bank of screens, scribbled Post-it notes and chewed biros. Brain of a geek, body of a rugby player, but despite his size, he always seemed nervous. He blinked almost non-stop, like he was sending a Morse code message, as he spoke.

'So the good news is whoever we're dealing with is no Gary McKinnon.'

Porter waited him out, hoping for an explanation. He looked at Styles, who shrugged. Morgan sighed.

'McKinnon? The man who hacked the US military, and NASA?' He rolled his eyes when Porter didn't respond. 'Anyway, we're dealing with relatively straightforward password encryption that I got past thanks to a nifty little program I wrote while I was at university. You see, it takes a modified approach to—'

Porter cut him short. 'It's not a shampoo advert, Morgan. You can spare us the science part.'

Morgan's blinking picked up speed. 'Yes, of course, sorry. Anyway, once you get into the file, it's just an Excel workbook with a dozen or so tabs on. The first just has strings of letters and numbers. No headings, no formulae. All nine digits. The other tabs are all blank but named after one of the strings. My guess is he has his own key to decipher these into something meaningful.'

'Could they be account numbers?' Porter asked. 'Maybe that's where he sent the money?'

'Hmm, maybe,' said Styles. 'Account numbers are usually just that, numbers. Could be anything. Travel bookings, parcel tracking references . . .' His voice tailed off as he leant forwards, staring at the screen. 'I recognise that one, though,' he said, tapping the third entry from the bottom. 'That looks like Jackson's National Insurance number.'

'You're sure?' said Porter.

'I'll double check, but I think so. It's the first two characters and numbers,' he said, tracing a finger across the screen. 'Same as Emma's initials and birthday. I noticed it when I did his background check.'

'They all follow the same sequence,' said Morgan. 'Two letters, six numbers, one letter.'

'If it looks like a dog, and barks like a dog,' said Porter. 'If Jackson's number fits, it's a fair assumption the others will too. Let's run them and see who else is mixed up in this.'

CHAPTER EIGHT

September 1988

He recognised them as older boys from school a split second after he rounded the corner. Walked smack bang into one of them, the larger of the two, before he knew what had happened. A cigarette cartwheeled from the startled boy's hand, a tiny explosion of sparks when it hit the zip of a dark green Berghaus jacket. His own heartbeat thudded like a bass drum, almost as fast as his footsteps when he turned and ran from the smoker and his friend.

They chased him into an empty factory and came within ten feet of catching him on a metal walkway, high above the warehouse floor. Almost certainly would have caught him in a matter of seconds, but for the gap in the criss-cross metal flooring, where rust had done its work, leaving a four-foot stretch weak and waiting. He'd spotted the kink in the floor, clearing it with an exaggerated stride. His pursuers hadn't been as fortunate.

It happened quickly. Footsteps punctuated by a thud. Sharp exhalation of air rushing out of lungs. Another thud, louder than the first. Howl of pain. They came in quick succession after the first one, strung together in a terrible symphony of sound. Smoker lay on the concrete below, one leg jutting out at an unnatural angle from the knee. The second boy left to get help.

The boy descended from the walkway. Stood half in shadow, ten feet away from where Smoker lay groaning. Even in the fading light, the boy saw the dark bloom growing on the lower part of Smoker's jeans. He supposed somewhere under the denim, bone pierced flesh. Smoker fumbled with his belt, trying in vain to loop it around the knee joint to slow the flow. After a full minute of trying, Smoker lay back, catching his breath, and saw the boy. He held up the belt.

'Please help.'

The boy took several slow steps towards him. Crouched down, took the belt. Looped it around his fingers. Hovered like that for a few seconds, then straightened up, retraced his steps into the shadow, slow and deliberate.

Ever since he could remember, people bigger than him had imposed their will. Told him what to do. Pushed him around. Not this time. This time, he was in control. He turned his back on Smoker's ragged curses, and by the time he was outside, they'd stopped altogether.

He didn't find out until teatime the following day that Smoker had died where he left him. Bled out on the factory floor before paramedics could reach him. He hadn't caused the situation, or created it, but he could have prevented the outcome. He'd consciously chosen not to, though. Life may well be all about choices, he reflected, and this had been his.

CHAPTER NINE

Twelve strings of numbers and letters, twelve names. Porter leant back in his chair, wafting the print-out in front of him. Two names he recognised, Jackson and Mayes, numbers nine and ten. All the others were new to him.

Andrew George
Kenneth Morgan
Daniel Fredrickson
David Marsh
Christopher Errington
Alan Bowles
Klaus Muller
James Singer
Stuart Leyson
Joseph Baxter

'Four main questions to start us off, then,' said Porter, counting off on his fingers. 'Who are the rest of these guys, and how do they link to Jackson? There's got to be a common denominator. If he's targeting them for whatever reason – which, taking Mr Mayes's current state of health into account, is not out of the question – why is his own number on here? Why are some cells green, and the others red or white?'

'How about we split them?' said Styles. 'Look for overlaps.'

'I'll take the second half, you run with the first six.'

'You mean you'll do five, then, seeing as I've already done Jackson for you.'

Porter did his best to look offended. 'Only because you're better at this part than me.'

'Oh, you smooth talker. Flattery gets you everywhere,' said Styles, batting his eyelashes, looking anything but feminine, as he pushed off in his chair back to his own desk.

Staring at a screen was part of the job Porter could do without. Crime scenes, interviews, anywhere he was in the thick of it was what pushed his buttons. Desk work was a necessary evil, though, and if he was honest, there wasn't enough to go on without it in this case.

Styles finished before him and wandered off, speaking to Emma on his mobile phone. When he came back twenty minutes later, carrying two coffees, Porter was finished, leaning back, hands behind his head.

'So, the plot thickens,' he said, taking a cup from Styles. 'First four are ghosts, literally for Mayes. The other three have dropped off the face of the earth. Closed down accounts, sold properties, never to be heard of again. They all live, and I assume work, in and around the City, so we can start by paying a visit to the two I've managed to find addresses for, neither of which, incidentally, are shaded in green. Make of that what you will.'

Styles perched on the edge of Porter's desk. 'I'll see your four ghosts and raise you two. Last trace of any of them was Alan Bowles. He closed his Lloyds account in November 2013 and hasn't surfaced since. Same story with the others dating back to 2009 and Andrew George. All similar ages, give or take a few years. Same general locations as yours. They drop off the map in sequential order, for what that's worth, but nothing else to link them.'

Porter said nothing for a beat, wading through what they'd learnt so far. 'OK,' he said finally. 'Family next, then employers and social media. There's got to be a link, we just need to know where to look.'

The prospect of more hours staring at a screen until the world went fuzzy at the edges was about as appealing as another session with Sameera Misra. He slapped a hand on Styles's leg, jumping up from his chair.

'Actually, I've got a better idea. Get Benayoun on it instead. Fancy a field trip?'

Twenty minutes in, and they had only made it as far as Madame Tussauds, impressive queue curling around the edge of the building, a good showing even for a Thursday lunchtime. Four flags high above it hung limp in the stillness of the morning. Faded green dome on the corner, standing proud like half a giant watermelon. A group of a dozen or so tourists stood outside, holding fixed grins like waxworks themselves for an impossibly long series of selfies.

A workman fifty yards ahead leant on an old-school stop-go sign, luminous yellow vest stretched taut over his gut like a boil waiting to be lanced. Traffic inched forwards, bumper to bumper, squeezing through the one usable lane. Porter twisted one of the AC vents so it hit him just under the chin, cool air trickling past his collar. What he'd give for one on his back as well. He shifted in his seat, shirt blotting the beads of sweat between his shoulders.

'Come on, then, talk me through what we have on contestant number one while we wait,' he said to Styles. Up ahead the workman flipped the sign back to red, after what couldn't have been more than ten seconds of painfully slow progress.

'OK, behind door number one we have Stuart Leyson. Forty-five-year-old former golden boy at Barclays, till he discovered the wonderful world of recreational drugs to help with the pressure. He had a run-in with us back in 2004, after a car accident. Cost him his licence, a fine, a stint in rehab and ultimately his job. Seems to be back on track now, though. Not even a parking ticket since then. Works for Credit Suisse as a risk consultant.'

'Bit ironic isn't it, seeing as he's taken a few over the years?' said Porter. 'Wife? Kids?'

'No, and no,' said Styles. 'You sure you don't want to call ahead and check he's about? At this rate, it'll take us another hour to get there. Long way to go on the off-chance.'

Porter thought it through for a second but shook his head. 'Nah, call me cynical if you will, but this whole thing feels off. Too many questions, not enough answers. Have you got any idea how hard it is to disappear these days, I mean completely disappear? If he knows anything, I'd rather not give him time to prepare any answers.'

'Fair enough,' said Styles.

'Then when you consider that this isn't just one missing person, it's eight, without Jackson and Mayes. That makes me suspicious and cynical.'

'You could use that as the opening to your lonely hearts ad,' said Styles. 'Suspicious and cynical would like to meet paranoid and distrusting.'

'What, and risk getting a response from your sister?' said Porter, straight-faced. 'That would just be awkward.'

Styles gave him a slow handclap as they edged a few feet forwards. One more rotation of the sign should do it.

'In all seriousness, though,' Porter continued, 'until we've got an idea of what the hell's going on, we assume everyone knows something they don't want us to know. Those names didn't end up on the list by accident. One of these guys today knows something that can help us, even if they don't realise it.'

'Speaking of the two of them, our second guy works at Canary Wharf as well. We could swing by after we see Leyson.'

'Joseph Baxter? What did we get on him?'

'He's an East End boy. Thirty-nine years old. Went to uni in Durham according to LinkedIn, to do accountancy, then landed a job with PwC. Worked his way up quickly by all accounts and got poached by KPMG in 2012.'

'Any priors?'

'Nope. Clean as a whistle as far as I can see.'

'What about what we can't see?' said Porter.

'Such as?'

'These other guys have disappeared. Passed Go, collected their two hundred and disappeared. Why isn't anyone looking for them?'

He paused, letting the question sink in, not expecting a reply.

'None of them have been reported missing. None of them have spent or borrowed a penny since they upped and left. Even if they'd just wanted a change of scenery, they'd need a bank account, change of address with the DVLA. One dead and eight missing makes me think being on that list isn't good for your long-term prospects, and nobody has bothered to ask where they've gone.'

'Might be stating the obvious,' said Styles, 'but what if there's nobody to miss them?'

'Maybe, maybe not. Let's see what Benayoun comes up with.'

Up ahead, the workman scratched at his gut, vest riding up, flash of white belly overhanging his belt, twirled the sign around, and Porter made it through, hitting the dizzy heights of thirty miles per hour on the other side. Who would miss him if he disappeared? His parents, his sister, sure. Even Styles might, to a degree.

He thought back to the hollow feeling after he lost Holly. Constant pressure, coming at him from all angles, compacting him down like a car in a scrap yard, until it felt like there was nothing left. Was that why he'd deflected Simmons's advance earlier this year? If he didn't let himself care about anyone, history couldn't repeat itself. What would Sameera Misra make of that? Even now, thinking about Holly, he felt a twinge in his gut, an echo of the churning stomach that had stayed with him for months after it happened. He'd grabbed on to his grief. Squeezed it in a bear hug. He couldn't imagine a world where he didn't miss her. Felt like if he let it go completely, then she would be gone with it, and what would that leave him with then?

Not much.

* * *

The Credit Suisse reception in the Cabot Square office was pristine, staffed by two women who could have been cloned in the same lab. Identical navy blue suits, ponytails scraped back from faces. Even though he and Styles both wore suits, Porter couldn't help but feel underdressed. Even a fashion agnostic like him could tell the group of four men who swept past them were wearing suits worth more than his last month's salary. Even their ties would probably run a higher bill at the checkout than his whole outfit, shoes included.

'Good afternoon, gentlemen, how can I help you?' The receptionist on the left greeted them with a smile.

'Good afternoon, Ms . . . Simms,' said Porter, clocking her name tag. 'Detective Porter, and this is my colleague, Detective Styles.' He flashed his warrant card. 'We need to speak with one of your colleagues, Stuart Leyson. Could you give him a call and see if he's free, please?'

'Certainly, Detective,' she said, eyebrows twitching at the prospect of something out of the ordinary. Inch-long nails pecked at the keyboard as she searched for his number.

'Mr Leyson? It's Melanie from reception. There are two gentlemen here to see you.' She paused, presumably while he spoke. 'No, sir, I know they don't have an appointment, but they're with the police. OK. Certainly, I'll let them know.' She ended the call. 'He's just with a client, Detective. He'll be down in about ten minutes, if you'd care to take a seat.'

She gestured to an area by the lifts – a small glass coffee table, four black leather chairs around it like points of the compass.

'Can I get you anything while you wait?'

'We're fine, thank you,' said Porter, wandering over to the nearest chair.

'You could have at least asked if I wanted a coffee,' said Styles, doing his best to sound hurt. 'I was going to ask if they had any of that civet coffee. Worth more per ounce than gold according to the *Sunday Times*.'

'You can read?' said Porter.

Styles chuckled. 'Good to have you back, guv.'

'Don't know what you mean,' said Porter, but he knew exactly what Styles was getting at. He could usually box things away, deal with them in his own good time, but that had felt nigh on impossible these past few months, and Patchett had been the mouldy cherry on top of an overcooked cake. Max, Jen, this whole puzzle of Gordon Jackson, was a welcome distraction from his own problems.

'Plan of attack, then?' asked Styles as they both took a seat.

'We need to know if any of the names ring a bell, especially Jackson or Mayes. See how it goes but might even ask him outright if he knows Max and Jen too. He doesn't need the detail around her kidnapping, or where we came across the names. Let's keep that part suitably vague for now.'

The ten minutes became twenty, and Porter was on the verge of going back over to reception when a slender man in a navy pinstripe came through the turnstiles and headed towards them. He looked every inch the City stereotype. Crisp white shirt, collar starched to within an inch of its life. Royal blue tie, with matching handkerchief that peeked out from his top pocket. His dark hair was a generic conservative cut, and Porter couldn't decide whether his shade of tan was natural or from a salon.

'Gentlemen,' the man said, offering a hand to Styles first, then Porter. 'Stuart Leyson. Can I ask what this is about?'

Porter cleared his throat. 'Detective Porter, and this is my colleague, Detective Styles. We're hoping you can help by answering a few questions relating to a case we're investigating. Is there somewhere a little more private we can go?'

'There's a meeting room behind reception,' Leyson said. 'Let's see if that's free.'

The barrier opened as if by magic when they walked towards it. The receptionist must have activated it. Porter glanced over, and she smiled in confirmation. The room could have catered for a whole task force, never mind three of them. A large oval table dominated the centre, sixteen leather chairs spaced around it. Every seat had a pad of paper, a brushed steel pen and an upturned glass on a paper coaster stamped with the Credit Suisse logo.

'Please,' said Leyson, pulling out the closest chair. 'Take a seat.' They followed his lead, a chorus of creaking leather. 'How can I help you then, Detectives?' Leyson unbuttoned his jacket, crossed right leg over left, and settled back into his chair. His poise and posture made Porter feel he was the interviewee, instead of the man here to ask the questions.

'Your name cropped up in the course of an investigation, Mr Leyson, and we're hoping you can help us understand why,' said Porter. 'Does the name Gordon Jackson mean anything to you?'

Porter studied him, watching a crinkle appear between Leyson's eyebrows as he processed the name.

'Sorry, Detective, can't say that it does. Should it?'

Porter looked for any sign that the name had registered but found none.

'That's the point of the question, Mr Leyson. We don't know if there's a connection or not. What about Harold Mayes?'

Leyson thought it over for a few seconds. 'Again, it doesn't ring a bell. Can I ask who these gentlemen are?'

'Afraid we can't say too much at this stage, sir,' said Porter, shaking his head. 'Suffice to say your name has appeared, along with others, on a list that's tied to Mr Mayes's murder, and Mr Jackson's disappearance.'

Leyson's jaw dropped a little at the mention of murder, but he stayed silent.

'Our first priority is to establish any connections between names on the list.' He turned to Styles. 'Let's see the pictures.'

Styles took an envelope from inside his jacket and spread the contents on the table. Two six-by-four colour photos.

'Do you recognise either of these men?' Porter asked.

'No,' said Leyson, shaking his head, sounding a little less confident than a minute ago. He fiddled with the knot on his tie. 'No, I've never seen them before. Who are they?'

'This is Gordon Jackson,' said Styles, pointing to the picture on the left, 'and this is Harold Mayes. You sure you've never seen them before, maybe using another name?'

'Positive, Detective. I'd tell you if I had.' Leyson was sweating now, not much, but Porter spotted a few beads had popped out on his forehead. He seemed genuinely rattled, though. The kind of misplaced nervous you get when a police car screams up behind you in the fast lane, until you realise they just want to get past you.

'How about any of the names on this list?' Styles asked, pulling a sheet of paper from the same envelope, flattening it against the table with his palm, sliding it across to Leyson.

Leyson pulled it across with his fingertips, flicking his eyes up and down. Porter was convinced it was a strikeout, but Leyson tapped the page.

'A couple look familiar,' he said, stabbing a finger midway

down. 'Let me check something.' He picked up his BlackBerry, flicking a thumb across the scroll button. 'I do know a Joseph Baxter. Not sure if he's the same one you're after, but we met a while back at a networking event. Turned out he did a stint at Barclays after I left, and we know a few of the same people. I say know' – he gave a nervous laugh – 'more like despised. Nothing like some mutual loathing to stimulate conversation.'

'And when was the last time you saw him?' asked Porter.

'Hmm.' Leyson pondered over it. 'I'd say about twelve months. We swapped business cards when we met at the AMT event, then he invited me to lunch a month or so later. He was less than complimentary about his current employer as I remember. I suspect he was working his way through his black book, looking for a new home. How's he mixed up in this anyway?'

'We can't say at this stage, sir. What can you tell us about him, work life or personal?'

'As I said, Detective, I barely know the man. Literally met him twice. Workwise he's like most of us in this game. Doesn't leave much room for personal life if you want to keep moving upwards. I don't remember any mention of a wife. I do remember the whisky, though.'

'Whisky?' said Styles. 'What about it?'

'We bonded over a love for single malt. They had a fabulous selection at the AMT event.' He glanced at his BlackBerry as it purred for attention but thought better of answering whoever it was just yet. 'This one too,' he said, pointing back at the list. 'Christopher Errington. Pretty sure I met him at the same event, although not seen him since.'

'You're sure of the name, though?' asked Styles.

'Pretty sure, yes. If it's the chap I'm thinking of, he's a fellow

Chelsea fan. We had a moan about never keeping a manager longer than a few seasons. Baxter was an Arsenal man, so we ganged up on him for a while.'

The fact that three of their names had met previously, however briefly, felt significant to Porter, even if he couldn't pinpoint why just yet.

'Do the names Max Brennan or Jennifer Hart mean anything to you?' said Porter.

'Sorry, no,' said Leyson, checking his watch. 'I don't mean to be rude, Detectives, but I really do need to get back to work.'

'Appreciate your time, Mr Leyson,' said Porter, holding out a business card as Styles gathered up the pictures. 'If you think of anything else about any of these gentlemen, I'd appreciate it if you'd give us a call.'

'Of course,' said Leyson, rising to his feet, confidence returning now his ordeal was nearly at an end.

Porter was halfway to the door when he stopped and turned around. 'One last question, Mr Leyson. AMT. You mentioned the name twice. Who, or what, are they?'

'They're headhunters. Placed me here, and I'm pretty sure they put Baxter at Barclays too. Everyone at that event was a client. Might be worth speaking to them. I had to fill out all sorts of personal information when I registered with them, so they might know where to reach the others.'

'Thanks, we'll follow up with them. I'm sure I don't need to spell out how sensitive an investigation can be. I'd appreciate it if you can keep our chat today between the three of us.'

Leyson nodded enthusiastically, desperate to get away from them at this stage, no doubt. They retraced their steps back to the barriers, and Leyson offered his hand again. His cockiness was back.

'You'll be OK to see yourselves out from here?' he asked.

'Of course,' said Porter.

'If you'll excuse me, then,' said Leyson, and scurried away into a waiting elevator, leaving Porter and Styles to make their own way out.

'What did you make of him, then?' he said to Styles when they were safely outside.

'Typical City boy,' said Styles. 'I'd trust a *Big Issue* seller with my money before I picked him. Bit smarmy for my liking but seemed on the level. I think he told us the truth.'

'Me too,' said Porter. 'It's got to mean something, the fact that he knows two of the others. I just wish I knew what.'

The visit to KPMG was a lot quicker. The receptionist called upstairs, grunted a few times at whoever was speaking on the other end, then told them Baxter had taken a few days' sick leave. Some kind of virus, but they expected him back on Monday. Porter promised to call and make an appointment next week, even though he had every intention of turning up unannounced again.

'Back to the station, then?' asked Styles as they climbed back into their car.

'We could,' Porter said, shooting a mischievous glance at Styles. 'Or we could swing by Mr Baxter's home address and see if he's feeling any better?'

'You're all heart,' said Styles, but his grin told Porter all he needed to know. 'Why not. Lead on, Macduff.'

'Not wanting to be pedantic . . .' said Porter.

'But you will be,' said Styles, a statement, not a question.

'Seeing as you ask so nicely. You're misquoting the Bard. Common mistake, but a misquote all the same. It's actually "Lay on, Macduff", but I'll let you off this once.'

'Lay on, lead on. You say toe-may-toe . . .' Styles's exaggerated American twang came out about as authentic as Dick Van Dyke's cockney accent in *Mary Poppins*.

'You'll thank me one day when it pops up in a pub quiz,' said Porter.

Buzzing, like an angry bee, from the cup holder. He looked down at his phone, saw Milburn's name, toyed with answering but started the car instead. Styles reached a hand towards it, but Porter covered the phone with his own.

'Leave it. I'll see him when we get back to the station.'

Styles raised his eyebrows but said nothing as he drew his hand back. Porter pulled away from the kerb, and it wasn't until the KPMG building was out of sight that either of them spoke.

'Everything alright, guv?' asked Styles.

Porter glanced at him, back to the road again. 'Yeah, everything's fine. Why?'

'Just not like you to ignore the big man's calls. You two had a lover's tiff?'

'Something like that,' said Porter.

'Can we skip the part where you tell me you're fine, and get to what his problem is?'

Porter gripped the wheel hard, fingers wrapped around until nail met palm. To share, or not share? He made his decision.

'The video clip. He thinks I've got issues, and wants me to see someone in OHU, a counsellor.'

'Really? A counsellor cos of Patchett?'

Porter hesitated a beat. 'That . . . and a few other things.' He ran his tongue across his teeth, stalling, deciding how much he wanted to say.

It's your partner, for Christ's sake. Not the OHU.

'Milburn thinks I should have spoken to someone after Holly,' he said finally. 'Reckons I've been bottling stuff up, that what happened to Evie pushed a few of the same buttons, you know, about someone you know getting hurt, and nobody getting banged up for it.'

He looked across, waiting for a reaction from Styles. Saw his partner give a few gentle nods but say nothing.

'You're agreeing with him? Has he spoken to you about it as well?' Porter's cheeks flushed at the thought of whispered conversations behind his back.

Styles whipped his head around. 'Really, you think I'd be Milburn's office gossip boy?'

Porter heard no trace of deceit in the words, and instantly felt bad for looking for any. 'Course not. Sorry, it's not you I'm pissed off at.'

'It's fine,' said Styles.

'Isn't that supposed to be my line,' said Porter.

Styles shook his head, smiled at the peace offering. 'I will say one thing, though,' he said. 'And I'm not saying you need to speak to anyone, that's your business, but you have been a bit off form these last few months. How you deal with stuff is your business.' He held up a palm to stave off any comeback. 'But if you ever need an ear to bend . . .'

No need to finish the sentence. Porter knew what he was getting at, even if he didn't like admitting it to himself. He knew he'd been wrapped up in his own issues, drawing them around himself like a cloak. He'd never felt comfortable opening up with anyone, even Holly, although she'd had a way of teasing things out of him regardless.

'Cheers. Honestly, I'm fine, but you'd be first choice if I do.' And he meant it as well. Maybe it'd help to air it all over a beer one night. Maybe not. A decision for another day.

They crawled along with daytime traffic, roads clogged like a smoker's arteries. Pedestrians scurrying off for midday meetings and early lunches, phones to ears, eyes fixed ahead. Things picked up once they got onto the A12, whisking past the huge doughnut-shaped London Stadium, and on up towards Stoke Newington.

Summerhouse Road was a tidy cul-de-sac. The properties might have been houses once upon a time, but they'd been carved into flats years ago. Basement windows peeked out from behind railings. Steps leading up to raised ground floor flats reminded Porter of New-York-style stoops, whitewashed bay windows jutting proudly out. A half-dozen willowy trees flanked the road at uneven intervals. Hardly what you'd call tree-lined, but that wouldn't stop creative estate agents claiming exactly that. The road ended abruptly in a wall that looked like it hadn't been whitewashed since Churchill was in Downing Street, branches from neighbouring Abney Park threatening to reach over and invade the street.

Baxter lived in the far left corner, at number seventeen. The curtains were drawn, downstairs as well as on the first floor. He ran a finger down the buttons of the intercom, jabbing at the one next to Baxter's name.

'Yes?' A disembodied voice floated through the air.

'Hi, I'm looking for Mr Joseph Baxter,' said Porter, leaning towards the speaker as if it was hard of hearing.

'Yeah, I'm Joseph Baxter. What can I do for you?'

'Detectives Porter and Styles, Mr Baxter, with the Met Police.

Your name has cropped up in the course of an investigation, and we'd like to ask you a few questions if you have a couple of minutes.'

Several seconds of silence, punctuated by a car horn from back on the main road. Porter was just about to press the button and ask again, when Baxter spoke.

'Bear with me two minutes, Detective. I was just getting ready to go out. I'll be right down.'

True to his word, Baxter opened the door minutes later and pulled it closed behind him. Porter gave him a once up and down. Three, maybe four days of stubble. Small scar running through the right eyebrow, giving him a slightly rakish look. Baxter wore a black overcoat, white shirt collar peeking out from underneath, pinstripe suit trousers and tan shoes that screamed designer label.

'Sorry, couldn't find my keys,' he said, holding them up in apology. 'What is it I can help you with?'

'Is there somewhere we can sit down for a few minutes while we talk, if you're feeling up to it?'

'Feeling up to it?' Baxter echoed.

'Yes, your office said you were under the weather, that you'd taken a few days off.'

Baxter looked sheepish, glanced at his feet and sighed. 'You've caught me out, Detectives,' he said, holding his hands out, wrists together in a *cuff me now* gesture. 'I'm actually on my way to a job interview with a rival firm. Wouldn't exactly look good if I asked for time off for that, would it?'

'Why don't we step inside for a few minutes, sir, and then we can be on our way?'

'I'm OK here if you are,' said Baxter. 'I'd invite you in, but my place is in a bit of a state, and I'm already running a little behind for my interview.'

Porter shrugged. 'As I said, your name came up in connection to a current case, and we're just trying to establish the nature of any connection. Does the name Gordon Jackson mean anything to you?'

Baxter's brow creased like a ploughed field as he pondered the name. 'No, sorry, doesn't ring a bell.'

'How about Harold Mayes?'

'No idea,' said Baxter, hands digging deep into his coat pockets. 'Should I know them?'

'That's what we're trying to work out, Mr Baxter,' said Styles, reaching into his coat, coming out with the photos.

Baxter's eyes flicked back and forwards between the two, but his face gave nothing away. 'Can't say that I do,' he said finally. 'Who are they?'

'It's the same two gentlemen. Just wanted to see if you knew them by another name. Their names, and yours, were found on a list at a crime scene, so we'd just like to understand how you're connected.'

'Does there have to be a connection?' said Baxter.

'If there's one thing you learn in my line of work,' said Porter, 'it's that very little turns out to be random. Where were you on Tuesday evening this week, between five and seven?'

'Tuesday? I was at the office until around eight, then went to the gym for an hour. What happened on Tuesday?'

'Is there anyone who can vouch for your whereabouts, sir?' said Porter, ignoring Baxter's question.

'I suppose you could check with the security guard on our front desk,' said Baxter. 'He's probably got me on camera. Same at the gym too.'

Styles reached back into his pocket, pulling out a sheet of

110

paper this time. 'What about these names, Mr Baxter, any of them look familiar?'

'Is this the list you mentioned?'

Styles nodded, handing him the sheet. Porter studied Baxter's face, looking for a reaction, a tell, anything that might signal he recognised any of the names. Baxter's lips moved, as if reading out the list. He touched a finger to the page, ran it down the names, shaking his head all the way to the bottom.

'Sorry,' he said, handing it back to Styles.

'You're sure?' Styles asked.

'Yep, I've usually got a pretty good memory for things like this, and none of them look familiar.'

'Really?' Porter said, surprised. 'You've met one of them before, or at least he remembers meeting you.' Something shifted behind Baxter's eyes, but Porter couldn't read it.

'Did I?' said Baxter.

'Stuart Leyson,' said Porter, nodding. 'You met at an AMT event last year. He remembers talking to you about a mutual love of good whisky.'

Baxter rolled his eyes. 'An AMT event? Anything's possible, I suppose, but have you ever been to one of those networking bashes? It's like career speed dating. I've been to a few. Met dozens of people at them.'

Porter could picture it now. A hundred suits crammed into a room, sizing each other up, throwing stories about deals they'd won into the conversation like a game of Top Trumps.

Baxter tilted his wrist, pulling back his sleeve to check his watch. 'Are we nearly done, Detective?' he asked Porter. 'I don't mind coming to the station another time to finish up, but I really do need to head off for my interview.'

Porter nodded, turning his body to face the park, leaving room for Baxter to pass by. 'One last thing,' he said, as Baxter walked between him and Styles. 'Do the names Max Brennan or Jennifer Hart mean anything to you?'

Baxter hopped off the last step onto the pavement and turned to face them, shaking his head. 'Afraid not. Sorry I couldn't be more helpful,' he said and headed towards the main road.

Porter sauntered down the steps, watching him go. Wondering if he'd look back. Whether it'd mean anything if he did. Baxter reached the corner and disappeared onto Church Street.

'What do you make of that, then?' asked Styles.

'Not much to go on, really.'

'You think he was telling the truth about Leyson, not recognising him?'

Baxter hadn't given much away and that bothered Porter. Most people get a little flustered when a pair of coppers turned up on the doorstep. Baxter had taken it in his stride. Then again, in his job he was used to pressure.

'No reason not to take him at face value. Not yet, at least,' Porter said as they headed back to the car.

'Any chance we can go back via Camden Town? I promised Emma I'd meet her for an early dinner at that Asian place, Gilgamesh. Seems pointless going all the way back to the station.'

'That's the third curry this week,' said Porter.

'What can I say, she's got a craving for spicy food.'

'Cravings? There something you're not telling me?' said Porter, raising his eyebrows.

Before Styles could answer, Porter's phone rang. Milburn, again.

'DI Porter,' he said, knowing it would annoy Milburn to think he wasn't saved in Porter's phone.

'Porter, where are you?' No introduction, no pleasantries.

'Just out doing a few interviews, sir.'

'Interviews? With who?'

Porter started to tell him about the attack on Max, finding Jen, and Harold Mayes. Got as far as the interviews before Milburn cut over him.

'Fine. You can brief me when you get back in. I hear your session with OHU was cut short. I suggest you reschedule sooner rather than later or you'll not be leaving your desk again until you do.'

Porter bit down on his lip. Counted to three in his head.

Pick your battles.

'Yes, sir, will do.'

'See that you do.'

The line went dead. Milburn was all heart. Porter swallowed his anger back down, gripped his phone so hard he thought the case might buckle. Turned to look across the roof of the car at Styles. No sense taking it out on him.

'Come on, can't have you being late on my conscience,' he said to Styles. 'Poor girl puts up with enough from you as it is without adding lateness in the mix as well.'

Hands balled into fists, pushing against the lining of his pockets. Fingernails cutting crescent half-moons into his palms. He ducked into Julian Reid Estate Agents, watched through the window full of cascading rows of house pictures as the two policemen drove past and disappeared along Church Street.

Breathe in. Breathe out.

He had always known this moment was a possibility, but never truly believed it would happen. His skin prickled, like an army

113

of ants scurrying up his back, across his chest, down his arms. He stifled a smile, thinking back to being close enough to reach out and clap a hand on the detective's shoulder, heart thudding a drumbeat against his chest.

The list surprised him. That should have taken them longer to figure out, if at all, but the fact they had changed things. The fact that they were looking into AMT bothered him as well, although that link was a little more obscure. Things needed to speed up, maybe even miss out a few steps to stay ahead of the game.

That's what it was now. A game. High risk, higher reward, similar to his style at the poker table. You don't just play the cards; you play your opponent. He'd looked his square in the eyes now, and knew he had their measure. Ten more measured breaths, then back out into the street, looking both ways. Back along Summerhouse Road, piles of leaves swishing around his feet. One more glance over his shoulder as he slipped the key in the lock. Two locks on the front door, both clicking into place, and he headed upstairs. Tired wooden steps creaked out a chorus. He fumbled in his pocket for a second key, an older brass one, unlocking the bedroom door. A patchwork of shadows leaked into the room, thick blackout curtains stretched across the window. Plastic sheeting taped to the floor behind the door, crinkled and crackled as he walked in.

The polythene Tyvek bodysuit rustled as he slipped it on. Legs first, arms and lastly head. Zip pulled all the way up. Leave no trace. Stick to a winning formula. Except it wasn't winning any more, not now they were looking for him. Well, not him specifically, not yet, but for someone. A pair of blue plastic shoe covers completed the outfit, the kind you find in show homes.

He flicked a light switch, blinked fireflies from his vision and pulled a chair across to the bedside. Stood silently, watching the man on the bed squirm against the plastic ties fastening him to the frame, chest stuttering up and down with uneven breaths.

'Now then,' he said, tugging the pillowcase up over the man's head, 'you know what they say about best-laid plans? Well, I'm afraid we've had visitors today, so we're going to need to finish our chat sooner rather than later.' He made a show of checking his watch. 'Now's good for me, and looks like your diary is fairly empty.'

Porter pulled up outside his house, weariness settling over him like a warm blanket. Behind the eyes, spreading soft fingers across his shoulders. Through into his legs, weighing him down, making his shoes whisper against the pavement. The house on Margaret Road had belonged to Holly's grandma, his by default now. A two-up two-down semi, half white, half pinkish brown, like a giant piece of Battenberg. It might as well be detached for all the noise he heard. Evelyn next door was in her eighties and made as much noise as a cat burglar. She loved to remind him that she'd been there since before he was born.

He'd barely hung up his jacket when the kitchen door creaked open a few more inches. A small black face peered out, unblinking emerald eyes staring through the gap. Nothing subtle about Demetrious, purr like an outboard motor, prowling around like he owned the place. Holly had named him, saying he needed something with a bit of swagger about it.

'OK, OK, D, you first. Where are my manners?'

Porter headed into the kitchen, grabbing two foil pouches from the cupboard, holding one out in each hand.

'Would monsieur prefer the fish or the duck tonight?' He jiggled the pouches as he spoke. Demetrious looked far from amused. 'I can highly recommend the salmon, freshly caught today.'

Green eyes blinked once, an unspoken threat if dinner wasn't served up soon. Porter squatted down and ripped the top off the salmon pouch, squeezing it into a bowl.

'*Bon appétit.*' Porter straightened up, blowing a chef kiss at the unimpressed cat. He watched for a second as Demetrious sniffed around the edges then tucked in, before turning his own attentions back to the fridge. A tub of margarine, half a pepper and a stack of out-of-date yogurts. Not exactly spoilt for choice. He pulled a Tupperware container from the bottom shelf, chilli that his mum had made a few days earlier.

'Should still be OK,' he muttered to himself, performing the obligatory sniff test. Two minutes in the microwave and he'd be in business. He killed time by grabbing the last Corona from the fridge door, popping the top off, draining half in three long, slow mouthfuls. He'd never been one to leave his baggage at the door, and as he wandered through to the living room, chilli and beer balanced on a tray, the events of the day flitted through his mind like mosquitos looking for a landing spot. Sometimes things got lost in the noise of the day, but moments like this, the calm between the storms, the mind slips into neutral, dots get joined. A wisp of an idea coalesces into something solid, workable.

Tough week. The copper in him said the obvious answer was the right one. Odds are that if Jen had arranged a meet with Gordon Jackson, then it was Gordon who'd arrived to pick her up. Gordon who'd abducted her. He flicked the TV on, chewing his chilli open-mouthed to save his cheeks being burnt from the inside out. Jackson may well be the main suspect, but why was his name

116

on the list? Jen wasn't on the list, so where did she fit into this? Had the others met the same fate as Harold?

The picture on screen cut to a reporter outside the Shard. The volume was low, but tickertape along the bottom said something about a fathers' rights group trying to climb it in protest. Shadows moved at the edge of the room as Demetrious glided over, in the way that only cats can. He sprang onto the sofa and Porter reached down, scratching the sweet spot at the base of the neck, the cat's back arching like a drawn bow.

Memories welled up. Holly putting on her best doe-eyed pout, holding up the cat, guilt-tripping Porter into expanding the family. Holly draped over him on this very couch, legs tucked underneath. Nuzzling into his chest, hand stroking lazy circles on his stomach, him stroking the cat, his gesture an extension of hers. God, he missed her. His mum had trotted out the cliché of time being a healer, but that was a lie. Time made it worse. Memories blurred around the edges. Faded like overexposed photos.

He tipped his bottle to the ceiling, drained the dregs and clicked the TV off. Demetrious looked at him with undisguised contempt as Porter brushed him off the couch. His limbs were like lead as he trudged into the bedroom, sloughing off his clothes like a snake shedding its skin. He raised two fingers to his lips, as he had every night for almost three years, transferring a kiss to the photo frame by his bed.

Holly had joked, saying it looked like a staged celeb shot from *HELLO!* or *OK*. Him with a hand resting on each of her hips. The dress, a pristine symphony of white, elegant in its simplicity. One of her hands caressing his cheek, the other on his bicep. Arched entrance to the church framing their heads. Snowflakes of confetti trapped in mid-air. A perfect moment, captured and preserved for ever.

The last thing Porter saw as his lids started to droop were Holly's chestnut eyes, gazing into his through the storm of confetti. Deep, rich brown pools, drawing him in, washing over him.

CHAPTER TEN

October 1995

Where Larchfield had been a game of survival, university was effortless by comparison. Sure, he'd had to interact to a degree in tutor groups and seminars, but he revelled in the anonymity of cavernous lecture theatres. One face amongst a hundred. There were occasional attempts at socialising, even an appearance at a party or two. More out of curiosity than craving for company.

By the time he graduated, there was no swapping of contact details with people from his course, or promises to keep in touch. Uni had been as much an escape as a chance to learn. Escape from Larchfield. From that life. He made a promise to himself never to return, and headed for London and the comforting cloak of solitude a city of that size could provide. The days of the 1950s, the suburban dream, where everyone knew their neighbours and left doors unlocked, was long gone.

These days, doors were bolted and windows locked. Travelling on the Tube was an eyes-down journey, barging your way to a destination. Suited him perfectly. He could go days without speaking to anyone. Let people in, and they'll hurt you given half the chance.

He still dreamt of the boy in the warehouse sometimes, although the outcome wasn't always how it had actually played out, like a director's cut of alternate endings. One time he'd dreamt that he'd applied a tourniquet, saving a life instead of watching it ebb away. Another time, he'd picked up a length of pipe, brought it down on the injured boy's head, over and over.

Whichever scene played out, the boy was still dead when he woke up, but there was no remorse either way. No rumpled nest of sweaty sheets from a restless night. No twisted knot of guilt. What he did feel, what he still felt after all these years, was a sense of being in control. Just by walking away, he'd made the choice for them both; him and the boy. It gave him an excited tingle up his spine. That hadn't faded with time.

CHAPTER ELEVEN

Porter called the hospital after breakfast, and they told him Jen had been discharged last night. There wasn't much to update Max on, but he left the house early enough to pay them a visit before work, as much as a friend as a police officer.

He stopped off at a cafe a few streets away and grabbed a black coffee for himself, latte and peppermint tea for Max and Jen, plus a few pastries. Worst case, if they were out, Styles would have the latte, and the tea would get him brownie points with Rose, who worked the front desk at Paddington Green.

Max's car was parked outside the front door but the curtains were still closed. He pulled up to the Audi's bumper, still debating whether or not to risk waking them, when Max opened the bedroom curtains. Porter got out, balancing the box of pastries on top of the cups to free up a hand as he walked up the path, but Max opened the door before he could make it.

'You must really need the good press if you're resorting to morning deliveries.'

'Like you wouldn't believe,' said Porter. 'How's she doing? You too for that matter?'

Max reached out for the box. 'Let me grab that before you drop something.' He motioned Porter inside. 'She's OK. Didn't sleep too good, mind. She's just in the shower. Should be down in a few minutes, though.'

'Has she remembered much more about what happened?'

'Nope. Talked about it some, but nothing you don't already know. I don't know if it's all sunk in yet.'

Max peered under the lids, held up the latte, and Porter nodded, reaching over for his own cup.

'What's new then?' Max said.

'Not much,' said Porter, with a slow shake of the head. 'Followed up a few leads, but still trying join the dots.'

He gave Max a whistle-stop tour of what they had: the laptop, the discovery of Mayes in the freezer, the list and the interviews. He pulled out a copy of the list, slid it along the bench towards Max.

'I'll need you and Jen to come down to the station and do this formally, but any of these names mean anything to you?'

Max shook his head. 'I barely knew my own dad, Jake. Why would I know any of his friends?'

'We don't know who they are, that's my point. We don't even know if your dad knew them.'

'So where do we go from here, then?'

'Early days, buddy,' said Porter. 'Every name is on there for a reason, we just need to find the common denominator.'

'I know what you'll probably say, but what can I do to help?'

122

'Well, if you do hear from your dad, call me straight away, but apart from that, you're just going to have to trust me. We still need to speak to someone from his office, see what they can tell us, but I'll keep in touch. You have my word.'

Max rubbed at his eyes, and Porter saw the pink blush to them, guessing Max had probably slept as well as Jen.

'I know, I know. You're right. I just feel so bloody useless, you know?'

'I know, mate, but you do have something to do. You need to convince Jen there's no monsters in the closet, and things can get back to normal. She's going to need to lean on you for a few days at least, maybe more.' He stood up, popping the lid back on his cup. 'Anyway, speaking of leaving things to me, I'd best make a move. Give her a hug from me.'

'Will do,' said Max, walking him to the door.

Porter shook his hand and sauntered off towards his car. A few days was wildly optimistic for Jen to bounce back. Not impossible, but unlikely. He should have been more honest with Max and made a mental note to dig out a number for a counsellor for the next time he saw them.

The irony wasn't lost on him. Encouraging others to exorcise their demons by talking, while he kept his under lock and key. Milburn wasn't going to let up about the OHU sessions any time soon. He'd have to see Sameera Misra again, at least once more anyway. Nothing to say it had to be today, though. An appointment for a fortnight's time should do the trick.

He glanced up as he pulled away from the kerb. Caught a glimpse of Jen, towel wrapped around damp hair like a turban, walking past the bedroom window. He'd heard it in Max's voice while she was missing. Disbelief, half an octave too high, straddling two realities. One where Jen turns up safe, the other too hard to think about. Both possible, like Schrödinger's cat. Porter was all too familiar with the dark flip side, that sense of the world tilting on its axis when you lose someone. Not something he'd wish on an enemy let alone an old friend, and until he figured out what was going on, she wouldn't be safe. Neither of them would.

Jen's mum, Tina, arrived around ten-thirty. Domestic whirlwind was how Max pictured her, unable to visit them without washing a few dishes or hanging out the laundry. Depending on the day, it swung from endearing to irritating, but her heart was in the right place, so he bit his tongue when he had to.

Tina was adamant that Jen's road back to normality included the Orchid Rooms spa, hot stone massages for both of them and afternoon tea at The Pear Tree cafe, near Camden Town. Max watched Jen as Tina fussed over her, ready to step in if he saw the slightest sign of tension in Jen's face, but she forced a smile, hugging him just a little bit tighter than usual.

Max watched them disappear upstairs and picked up his phone. Work wasn't expecting him back till Monday at the earliest, but he called Callum Carr's mobile.

'Hey, how you doing? How's Jen? Is everything alright?' The way Callum wrapped his tongue around each 's' made him sound like a poor man's Sean Connery.

'You journalists are all the same. Questions, questions, questions,' said Max. 'But we're OK, I think. Not much sleep, but she's a tough cookie.'

'And you?'

'To be honest, mate, I haven't a clue what's going on, or

what my dad's mixed up in. That's partly why I'm calling.'

'And there was me thinking you just loved listening to my velvety tones,' said Callum. 'What do you need?'

Max ran him through what he knew so far. Porter had taken the list with him, and he could only remember a handful of names, but it'd have to do.

'I'm thinking we, and by we I mean you, could do a little digging, see if there's any connection between them.'

'What about your pal, the copper?'

Max paused. 'Jake's a good guy. I trust him one hundred per cent, but they've got nothing to go on. I mean, this guy came to my house. How can Jen feel safe in her own home if . . .' Words came through gritted teeth, free hand clenching into a fist. 'I can't sit and wait for them to try anything else. I could pay a visit to Gordon's office, and you could see what you can turn up on the rest.'

'As if you don't have enough going on, you want to play cops and robbers?' said Callum. 'What the hell, I'm in. Gimme a few hours and I'll give you a call.'

'How about a coffee later,' said Max. 'Tina's taking Jen out for the day, so I'm at a loose end.'

'As long as we're clear on two things,' said Callum. 'It's most definitely your turn to pay, and I don't put out on the first date.'

'Your virtue is safe with me,' said Max, smiling. Callum's speak-before-you-think approach was usually good for at least one.

They agreed to meet at YO! Sushi at one o'clock. Close to the office, if a bit of a hike for Max, but Callum was doing him a favour so he didn't mind. Besides, there were worse ways to spend an afternoon than grazing from a conveyor belt. He grabbed his car keys and took the stairs two at a time. The whine of the hairdryer was a dead giveaway, and he found Jen bent over, head down, running her fingers through dangling hair in front of the bedroom mirror.

'I'm going to meet Callum for lunch while you girls get pampered,' he said, sliding arms around her waist, pressing his chest to her back as she straightened.

She flicked a blast of hot air over her shoulder. Instead of ducking away, he did a slow-mo head roll, pretending to flick his fringe.

'If the day job doesn't pan out, I could totally have a career in shampoo commercials.'

She bumped backwards into his thighs, nudging him away, but not before he saw half a smile in the mirror.

'First smile of the day,' he said, backing away. 'My work here is done.' He took a step backwards, bowing, hands out.

She tapped him lightly on the head with her hairbrush. 'What time will you be back?' she asked, serious face again. She wasn't needy by nature, but there was a nerviness to her. Hardly surprising, given what she'd been through. She was trying her best to hide it, but he knew her too well. It was the little things. Voice that bit softer. Eyes flicking around the room, as if checking all exits.

'Meeting him at one, so I'd say about three-ish. Should be back before you are, if you want me to sort tea. Will your mum be joining us?' He made a sign of the cross, pressed his palms together, slight shake of the head.

'Cheeky,' she said. 'As it happens, she and Dad have friends going round tonight. She wanted to cancel, but I told her not to. I think I just want to curl up on the couch, if that's OK with you?'

He stepped in close, pulled her to his chest. 'Course it is.'

'What are you up to this morning, then?' she asked, words muffled, speaking into his jumper.

He paused, wondering how much to tell her. Decided honesty was what she needed. 'I thought I'd swing by where Gordon works,' he said. 'I want to see if there's anything they can tell me that might help Jake.'

Jen pulled back, arms still around his waist. 'Help Jake? Do you really think that's a good idea? We need to let him do his job.'

He smoothed a stray hair away from her eye, tucking it behind an ear. 'I know, sweetheart, and I'm not going to stick my nose in, I promise. He said that they'd not been returning his calls, though, so maybe I'll have more luck playing the concerned family member card.'

She held his gaze for a few seconds. 'As long as that's all you do,' she said. 'After everything that's happened, I'm scared, Max. Promise me you won't go around playing detective.'

'Scout's honour,' he said, lifting a three-finger salute to his temple, leaning in to kiss her. She felt tense at first, but he let the kiss linger, feeling the tightness melt out of her. When he pulled away, she was still looking at him, wide eyes full of concern.

'You crazy kids have fun at the massage parlour,' he said, lifting her hand to his lips, planting a loud squeaky kiss on her knuckles.

'Parlour?' She rolled her eyes. 'It's a spa, not one of those seedy dives you'd choose.'

'Cheerfully withdrawn,' he said.

'Go on, get out before I decide to drag you with me.'

It felt wrong letting her out of his sight after the last few days, but all the unanswered questions bouncing around inside his head were like flies against a window. He said a quick farewell to her mum and pressed two twenties into her hand for lunch. She tried to protest, but he was out the door and half way to his car before she finished her sentence, walking with more energy and purpose than he'd felt since all this kicked off. Time to find out what kind of man his dad really was.

Styles looked deep in conversation with another officer when Porter pulled up a chair next to them.

'I miss anything interesting?' he asked, as Styles turned to face him.

'Yep, all solved. Colonel Mustard, in the library, with the candlestick.'

'The sooner you swap policing for stand-up the better.'

'You'll miss me when I'm gone,' said Styles, doing his best to sound hurt. 'Did you sleep in?'

The younger officer, whose name Porter couldn't place, took this as their cue to leave.

'Been to see Max and Jen. They let her out last night.'

'And?' said Styles.

Porter waggled a hand. 'Hmm, hard to say. I'm going to ask the pair of them to come in today or tomorrow, get them on record. Guess we'll get a better sense then.'

Styles nodded. 'I'll give them a call if you like, set things up?'

'Yeah, that'd be good,' said Porter.

A long, low grumble from under his shirt reminded him of the box of pastries, left on Max's bench. No breakfast yet, but no real appetite, despite his body's protests.

'Anyway, while you've had your coffee morning,' said Styles, nodding at Porter's takeaway cup, 'the rest of us have been doing some good old-fashioned police work.'

'Do tell,' said Porter, sitting back in his chair, arms folded.

'OK, good news first. We've got a good set of prints. Bad news, there's no match for them.'

'Where did we get them from?'

'Few partials on the laptop keys, but three clean ones from the phone, and a glass he used. We're assuming they belong to whoever did this, anyway. They're not Harold's.'

'You're probably right but keep an open mind. You're assuming it's only one person we're after as well. Could be two or more working together.'

'Fair point.'

'What about Jackson? Any prints lifted from his house?'

'Way ahead of you. Checked that straight away and no match. There is a bonus find, though. Phone screen had a crack, and we've got DNA from that. Skin cells from where it's been swiped. Again, no match for Jackson.'

'So is he nothing to do with Jen, or working with a partner?'

'Without discounting him completely,' said Styles, 'I'd keep him on the back burner, until we actually get something solid linking him. I know Max doesn't really know him, but I struggle to see a father going from wanting to reconnect to attacking a son and his girlfriend. He could have just ignored Max's letter if he didn't want anything to do with him.'

'I've seen more far-fetched things on *Jeremy Kyle*,' said Porter.

'Which is why you need to watch less TV and get out more.'

'OK, OK, point taken. We still need to link the other names, though.' Porter took a long swig of lukewarm coffee. It'd have to do for now. 'I just don't see a scenario where they're not all linked. Whoever made the list had their reasons. Let's keep an eye on the two we've found. Get a car on Baxter and Leyson, low key though.

No need to alarm them. A couple of PCs in civvies on each. Just do it this morning and I'll clear it with Milburn later.'

Styles nodded. 'I was thinking about this idea of connecting them, before you came in . . .' he began.

'Careful,' said Porter. 'Much more of that and I'll expect it on a regular basis.'

Styles gave a forced smile but continued. 'We might not be able to connect all twelve yet, but we can connect at least three of them . . .' He left it hanging, raising eyebrows to prompt Porter.

It took a few seconds, but he got there in the end. 'Of course,' he said, snapping his fingers. 'The recruiters. Leyson, Baxter, Errington, they all used them.'

Pure coincidence? Maybe, but worth looking into. His stomach protested again. Felt it was bubbling like an overheated pan, but Styles didn't seem to hear it.

Should have seen that yesterday, he thought.

Maybe Milburn was right. Something as simple as that, missing connections like the recruitment firm, wasn't exactly the sign of someone on top form. Sign of a slow slide.

Pull yourself together man. Can't let them down like this.

He realised Styles was staring at him.

'OK, let's, um, let's head over there this morning, see who there is to talk to.'

'Thought you might say that, so I took the liberty of calling them. We've got an appointment with Nicholas Glass, he's the MD. I had to practically beg his PA for fifteen minutes as well so we'd best make a move.'

Porter felt the first twinge of a headache, starting at the base of his skull, edging down into his neck. Too much caffeine, too early? Not enough sleep? Bit of both. He rubbed a hand across the back of his neck, digging fingers in and tilting his head till he a heard a crunch.

'You OK, guv?'

'Yeah, I'm fine. Give me fifteen minutes, and I'll meet you downstairs.'

Styles nodded. 'I'll call Max first, then. See when they can come in.'

Porter left him at the desk, pulling out his phone as he walked out into the stairwell, muttering a pep talk under his breath. Two missed call notifications. He dialled his voicemail.

'Jake, it's your mum.' As if he wouldn't have worked that out from her voice. 'Just wondering if you want to pop around for dinner tonight. Your sister's coming as well. Anyway, let me know either way.'

The thought of his mum's cooking had the desired effect, kickstarting his appetite, and he knew he'd have to grab something from the canteen before he went to AMT. The second message was from Misra.

'Detective Porter, it's Sameera Misra here. Just calling to see if you'd like to reschedule our session. I'm in all day, so look forward to hearing from you.'

'Like' wasn't the first word that sprang to mind. He'd do it, but in his own time. The prospect of making progress this morning at AMT was too real, too immediate, to ignore.

Stairwell acoustics made it sound like he tap-danced his way down a floor. He'd call her, but after their visit to the recruitment firm. He'd worked enough cases, seen enough people coping with life-changing events, to know that bottling things up rarely ended well.

What scared him most wasn't even the prospect of having his

feelings picked apart in a cosy office. It was what he'd be left with afterwards that worried him. He was the strong, stoic widower, still grieving. Without that, who would he be? He wasn't sure that he wanted to find out, but either way, something had to change. Max and Jen both needed him to be on point, and things were starting to slip. Badly.

Sound was all he had to go on. Squeaking tap. Splash of water on enamel, morphing to the heavier slap of water on water as the bath filled. The pillowcase clung to his forehead, mopping his brow, the air inside hot, heavy, claustrophobic.

No sense of time, but light filtering in through the cotton felt artificial. He could have been here for two days, or a week. Who knew? Hard plastic edges dug into his wrists. He'd twisted his head and seen them cutting pink furrows last time the pillowcase was off.

He closed his eyes, tried to slow his breathing rather than suck in a mouthful of cotton. Footsteps off to his right. Heels clicking on bathroom tiles, dulling as they moved onto carpet, getting closer.

Fingers clamped around his right ankle, lifting it up. He kicked out, but too late. Strong hands pushed it back down. Something squeezed it, tight like a tourniquet. He felt it bite in, same harsh edges as his wrists. Left ankle now. He bucked like a rodeo bull, but only made the plastic ties dig deeper.

He yelped in pain, yelp turning into a shout. No words, just noise. A raking growl that burnt his throat on the way out. Both legs were forced together, weight pinning them from above. Rasping clicks that sounded like plastic ties cinching into place. He tried to lash out a kick again, but his legs moved as one, stuck together, the deadweight of his captor pressing down. It was like being buried on the beach as a kid, sand pressing in on all sides. His hands already bound and fastened above his head. A momentary absence of tension in the bonds, short-lived, as both wrists were slapped back together, even tighter than before.

He found his voice, shouted into the cotton. 'Jesus, man, what the hell do you want?' Fabric invaded his mouth like an inverted bubble as he sucked in a deep breath. 'I've told you everything. Everything you wanted. You said—'

A sharp tug rolled him towards the edge of the bed. For a second, face down on the mattress, he couldn't breathe at all, until he was flipped onto his back again. Legs pulled around roughly so they dangled from the edge of the bed. Hands on his jumper, pulling him into a sitting position. Pulled forwards, and up. Blood rushed to his head. Hands gripped his legs. Hard ridge digging into his stomach. Slung over a shoulder like a sack of laundry.

He counted a dozen steps, felt his legs bounce against the man with every one of them, then a hard stop. The bony shoulder beneath him shrugged him off, and he was sliding feet first back to ground. Except it wasn't ground. Too cold. Ice-cold water splashed up his calves, plastering heavy denim against his legs. Then he was falling, at least that's how it felt, but only a few feet at most, backside smacking against water, hitting the bottom of the tub with a barely cushioned thump.

The cold took his breath away. Sucked it, quite literally, from his lungs, but before he could inhale a mouthful of pillowcase, it was whisked away. After a few days of light filtered through his cotton hood, the glare of spotlights embedded in the ceiling made him screw his eyes closed. The cold wrapped around his chest, squeezed like a python, as he fell back against the bath. A blanket of ice cubes bobbed on the surface, little sub-zero pebbles, bumping against his cheeks, chin, Adam's apple.

His breathing kickstarted again, rapid and ragged. He tried to sit up, but with his hands and feet still bound he might as well have been limbless. He pushed out with his feet, found the far end, used it to push his shoulders back against the bath to keep himself above water.

That won him a precious few seconds' respite, and he saw the man's face for the first time.

'T . . . t . . . tell me what you want me t . . . to say.' He heard the fear in his own voice. Hated the weakness but could no more hide it than he could snap the ties that bound him.

'Focus on your breathing,' said the man. 'You've been rather cooperative so far. I just need to be sure you've not left anything out.'

He disappeared back into the bedroom, returning a few seconds later with a chair, and sat, legs crossed, pad of A4 paper in one hand.

'Let's start from the top again, shall we, and we'll see where we go from there.' He checked his watch. 'You've got around thirty minutes before you're in any real danger of hypothermia, so probably in your best interests to be as precise as you are honest.'

Max decided not to call ahead. Nobody at Marlin had bothered to return Porter's call, so he'd try the element of surprise instead. Images of the *Monty Python* crew dressed as the Spanish Inquisition sprang to mind. Marlin had their headquarters just off High Holborn. A three-storey whitewashed building, that gave nothing away about its occupants, save a brass name plate by the door. A short corridor opened up into a reception area

134

that reminded him of a dentist's waiting room. Matching tables with four chairs on either side of the room, dark grey fabric. Each table sported a copy of *The Economist*, sitting on top of a broadsheet, maybe *The Times*, both dead centre like they'd been positioned with a set square.

Someone's got a little too much time on their hands.

A polished wooden reception counter was set into the far wall. Frosted glass doors off to the right and left. The woman behind the desk looked up as he approached. She was as well-groomed as her surroundings. Late twenties, minimal make-up, thin-framed glasses and eyes the same shade of blue as a Bombay Sapphire bottle.

'Hello, sir,' she said, sounding too chirpy to be true, 'how can I help you today?'

'Hi,' said Max, wishing he'd spent a little more time on the way here deciding how to explain his visit. Her fixed smile didn't budge a millimetre while he chose his words. 'My dad works here, Gordon Jackson.'

Dad. The word still felt awkward when he said it. Clunky.

'He hasn't been in touch for a few weeks,' he went on, feeling a slight flush in his cheeks, being more than a bit economical with the truth, 'and I'm getting a little worried. I'm hoping I can speak to someone he works with to see if he said where he was going.'

Her smile faded, lips parted slightly, as if ready to say something but unsure of the right words. 'If you can bear with me a moment, sir, I'll just see who's free.' She picked up the phone, fingers hovering over the keypad. 'Who shall I say is asking?'

'Max. Max Brennan.'

'OK, thanks, Mr Brennan. If you'd like to take a seat,' she said, tilting her head towards the chairs.

She spoke low into the handset as he sat down. He couldn't make out most of it but heard his dad's name twice. Saw her eyes flick over to him as she said it. Giving him what he guessed was supposed to be a reassuring nod and smile as she finished the call.

Max slid the newspaper out from under the magazine, today's *Times*. The front page was dominated by the latest humanitarian crisis in Syria. Max's eye was drawn to the pictures first, text second. Professional curiosity. He clocked the name underneath the photograph. Decent enough photographer. Max admired his work but wondered if anyone would notice if they just reused the same pictures every few days. Shock value had peaked in the eighties, around the time of Geldof and Band Aid. People were just overexposed to this kind of thing now, desensitised to an extent. Immune, like germs to a vaccine. Had he really just likened the great British public to a germ?

'Mr Brennan?'

A voice cut across his thoughts. A man stood by the reception desk. Max stood, took a little too much pleasure from replacing the paper at an angle, and walked across to shake hands.

'I'm Thomas Phillips. Why don't we go through to my office?'

The receptionist smiled again as he walked past her. Hard to read for sure, but it reminded him of the one a teacher gives on parents' evening, right before they tell you your perfect little angel could pay more attention in class.

He followed Phillips along a corridor, and through a door at the far end. The office was a mash-up of clichés. Framed degree on the ego wall. Framed artsy prints on the others. Bookcase off to the right, stocked full of sleep-inducing leadership and management bibles, mixed in with financial and regulatory-sounding titles.

Obligatory family photo on the desk as the cherry on top, the human touch. The message was clear. Our firm is trustworthy. I am trustworthy. Solid. Dependable.

'So, you're Gordon's son?' said Phillips, sinking into his high-backed chair. The way he said it, could be a question or a statement. Max answered as if it was the latter.

'Yep, I am indeed. Look, Mr Phillips, I don't know how much your colleague told you about why I'm here . . .' Max trailed off, hoping that Phillips would step in, tell him exactly that. Phillips didn't disappoint.

'Yes, Amanda said you hadn't heard from him for a little while, and you wanted to know when he was due back at work.'

'That's right.' Max nodded.

'I hope you don't mind me saying so, Mr Brennan,' said Phillips, leaning forward, elbows on the desk, fingers steepled, 'but Gordon worked here for almost six years, and never mentioned any family.'

'Here's the thing,' said Max, mirroring the body language, 'I didn't know who my father was, growing up. He didn't know I existed. My parents were both young, and didn't part on good terms, so he and I only became acquainted recently.'

Phillips's eyes widened, and he leant back, folding his arms.

'We haven't actually met yet, just swapped letters. I was supposed to meet him this week, but he never showed, so I'm hoping you can help.'

Phillips said nothing. Just stared at Max, eyes narrowing just a touch, choosing his words carefully.

'Wow, OK. That's quite the story. I had no idea.'

Max shrugged. 'Neither did he until recently. So, can you help me?'

'I wish I could, Mr Brennan, genuinely I do.' Max heard the tone, knew he wasn't going to get what he'd come here for. 'However, I'm afraid Gordon resigned a few weeks ago. Quite out of the blue to be honest, but I'm afraid your father doesn't work here any more.'

CHAPTER TWELVE

February 2008

He was good at what he did. Good without being great. Head down, get on with life, nothing to be gained by standing out from the crowd. Everyone came to crossroads in their life. Being abandoned by his mother had been one, the incident in the warehouse another, but he'd taken each in his stride, moved on past them. Spring 2008 was more of a derailment.

He went out jogging late one night. Winter still hadn't given up the fight, pavements glazing over as the temperature dropped. Patches of ice sparkled in the street lights. That was the problem. He was so focused on the ground, ten feet or so ahead, that he hadn't seen them until it was too late.

There were five of them. Two inside a parked car, three more waiting around the corner, working as a pack. The car door clipped him as it swung out. No chance to avoid it. Momentum made him spin clockwise, into the wall to his left. They were on him before he hit the pavement.

He'd never been able to submit, even as a child, always swinging for the bully rather than cover up, and he'd taken a few beatings for his troubles. This went beyond a beating, though. He caught the nearest one square under the jaw with an up-kick, sending him sprawling. The remaining four set upon him, overwhelming him in seconds. Fight or flight spluttered to a halt, in favour of curling up and waiting for them to stop.

He had no idea how long he'd lain there for after they left. Vague recollections of them rummaging in his pockets, taking phone and watch. Minutes later, fresh hands rummaged, cursing when they found nothing. He didn't have the strength to stop them. He never saw what his attackers had used, but doctors told him afterwards the breaks in his legs were consistent with a blunt object, maybe a baseball bat.

For the first time in his life, he needed the help of others, but there was nobody there. Sure, the NHS looked after him in the beginning. Several weeks in hospital, discharged on crutches, but the real struggle began when he got home. Try asking anyone who's attempted to carry a cup of coffee from the kitchen, while on crutches, how their day's been. Three months of rehab turned into five, and two weeks before he was due back at work, the *Dear John* letter hit the doormat. Laced with phrases like *with great regret* and *organisational restructure*, signed by a name he'd never heard of, someone he'd never met assuring him that the severance package attached was more than generous. How fucking magnanimous of them. Not a single phone call for at least ten weeks, and now this.

Between the faceless cowards in human resources and the anonymous passers-by who had turned a blind eye to his beating, they could all, every last one of them, go to hell.

CHAPTER THIRTEEN

Porter's driving got them to the Shard five minutes early, and he couldn't help but tilt his head back to take it all in. It jutted into the sky like a giant stalagmite of glittering glass. Defiantly different than the blocky right angles that dominated most of the skyline. They made it up to the AMT office bang on time but had to wait another twenty-five minutes before they were ushered into a spacious room by a PA who glided across the carpet like she was on a catwalk.

Nicholas Glass rose and walked around from behind his desk to meet them. Glass was one of those people who oozed success. Suit that would look the part in Savile Row, shoes shined to a military sheen. Did he even have to do his hair in the morning, or did he just roll out of bed like that every day? The kind of man whose only brush with austerity was if it appeared in *The Times* crossword.

The office decor was minimalistic, which only served to emphasise the impressive square footage. An oval-shaped walnut conference table served as the centrepiece, framed by a floor-to-ceiling window. A large triptych dominated the right-hand wall. Three canvases, whorls of colour, each flowing into the next. Could just as easily have been from Camden Market as far as Porter knew, but he was pretty sure they'd amount to a down payment on a nice flat.

Glass gave a smile that Porter took as all teeth and show, rather than any real warmth. 'Good morning, Detectives,' he said, pumping Porter's hand, going for the alpha male handshake. 'So sorry I had to keep you waiting.'

'No problem at all, Mr Glass,' said Porter. 'DI Porter, and this is my partner, DS Styles. Thank you for seeing us on short notice.'

Glass gave Styles a few seconds of the same vigorous handshake, then gestured to the conference table. 'Please, have a seat.'

They all settled into comfortable high-backed chairs, the kind that made Porter feel like a Bond villain.

'So,' said Glass, unbuttoning his jacket, 'how can I help you gentlemen?'

'Your firm has cropped up in a case we're working, Mr Glass,' said Porter, watching Glass's eyebrows twitch at the mention. 'More of an indirect link, really. We're trying to locate a few individuals in connection with our case, and several of them have used your firm.'

Porter nodded at Styles, who reached into his jacket pocket. 'Do you recognise any of the names on this list?' said Styles, smoothing the creases out against the table, sliding it across to Glass.

Glass leant over the paper, scanned it, shook his head. 'Sorry, Detective, none of them look familiar, but then again we have thousands of clients. I can have Ellie check against our database if you like?'

'That'd be a big help,' said Porter.

Glass scooped up the sheet of paper. 'Not at all.' He walked over to his desk, jabbed a button on the phone, and Ellie appeared at the door like a genie. 'Ellie, can you check these names to see if any are clients, please?'

'Of course, sir. I'll do it now.'

'Oh, and Ellie, could you grab me a coffee on your way back in, please? Detectives, can I offer you a drink?'

Porter looked at Styles, shrugged. 'Black, no sugar, please.'

'Make that two,' said Styles.

It was hard not to watch her as she turned to leave the room. Navy blue pencil skirt clinging to her hips. Glass had a hint of a smile when Porter looked back but said nothing.

'Might I ask what these men have to do with your case?' he said after Ellie closed the door.

'We can't go into too much detail,' said Porter, suitably vague, 'but one of the men has turned up dead, and several others are missing. We spoke to Stuart Leyson yesterday. He remembers meeting Joseph Baxter and Christopher Errington at one of your events.'

'We run quite a few of those, at least one a month. Networking over a few drinks, that type of thing. You'd be amazed how many people line up their next career move at these things.'

'So if I come to you for help finding a job, what happens? Do I work with you directly? One of your team?' said Porter.

'We've got around fifty consultants. You'd be allocated to one of them. If you come back to us a second time around, we try and place you back with the same one. Personal touch, you know.'

He smiled, cranking up the wattage this time, almost blinding Porter with a flash of porcelain veneers that could probably pay for an extra copper on the beat for the next six months.

'And is there a particular industry you recruit into, Mr Glass?' asked Styles.

'Finance sector mainly, accountants up to executives, but we do IT and architectural as well.'

Porter noticed Glass's eyes stray over his shoulder and turned to see Ellie reappearing with a small tray. The conversation paused as she set three cups on the table, slipping a sheet of paper from under the tray like a magician producing the rabbit.

'The names you asked about, sir.'

'Thank you, Ellie, that's all for now.'

Porter made a point of not following her exit this time, although caught Styles's head twitching around.

Porter tried to read the expression as Glass studied the sheet, but he had a solid poker face. After a pause, he broke the silence.

'Well, Detectives, looks like you're in luck. I have no idea what this means as far as your case is concerned, but you've scored twelve for twelve.'

Glass slid the paper across to him, and Porter's eyes widened as he saw the twelve names, now complete with addresses and phone numbers. All twelve. He'd hoped for one or two to be linked through AMT, but all twelve was like a full bingo card.

'Do you mind if we keep this?' Porter asked.

Glass shrugged. 'I don't see why not. Nothing you couldn't find yourself, really.'

'I'd appreciate it if you didn't make any contact with these men before we speak to them,' said Porter. 'Just for the next few days.'

'Fine by me, Detective. They tend to come to us anyway, rather than the other way around. I will have to call my head of legal and our PR manager, though, work out how we manage any fallout.'

'That's fine, as long as they keep it to themselves for now, but I wouldn't say you have anything to worry about at this stage.'

Glass shook his head. 'We trade on reputation, Detective. If it turns out that any of our clients have been up to no good, we need to be ready to respond. I'd appreciate any heads up you can give if it's going that way, you know, before anything goes public.'

'There's a limit to how much I can tell you about an ongoing investigation, Mr Glass, but the fact you've been helpful goes a long way to showing your firm in a good light. Speaking of being helpful . . .'

Porter reached into his pocket, pulled out a card between finger and thumb, and passed it to Glass.

'Here are my details. It'd be a big help if you can send over what you have on these men. Jobs they secured through you, any personal information you can share.'

For the first time, Glass was starting to look uneasy, creases on his forehead that weren't there before, chewing on his lower lip as he took Porter's card.

'I'll need to speak to Dean first; he's the in-house counsel I mentioned before, but I'll send what I can.'

'Mr Glass, sir?' Ellie's voice floated over from the door. Porter hadn't even heard it open. 'Sorry to interrupt, but they're waiting for you in the conference room.'

Glass looked relieved at the excuse and was quick to his feet. 'Tell them I'll be two minutes.' He looked down at Porter, smile back now. 'Sorry, Detective, I really do have to go, but I'll get Ellie to send over what we find.'

Glass ushered them back out to reception, where Ellie had already returned to her seat. She flashed a smile that could have graced any toothpaste ad as they walked past. Glass went for the

145

full-force handshake again, only this time it was a little on the clammy side, and he turned on his heel, disappearing through an adjacent door.

They waited patiently for the lift, and Styles turned to Porter once the doors closed. 'You must teach me how you do that,' said Styles.

'Do what?'

'Reel them in by ignoring them.'

'What the hell are you talking about?' said Porter.

'Ellie,' he said, eyebrows raised.

Porter rolled his eyes. *Here we go again.*

'I can only assume women these days go for the brooding, moody types that pretend they don't exist. More of a challenge, I suppose. All smiles on the way in, another one with your coffee, third for good luck on the way out.' Styles counted them off on his fingers.

'Jealousy is such an ugly trait.'

'Not at all,' said Styles. 'I'm happily married. Wouldn't dream of ignoring any woman other than my beautiful wife.'

'Well, if ignorance is bliss, then you've got the happiest marriage going.'

The air outside was heavy as they exited the building, noticeably warmer than when they went in, or was it just the office air conditioning wearing off.

'Bite to eat on the way back?' said Styles.

'Can do. What do you fancy?'

'I'm easy.'

'So the boys at the station tell me, but let's focus on food.'

This is what Porter had missed. Back and forth, verbal sparring. It felt good. Normal, and that wasn't something he'd felt in a long time.

'How about that place Charlie bleats on about?'

Charlie Moore, one of the longer-serving officers at the station, bent their ears at every possible opportunity, raving about the coffee at a little place about ten minutes' walk from the station.

'Works for me. Went there with Emma a few months ago as it happens. Quite nice, actually. One condition though.'

'Yep?'

'No matter how good it is, we tell Charlie it tastes like someone cleaned out a hamster cage and used the leftovers in the espresso machine.'

'Done.'

Twenty minutes later, they pulled up outside Café Blanca. Even from the street, Porter could see it wasn't his usual type of place. Stark combination of black chairs and white tables framed in the window. No better when they went inside. It looked like someone had bleached the character out. The waitress came over to take their order. All business. Not even a forced smile to finesse a tip further down the line.

'Come on, then,' said Styles, when she'd retreated out of earshot, 'you like a flutter at the bookies, which way is this one going?'

'The AMT link has to mean something, not sure what, but even two names in a city this size would be something, never mind all twelve. There's got to be a reason it's those twelve, though. Have they all worked for the same company once upon a time? Do they drink in the same pub? There's got to be something more.'

'I'll plough through the stuff Glass has sent over when we get back, if you like?'

Porter nodded. 'Yep, that'd be good. I've got a few things to take care of, so I'll leave you to it. Also, the more I think about it, the more I reckon there's another player in the game here. I just don't see whoever shoved Mayes in that freezer sticking their own name on next to his, can you?'

'I know we need to keep an open mind, but, yeah, I'd say you're right there. By that logic then, Gordon Jackson would be off the hook as well.'

Porter nodded. 'That's what my gut tells me. Not enough to say that to Max just yet, but I'm more bothered about the fact the others have literally dropped off the map. Everyone leaves some kind of trail these days. And why are none of them on a missing persons list?'

The dour-faced waitress came shuffling back over, coffee sloshing over the rim as she practically dropped the cups in front of them, turned on her heel and left again.

'Maybe they've all met the same end as Mayes?' said Styles.

'Hmm, maybe, maybe not,' said Porter, 'but you'd think somebody would be looking for them regardless, wouldn't you? Wife, brother, parents?'

Styles looked down as his phone buzzed, back up at Porter and down at the screen again.

'Everything OK?' said Porter.

'Yeah, just Emma. Everything's fine.' There was definitely something on his partner's mind. Porter had worked with him long enough to read him.

'In fact, everything's a little better than fine,' said Styles after a pause. 'Been meaning to tell you this week, but I'm, um, I'm going to be a dad.'

'Mate, that's great news,' said Porter, reaching across, squeezing his partner's shoulder. 'Explains her curry cravings.'

'Thanks. We've been keeping it quiet till she got past twelve weeks. That's today by the way. I need to dodge out for an hour for the scan.'

Porter picked up his cup, blew across the surface, and watched Styles. Sure, he was smiling. Who wouldn't with news like that? But there was something else, something he was holding back. He'd tensed up when he spoke. Nothing drastic, but a tell all the same. Hard to say what it could be, but it didn't take a genius to work out that people don't tend to tense up with good news.

How bad can it be?

Emma's car was already there when Styles pulled up. He followed the signs for the antenatal department, and caught Emma's glare full force as he came through the doors

'Sorry, sorry,' he said holding his hands up in surrender. 'We had an interview that ran over.'

'Did the suspect ask for extra mustard?' she said, staring at a point on his chest.

He looked down. Saw the yellow splodge front and centre next to a shirt button. Busted.

'I had to grab a quick bite on the way here. I'd had nothing since breakfast.'

'It's fine,' she said, stern face melting away in favour of sly smile, 'I'm just messing with you. Come here.' She patted the seat next to her and he slumped into it, twisting to give her a kiss on the cheek.

'Running late?'

'Yes, thank God,' she said, and his cheeks flared up pink again, even though he knew she wasn't being serious. Force of habit. His mum used to tell him he had the timekeeping ability of a sundial in the shade, and he didn't usually disappoint.

'Anyway, how's your day been?' she said.

'Told him today, about the baby.'

Emma reached over, squeezed his arm. 'How did he take it?'

'He was happy for us.'

'That's not what I mean,' she said, digging her nails into flesh, 'and you know it.'

'He's fine.'

'So you've told him, then? About switching jobs?'

'Emma Styles?'

Her head whipped around. 'Yes,' she said, rising to her feet. A nurse in navy blue scrubs smiled in their direction and beckoned them into an examination room.

Styles realised his mouth was half-open and swallowed down the half-truth he was about to try and fob her off with. Saved by the bell, or by the nurse who looked like Hattie Jacques reincarnated, to be more precise. Only a temporary reprieve, though. Emma had asked him every day this week, and there was only so long he could stall for.

Emma hopped up on the bed, peeled her waistband down and held her breath as the nurse squirted a dollop of cold gel on her tummy. Styles felt her fingers scrabbling for his, squeezing his hand as the nurse touched the ultrasound transducer to her skin, spreading the gel like wallpaper paste across a wider area. Styles realised he was barely breathing and forced himself to relax. It seemed to take for ever, but the nurse reached up, spun the screen around to face them, and Styles had his first glimpse of the baby in all its grainy black-and-white glory.

Emma's fingers relaxed for a split second, then closed back around his like a vice. She looked up at him, blinking back the tears, and he realised his own eyes were starting to fill. Not what he had expected, but the small shape on screen twitched, something that looked like an arm waved, and he swallowed back a lump in his throat the size of a watermelon. The midwife pointed to a flickering dot in the centre. The heartbeat. Any thoughts of work, Porter, Gordon or Max shrank to a pinprick. All that mattered was right there in front of him for those few seconds. He could happily have stayed there staring at the screen for hours, but a buzz from his pocket pulled him back to reality. Emma shot him a stern look as he pulled his phone out, expecting Porter's name to have popped up, but it wasn't his partner.

Milburn? What the hell could he want? Nothing good.

Max arrived at YO! Sushi before Callum, ordered a bottle of water and managed to grab the last two seats in the place. Callum sauntered in five minutes later, tan trench coat tangling itself around his legs. Combine that with his carpet of stubble and hair fresh from a wind tunnel, he had the look of a man who'd fallen out of bed, headfirst into a pile of clothes.

'Well, hello there, Miss Moneypenny,' said Callum, looking as far from Bond as a man could get.

'If I close my eyes, you could almost be him, if he stunk of cigarettes.'

Callum shrugged off his coat onto the back of his chair and plucked a plate from the conveyor belt as they crawled past.

'I could live here,' he said, mouth full of what looked like duck and mango roll. 'Really could.' He reached out again, a plate of salmon maki this time. 'Makes you feel all hunter–gatherer, pouncing on your food like this.'

'The only hunting you do is in the drawer for a takeaway menu,' said Max, nodding at Callum's straining shirt buttons.

'First you offer to buy me dinner, now all the compliments. You know how to make a girl feel special.'

Max bided his time, grabbing for the plate of chicken katsu that trundled past. 'Anyway, enough pillow talk,' he said. 'How was your morning? Find anything interesting?'

'Mm,' Callum grunted, doubling his chewing speed. 'So, I made a few calls, and it's a funny old situation you've got here. I got a few hits on Google for where some of these guys worked. Called up saying I was doing an article on City high flyers. Funny thing is, none of the ones I called about work for those firms any more.'

'Did they say where they'd gone?'

'Afraid not. All a little sparse on the info. All they'd say is that they left for "personal reasons",' said Callum, making air quotes. 'I tried to push it, asked if they had any contact details so I could still feature them, but no joy. How'd you get on with your dad's firm?'

'Snap. He resigned a few weeks ago. Only difference is I managed to persuade them to tell me why.'

'Oh, do tell,' said Callum popping the last duck roll in.

'Well, I say they told me why; the guy I spoke to showed me the email he'd sent in. Health related, apparently.'

'I know you two had only just got back in touch, but I'm assuming he'd not mentioned anything like that to you?'

Max shook his head. 'Nope, but then again, I'd hardly expect him to write back saying, "Hey, let's meet, and by the way, I'm terminal."'

'OK, OK, just asking. What about your pal, the copper?'

'Jake? We spoke this morning, but not heard from him since.'

'I did take the liberty of trying one more wee trick as well,' said Callum, looking over his shoulder for effect. 'I called that firm you mentioned, AMT, gave them the same line about an article. They sent me CVs and bios for three of them. There's a guy at one of the big credit agencies, owes me a few favours. Weird thing is, none of them have taken out any new credit since they left their jobs, but all of them paid off any mortgage and cards in full right before they dropped off the map. What do you make of that?' he said, leaning back, arms folded.

Max rubbed his forehead. It felt tight, pressure building inside. Why was nothing straightforward?

'Who knows?' he said eventually. 'They must all be in the same boat, whatever that is. Too much of a coincidence for them to all just vanish like that.'

'Only ones I can think of are folk in trouble with the law,' said Callum.

'Or ones who owe the wrong people,' Max ventured.

Callum shook his head. 'If they owed money to bad people, I can't see them settling their credit cards first, can you?'

He was right there, but if none of those things then what? What was his dad mixed up in that was so bad, he'd walk away from his son for a second time?

'You're right. Besides, if they were in bother with the law, Jake would have turned up something by now.'

'There's another option you've not thought of yet,' said Callum, wiping a napkin across his mouth, surprised how much soy sauce came out of his stubble. 'Maybe wherever they are, it's not exactly a voluntary thing.'

'You mean like kidnapped?' said Max. 'Like Jen was?'

'Actually I was thinking more like that chap they found in the freezer.'

'Hmm, that's a bit of a leap.'

'Really?' said Callum, arching his eyebrows. 'I know it's one you'd rather not think about for obvious reasons but think this through. If they all had to vanish to avoid bad people, why hang round and sell their houses first, let alone pay off credit cards? What if someone's making them disappear? What if they're paid off so nobody comes looking, not even the bank?'

Max opened his mouth to answer back but stopped. What Callum said made sense. As far-fetched as it sounded, it was as plausible as any other theory they had. Something uncoiled in his stomach at what that could mean. The realisation hit him like ice-cold water over the head. His father could well have met the same end as Harold Mayes, before they'd even had a chance to meet.

Styles felt like a suspect about to get grilled. Milburn had yet to look up from a stack of papers on his desk, and Styles crossed and uncrossed his legs, waiting for the interrogation to begin, although about what he didn't have a clue.

He'd never seen Milburn look relaxed, not even sitting at his desk, head bowed down. Something about his posture always seemed rigid, forced. Milburn scratched a pen across the bottom of a page, more an ECG than signature. He shuffled the papers together like a dealer, clicked the top back on his pen and set it to one side.

'So, Detective,' he said, leaning back in his chair, 'I'll cut to the chase. I heard a rumour that you're eyeing up a move back over to Specialist, Organised and Economic?'

Styles's tongue felt grafted to the roof of his mouth. How the hell had that gotten back to Milburn? He'd only spoken to two people about this. Both knew not to breathe a word. He'd be having words with both later, that much was for sure. He toyed with denying it, but what was the point. For now, he swallowed, nodded, wondered where this was headed.

'Have to say, it'd be a shame to lose you if you did. You've done some good work here, son. Any particular reason?'

I can hardly say it's because my pregnant wife doesn't want me getting hurt, can I, he thought.

'Just a personal preference, sir. I've thoroughly enjoyed my time here, but that's where I think my strengths lie.'

'I see.' Milburn folded his arms, looking as convinced as if Styles had just told him that he was joining the circus. 'Well, if that's what you've got your heart set on' – he shrugged – 'I'm sure we can work something out sooner or later.'

Is this why Milburn had called him in? To wish him luck for a move he hadn't even asked for yet?

'But while you're still with us,' Milburn continued, fingers drumming against his arm, 'I need your help on something, how can I put this, a little delicate.'

Styles fought the urge to mirror body language as the superintendent leant forwards, one of his patient, politician's smiles starting to spread.

'I'm worried about Detective Porter,' he said, voice heading down towards a stage whisper. A confiding tone. 'This business with the video, with Patchett . . .' Milburn wrinkled his nose, as if he'd just sniffed week-old meat. 'It's hard not to wonder how he's coping with it all, you know, after what happened to his wife, then that mess earlier this year. You almost can't blame him for snapping like that.'

Styles noted the use of *almost*, inference being that blame was exactly what Milburn was doing. What did he want to hear? That losing your wife can mess with your head? That Porter had had an Alexander-Locke-sized chip on his shoulder since the colossal cock-ups at the start of the year? Locke had been at the

155

centre of a whirlpool of colossal cock-ups. People in his way had gotten hurt, Evie Simmons for one, and when Locke had died without seeing the inside of a courtroom, Styles knew Porter felt as cheated as he did.

Defeat snatched from the jaws of victory. It stung, sure, but it didn't make Porter a bad copper. Didn't mean he was a liability.

'All I'm asking is that you help him by keeping an eye, you know, making sure he doesn't lose it like that again. The last thing we need is a good copper, gone bad for the press to crucify.'

We. *Us* against *Them*. Which side did Milburn see Porter on right now?

'If you see anything that worries you, anything you think I should know about, you'll come and see me.'

And there it was. Subtle, like a dig in the ribs when no one's looking. Whisper behind your partner's back, but for the greater good, of course. Styles saw now, clear as day, why Milburn had mentioned his move first. Saw the underlying threat for what it was. Do for me, or I'll do for you, and not in a good way. Styles ran a finger under his collar. When had it gotten so warm in here?

This was turning into more of a lecture than a conversation. Styles cursed himself for not speaking up. 'He's a good copper, sir. I've learnt a lot from him. I'm sure he's fine. Just one bad day, that's all.'

'Your loyalty is admirable, Styles,' Milburn said with the slightest of headshakes, like a disappointed parent. 'But we can't afford to have bad days like that. This is bigger than just Detective Porter. If we don't have people's trust, how much harder does it make to keep them safe? Anyway,' he said, sitting back in his chair, 'I know I can count on you to do the right thing, for as long as you're still with us, anyway.'

That last part hung over Styles like an executioner's axe. Become Milburn's eyes and ears, or any sideways move might take longer than you think, if it happens at all. Would that be so bad? There were plenty who'd give their right arm for a stint in Homicide and Serious Crime Command.

'Anyway, I'm sure you have things to be getting on with. That'll be all, Detective.'

Milburn gave a curt nod, didn't bother getting up, and turned to look at his laptop screen. Styles stood up, picturing Emma's face as he went back out to his desk. Could practically hear her grumbling like Marge Simpson as he told her he was staying put.

Maybe he could have another chat with her tonight. Persuade her that he wasn't exactly getting shot at on a daily basis. Truth be told, he loved working here, with Porter, even if he had been a grumpy bastard at times. He made a mental note to pick up some Ben & Jerry's on the way home, to waft in front of her as he argued his case.

Ground his career. Talk behind his partner's back. Let his wife down. Rock and hard place? More like standing in the hard place, waiting for the rock to fall on his head.

He'd take shouts and insults from hardened criminals any day over a dressing-down from his mum. He'd called her back, fully intending to politely decline dinner, but she had a knack of getting her own way, always had. His dad would call a spade a spade, pull you up, quite bluntly sometimes, if he disagreed. With his mum, it was perfectly placed pauses, sighs, telling you how disappointed she was. A true passive-aggressive black belt.

'Really, Jake, I can always freeze the extra if you've got other plans.'

'It's fine, Mum, I'll be there.'

'Don't feel you have to just because I've cooked enough.'

'I'll be there for half seven, Mum.'

He could practically hear her smiling down the line. 'If you're sure, then.'

It wasn't a case of avoiding his parents, more that he could practically hear the eggshells crunching as they trod on them. The way they, or more specifically his mum, threw in hopeful questions about what he'd been up to, who he saw outside of work, that kind of thing. He'd told her not to worry more times than he could remember, but he might as well have asked her to stop breathing.

He ended the call with promises to not be late. *Because you know what your dad's like for timekeeping.* He looked across at Styles's empty desk. How long did those antenatal appointments take? He picked up his phone to text and ask exactly that when he heard a door open and close. He looked up in time to see Styles letting go of the handle to Milburn's office door.

His partner's shoulders rose and fell with a deep breath, staring down at the carpet. Must have gotten a grilling over something. If Milburn spent half as much time singing people's praises as he did pulling them up on things, the world would be a better place. Styles looked up as he started towards where Porter sat. Was it Porter's imagination, or did Styles flinch when he saw him? Poor bugger had probably taken one for the team in the absence of Porter himself to shout at.

Porter decided to call Misra before he left for the weekend. It was one thing for Milburn to pick away at him, but no reason why Styles should get tarred with the same brush.

'Everything alright?' he asked as Styles slumped into his seat.

Porter nodded towards Milburn's office, making the gist of his question clear.

'Yeah. All good, I was just, um, telling the super about needing some paternity leave next year.'

Styles was one of the worst liars Porter had ever come across, and he'd seen more than his fair share. They'd eat him alive if he ever braved the monthly station poker game. Most people had a tell. Styles had a full bingo card of them. Flushed cheeks. Tongue darting out to lick at dry lips. Eyes zig-zagging all over the room.

Porter toyed with asking, but let it slide. Whatever it was, he'd talk in his own good time. Porter could hardly take the moral high ground while avoiding Milburn, Misra and his mum at every turn.

'So while you've been swanning around the hospital, I had Benayoun print that stuff off that Glass sent through.'

Porter got up and gestured for Styles to follow him into one of the incident rooms at the far side of the office. Neat stacks of paper lined up along the table inside, like exam papers waiting to be turned.

'Alright, let's think this through,' said Porter. 'What do we need to prioritise? There's one stack per name. Headshot, CV, personal info.'

Styles stared at the sea of paper for a few seconds, then picked up the top sheet of the nearest pile and walked over to the whiteboard on the far wall. A series of magnets, round and coloured, like giant Smarties, ran in a line down the side of the board. He slid the page under the nearest magnet. A photo, courtesy of AMT, of one of the missing men, Andrew George. Tan that looked more store-bought than natural. Bald, with patches of hair over each ear, giving him a monk-ish look. Mid forties maybe?

Styles stepped back, studied the picture, reached forwards and straightened it. A minor quirk that Porter had noticed a few times now. Next, he grabbed a marker pen, writing George's name in block capitals under the photo. Porter stood and watched as he went through the same process again and again, until he ran out of room, and had to drag a flip board over from the corner of the room to fit the last few on.

'Right, we said we needed to know who their contact was at AMT,' he said, looking over at Porter. 'What else?'

'Let's start with their age, any family, and date anyone last heard from them,' said Porter.

Styles found them on the printouts, scribbled these under the left-most picture, adding a few of his own as he went. Previous employers. AMT event attendance.

'I'll do mine, you do yours?' said Styles. Whatever awkwardness he'd left Milburn's office with had evaporated now.

Porter grabbed a pen of his own, and they continued shuffling papers, scribbling away for almost half an hour without much conversation. Styles finished first and headed out to grab a couple of coffees. By the time he came back in, Porter was done, leaning back in a chair, hands behind his head, staring at the boards. Pictures, text and coloured magnets gave it the look of a collage displayed on school walls for parents' evening.

'Where to start, then?' he said, as Styles passed him a cup.

Styles pulled up a chair beside him, and they sat like that for a full minute, staring at their efforts like critics appraising artwork. Some of the similarities were obvious, if nothing to get excited about. They'd all attended at least one AMT event, but then again Glass had said that was par for the course. They were spread across four recruitment consultants. Porter made a mental note to speak to all four. Apart from that there didn't seem to be any pattern to speak of.

Styles broke the silence. 'All a bit bland, really.'

'What do you mean?'

'To look at,' said Styles.

He was right. They were all cut from the same generic City boy template. Short hair. Clean-shaven. Lined up alongside each other like a DIY game of Guess Who. Porter kept staring at each picture in turn, willing something to pop out, a case-defining fact to slap him across the face.

'What about . . .' he began but trailed off.

'What about what?'

'The ages. It's not a fixed pattern as such, but look.' He pointed at the first picture, Andrew George. 'Youngest first, then they get older. There's a few who don't quite fit that, but broadly speaking, they get older the more recent we get.'

'What does that mean, though?' said Styles.

'If I knew that, I'd have the case cracked by teatime,' said Porter.

They lapsed back into silence, but this time it was Porter who spoke first.

'Family,' he said. 'Or lack of. No kids. No wives, at least none they still live with.'

'What about Gordon?' Styles asked.

'He's different. He didn't know about Max till around a month ago. Stands to reason that whoever put his name on that list didn't either.'

'That would explain why nobody's looking for any of them,' said Styles, nodding.

'That, and the fact they all signed off with a farewell note before they upped and left. Have we seen copies of them yet?'

'We've not been asking,' said Styles, looking a little sheepish at missing something so obvious. 'I'll get on it.'

'Yep, do,' said Porter. 'Did we get cars sitting on Leyson and Baxter yet?'

As he said this, he glanced at the door, patches of frosted glass obscuring part of the office beyond. He recognised Milburn's grey Brillo-pad hair, even though the body was blurred. Watched him head over to their desks, stand there for a second, then move off towards the exit.

Styles winced. 'Sorry, guv, hadn't got round to it yet, what with the appointment and everything.'

'Let's get that sorted from tonight,' said Porter.

Styles puffed out his cheeks. 'You think the super will sign it off, guv? He's tight enough when it comes to getting drinks in, never mind overtime.'

'He's gone for the weekend now. I'll square it with him on Monday,' said Porter, even though he knew the only thing Milburn would want to talk about on Monday was whether he'd seen Sameera Misra yet. Easier to beg forgiveness than ask permission.

CHAPTER FOURTEEN

July 2009

He'd always been a solitary figure before the beating, but he lived like a hermit in the months that followed. Apart from buying food, the only thing that lured him outside were his appointments at the doctor, or physio, and soon not even them. His pay-off from McCallum was enough to eke out an existence, but that wouldn't last for ever.

He started filling out job applications, but the first tremors had already hit the City. Words like collapse and sub-prime were spoken with pained expressions by newsreaders on every channel, and jobs, decent jobs at least, seemed to be on the endangered species list.

London still lured people in, like the Pied Piper, but by God you had to pay that piper to stay. For every one that made it, two or three had their dreams trampled. Some limped off, licking their wounds, others stayed, unwilling, or unable, to admit defeat.

He approached recruitment firms, one after another, scant pickings thrown his way. Nervous waits in reception areas, leg-bouncing, fidgeting, stumbling through his answers, words tangled together like vines on a trellis. Bank balance draining away like sand in an hourglass, he even resorted to working evenings as a delivery driver for a local takeaway.

This half a life, day-to-day existence ended with a ping of his inbox. He barely remembered the mail he'd sent to AMT, but they were now taking on new clients. Short and to the point. This Friday, their office. He realised he was holding his breath as he read it. Let it out in one long whoosh. The thought of getting suited up for yet another rejection made his shoulders slump an inch, and legs fill with lead. But what was the alternative? A lifetime of delivering pizzas? He was due a break. Owed one. Time to man up and collect.

CHAPTER FIFTEEN

Porter glanced at the dashboard clock as pulled up at his parents' house. Eight minutes late, the best he'd managed in a while. They still lived in the house he'd grown up in, a four-bed detached just outside Pinner. A street lined with lawns like bowling greens, borders weeded to within an inch of their lives, and curtains that twitched like they were sending Morse code messages.

All their cars were there, Dad's Beemer practically kissing the rear bumper of Mum's postbox red Mini Cooper in the driveway, his sister Kat's people carrier blocking them both in. He pictured them waiting at the dinner table for him, all eyes on the clock. The street seemed to be holding its breath as he trudged up the driveway. Nothing more than a drone of cars from St Thomas' Drive a few streets away.

Food, one drink, then home. Tomorrow was a vague concept at the moment. Nowhere to be. No one to see. Not due back at the station until Monday. The notion of switching off for the day felt decadent. Good in theory, God knows he could do with the downtime. Realistically, it rarely happened. Cross that bridge as and when.

He walked straight in without knocking. His parents, bless their trusting souls, had never been ones for a locked door if they were in. A luxury in this neighbourhood, a liability most other places. He followed murmured voices into the kitchen. Three sets of eyes turned to him as he walked in. Mum was stirring something on the hob, like a mini witches' cauldron. Kat's legs dangled from the workbench as she swung her feet like a kid in a playground. His dad was halfway through pouring a glass of red wine. The glance at Porter nearly cost him, but he looked back just in time to stop it from overflowing.

'Speak of the devil,' said Kat, holding her arms out like a kid demanding a carry.

He couldn't help but smile as he walked over and gave her a hug. 'Alright, sis.'

She wrapped her arms around his shoulders, squeezed, held it for a few extra seconds, even when he tried to pull away. His mum had stood her spoon against the pot, waiting her turn, and he moved on to her next, bending down to hug her. She smelt of whatever was in that pot, a vegetable mish-mash of some sort. Mum and Kat couldn't be mistaken for anything but mother and daughter. Same high cheekbones, same almond-shaped eyes. A hand clapped him on the back, and his dad held out a second glass of red when he turned, not as dangerously full as his own on the bench.

'You can have one, can't you, son?'

Porter eyed the glass, wished for something stronger, but took it with a smile.

'Got the car, so just the one.'

'Looks like you managed to stop trending on Twitter,' Kat said, raising her glass in a toast.

'Katherine!' Harriet Porter gave her daughter a glance that could wither flowers.

'It's fine, Mum,' said Porter. 'I get far worse than that from the lads at work.' He stuck his tongue out at Kat as he walked over to where she sat, leaning on the counter next to her. 'Where are the boys?'

'Tony's taken them to see *Despicable Me 3*, so I get a night off, and you' – she leant over, play-punching his shoulder – 'you get the pleasure of my company, you lucky bugger.'

'Dinner should be ready in half an hour,' said Harriet, turning back to the hob. 'That's plenty of time.'

Kat's smile disappeared. Richard Porter cleared his throat, glanced at his wife, then back to his son.

'Plenty of time for what?' Porter asked, narrowing his eyes, wondering why his family were suddenly looking like shifty suspects about to be interviewed.

'Your mother and I,' his father began, 'well, I mean we all' – he held out his glass towards Kat, roping her into whatever was coming next. 'We're just a little worried about you, you know, with this mess with that man, the video on Twitter.'

Porter took a long swig of his wine. 'What is this? Some kind of intervention?' he said, half smiling. He looked at each of them in turn. His mum had turned to face him now, wearing the same worried face he'd seen a hundred times as a kid.

'You never talk, Jake. You never tell anyone how you're feeling. People make themselves ill like that, you know. Bottling it all up.'

167

'Maybe I don't talk about how I'm feeling, because I'm actually fine, and there's nothing to say,' he said, doing a poor job of convincing himself, let alone the three of them, by the looks they all gave.

'All I'm saying is that we're here for you if you need us. Those . . .' He watched his mum struggle for something other than a swear word. 'Those fools that say you've lost the plot, well, they don't know you like we do. They don't know what you've been through.'

Lost the plot? He'd read a damn sight worse already this week. He knew everything she said came from a good place, but it was like the first six months after Holly all over again. Killing him with kindness, smothering, offering him everything but the space he wanted.

He stared down at the pool of red wine left in his glass. Breathe. Count to ten. She meant well. They all did. Silence, except for a ticking kitchen clock, and wet popping noises from the pan.

'Well, this got awkward real quick,' said Kat, pushing off the bench, padding towards him on bare feet. 'You don't want to talk to us, you don't have to,' she said, cupping his face in her hands. 'But you should talk to someone.' She gave him a light double tap on each cheek, scooped up a packet of cigarettes from her handbag and went out into the back garden.

'Anyone for a top-up?' said Richard, holding up the bottle of Merlot as an olive branch.

Harriet sighed like a deflating tyre, turning her attention back to the pans on the hob. Porter shook his head.

'I'm OK, thanks, Dad. Back in a sec.'

He walked past his mum, touching a hand to her shoulder, felt her tense then relax. He had his way of dealing with things. She had hers. He stepped out into the dimming twilight and slumped into one of the patio chairs next to Kat. She'd slouched down low, almost horizontal, staring up at the sky, one hand dangling towards the ground holding a cigarette.

He reached over, plucking it from her fingers before she could stop him.

'Oi, give that back,' she said, eyes wide in surprise. 'You don't even smoke!'

'Only once in a blue moon. I won't tell if you don't,' he said, glancing across at the kitchen window to make sure they weren't being watched.

'You're asking me to lie for you, Detective?' she said in a faux-breathy voice.

Porter took a drag on the cigarette, held it in for a three count, then let it out in a messy plume. How long since his last one? Couple of weeks? Used to be no more than a couple a year, and even then only when blind drunk. They sat side by side in silence for a full minute, passing the stump of a cigarette back and forth like a baton.

'I miss her too, you know,' said Kat finally. 'We all do, and I know what you're going to say. It's not the same.' She twisted around in her chair to face him. 'She was your wife, and I get that. It must have been shit. Still is, I bet, but you know what I'd be asking myself if I was you?'

Porter said nothing, just stared up at the clouds, lumpy like cold mashed potato.

'I'd ask myself, what would Holly want me to do, and it sure as hell wouldn't be to fade away like this, piece by piece.'

'I'm hardly fading away, Kat!' he said, louder than he intended, and glanced at the kitchen window to check his parents weren't eavesdropping. 'What do you want me to say? That it hurts? Of

169

course it bloody hurts. What do you want me to do? Cry? Crawl into a bottle?' He shook his head. 'That's not me. I'm out there every bloody day, grafting my backside off to make sure that other people don't have to deal with shit like this.'

'And that's my point, Jake. All you do is work. You finish one case and sink your teeth into the next one. We hardly see you. When was the last time you came and hung out with the boys? Properly hung out, for more than half an hour.'

Porter sat forwards, practically stubbed the cigarette on her arm as he passed it over. He wasn't angry at what she was saying. Fact was that she was bang on the money. What would Holly say if she was here? He closed his eyes. Pictured her, pursed lips, shaking her head. She'd call him a muppet. Tell him to crack on with life, and that life meant more than just work.

He felt a hand on his arm. Turned to see her looking over at him, genuine concern etched in her face. 'Why don't you come over tomorrow? The boys would love to see you. Tony's been looking for an excuse to fire the barbie up.'

She only held the serious face for a few more seconds, fluttering eyelashes and sticking out her tongue to lighten the mood.

He tried his best not to smile but failed miserably. She'd always been able to drag one out of him.

'Fine, you win, I'll come,' he said, standing up. 'Come on, before they send out a search party.'

She bounced up, gave a happy squeak and wrapped her arms around him. He barely had time to return the hug before she pulled away. He saw the mischief in her eyes, narrowed his own.

'I know that look. What are you up to?'

'*Moi*?' she said, spinning away and towards the house, vanishing inside before he could ask anything else.

He'd seen that look a hundred times growing up. It usually meant she was up to no good, and more often than not, at his expense. What with everything else he had going on, how bad could it be? He'd find out soon enough.

CHAPTER SIXTEEN

Porter squatted down by the graveside, resting one hand on the headstone. The tulips were a blaze of reds and oranges, Holly's favourites. He slotted them through the holes in the colander-style lid of the steel vase, like straws into a drink. Late in the day was his favourite time to visit. Fewer mourners, more peaceful. He preferred the place to himself. Alone with his thoughts.

Once the last flower was in he stood up, knees creaking, and took a step back to admire his work. An engine revved in the distance. He glanced over his shoulder towards the main gate, but he still had the place to himself. That was the problem, though, according to Kat at least. Too much time with just himself for company. Sign of the times that, outside of work, the person he spent most time talking to was his dead wife.

Maybe Kat was right. Maybe he needed a good slap. Everyone else had gotten on with their lives and left him wallowing. It wasn't that he couldn't see it for himself. He wasn't stupid. It was easier to squat in his grief like a troll under a bridge than to let anything about her go, even this.

'What do I do, Hol? Can't do right for doing wrong. What do I do?'

Porter checked his watch. Two hours before he was due at Kat's. He toyed briefly with crying off. Blame work. That would only be a stay of execution, though.

He turned and walked back towards the main gate, between rows of marble, picking his way around a carpet of flowers at a recent grave. *Sister. Daughter.* He glanced at the writing on the headstone. Only twenty-six. How many had stood here? Holly's face swam into his mind, only this time the edges blurred, shifting into another. Evie. It could easily have been her name carved in marble.

His stomach churned like a rough sea, but with what he wasn't sure. Guilt at thinking of someone other than his wife? Worry at the thought of what Evie had gone through, was still going through? As if things weren't complicated enough already.

He caught a whiff of charred meat and charcoal as soon as he opened his car door. Tom and James were out the door and halfway down the path before he'd even locked his car. Five-year-old limpets, clamping around his arms as he walked.

'Uncle Jake, Uncle Jake, have you arrested anyone today?' asked James. It always took Porter a second or so to tell them apart.

'Not yet,' said Porter, looking down at them with what he hoped was a passable snarl, 'but there's still a free cell that would be just the right size for you two.'

He bent down, scooped up one in each arm, wincing as they part-roared, part-laughed, one into each ear. Surround sound schoolyard style. Kat stood at the door now, black-and-white-striped apron with a streak of what looked like tomato sauce along the hem.

'Gunshot wound?' said Porter, nodding at the stain.

'Why do you think I invited you? It's like the Wild West back there. We need some law and order.'

'Off the clock today, sis.'

'That'll be a first,' she said, heading back into the house and through into the kitchen.

Porter followed her, twisting sideways to get his passengers safely through the door, depositing them on the kitchen floor. He followed Kat outside, where Tony was manning the barbeque, beer in one hand, spatula in the other. He'd been expecting just Tony and the boys, but there were five others around the patio table as well; three women and two men. No familiar faces. Kat reached the table ahead of him and turned back to face him.

'Jake, meet the gang from work. Everyone, this is my brother, Jake. Jake, this is Andy and Tasha.' She placed a hand on the shoulders of the nearest two, presumably a couple if she was introducing them like that. 'That's Greg and Martha,' she said, flapping a hand towards the couple furthest away. 'And this is Rachel.'

They all said hello, voices overlapping. There was something about the way Kat said the last name, the way she held her smile and Porter's eye a fraction too long. Then it hit him. She really had no shame. First the family ambush last night, now this. Rachel would be single. Two unattached people at a couples' barbeque. No pressure. If there'd been any doubt, it was dispelled when Kat arched her eyebrows, looking down at Rachel, who had thankfully turned her attention to her drink, then back at him.

174

Porter stared back at Kat, trying for the *you'll pay for this* look. She went wide-eyed with innocence, then pulled out a spare chair, patting the back of it.

'Have a seat, Jake. I'll get you a beer.'

Rachel smiled as he sat down, and Porter found himself returning it, all the while inwardly cursing his sister. Rachel looked around thirty, sandy curls tied up in a ponytail and a splash of freckles across both cheeks.

'Nice to meet you, Jake,' she said, tipping her glass towards him.

'Yeah, you too,' he said. Sweat prickled on his back, but nothing to do with the evening sunshine.

'So, Kat tells me you're with the police?'

As if on cue, a hand appeared over his shoulder, holding a bottle of Budweiser. Kat disappeared before he could even say thank you. He had to give her credit. Her set-up was near perfect. Spare seat next to the single friend. Two couples chatting amongst themselves, she and Tony playing host and hostess. Well and truly stitched up.

'Mm-hmm,' he said, taking his first swig from the bottle.

'What kind of cases do you work?'

'I'm, um, I'm in Homicide and Serious.'

'So, murder through to shoplifting?'

That squeezed a smile from him. 'Yeah, something like that.'

They both reached for drinks at the same time. The dance of the singleton. Sip, then small talk.

'How about you?' he asked her.

She shook her head. 'Nope, I'm not into shoplifting.'

They both smiled this time. She had one of those faces that beamed from cheek to cheek when she did. He lifted his bottle again, took three long swallows this time. This didn't feel so bad.

Would it hurt to leave the car, have a few beers, press pause on the jumble in his head? What's the worst that could happen? He could feel the half a bottle he'd drained already melting away the top layer of tension.

'Uncle Jake,' a voice piped up from over by the house. 'Will you read us a story?'

He squinted against the sunlight that reflected off the kitchen window. Tom this time, he thought. Saved by the bell.

'Duty calls,' he said to Rachel as he stood up.

He followed Tom and James upstairs into a room that could easily be a Disney store, with the amount of merchandise. Toys, duvet covers, even their matching pyjamas had Lightning McQueen from *Cars* splashed across them. Tom thrust a book into his hand.

'This one please, Uncle Jake. This one's our favourite.'

He looked at the cover. *George's Marvellous Medicine* by Roald Dahl. Memories of Mum reading this to him as a kid. Kat's voice was faint but audible from the bottom of the stairs.

'One story, boys, that's your limit.'

Choruses of grumbling as the boys clambered into bunks, Tom on top, James on the bottom. Porter gave them a wink.

'Mum didn't say how long the one story should last for, though, did she?'

Their faces lit up at the prospect of a conspiracy, and they wriggled under their duvets until only their heads popped out, caterpillars in their cocoons. They were still wide-eyed, soaking up every word when Kat's face popped around the door twenty minutes later.

'You' – she pointed at Porter – 'are a bad influence. Lights out time.'

She stepped in, waited while they threw their arms around Porter, gave them both a hug of her own, then guided him out the door.

'I know what you're doing,' he said, halfway down the stairs.

'Looking after my big brother.'

He turned to look at her when he reached the bottom. 'You know what I mean. Doesn't exactly take a detective to see through your plan.'

'Yet here you are.'

Porter grumbled, kept walking, but stopped short of the door to the garden, guiding Kat past him. 'Back in two, sis, just got a quick call to make.'

'The front door's locked.'

He shot her his best sarcastic smile and headed through into the living room. Truth be told it wasn't a call he wanted to make, but better now than Monday. Milburn wasn't going to let things lie, and that meant Sameera Misra wasn't going anywhere either.

Just hoops to jump through, he thought. *But I'll jump when I'm ready, and not before.*

He'd meant to call her yesterday, but it worked out better that he'd forgotten. He was pretty sure the OHU kept office hours, so the chances of getting anyone, let alone her, were as slim as they'd get. He dialled Misra's number, counted eight rings before her voicemail kicked in. He waited for the beeps, choosing his words.

'Ms Misra, hi, it's Detective Porter here. Sorry we keep missing each other. I was wondering if you had any time free on Thursday for us to pick up where we left off?'

Friday would be too obvious a tactic. Thursday felt arbitrary enough to put it off, give him time to focus on Max's case. Should work, for her at least. Whether it would satisfy Milburn was another matter entirely.

'Anyway, if you can let me know what works for you, and I'll see you soon.'

The mere thought of his boss, his holier-than-thou tone, made Porter's scalp itch. To hell with him. He could pick Porter apart all he wanted on Monday, but right now, there was plenty waiting for him outside. He smiled at Kat and her scheming. Everything she did came from a good place.

Deep breath. One more for good measure, and he headed back outside, surprised at finding a lightness in his step. How long since that had been there? Too long.

CHAPTER SEVENTEEN

'Do you think I'm stupid, Porter?'

Honesty would definitely not be the best policy here. 'No, sir, of course not.'

'Then why go and do the opposite of what I asked?'

'Sir?' Porter's face was a mask of innocence.

'You know damn well what I mean. I want you in that OHU session, I want it this week, and if you walk out again, I'll speak to the IOPC myself, and that won't end well for you.'

Porter chewed the inside of his lip. Stayed silent, even though every inch of him wanted to reach across, staple Milburn's tie to the desk, feel crunching cartilage on fist.

'Is that clear?'

'Yes, sir,' said Porter, words pushed out past gritted teeth.

Milburn stared him out, waiting for Porter to blink or look away, but Porter held it. Waited him out. Willed even a fraction of his dislike for Milburn to register. If it did, Milburn didn't show it. Too far up his own arse to acknowledge that people saw him in anything other than a positive light.

'I'll be checking in with OHU on Thursday. That'll be all.'

Milburn looked away from Porter, at whatever was on his laptop screen, but Porter stayed put, cleared his throat.

'There is one other thing, sir.'

Milburn gave him a stern look, the kind reserved for a kid on the naughty step who's just asked for sweets.

Porter ran him through last week's events, the trip to AMT, and finished with the two cars currently keeping an eye on Leyson and Baxter. Milburn scowled at the last part.

'So basically, what you're saying is that, without my say-so, you've authorised hundreds of pounds of overtime to babysit two people, in a case where we have no credible leads, no sense of what's actually going on, and no suspects even if we did?'

Porter opened his mouth to speak, but Milburn cut him short.

'First the fiasco with Patchett, now this. Give me one good reason why I shouldn't stick you on a desk while we wait for the IOPC to come after you.'

'Because we're getting enough bad press already, sir.'

'What the hell is that supposed to mean?'

Men like Milburn responded best to self-interest, so why not give him a healthy dose. 'Every other name on that list is missing, sir. The two that are left are our best chance of figuring this out. I can't imagine it'd sit well with the press if it got out that someone was targeting them, and we sat back and watched, all for the sake of saving a few pennies.'

Milburn's mouth twisted. He was all about the image. Porter was sick of hearing his mantra about the public image of policing – *perception is reality*. The press wouldn't care that they had no clue

180

about what was actually happening. They'd swarm like piranhas, tearing strips off the Met, and Milburn by proxy, crying out that money was more important than public safety. The kind of thing that would hit Milburn where it hurt: his ego.

'You should still have cleared it with me first,' he said finally. Porter fought the urge to smile as Milburn beat a tactical retreat. 'You've got until Thursday. If there's nothing by then, by the time you've seen OHU, you pull the cars off.'

A small victory, but any over Milburn tasted pretty sweet. Probably didn't hurt that the super thought it was a dead-end case either, or he might have ordered Porter to hand it to somebody else.

'Yes, sir.'

Porter left Milburn to stew, and found Styles at his desk, talking to Farida Benayoun, the young constable who'd been with them at Max's house the night of his attack. She was still fairly new, only twelve months on the force. Not long enough to have had the optimism knocked out of her like stuffing from a toy. She stood up as Porter approached, the top of her head barely reaching his chin.

'Morning, guv,' said Styles. 'Benayoun has been calling around the companies these guys worked for.' Porter took the sheet of paper Styles held out to him. 'You want to start from the top again?' Styles prompted Benayoun.

Benayoun did a double take between Porter and Styles, and stuttered back into life. 'Yep, of course. So, of the ten companies for those missing, only six keep personal info going that far back. Of those six, we've had two send us copies of their resignation emails through, plus a few other bits and pieces, and the other four have promised it by the end of the day.'

Porter looked at the summary sheet she had prepared. Kenneth

Morgan and David Marsh were the two they'd had returns for so far. He scanned Morgan's first. It had come from a personal account.

Date: Monday 15 February 2010
From: kmorgan_1970@gmail.com
To: a.saunders@GKR.com

Dear Anthony
It's with regret that I am writing to tell you of my decision to resign, effective immediately. I've greatly enjoyed my time with the firm, and my decision is no reflection on the firm, or its people. I've had some troubling news about my health recently and am taking an indefinite career break on medical advice. I understand that the lack of notice means I forfeit the three months' contractual pay I'm entitled to, but sure you understand, I need to put my health first.
Yours sincerely
Ken Morgan

Fairly vague, Porter thought. Didn't give much away. He made a mental note to check on who Morgan's doctor was, and flipped over to the second email, this one from David Marsh.

Date: Wednesday 16 March 2011
From: david.marsh@santander.com
To: david.pollard@santander.com

Dave,
Sorry for the short notice, but I've had to rethink my priorities after a recent trip to the doctor's, and some unexpected news.

As part of some treatment I need to go through, I'm taking a step away from my career for a while, so please treat this as my notice. Sorry I can't do this in person, but I've been advised against coming into the office, so will arrange to have my laptop and security pass returned by courier.
Best regards,
David

Equally as vague as the first one. Porter felt deflated. From the excited look on Benayoun's face, he'd expected something a little more conclusive. It must have showed in his face.

'I know it doesn't exactly send us past Go and collect two hundred,' Styles said, 'but Benayoun here also went back to them and asked about pre-existing health conditions. Most of them, these two included, were covered by company health plans. None of them could give any specifics, obviously, doctor–patient confidentiality and all that, but they did all confirm that no claims had been made under the policies. What do we make of that?'

'I have to say, guv,' Benayoun cut in, 'I can't really see people with access to help like that going through the NHS instead.'

Porter gave her an encouraging nod. 'I'd have to agree. So, the next question is, did they get any treatment at all, and if not, why not?'

'Even those who haven't sent copies yet have confirmed that they all resigned for health reasons,' said Benayoun.

'Good work, Benayoun,' said Porter, watching her practically preen with pride at the compliment. 'I'm going to head out for a bit. Let me know when the others come through, yeah?'

'Where to, guv?' said Styles.

'Just a social call,' said Porter. 'You hang fire here in case anything juicy comes back from any of those companies. I'll be back by lunch.'

Styles looked like a puppy about to be locked in its cage but stayed sitting as Porter headed for the door. He had been a little economical with the truth. He was heading to Max's, which was a mix of work and social. That wasn't the only reason for being out and about. A longer absence meant less chance of an encounter with Sameera Misra, or any more earache from Milburn.

His phone chirped as he reached the door to the car park. Styles, an invite to dinner with him and Emma tonight that he'd forgotten to mention. Porter fired back his RSVP, a simple *Yep. Time?* He'd barely taken another step when a second text came through. Not Styles this time, though. Kat.

Well???????

He'd ignored three from her already – fishing, stirring, a combination of the two. What did he think of Rachel? Truth be told, he'd enjoyed himself more on Saturday than he'd been prepared for. One beer had turned into six, washing down Tony's home-made burgers. The other couples, contrary to his suspicions, hadn't been instructed to ignore him by Kat. They were an easy bunch to be around, to relax around. Whether that last part was due in no small measure to the beer, or to Rachel, didn't matter to him. What mattered was that the weight, or some of it at least, of the previous week had melted away.

This morning's run-in with Milburn had added a few rocks back in his pockets. Kat playing Cupid could wait. He still had his head bowed over his phone, so didn't see the figure until he was on the bottom step, less than a foot away. His head jerked up, fingers clenching reflexively around his phone.

Evie Simmons looked up at him, wide-eyed, leaning off to one side, weight on one crutch to lean away from a head-on collision, the other six inches off the ground, about to tip like a felled tree. Porter reached out, grabbed an arm to steady her. Didn't take much, her being a fraction of his size. Embarrassed smiles all round.

'Sorry, didn't see you there. You OK?'

She waggled a crutch towards him. 'Yeah, I can be hard to spot with these babies.'

Porter saw her glance down, realised he still had hold of her arm, let go of it like it was a hot kettle.

'Sorry.' *For nearly mowing you down. For grabbing you.*

'Yeah, you said that bit already.'

He held up his phone. 'Had my head stuck in this.'

He realised as he waved it around that Kat's text was still on screen. Felt knots cinch tight in his stomach. At what? Guilt? What was there to feel guilty about? Nothing to even see there, just a one-word question. It was more the subject of the enquiry. Rachel. Porter felt the heat in his cheeks. At what, though? Wasn't like he'd made promises to her. To either of them. He'd gone home on Saturday with nothing more than a brief hug goodbye. Not even so much as a 'hope to see you again', let alone a phone number, so why feel bad?

A flash of memory. Darkness and drizzle outside a bar. A drunken kiss, no more than a second or two. So why did this feel like a betrayal? She must have seen something in his expression, her own forehead creasing in concern.

'Everything alright?' She flicked her eyes at the phone.

'Hmm? Oh, yeah, everything's fine. Just getting grief from my sister.'

185

She pushed down on her crutches, shifting her weight. 'Feel your pain, I've got two.'

One second stretched into three, felt like thirty. 'You here to see Milburn again?' Porter said finally.

'No, today's part of my grand reappearance on the job. Just a few hours getting back up to speed, finding out what you lot have been up to without me.'

Porter nodded, hands in pockets now. 'Not much really.' *Way to go, smooth talker.* 'Anyway, I should let you get inside,' he said, stepping to the side to give her room.

She hopped one step forwards, turning to face him as she drew level. 'I looked for you on Wednesday, after I'd seen Milburn. Coffee, remember?'

He looked up and away, eyes screwed shut, part embarrassment, part frustration at having forgotten. He'd gone to see OHU while she was in with Milburn, and when Max had called him, he'd left without a second thought.

'Shit, sorry, something came up. I had to split. I . . .'

She shook her head. 'It's fine, I work here too, remember? I know what it's like. Tell you what,' she said, letting go of one crutch to fish around in her bag. She pulled out what looked like a receipt, and a pen. 'I can always pop back in another day if you're off out now.' She scribbled as she spoke. 'Here's my number. Just drop me a text when you're free.'

Porter took it, not sure what to say. Her head bobbed down, looking at her bag as she dropped the pen back in, but he caught the rosy tinge spreading across her cheeks, as if they'd been pinched by an overenthusiastic auntie. She took the steps surprisingly quickly, vanishing inside before his tongue became unstuck.

Porter puffed out his cheeks, blowing out hard, like cooling down an imaginary cuppa. As if life wasn't complicated enough.

Would he still be there if she turned around, watching her leave? Would it mean anything even if he was? She forced herself to keep moving until she was through the door and around the corner. Her face still felt flushed, uncomfortably warm, as if she'd been sitting too close to a radiator, but she knew it was nothing to do with double-timing it up the steps.

Six months ago she would have asked him outright, outranked or not. At least that way she'd know. Self-confidence had been just another casualty that hadn't survived her accident intact. Readjusting to life back at work felt like a steep enough slope to climb without the thought of awkwardness in briefings, avoided eye contact whenever they passed in a corridor. Even just passing him her number had felt like walking the plank, waiting for the swoop in her stomach if he hadn't taken the piece of paper.

She stepped into the lift, using the precious seconds of privacy to slow her breathing. Inhale. Exhale. A problem for another day. The lift jolted to a halt, and as it opened she saw Farida Benayoun standing there, smile growing like it was keeping time with the widening doors.

'Evie! Didn't think you were back in till Wednesday?'

'That was the plan, but I've got a doc's appointment then, so switched it around.'

'What you up to, then? You got time for a cuppa?'

'Yeah, sounds good. Gimme ten minutes to sort a few bits?'

Benayoun checked her watch. 'I'll come find you. I've got an hour before I've got to head out anyway, so no rush.'

Benayoun stepped way off to one side, as if Simmons needed the clearance, like a wide-load lorry. Something she'd look forward to seeing the back of. These damn crutches had been nothing but an irritation for the last few weeks. She felt strong enough to throw them to one side, like one of those people healed live on TV by a preacher, but she'd made a promise to her dad. Doctors' orders to be followed to the letter. Two more days and they were history.

She made her way through the office, returning smiles and nods, until she reached her desk. She'd avoided it last week. Just being back in the office for the first time had been a big step. She still felt out of place. Couldn't quite explain why. It was the same faces and surroundings as before. Familiar, but at the same time unsettling. She leant her crutches against the desk and sat down.

Baby steps. She'd be fine. Had to be. What else could she be if she wanted to get her life back on track? It'd be a while before she was anywhere other than a desk, so that would give her time to readjust. Could be worse, she could have ended up like Mike Gibson. He had charged into the same building she had, but while she'd left on a stretcher, he'd left in a body bag.

That thought of Gibson washed away her self-pity like a cold shower. She'd make this work, one day at a time. As for Porter, she'd wait till the end of the week, then give it up. His loss.

It occurred to Porter as he pulled up outside Max's house that he should have called ahead, but the chance meeting with Simmons had thrown him off stride. Would a coffee just be a coffee? Would it be fair to her to make her think it could be? He wasn't sure he had enough headspace for himself, let alone letting anyone else in. What kind of insensitive idiot would he be if he fobbed her off after all she'd been through? He had kissed her back, after all.

He was still wrestling with his thoughts, as Max opened the door. Porter could see the signs of wear and tear creeping in around the edges. Shoulders hunched ever so slightly forwards, dark hint of stubble coming in stronger like a bruise. Even the smile he gave when he saw it was Porter looked like it taxed him.

'Hey, wasn't expecting you. Has something happened?'

'Not exactly, nothing significant anyway. Just passing,' he lied, 'and thought I'd update you face-to-face.'

'Come in, come in,' said Max, standing back to let Porter past. 'Timing is perfect as ever. Kettle's just boiled. Jen? Honey? Jake's here.'

Max walked through into the kitchen without waiting for a reply. Porter heard signs of life from upstairs as he followed. Flushing toilet, creaking door, soft footsteps. Max pulled three cups from the cupboard.

'It'll have to be instant, I'm afraid. Machine's broken.' He shot a glance across at the silent contraption on the bench, as if he'd taken its malfunction personally.

'Let you off this time,' said Porter, pulling out a chair to sit down.

By the time Max had dumped a heaped spoon of Nescafé into two cups and a herbal teabag into the third, Jen ambled through the door, hair still wet from a shower or bath. Porter figured the rosy cheeks made the latter more likely. Score one for the detective. Damp strands of hair laced a pattern across a grey hoodie at least two sizes too big for her. Probably Max's. It hung off her like a kid wearing their father's jacket.

'Hey, Jen,' said Porter, rising to give her a hug. 'How you doing?'

'I'm OK,' she said in a voice too quiet to convince anyone. There was a surprising strength when she returned his hug, and she gave a quick squeeze, then let go and headed over to where Max held out a cup for her.

'What's the latest, then?' said Max. 'I'm assuming there's something or you'd have just called.'

Porter hesitated. He'd thought this through on the way here, in between hating himself for the way he'd clammed up around Simmons. He had to be careful not to raise any false hopes, or to cross a line in terms of how much he was allowed to share. At the same time, he knew if he were in Max's shoes, he'd want to hear it, whatever it was, warts and all.

He ran Max through the trip to AMT, finishing with what they'd found out about the resignations.

'So basically' – he sat back in his chair as he finished – 'it's like doing a jigsaw, except without the bloody picture on the box for help. I'm assuming you've still heard nothing from your dad?'

Max glanced over at Jen. She walked over, stood behind him, hands on his shoulders. 'Tell him, Max.'

'Tell me what?' said Porter, looking at Max through narrowed eyes.

Max licked his lips, looked up at Jen, and back to Porter. 'I'm guessing you'd have said if you'd already found out, so now's as good a time as any to mention it.'

'He's been in touch?' Porter jumped in.

Max shook his head. 'No, but I went to his office yesterday.'

Porter rolled his eyes. 'Max—' he began, but Max held up a hand.

'I know what you're going to say, but just hear me out. I've not said anything that could mess up your investigation. All I told them was how we'd only just got in touch. All I asked was if they knew where he was, just a concerned son, that's all. I'm not daft.'

'Didn't say you were but I told you, you need to let me handle this.'

'He doesn't work there any more, Jake. He resigned, just like your other guys.'

That knocked Porter sideways. 'Did they say any more than that?'

Max shook his head. 'Health reasons, apparently. Left a few weeks ago.'

'Did you get to see the letter?'

'Eventually, yeah. I took a few of his letters along in case they doubted who I was.' Max slid his iPhone across the table, mail app open. Porter scanned it, read it a second time. Almost identical to the others. True, Gordon could have done that deliberately to blend in with the others, but Porter had serious doubts now that he was their man. He reread the email a third time.

Date: Monday 3 November 2014
From: gordon.jackson@marlin.com
To: thomas.phillips@marlin.com

Tom,
It's with a heavy heart that I must tender my resignation with effect from today. The circumstances are personal and health-related so hope you will understand the abrupt nature of my decision. I'm aware that in doing so I forfeit any salary stipulated in my contract re: notice period and accept that. I've made arrangements to deliver my laptop and company phone back to head office – confirmation email to follow.

I've greatly enjoyed being part of the Marlin team and wish you all well in your future endeavours.

Best regards,

  Gordon

Porter pushed the phone back across to Max. 'You shouldn't have gone there, Max.'

'But?' Max hunched forwards, elbows on the table, re-energised now. 'Is it the same as the others?'

Porter paused, nodded. 'Almost identical.'

'What does it mean, though?' said Jen, a hint of a tremor in her voice.

Porter pressed on, ignoring her question. 'What else did they say, Max? Think back to what this Phillips guy told you.'

Max stifled a yawn, blinking back the tiredness. How long before it caught him up, overtook him? Porter wondered. 'Just that he'd been there nearly six years. Got on well with everyone but kept to himself outside of work. They tried calling and emailing after they received that.' He nodded towards the phone. 'But nobody's spoken to him since.'

A dozen questions and theories fluttered around, with no chance to settle, like leaves in a strong wind. 'I'm going to need you to forward me a copy of the email.'

Max nodded, tapping at the phone, eager to please.

'I also need you to promise me you'll stop playing detective. If there's something to look at, someone to talk to, you call me. Understood?'

Max was nodding, but Porter knew he'd have to keep a close eye on his friend. Max had a vested interest, and the best of intentions, but any repeat of the trip to Marlin, no matter how well-meaning, could play havoc with any case they might eventually take to court.

'Do you still think he did this, Jake? Kidnapped Jen?' Max spoke more softly now.

Porter weighed up his choices. Went with blunt honesty, wondering if he'd come to regret it. 'No, Max. No, I don't.' He saw the relief ripple across Max's face.

'You're sure of that?' said Jen.

'Can't be sure of much at this stage, but whatever's going on, my gut tells me that Gordon is in the same boat as the rest of them, not the one pulling the strings.'

'And what boat is that?' asked Max.

Porter had hoped he wouldn't ask anything quite so direct. 'I know what you're asking, Max. We've found one body, so will we find more? There's not enough to suggest everyone has ended up like that. Do I think these guys are in trouble? Yes. Why else would they disappear? Could they have stashed themselves away somewhere, waiting till it's safe to come back? Yeah, it's possible.'

He left it there. Possible. Unlikely in his view, but it served no purpose to hit Max with that head-on. Not unless he had to.

Stashed themselves away, or been stashed away?

That was the unspoken question. Harold Mayes hadn't willingly been stashed in the freezer. That much was for sure. Time, and an autopsy, would tell if he'd had any serious health issues worth resigning over. If he didn't, well, that opened up a darker set of questions. He hoped Max couldn't read too much of this in his expression. Nobody wants to be the person who slaps down what little hope there is hovering around. Despite all that Max had said about his dad, the confusion and anger of growing up without him, Porter knew it was there, and he'd do what he could to keep that hope alive, until something or someone else snuffed it out.

* * *

They all cracked in the end, and this time had been no different. He'd lasted longer than most, but they all caved when base survival instinct kicked in. There was never going to be any last-minute reprieve, of course, but they weren't to know that. Eventually, they all gave him what he wanted. Every last detail. A free pass into their lives. Once they'd accepted the trade, life in exchange for information, they talked willingly, eagerly even. Carrot and stick worked every time. Give a taste of the latter, then dangle the former.

The visit from the police had thrown him, but he worked well under pressure. This would be no exception. Plans would need tweaking, sure. What was set to be a summer break would be an indefinite leave of absence. None of the changes would benefit the unfortunate soul in the boot of his car, but the less they knew the better.

He waited till 3 a.m. before making a move. Not without risk, granted. This had never been part of the plan, but there was no telling how quickly the police might start piecing things together. The subject hadn't been keen on the idea of being locked in the boot but promises of a release within twenty-four hours had smoothed the waters.

The drive to the industrial estate took forty-five minutes. Navigating the criss-cross of roads running through it, only two. At this time in the morning, it had the feel of a deserted movie set. He pulled up outside unit 173 and wound down his window. Nothing on the outside to mark it out, no logo, no signage. Just a grey-slatted roller door, a little higher than a transit van, single door set off to the side of it. He sat for a moment, head cocked, listening for sounds from outside. Nothing, not even the hum of traffic from the main road half a mile back.

Even though his footsteps were the only sound, he still looked left and right as he slid a key into the door, stepped inside and hit a switch. Fluorescent strips strobed to life. He took a half-dozen steps inside. Stopped. Listened. Looked. Just as he'd left it. A second switch sent the corrugated rolls of the main door grumbling upwards, unnaturally loud in the silence, revealing his car inch by inch. He pulled the car inside and tapped the switch to bring the door back down, world's slowest theatre curtain, slight ripple spreading upwards through the door as it clunked against the floor.

The space inside was a thousand square feet, carefully chosen. Too expensive meant a prime spot, too much security, too many potential sets of eyes watching him coming and going. Too cheap meant small, poor location, more likely to be broken into. No insurance policy would pay out for theft of these contents.

He popped the boot open, saw the man inside wincing against the sterile brightness of the strip light. He lifted him out, checked the cable ties that pinned his hands together behind his back were still tight, then led him to a storeroom at the far side. Ignored his questions as they walked past half a dozen large, boxy, white containers. Placed a hand square between his shoulders and shoved the subject into the room, pulled the door shut, checking the lock twice.

Satisfied the subject wasn't going anywhere, he went over to a desk butted against the right-hand wall, opening up a laptop he'd brought with him. There was no phone line, no broadband. Utilities meant paperwork, bills, a trail. He'd read a blog a while back that claimed service providers can log all sites you access via your router. Didn't know if it was true or not, but he wasn't a man to take unnecessary risks. Speaking of risks, he'd decided to keep the subject alive. Not a decision made with any emotion, or moral hesitancy. Quite the opposite. Just so happened that keeping them alive was part of his exit strategy. For now, anyway.

He pulled out a pay-as-you-go smartphone, scrolled through the settings to turn it into a hotspot, his piggyback onto the Internet. He opened up a browser window. HSBC first, tapping in the subject's username and password. Nodding as he saw everything was just as he'd been told. Two minutes was all it took to issue instructions to sell when the market opened, proceeds to be transferred into an account of his own. Not his actual name, of course. Years of practice had helped weed out schoolboy errors.

The cash would only rest there, pause for breath, then splinter off into smaller chunks, each heading to a numbered offshore account. Shame about the flat. Another few weeks and he could have sold that too, but he had days, not weeks.

His next stop was the British Airways homepage. He paused, closed his eyes. *Eenie, meenie, minie, mo.* Chose a destination. Three days from now should do it. Enough time to tie up loose ends. Time to head back to the flat in Bromley, pick up a few things. Maybe even time to figure out where he'd gone wrong, what he'd overlooked. He wasn't sure he could do it without sticking his head too far above the parapet, but the seed of an idea had started to germinate. A little audacious, perhaps; doable, though.

He made one more trip to the storage room, squeezed a few carb gels into the subject's mouth, held a bottle of water to wash them down. Checked the lock twice again on the way out. He shut down the laptop, stared at the car for a few seconds. It could stay here. Better that he head out on foot, walk a couple of miles to the nearby train station and head back to the subject's flat. Made more sense that he used their car now, not his own.

He needed to have a conversation with Max, that much he had decided, but no home court advantage this time. He knew now that Max could handle himself, so he'd need to take that out of the equation, and he knew just how to do it.

CHAPTER EIGHTEEN

Porter and Styles arrived promptly for their noon follow-up at AMT. Glass's assistant had sounded stern when she'd said all she could give them was fifteen minutes, as if there would be a forfeit attached for non-compliance. When they walked into the reception area, it looked as if she was muttering to herself, but as they approached, Porter spotted a Bluetooth headset tucked into her ear. She looked up as they got closer, smiled and held up a finger, mouthing silently that she'd be one minute.

After Styles's comments about her on the previous visit, Porter made a conscious effort not to look her way, but it was like trying not to look at a car crash on the opposite side of the road. His eyes kept flitting her way.

Did you just liken an attractive woman to a car crash? Smooth, Jake, smooth. No wonder you're fighting them off.

The idea of actually flirting with anyone new, anyone not Holly, still felt awkward to him, like trying on a suit that was out in every measurement. All the same, even he had to admit that Glass's PA would turn every head in a bar. She finished her call, glanced up and caught him staring. She smiled, like full beam headlights, and he looked away for a second before giving a sheepish one of his own in return as he stood up.

'Good morning, Detectives. I'll let Mr Glass know you're here.' She pressed a button on her phone. 'Yes, sir. They're here. Mm-hmm. Will do.' She stood up. 'If you'll follow me, gentlemen, he'll see you right away.' Like he was doing them a favour, as if they'd just walked in off the street.

Porter fell in behind her, stopping when she did, and waited as she gave a polite two-tap knock with one hand, pushing the door open with the other. Glass sat at the conference table, fingers furiously pecking at a BlackBerry. He spoke without looking up, no pause in his attack on the keypad.

'Take a seat, please. I'll just . . . be . . . one . . . moment.' The sentence stretched out, Glass typing three words for every one spoken.

'Can I get you a coffee, Detectives?' Ellie asked from behind them.

'We're good, thanks,' said Porter, answering for both, seeing disappointment on Styles's face.

They sat down as Glass slapped his phone on the table. 'Good to see you again, Detectives. I hope the information I sent over was useful?'

Porter nodded. 'Interesting reading, Mr Glass. We've come across something as a result that you might be able to shed some light on.'

Glass spread his hands, a magician with nothing up his sleeve. 'Of course, if I can, I will.'

'One of our colleagues has been in touch with the companies these men worked for, and there's something else in common apart from the link to AMT. They all left, blaming poor health. All resigned by email. Does any part of your profiling cover their physical or mental health?'

'Afraid not, Detective.' Glass shrugged. 'Most companies we place people at offer healthcare as part of the package. Have you tried asking them if they'll share?'

'We have. Still waiting for replies, though, so hoped you might have been able to help speed things up.'

'I hate to rain on your parade, but might it just be that they all had their reasons, and that's where the similarities end, with the fact they don't want to be bothered while they work through whatever's wrong with them? We had a similar thing a while back with one of our chaps.'

'What do you mean, similar thing?' said Porter.

'One of my recruiters, he did the whole email resignation thing. Suppose it avoids the stress of doing it face-to-face, or the pity you get if it's anything serious. Some people are just too proud to let that happen.'

'When was this, Mr Glass?' said Styles.

Glass leant back in his chair, absent-mindedly swinging a few inches either way. 'A while back now. I'd say summer 2009 or 2010. It was back in the recession. To be honest, and I feel bad for saying this, but business was slow then, and Michael leaving probably saved us from having to let someone go.'

'Can you be more specific, sir?' Styles asked. Porter could hear it in his partner's voice, questions coming slightly quicker, leather seat squeaking as he leant forwards. Was this something, or nothing?

Glass shrugged. 'I can have Ellie find out if it's that important, but I don't see what that has to do with what's happening now. That was years ago.'

'Even so, can you remember his name? You said Michael. Michael what?'

'Michael Fletcher,' said Glass, looking a little bemused at the direction the conversation was taking.

'And you literally got an email one day saying he wasn't coming back?' asked Porter.

'Mm-hmm. Little unorthodox as I say, but . . .'

'Is it possible that Mr Fletcher could have had dealings with any of the people we're looking for?' said Styles.

'Anything's possible,' said Glass, although the slight roll of his eyes suggested he thought they were wasting their time. 'It'll all be archived now, after all this time, but I can ask Ellie to check. Probably won't be until tomorrow now, though. She's in meetings with me all afternoon.'

'Tomorrow will be fine,' said Porter. 'If we can get an address or phone number as well, that'd be appreciated.' He asked out of habit as much as anything. There was every chance that Fletcher would have changed one, or both of those, in the last eight years.

Glass glanced at his watch and pushed up from the table. 'I'm afraid I've a meeting starting in five minutes.' He shrugged an apology.

'Of course,' said Porter, both he and Styles standing in tandem, following him out of his office.

'Just give Ellie details of what you need,' he said, as they passed her desk. 'Really must dash.' With the briefest of smiles, Glass turned and left.

They did as he suggested, and Ellie promised to look into it first thing tomorrow. It was just the two of them in the lift for the ride down. After a few floors of silence, Porter turned to face his partner.

'Why do I feel like a small piece of the puzzle might have just fallen into place?'

'Maybe one of those corner pieces,' said Styles. 'Not the tricky bits in the middle that look like they fit everywhere.'

'Had no idea you were such a jigsaw black belt.'

'Oh, I'm full of surprises' said Styles with a wink. 'But yeah, I think you're right. Too many coincidences mounting up for them to only be that and nothing more.'

'There's another one we've not talked about yet,' said Porter. Styles's puzzled look suggested it hadn't occurred to him yet, so Porter pressed on. 'I did some quick sums in there, and I can't believe we missed it when we did the whiteboard grid.'

'Should I be doing a drumroll while you keep building up to this?'

'It's the dates,' said Porter. 'The dates they resigned. Dates they last showed up anywhere. The first four were spaced out by roughly six months. Ones after that were a bit faster, then we get Jackson and Mayes practically on top of each other. If this Fletcher chap is linked, then he disappeared around six months before our first name.'

'That's still an if, though,' said Styles, sounding cautious.

'You know as well as I do that the chances are he will be,' said Porter. 'It's a pattern, Styles, a bloody pattern. Someone is making these guys disappear, and they're getting better with practice. Speeding up.' Porter felt a flutter of excitement in his chest.

Styles stayed quiet for a moment, then nodded. 'Alright, that

202

makes sense. I don't envy Baxter or Leyson if you're right, because if you are, they won't have to wait long before he pays them a visit, and we still don't know who he is, or what he looks like to be able to stop him.'

He waited until nightfall. Outside the window, shadows appeared on the ground as if by magic. Dark stains on a grey concrete carpet, thickening into inky black as they oozed over the neighbourhood, matching the sun's retreat stride for stride.

He slipped on a black fleece, stuffed a handful of cable ties into the pocket. Shouldn't need any more than that. He had no idea of Max's plans tonight, but there was no hurry. He could park up along from the house, wait all night if he had to.

Quick pat of pockets for car keys, and he headed out. The *pip-pip* of the doors unlocking echoed along the street. He hadn't driven an automatic for a few years, and his hand reflexively reached for the gearstick. Second time lucky, he pulled away from the kerb and off into the night.

Two officers sat in a plain unmarked Volvo. No uniforms, no fuss. Strictly a watch and observe brief. The tail lights of the black BMW glowed like twin cigarette butts as it cruised past them, turning left onto the main road. The Volvo pulled out, made the same turn, and slotted in three cars behind the BMW. Perfect. The officer in the passenger seat yawned, stretching his legs as far as the footwell would allow, settling in for the ride.

Porter's mouth watered like Pavlov's dog as he walked past his partner and into the house. Emma Styles popped her head out of the kitchen door as he shrugged off his jacket.

'Jake! We were beginning to think you weren't coming.'

She was closer to the truth than she realised. He'd nearly had a change of heart an hour ago, but the chance to bounce a few more ideas around with Styles won out over a microwave dinner and a night on the sofa with Demetrious. Just.

Emma came out to take his jacket, wrapping her arms around him for a quick hug. He caught a whiff of garlic and onion that clung to her from the kitchen. She passed his jacket to Styles and dipped back into the kitchen to finish up.

Being late meant that she plated up after only a few minutes. Her dish of the day was Bajan rice and peas, dotted with big chunks of salted beef. Styles had warned him that Emma had been experimenting with recipes ever since they got back from visiting his grandma in Barbados, and his stomach gurgled its approval. It was only as the plate was slid in front of him that he realised just how hungry he was. Something felt off, though. Emma and Styles were both smiling, making small talk, but there was an awkward edge to it. Maybe they'd argued before he arrived? Had his invite been more Styles's idea, with Emma just wanting a quiet night? Best not outstay his welcome either way. They could hash out whatever it was after he left.

Conversation over dinner felt the same, clumsy at times. The couple of looks that Emma shot at her husband weren't lost on Porter. Emma scooped up the empty plates and rattling cutlery.

'The sofa's calling me. I'll leave you two to talk shop,' she said. 'Shout if you want anything.'

Porter waited until the door clicked closed behind her. 'Everything alright?'

Styles glanced at the door, then back to Porter. 'What? Oh, yeah, course, everything's fine.' The response was flat, without conviction.

'You sure? Em seemed a bit off her game.'

'She'll just be tired, you know, what with the baby and everything.'

Porter thought about pressing it, but let it drop. Who was he to offer advice anyway? He scooped stray grains of rice from the tablecloth, dropping them onto the plate.

'Don't know about you, but I'll be more surprised if there's no mention of this Fletcher guy than if there is.'

Styles nodded. 'You thinking victim or perpetrator?'

'Could be either, but I'd stick my mortgage on him being one or the other.'

'You know I'm normally more of a hard facts kind of guy, but you're starting to win me over to the dark side with the occasional speculation.'

'I'm thinking of asking Jen Hart if she'll consider hypnosis to see if she can remember anything else,' said Porter. 'Might be a dead end, but this is starting to feel like wading through treacle, so anything we can shake loose is fine by me.'

'Anything's worth a pop,' Styles conceded. 'Want me to set it up?'

'Let me speak to her and Max first. She was full-on deer-in-headlights still when I saw her, so need to be careful how we approach it.'

'Fair enough,' said Styles. 'Makes sense, what with you knowing them. Anyway, plan of attack tomorrow?'

Porter leant back. The rice and meat sat heavy in his stomach, like he'd swallowed a lead weight. Too much, too quickly, but too good to leave anything but a clear plate.

'Let's see what AMT comes back with. We'll chase them if we haven't heard by lunch. Failing that, we should get around a few more of the old employers. See if we can speak to bosses, co-workers, that kind of thing. I'm not writing them off like Mayes just yet.'

The words rang as hollow as a smoker declaring today was the day to quit. No wager of a mortgage this time.

Styles leant forwards again, elbows on table, for the fifth time, or was it the sixth. Like a bloody see-saw. He willed himself to sit still as he listed to Porter talk, eyes fixed on the door, expecting Emma to come back through any minute. This was her way, he supposed, of giving them some time alone, time for him to tell Porter that he'd spoken to Milburn about a transfer. Well, strictly speaking, he'd been spoken to by Milburn. He hadn't actually raised the subject himself, although Emma thought he had. One little white lie to keep her sweet while he worked up to it.

That was the thing; any move wouldn't be his choice. He loved Homicide and Serious. Loved working with Porter. But he also loved his wife, and the way she saw it, those were circles on a Venn diagram that just didn't intersect any more. He caught himself drifting, heard the tail end of a sentence, something about Harold Mayes.

'I said I'm not writing them off like Mayes just yet,' said Porter.

'Oh, yeah, I mean no, course not.'

He saw the way Porter looked at him, the same way he'd seen him look at countless suspects, trying to work out what was going on behind the eyes.

'You sure you're OK?' Porter asked.

Styles nodded, a little too enthusiastically. 'Yeah, why wouldn't I be?'

Porter shrugged. 'Just seem a little distracted, that's all.'

'Nah, I'm fine, honestly. Just tired, that's all. Been a long day. You old timers of all people should know how that feels.' He forced out what he hoped was a convincing enough grin.

Seemed to do the trick, and Porter blew out a breath. 'Sad but true. I'll take that as my cue.'

'No, no, I didn't mean it like that,' Styles said, feeling bad now that his boss had thought he was hinting.

'Honestly, it's fine. I was going to make a move in a few anyway,' said Porter, pushing back from the table.

Styles almost suggested one for the road, but Porter had already turned towards the door, so he let the words slide back down. Tonight hadn't felt like the right time to say anything anyway, no matter how many hints Emma had dropped before Porter had arrived. Porter popped the door to the living room open a foot and stuck his head around.

'I'm off, Emma. Thanks again for the pity invite. Great grub.'

Styles heard his wife scoff at Porter's parting shot. 'Playing the victim doesn't suit you, Jake. Night night.'

Porter left the door open and headed into the hallway towards the front door. 'See you tomorrow.'

'Will do, guv,' said Styles. He heard the whisper of socks on carpet and turned to see Emma joining him as he started to close the door.

'You didn't tell him, did you?' she asked, studying his face as he pushed it closed.

Styles glanced back at the door, seeing the blurred silhouette through opaque glass, lit up by the security light. Had he closed the door before Emma spoke? She hadn't exactly whispered. He fancied he saw Porter's outline pause, only for a second.

Had he heard? Shit. He hoped not. Should have taken his chance at the dinner table. *Tomorrow*, he thought. *I'll do it tomorrow. If she hasn't already done it for me.*

* * *

207

His cautious approach had nearly cost him dearly. He'd always been more of a night owl. Came in handy during the research phase. Passers-by remembered less at night, were less inclined to poke their noses in. A dozen different shades of car colour, all faded into vague dark splashes as they drove past.

These things and more had served him well in the past, slipping through streets and towns unnoticed. Tonight, though, he'd almost come undone by the very darkness that he sought out. Nobody's fault but his own. Hadn't even been looking at first. Didn't feel the need to. He glided along the roads, enjoying the gentle growl of the BMW's engine. That somebody could be following him didn't register until it was almost too late. Maybe it was already too late. Depended on who it was and why there were there.

He'd only been vaguely aware of what happened behind him a few minutes back. A few short, angry toots of a horn made him glance in the rear-view mirror. Someone had chanced it on amber, avoiding a T-bone by inches. He made a left turn seconds later and glanced through the passenger side window, seeing what looked like a Volvo, hand held out of the passenger window in apology.

Five minutes later, he pulled up at another set of lights, in the glare of a huge twenty-four-hour Tesco, with car park floodlights that wouldn't look out of place at a stadium. Another glance in the mirror. Was that the same Volvo, two cars back?

Amber joined red, both yielding to green. He hesitated. Less than five minutes to Max's street from here. Could be coincidence. Might not even be the same car. He rolled slowly forwards, leaving his turn until the last minute. Pulled the wheel to the left and headed towards the supermarket. A white Mini that had been tucked in behind him cruised straight over. His eyes flicked from road, to mirror and back to road again. Felt his breath catch as the

Volvo eased around the junction, tucking in behind him.

Could just be somebody doing a late-night shop. An image of the apologetic hand swam to mind, sticking out from the passenger side. Two people in the car, not one. He followed the signs for the petrol station, pulled alongside a pump and climbed out. Nobody followed him onto the forecourt. A slight twist to either side, loosening up as if stiff from the journey, and he saw the Volvo in the main car park. Hard to see past the glare of artificial light off the windscreen.

He went through the motions, pumped a few litres in, half expecting a hand on his shoulder. Were they here for him? No, they'd be out of their car. Watching him, then, but why just watch, and not act?

He paid for his fuel and a pack of Marlboro Lights, peeling off the cellophane as he walked back to the car. Max could wait for another day, maybe two. Now he knew he had babysitters, he could slip past them another time. No reason to take any chances tonight. Pulling away from the pump, he shook a cigarette loose from the pack, left it dangling from his lip while he waited for the lighter to heat up.

The Volvo followed him back out onto the main road, always a few cars behind, as if that granted them invisibility. Amateurs. They'd get a lesson soon enough.

CHAPTER NINETEEN

For the second time in four days, Porter stared at his wife's name carved in marble. He stifled a yawn. Last night had been three hours of sleep, and not great sleep at that. Holly had danced her way through his dreams again. Cruellest of all, he'd woken from one where she'd been lying next to him in bed, and he'd opened his eyes, confused for a second as to where she'd gone. Double-edged sword, though. At least on nights like that he got to hear her voice again, feel her hand in his. The gold inlayed writing caught the early morning sun. He could recite the words with his eyes closed.

Only a life lived for others is a life worthwhile.

She'd always loved a meaningful quote, and Einstein's words might as well have been written with her in mind, the way she lived her life. She would have been thirty-one today. Porter thought back to when she met his parents. How she'd blushed when they pressed her into telling her age. He closed his eyes, savouring the memory, letting its warmth wash over him.

The flame-coloured tulips were still fresh from Saturday's visit, poking through the holes like candles on a cake. The irony wasn't lost on him. There was so much he wanted to say every time he came. Tell her that her folks were OK, that he still visited them from time to time. That Demetrious still sniffed at her side of the bed most mornings, looking accusingly at Porter as if he'd hidden her somewhere.

He didn't say any of it out loud. Just pressed index and middle fingers of his right hand to his lips, touched them to the cool stone.

'Happy birthday, sweetheart. Love you.'

Porter wound his way back through the lines of marble, moving from his past back to present, and slid into the driver's seat. The eyes looking back at him from the rear-view mirror were red-rimmed and heavy. He dug a knuckle into each, rubbing some life into them.

Time to get your head in the game.

He pictured it all, everything that had happened in the last week, all the coincidences, circumstantial titbits, like a cloud, swelling in size. Hoped today would be the day it burst. Wondered what would spill out from it when it did.

Styles sat perched on the edge of the desk, fidgeting like a kid in detention, as Porter read the email on his screen. He saw the moment it registered, Porter's eyes widening as he looked up.

'Keep going,' said Styles. 'Read it all.'

Porter turned back to the screen, lips moving but no sound as he hurried through the rest of the message.

'I knew it. I bloody knew it. They were all his clients,' he said, pushing back from the desk, bouncing to his feet, a ball of nervous excitement. 'Used to be anyway. He had them all before he went missing, then they got passed on to other recruiters. We need to find Fletcher before anyone else gets hurt.'

'That we do,' said Styles. 'And because I'm a model professional, and the fact that Emma woke me up at six this morning on the way to yoga, I've already made a start on that.'

'Come on, then,' said Porter, 'don't keep me in suspense.'

'Seems there's still a good chance that our Mr Fletcher might be just another monkey rather than the organ grinder.'

'How do you mean?'

'Well, after he jumped ship, he decided not to spend another penny, and vanished like a fart in the wind. At least that's what it looks like at first glance.'

'What do you mean, first glance?' Porter's excitement gave way to uncertainty.

'There are differences,' said Styles, opening a black notebook from the desk. 'Fletcher didn't own his place, he rented. All the others owned theirs and sold up before they vanished. Secondly, he's the only one who didn't pay off what he owed before he split, credit cards, loans, that type of thing.'

All circumstantial, like everything else. Practically meaningless without context.

'And lastly,' Styles said with a flourish, 'he was the only one reported missing.'

That got Porter's attention back on track. 'Who by? When?'

'We took a call back in 2009 from Fletcher's sister, apparently.'

'Who took it? What happened?'

'Not a lot, apparently,' said Styles. 'She reported it, but we closed it down.'

'What do you mean, closed it down?'

'Exactly that,' said Styles. 'It's logged as missing persons, but Harry Archer took it. You remember Harry, don't you?'

Archer had been a lifer who took his pension a few years back, and left to tour around Europe in his mobile home. Wouldn't be easy to track down, to say the least.

'Harry had a look, but from the notes, once he saw the guy had resigned, he took the easy way out and said there was nothing to investigate. Just a bloke of sound mind wanting their privacy. The sister let him in to have a look around Fletcher's apartment. Apparently, there were some clothes, a suitcase and passport missing.'

'What about the sister?' Porter asked. 'Where does she live?'

'You want to speak to her? No can do. She's currently residing in the family plot at a cemetery not far from Oxford.'

Currently. Like her situation was likely to change any time soon.

Porter scowled, dropped back onto his chair with a solid thump. One step forwards, two back.

'There is more, though,' said Styles. 'I called and spoke to Glass's PA again, Ellie. Asked her to see what else she could give us on Fletcher. Funny thing is, despite disappearing, it seems Mr Fletcher still felt the need to log in and view client files, some as recently as six weeks ago.'

'Does that mean he's been in the office, or can they do that remotely?'

'Either's possible, but remotely makes more sense.'

'And he's viewed every name on our list since he left?'

Styles nodded. 'She said – she being Ellie – that she'd have to tell Glass, so I suspect the access will be revoked soon enough, but yeah, he's looked at them all.'

Porter let this filter in as he considered his next move. 'OK,' he said finally, 'we keep looking for Fletcher, and see who we can talk to who knew him in the meantime.'

213

'I'll see if there's anyone still at AMT that worked with him back then,' said Styles.

'Good. While you're at it, get his address. If it was a rental and he skipped town, might be worth having a chat with the landlord. Anything from the cars on Baxter and Leyson yet?'

'Not heard anything,' said Styles, shaking his head. 'I'll check in with them, though.'

Porter ran a hand over his chin, two days' worth of bristles rasping against his palm, the price to pay for feeling sorry for himself this morning. He looked at Styles, noticing for the first time that his partner seemed a little subdued. He thought back to last night, walking towards his car, Emma's voice cut off by the closing door.

You didn't tell—

Tell who? Tell what? Styles looked up, caught Porter studying him, and his forehead creased, somewhere between question and confusion.

'Emma OK this morning?'

'Hmm?' Styles made a face as if the question had caught him by surprise. 'Oh, yeah, she's fine. Good night's sleep worked a treat.' But his smile didn't carry the same confidence as his words.

You didn't tell—

Only half a sentence, but the edge to her voice left little doubt that the words he'd missed weren't happy ones.

CHAPTER TWENTY

July 2009

The meeting was shorter than he expected. Diary mix-up, only fifteen minutes instead of the original hour. Confidence rolled off the consultant in waves as he raced through his pitch, how the perfect job was just around the corner. He tried his best to mirror the consultant's poise, his assertiveness, but it felt awkward, like an ill-fitting suit.

He hesitated at the suggestion of continuing the meeting over a drink after work the following day, a peace offering for the diary mix-up. Socialising, networking, wasn't really his thing, but he couldn't afford to be choosy.

By the time he entered the bar the following evening, the consultant had plainly made a start without him. Glassy-eyed, at the tipping point from a few sociable ones to a serious night's work.

Even in the open-plan bar, he felt penned in, bordering on claustrophobic, by the consultant's constant invasion of his personal space. Forever leaning in, half shouting slurred anecdotes above the background mash-up of the Friday night crowd. He nursed his own drinks, tried to laugh at the right intervals, tried to turn the conversation back to jobs.

He'd decided to tell the lie after one more drink. Say that he had to meet a friend, and scurry back to the solitude of his flat. Before he had a chance, the consultant leant in, finger crooked, ready to share a secret. There was a job, perfect for someone like him. He had the details back at his flat, only five minutes from here.

There were a thousand things he'd rather have done than go back for another drink. This would be the moment he'd go back to many times over the years that followed, turn it over, look at it from all sides. How different would life be if he'd just said no? Declined the drink and left. The answer was always the same. What could have happened didn't matter. Never did. Pointless dwelling on what might have been, because he had gone back to the flat, and, when he did, everything had changed. Everything.

CHAPTER TWENTY-ONE

Max poked through the loose change on his palm while the barista waited patiently. This was the longest he'd left Jen alone since her ordeal. *Such a subjective word*, he thought as he grabbed a sachet of sugar and sauntered over to a free table. For some people, an ordeal is a delayed flight, or fighting your way through hordes of Christmas shoppers.

It'd be a while before she could properly put this behind her, if ever. She was doing a good job of toughing it out so far, though. Sure, she was a little more tactile than usual, but he couldn't have blamed her if she'd gone to pieces and felt a surge of pride at the way she was fighting through it.

He glanced at his watch. Callum was already five minutes late. Not bad by his usual standards. Max slouched back in his chair, settling in for a spot of people-watching, when his phone rang. Porter.

'Morning, mate,' he said, hearing the hint of wariness in his own voice. A call from Porter could be anything from *just checking in* to *we found another body*.

'Hey, how you two holding up?'

'We're good,' said Max. 'All things considering, anyway. What about you, any news?'

There was the briefest of pauses. Was Porter deciding how much to share? 'We've got another link at AMT,' he said finally. 'Guy by the name of Michael Fletcher. Name mean anything to you?'

'Nope,' said Max. 'Never heard of him. Who is he?'

'Used to work there. His name only came up yesterday but looks like he worked with every person on our list, including your dad.'

'So what's this guy had to say for himself?'

'That's the thing – turns out he disappeared in similar circumstances eight years ago. Might just be a coincidence, but you know how I feel about too many of them stacking up.'

'So he might be in trouble as well?' He couldn't quite bring himself to badge it any worse than trouble for now.

'Maybe,' said Porter, 'but he's not on the list, so I'm thinking something about him has to be different. Just need to work out what.'

'What about the other two, the ones you spoke to that haven't vanished yet?'

'Still both very much around, and we've got someone keeping an eye to make sure they stay that way. That last part is just between us, though, yeah?'

'Who am I going to tell?' They both lapsed into silence for a few seconds. 'Look, I just want to say I really appreciate you telling me all this.'

'Feels like the least I can do. Anyway, got to go. Give my love to Jen.'

Max barely had time to reach for his cup when Callum strolled in, hair like a smashed bird's nest thanks to the wind.

'Hey, pal, how's tricks?' said Callum. 'Another?' he said, pointing at Max's cup.

Max shook his head, and Callum sauntered over to the counter, returning a minute later, takeaway cup in hand.

'Sorry to be that guy,' he said, holding up the cardboard cup, 'but I've only got fifteen minutes. Finally managed to get an interview with the good councillor.'

Councillor Neil Lindsay was the latest sacrificial lamb, hounded by the press after claiming expenses for a trip that turned out to include hotels for him and his mistress.

'Fifteen will do me fine. What's your plan of attack with our lovely political poster boy, then?'

They settled into an easy back and forth, and Max felt himself unwinding, talking about normal life, instead of the mess this past week had become. Max wondered how long it'd be before things could genuinely feel normal again.

'I know you're probably sick of being asked, but any news about your dad?' said Callum.

Max hesitated, faced with a similar dilemma to what Porter had no doubt been through with him. How much to reveal? Sod it, if he couldn't trust Callum, who could he trust? Max gave him a run-through of the call he'd just had from Porter.

'You want me to see what I can dig up on this Fletcher bloke?'

'Hmm, I dunno, mate. I'd hate to piss Jake off if it got back to him.'

'Please,' said Callum, sounding offended, 'I'm the soul of discretion. Besides, I know a man, who knows a man, who owes me a few favours. Wouldn't even come back on me, let alone you.'

'And what do you think there'll be to find that the police won't come across anyway?'

Callum took the lid off his cup and sipped at his latte. The foam left a tidemark on his lip, and he wiped at it with the back of his hand.

'I'm thinking there might be a way to see where those files were accessed from if Fletcher wasn't in the office. Maybe my man can track down an IP address?'

'I don't know, Callum,' Max said, playing for time, weighing up the risks.

'This guy is as good as they come. He's like the guy from the old Cadbury's Milk Tray adverts. In and out, never spotted. Doesn't even leave a rose.'

Max smiled and shook his head. 'Alright, why not. If you say he's good, then that's enough for me. How long do you think it'll take?'

'I'll call him on the way to my interview,' said Callum. 'With a bit of luck he can crack on straight away. He's usually pretty quick, and he owes me. I got him Beyoncé tickets at the O2.'

'Beyoncé?' said Max, raising an eyebrow.

'Don't you dare judge,' said Callum. 'Might even have been there myself that night. She puts on a hell of a show.'

'*Et tu, Brute?*' said Max, holding a hand over his heart.

'Hey, we're not all stuck in the seventies with The Eagles,' said Callum.

'Who are still going strong by the way, albeit minus Glenn Frey. Let's see if Miss Beyoncé is still strutting her stuff in forty years.'

'Yeah, yeah, anyway, I need to get going,' he said, checking his watch. 'I'll be in touch as soon as I hear back from my guy.'

'Cheers, mate,' said Max, and he leant forwards to shake hands as Callum walked past. 'Tell him to be careful, though, yeah?'

Callum winked, then left, swallowed up by the flow of shoppers streaming past. Max settled back into his seat, watching the world go by, blissfully unaware of the chain of events he'd just set in motion.

Evie Simmons counted off the laps in her head. Before her injury, she only ever swam on holiday, but she looked forward to these sessions. Blocked everything else out except the slow, steady rhythm, the rise and fall as she bobbed along in the slow lane. She pushed herself as hard as she dared, what passed for a sprint finish to her last length. Felt the ache across her shoulders. Different to those she'd felt months ago on her first trip here. Those had been harder to work through, limbs weak from a hospital bed. Today's was a good ache, sign of another milestone reached. Forty lengths, unthinkable a few months back.

She climbed out, grabbed her towel, stared at her crutches for a moment. Two hours' time, all being well, the doctor would let her hand them back. Confirmation that she was almost there. Almost back to normal, or as close as anyone could be after what she'd been through. She switched her towel to the other hand, picked up her crutches, carrying instead of using. One small act of rebellion, but it made her feel good.

She changed back into her jogging bottoms and jumper, taking her time with the hairdryer. Nowhere else to be until after lunch. The dull ache at the base of her back was still there, ever-present. She'd been assured it would fade eventually, an unfortunate side effect of the way she'd fallen when she was attacked six months ago. Damage to two of her discs, not permanent they said, but a constant reminder that she wasn't invincible.

Her dad's car was outside, parked just along from the main entrance. She rolled her eyes. Even though she'd told him she wanted to get the bus home, she wasn't altogether surprised he'd ignored her. Overprotective in the extreme, but she wouldn't have him any other way. He reached over, popping the door open as she approached.

'Alright? Thought we could grab some lunch before your appointment.'

She saw his eyes narrow, realised he was looking at her crutches, rattling together in her right hand.

'Evie,' he said, as if she was a toddler who'd drawn on the walls. 'What did the doctor tell you?'

'What?' she said, dropping them onto the back seat then sliding into the passenger side beside him. 'It's not like I need them any more after today.'

'You don't know that for sure just yet.'

'Yes, I do, Dad. I'm giving them back today.'

He huffed his disapproval but said nothing, pulling away from the kerb. They drove in silence for a minute before he spoke again.

'What do you fancy for lunch, then?'

'Anything really. Don't mind.'

She said it knowing all too well where they'd finish up. Her dad was a creature of habit. Same cafe every time he'd driven her to an afternoon appointment.

'How about a sandwich from that little deli around the corner from the doctor's?'

'Yeah, why not.'

'I was wondering . . .' He paused, and she knew what was coming. 'Have you given any more thought to what we talked about last night?'

He had never wanted her to join the police in the first place. What had happened to her proved his point, in his eyes at least. Too dangerous. Why would she want to put herself in that position again? She bit down on the inside of her lip. Counted to three before she answered.

'*We* didn't talk about it, Dad. You did.'

'I'm just worried about you, Evie.'

'I'm a big girl, Dad, I can look after myself.'

'Really? Tell that to men like James Bolton.'

Bolton was the man who had slammed her head into a wall six months ago. Just the mention of his name made her clench her fists, grit her teeth, wish for something to lash out at. She stared at her dad, biting back the urge to tell him where to shove his concern. He glanced over at her.

'OK, I'm sorry, that was a low blow.'

'You think?'

'There's just so many other things you could do. Things that don't end up with you in a hospital.'

'Yeah, things you want me to do. What about what I want?'

He huffed out a loud breath but said nothing. Truth be told, she didn't know what she wanted; not for sure. The thought of charging into a building like she had six months ago, no idea of who or what might be waiting for her, made her break out into a cold sweat. She loved her job, but what if she couldn't do it any more? Quite literally, what if she froze up in the heat of the moment? She'd be no good to anyone. Worse than that, she'd be a liability. Was it selfish to put others at risk, just to see if she still had what it took?

The uncomfortable silence lasted all the way to the cafe. She was about to get out of the car when a text pinged through.

She rummaged in her bag for the phone, wondering as she had for the last few days if it might be Porter, but it was another PPI spam message.

She had almost texted him this morning. Almost, but managed to stop herself. Even with a few days off her Friday deadline, she couldn't help but feel annoyed. Why say he wanted to grab a coffee, and not get in touch? After everything she'd been through, life was too short to get messed around. Maybe she'd send him one first saying she'd changed her mind. Time to start taking back control of her life.

Fletcher's old apartment was a stone's throw from Regent's Park, on Oval Road, and comfortably above Porter's price range. Pretty much what Porter had expected for a City boy, which by all accounts, Fletcher had been. *Had been?* Porter scolded himself for using the past tense, although even as he corrected himself, he knew it felt uncomfortably right.

He had spoken to the agency that managed the property. The owner turned out to be a faceless company, headquartered in Dubai, where nobody, the agency assured him, would have the first clue about a man who rented a flat eight years ago. This place was just one of over two hundred, managed lock, stock and barrel by Turner Property Consultants.

The flat was currently occupied, the third tenant since Fletcher had vanished. No chance, then, that anything in there during his time that had survived through to now would be of any use. The lady he'd spoken to did give him one glimmer of hope. A storage facility just off the North Circular Road, near Brent Reservoir, home to boxes of whatever oddments tenants left behind.

The storage unit was just one in a row that stretched for five hundred yards or so, one dark green splodge in an otherwise grey alley of corrugated grey. A petite blonde wearing a navy trouser suit leant against the bonnet of a cream Mini Cooper. She was lost in her phone, but the sound of his car door closing snapped her head up like the click of a hypnotist's fingers.

'Miss Stanley?' Porter fished in his pocket for his warrant card, holding it open as he walked towards her. 'DI Porter. We spoke on the phone.'

'Hello, Detective. Please call me Marissa.' Her smile wobbled nervously as she held out her hand. That nervous edge even the most innocent of people sometimes developed when they were dealing with the police. He tried to pack as much warmth into his own to set a lighter tone.

'Thanks again for meeting me here. I'm sure you've got plenty of other places you'd rather be, so I'll try not to keep you.'

'It's no problem,' she said, tucking a stray wisp of hair behind an ear as it made a break for freedom. He tried to place her accent, a hint of Eastern Europe maybe. She reached into her handbag, pulling out a set of keys the size of her fist.

'This way,' she said, and he followed her towards the door to what looked to be the size of a small aircraft hangar.

'Looks a fair-size place,' said Porter as she jiggled a key in the lock.

'Yes, it's rather large. Has to be. It's not just things that get left behind. A lot of our places come furnished, but some people prefer to have their own stuff, so we store our items here until they move out.'

The door squeaked against the frame as it opened, and Porter followed her into the dimly lit interior. She flicked a series of switches and strip lights spluttered into life, revealing wide aisles, lined with containers, the type you see in shipping. He narrowed his eyes, squinting at the far end of the building, a hundred yards or so away. A quick look left and right showed eight aisles, and God only knows how many containers to each.

'Do we know which one we need?' he said, dreading her answer.

'Not yet, but we will in a minute.'

There was a small office to the right, 'office' being a flattering term for what was the size of hotel bathroom. A small wooden desk was crammed in to one side. The computer looked so old it could have been one of Steve Jobs's first prototypes. Marissa pressed the power button and waited while it chugged into action. Two minutes later, with something resembling a floor plan on screen, she grabbed a Post-it and scribbled something down.

'Got it.'

She held up the yellow square like a referee cautioning a player. He stepped back to let her past and followed her across to the right-most aisle. Every crate had a code stencilled on in a military-style font. They walked half the length of the aisle and she stopped abruptly, so that Porter almost walked into the back of her.

'Master key,' she said, plucking another from her bunch. The door to the container squeaked like something from a Hammer House of Horror episode, to reveal stack after stack of cardboard boxes along both sides and across the back. She flicked a switch, and a single bulb came on overhead.

'Those were Mr Fletcher's,' she said, sweeping an arm up and down twin stacks by the left-hand wall. 'If it's OK with you, I've got a few clients I need to call to let them know I'm running a bit behind, if you're OK to take a look by yourself?'

'Sure, no problem,' he said, stepping back to switch places with her.

She wandered towards the front of the building, phone stuck to her ear. He looked back inside the container. Might as well start at the top and work his way down.

The first one was all books, mainly paperbacks, and an eclectic mix at that. Everything from Penguin classics like *Jane Eyre* through to Sophie Kinsella. The bottom layer was autobiographies. Nelson Mandela. Stephen Fry. More his type. For the briefest moment, he wondered if anyone would miss them if they found their way into his car.

The next box was full of clothes. Styles had mentioned that it looked as if Fletcher had packed a case before he left, but there were still plenty here. The comment his partner had made about the passport bothered him more. There'd been nothing to suggest Archer had even checked whether it had been used to leave the country. Not exactly a shining example of police work.

Box three was a little more interesting; a mix of stationery and paperwork, as if a desk drawer had been tipped up into the box. Porter lifted out a stack of bills and card statements, stacking them neatly on the floor. Three photo frames next, one on top of another.

The first had a picture of two men. He recognised Fletcher from a picture AMT had provided: mid-thirties, arm around an older man, who Porter guessed was around sixty-ish. A relative? A friend? There was a vague similarity between the faces. Something in the eyes. Could be Fletcher's dad.

Picture two was Fletcher by himself, standing on a beach, like something from a holiday brochure. Azure sky, sand so white it could be flour. Fletcher standing hands on hips in a pair of red shorts straight from an episode of *Baywatch*.

The final snap was Fletcher again, this time with a younger man, more his own age. Both men had an arm draped over the other's shoulder. Looked to be in a bar, but not one Porter recognised.

He looked back down at the box, papers, pens and Post-its scattered like confetti. A black corner of something poked up from underneath. He brushed the top layer aside and saw it was a notebook. No, scratch that, a diary. Porter riffled through the pages, most of which had entries in.

When had Fletcher resigned? July? Porter flicked to the beginning of the month and started reading. Mostly times and names, meetings he presumed. Lunch at Café Rouge with Glass. Session at the gym. He skipped forwards to the last week of the month. Friday 31st had been the last time anyone saw him. A run of meetings, times and names, right up to 5 p.m. There was one right at the bottom of the page.

9 p.m. JB. Mardi Gras.

Porter called up Google and entered 'London' and 'Mardi Gras' as the search terms. First hit was a bar not far from Fletcher's flat. Porter frowned. Would you expect a man with health problems bad enough to make him quit his job to be out partying the night before? Maybe he'd just gotten whatever the bad news was, and needed a drink to help it sink in.

Who or what was JB? A friend? A client? Porter set the diary aside and carefully put everything else back in the box. He made a mental note to email copies of the pictures to Glass to see if he recognised either of the men photographed with Fletcher in them.

The last two boxes yielded nothing of interest; mainly ornaments and some kitchenware. Porter stacked the boxes back the way he'd found them and stepped out to where Marissa stood chattering away on her phone. He pointed to the diary, and she gave a thumbs up, not missing a beat on her call, and gestured for him to follow her back outside.

Porter couldn't help but wonder as he looked at the rows of containers, how many other people's lives were tucked away in a box, an Aladdin's cave of abandoned knick-knacks. How many boxes could his life be condensed into? Truth be told, he could walk away from most things he owned if he had to. Was that liberating, or just plain sad?

Porter slung the diary across the desk towards Styles, wincing as it knocked a stack of papers off the edge, sheets falling to the floor like flower petals.

'Whoa, whoa, whoa,' Styles said, kneeling down to pick them up. 'That took me ages to sort.'

'Sorry,' said Porter, moving to help him, but Styles waved him away.

'It's OK. It'll be quicker if I do it. They were all in order.'

'What's with the half a rainforest anyway?'

'Fletcher's appointments for the four weeks before he left. Turns out that not having his access revoked has worked in our favour. They were able to pull all this from his Outlook calendar.'

Porter watched on as Styles shuffled the scattered sheets into four piles, then parked two of them in front of him.

'Here, these two are yours. One pile equals one week. Knock yourself out. I made a start on mine before you got back, but nothing's jumped out yet.'

Porter settled into his chair and started leafing through his first pile. Everything from reminders about gym membership renewal to clients' CVs. Fletcher had used his email calendar to organise his personal life as well, by the looks of it. Some of his appointments outside office hours were one-liners. A name, a time, a restaurant. Porter wondered, not for the first time, if Fletcher had anyone.

Girlfriend, boyfriend, someone who hadn't quite earned a title yet? He assumed not, as the only person who'd contacted the police had been his sister.

The second pile followed a similar pattern: work, gym, eat, repeat. Twice, he noticed an evening appointment matching a name against one of the CVs and jotted the names down to come back to later. Both CVs had contact details. Maybe they remembered Fletcher, maybe they didn't, but if they were meeting him after work, chances are they might even be friends.

His head started to throb like an idling engine, information overload from a rainforest's worth of paper, so much so that he nearly missed it. Fletcher had had a series of sessions that Friday afternoon. Porter had been focused on the CVs themselves, but now he saw they were all named using the same convention.

Will Hutton – WH27334

Greg Smith – GS26331

James Bannister – JB27889

Dan Lane – DL25112

Joseph Baxter – JB11326

The last one made him do a double take. Porter's mind flashed back to the diary. *JB Mardi Gras 9 p.m.* JB. Joseph Baxter. Too much of a leap? He scribbled Baxter's name down next to the other two, scratched a double underline to highlight it, and set the pile back on the desk. He'd ask Baxter about that the first chance he got. He turned to Styles, who was still hunched over his printouts, spread across the desk like a messy deck of cards.

'Nearly finished?' Porter asked.

'Just about,' said Styles, not taking his eyes from the sheet in his hand. 'Got about a day and a half left to get through.'

'I meant to ask you, what did our babysitters say about Leyson and Baxter?'

Styles let out a low moan. 'Ahhh, sorry, guv.'

Porter felt the first stirring of irritation. Whether it was the headache, or Styles getting distracted by whatever he had on at home, their lack of progress was frustrating him enough without Styles contributing to it.

'I'll get Benayoun to do it,' he said, hearing the impatience in his own voice.

Styles clearly saw it for the dressing-down that it was, opened his mouth to speak but thought better of it and turned back to his stack of papers. Porter's phone buzzed, and he glanced down at the screen. Shit. Call from Sameera Misra. She'd been trying to return his weekend call. He sent it to voicemail for now. He was still working out how to stall her further when a text came through. Misra again, offering him a 5 p.m. slot, today of all days. What better day to talk to a stranger about his dead wife than her birthday?

He spotted Benayoun on the far side of the office and headed over to intercept her before she disappeared. She had one hand on the door when he reached her, scrap of paper in his hand.

'Need you to do something for me. Fletcher met with everyone on this list the last day he showed up for work. Track them down, see what they can remember about him.'

'Will do,' she said, looking at the paper like it was the case-cracking clue. She headed back to her desk, whatever errand she'd been about to do forgotten. Oh, to have that level of enthusiasm. He supposed he'd been like that once upon a time. Trying to remember that version of himself was like looking through a fogged-up window. The dull heartbeat of a headache picked up pace, like someone knocking at his temple, trying to get inside.

He looked down, realised he was still holding his phone, text from Misra still on screen. Between her and Milburn they were slowly backing him into a corner, if he wasn't already there. Ignoring her again would only delay the inevitable, Milburn coming for him like a fire-breathing dragon, ready to throw him to the IOPC. He'd seen too many TV dramas to know that all-out war with the boss man rarely ends well. Is that what he was in this story? The hero? Whatever happened next, it had to be on his terms. He clicked into Misra's contact details, pressed call, and took a deep breath.

CHAPTER TWENTY-TWO

July 2009

The flat reminded him of a show home. Everything new and perfectly positioned. Shiny, but soulless. Prints on the walls, shapeless splashes of colour. Footsteps behind him. He turned, saw his host heading across the room, glass of whisky in each hand. He took the one that was offered, letting himself be ushered towards an enormous sofa, big enough for him to lie down full length, arms and legs stretched out.

True to his word, the recruiter did indeed have a job. Michael Fletcher handed him a printout, practically dropped his own whisky onto the glass coffee table with a solid *thunk*, loud enough to make him flinch. Fletcher fell backwards onto the couch next to him, breathing a toxic mix of cigarettes and whisky on him as he leant in, almost enough to make his eyes water.

For all he hadn't wanted to be here, he had to admit, the job did look a pretty good prospect. That, and the fact that Fletcher had practically begged him to come back and look at it, had to be a positive sign, right?

He read on, trying to tune out Fletcher's slurred speech, mumbling something about claiming his referral fee, then giggling to himself. He didn't quite catch the rest of what Fletcher said, and turned to ask him to repeat it, when it happened.

Fletcher moved in to match his turn, and their lips met. He felt Fletcher's tongue probe at his lips, a hand on his knee, sliding upwards. He jerked his head back, scooted a few inches back on the couch.

'What the hell was that?' His own voice went an octave higher, shaky and shrill.

'Ha!' Fletcher spat the word out like an accusation. 'Don't go all shy on me now. That, dear boy, is why we came back here.'

'But . . . the job . . .'

'Yes, yes, you'll get the job, but one good turn deserves another, don't you think?'

Fletcher shuffled forwards, trousers squeaking against the leather sofa, making him jump up to his feet. Fletcher mirrored, albeit a touch more unsteady. Two feet apart, no sound apart from his own breathing, shallow and fast. Gave the whole scene a strangely intimate feel. Fletcher broke the tableau, reached out, as if to pat a shoulder, and he reacted instinctively, batting the hand away, making more solid contact than intended.

Momentum plus alcohol made any attempt at balance an impossibility. Slow motion, Fletcher spun, arms windmilling, grasping air. Toppling like a felled tree, slow, picking up speed as he passed the point of no return. Fletcher's shoulder smashed against the edge of the coffee table, and a maze of cracks appeared as if by magic, running through to the centre. His cheek connected with the corner, carving a line that stretched around to his ear.

Fletcher lay there, stunned, open-mouthed, eyes fluttered half closed, then wide like pools as pain kicked in. He touched a hand to his cheek, saw it come back red, and pain gave way to anger.

'You fucking idiot,' he roared. 'You're finished. The only job you'll get is washing dishes when I'm through with you.' He winced, wiggling his jaw from side to side. Ran his tongue over his teeth.

He looked down at Fletcher. The glass had cut deep, a red curtain of blood seeping down to the jawline like war paint.

'Well? Don't just stand there, you useless piece of shit,' Fletcher yelled. 'Either help me up or get the hell out of here.'

The blood. The man sprawled on the floor. He blinked, and he wasn't in the flat any more. He was back in the warehouse, bully at his feet.

Blink. Back in the room. He bent down, picked up Fletcher's whisky glass. He was the victim here. All an accident, a misunderstanding.

Blink. The feeling of injustice turning to justice. Of standing up for himself. Hesitation into righteous indignation.

Blink. The realisation, an epiphany of sorts, that the dreams he'd been stuck with since that day weren't just dreams. No, they were fantasies, alternate realities, of what should have happened. Not this time. The glass was reassuringly heavy in his hand, thick base snug against his palm. Fletcher groaned, pushing himself up, palms on the floor.

That movement triggered something in him. Acting without thinking, the hand holding the glass stretched out behind, then whipped forwards, like a baseball pitch. It flew straight and true, heavy base connecting with Fletcher's temple. He saw the recruiter's eyes roll back in his head, supporting arm giving way, and he face-planted into the floor.

He stood motionless for a ten count, barely breathing himself. Fletcher lay still, not so much as a twitch. Slowly, he inched towards Fletcher where he lay. Placed two shaky fingers to his neck, felt the faintest of pulses. Touched the same two fingers to the spot that the glass had connected with. Traced the concave dent, felt something grate when he prodded. No reaction from Fletcher.

He stood up, looked around, saw his own drink where he'd left it on the table. He pulled the glass towards him and drained it in one. Focused on his breathing. In through the nose, out through the mouth. Felt the heat of the whisky spreading through him.

Two choices. Call for an ambulance, report it as an accident. Deal with the consequences. No way that ended well for him, though. Option two, take care of things himself, whatever that entailed.

Of all the crossroads he'd found himself at, this was the most defining, even more so than the warehouse. Two choices, but the decision had been made the second he threw the glass, and he set about doing what needed to be done.

CHAPTER TWENTY-THREE

The BMW hadn't moved since they came on shift, so, consequently, neither had they. No need to. Only one way in, one way out. Abney Park lurked beyond the wall at the far end, sealing off the street with a dense green wall. They'd parked up outside an estate agents on the corner, giving them a full view of Summerhouse Road.

Neither officer had seen so much as a twitching curtain since they'd taken over earlier this morning. At least last night's crew had had a field trip, even if it was only following Baxter to the shops and back. The man in the driver's seat, PC Glenn Waters, was the proud record holder of today's highest score on Angry Birds. His passenger, PC Dee Williams, swore under her breath, stabbed a finger at the screen, muttering something about it being a stupid game anyway.

Waters's grin dropped as he jerked his head around to catch movement in the wing mirror. False alarm. A young mother struggled past them, bumping a pushchair up the kerb, her son's hand in her left, the hand doing the steering weighed down by two heavy-looking shopping bags that cut into her wrist.

He had just looked back across to Williams when a jogger came out of the back lane, past them and off onto the main street before he had a chance to twist in his seat for a better look. Light grey hoodie pulled up over their head, a dark grey inkblot of a sweat patch on their back. A man, he thought, judging by the build. Must have just cut through the lane if he'd already got a sweat on.

Waters jumped as something landed in his lap. Looked down at his phone, where Williams had thrown it, scrubbed the jogger from his mind and tapped the screen to start a fresh game.

'Here, I'll show you how it's done.'

He kept running for almost ten minutes, criss-crossing streets to check for unwanted followers. The liberal sprinkling of water on the hoodie had given a sweat patch like a Rorschach test. A small sports pouch around his waist held a few essentials, including a key for the BMW a few more minutes away, bought for cash a few weeks back.

Patience had always been a strong point. Over an hour of watching them through the narrowest of gaps where the curtain met the wall, waiting until they'd both taken a comfort break, unlikely to leave the car again until the next shift change.

He slid into the driver's seat of the BMW, peeled his hood back. Quick check in the mirror for traffic, and he was on his way. First stop would be his place for a change of clothes, then on to Max, and the answers he needed to put an end to this once and for all.

* * *

238

Porter's stomach gurgled like water down a drain. When was the last time he'd eaten? He checked his watch. Three hours until he was due in Misra's office, and he was looking forward to it as much as most people look forward to visiting the dentist. He knew she couldn't force him to say anything, but it wasn't her he was worried about.

Everywhere he turned, someone mentioned Holly. Milburn, Misra, Kat, parents, even Styles. Their concern for him was like a fist around a tube of toothpaste, squeezing him, pressure building. No telling what might come out eventually.

He had dealt with losing Holly like he coped with everything. By putting it in a box, tucking it away somewhere safe. The grief was there; he just chose not to let it wash over him, to paralyse him. Too many people relied on him every day to let that happen. He would cope with it a damn sight better, had been since it happened, if they'd just all leave him be.

Enough of the self-pity. He turned his attention back to Benayoun's notes. She'd tracked down all bar one of Fletcher's appointments from the day he disappeared and arranged times for them to be interviewed. The exception was James Bannister. Porter studied his AMT profile. He had been some kind of finance expert, although the jobs on Bannister's CV looked more like temp roles than anything significant. The address they had for him was near Bromley, a little over an hour's commute from the City. He was still on the electoral register there. Had anyone been around to check? Nothing to confirm either way.

He clicked through to the financial information they'd tracked down for Bannister. He hadn't paid any taxes since April 2009. That only made sense if he was working cash in hand. Would there be enough of that to fund a flat in that area? Porter doubted it.

Bannister's lack of a footprint niggled him, like sand in a shoe after a trip to the beach. It wasn't quite the same as the others, but at the same time there were enough questions to make him as much of a potential victim as anyone else, maybe even the first. Whoever was making these men disappear could have started with Bannister and gotten a taste for it.

Porter was loath to think of this as yet another coincidence, but whatever was going on, it felt like it was reaching a critical mass, a boil about to burst. There was a trail to follow, even if he hadn't a clue where it led.

Porter decided he and Styles would pay a visit to Bannister's flat this afternoon, and he scribbled the address on a bright orange Post-it, slapping it next to the original list of names on the whiteboard. He called out to Benayoun, and she appeared beside him a few seconds later, like a genie from a lamp.

'Quick job for you,' he said, pointing at the orange square. 'That chap there, we need a photo. There'll probably be one with his CV like the others. Can you print off a few for me?'

'No worries, I'm on it,' she said, wheeling away to get started.

It occurred to him as she disappeared that he'd meant to ask her to get an update from the cars watching Leyson and Baxter. He opened his mouth to call her back but changed his mind. Want a job doing properly, do it yourself. He picked up the phone, punched in the extension for the control room, and asked to be patched through to the officers watching Leyson.

The constable he spoke to made no effort to hide his boredom as he walked Porter through in a monotone like he was reading the football scores. Office, wine bar, home and back to the office again. Porter thanked him and pressed redial, this time asking for the car keeping an eye on Baxter.

'Still holed up at home.' PC Williams had a nasal drone to her voice that reminded Porter of one of his school teachers.

Porter wondered if Baxter was taking an extra few days to make the line he'd fed his employer about being sick more convincing.

'Not left the street all day,' Williams continued. 'Night shift get all the fun.'

'Fun?' Porter felt a trickle of uncertainty run down his insides, pooling in his gut.

'Slight exaggeration, guv.' Williams chuckled. 'They had a late-night trip to the shops. Long way to go for a pack of smokes, mind.'

'Where's a long way?'

'Finished up at that big new Tesco in Harrow. Topped up the tank, bought some cigarettes then headed home.'

'The one on Station Road?' Porter asked, even though he knew the answer.

'That's the one.'

Station Road. Minutes away from Max's house, but a good forty-five minutes from Baxter's flat. An hour and a half round trip instead of one of dozens of petrol stations closer to his own home. Porter had mentioned Max's name to Baxter when they'd met, but nothing more than that. The only way he could know about Max, specifically where he lived, would be if he was part of whatever was going on. He hadn't gone out for cigarettes. He'd gone there for Max. Must have clocked the car following him and changed his plans.

Porter sat up rigid in his chair. 'You're sure he's still at home?'

'Yep, not crossed the doorstep since we got here.'

'Make sure he doesn't,' said Porter, springing to his feet. 'He doesn't leave till I get there. Understood? And put a call in for a car

241

to go to Max Brennan's house. I want him and his girlfriend at the station within the hour.'

Porter didn't wait for an acknowledgement. No time. If he was right, this ended today.

Styles drove while Porter called Max's mobile, but it went straight to voicemail.

'Max, it's Jake. Call me now.' Short and to the point.

Styles darted through a gap in the traffic to take the turn into Summerhouse Road, pulling up behind the unmarked Volvo. He and Styles trotted along to where Williams stood by the stairs leading to Baxter's front door.

'Anything?' said Styles.

'No sign of life,' said Williams, shaking her head. Her face was somewhere between confusion and contrition, like she'd messed up but didn't know how.

Porter strode past him and jabbed a finger at the intercom, staring at it, willing it to speak. Seconds of silence oozed past. Nothing. Pressed it again, holding for a five count, but the result was the same. He stepped back to where the others stood. Looked up at the rows of windows, curtains drawn like stages waiting for their actors. He took out his phone and redialled Max. Still nothing. Where the hell was he? Beads of sweat popped across his shoulders and down his back. This, whatever this was, felt all kinds of wrong, like things were playing out right under his nose that he was powerless to stop.

He looked back at Styles, at the two officers, shuffling nervously from one foot to the other, and made his decision. There was a good chance he'd end up regretting it, but if he was right, what he had in mind was the least of his worries.

* * *

Max had just pulled his T-shirt on when he heard the doorbell. He had pushed himself on his run around Kenton Rec, sprinting stretches, pumping arms and legs, breathing hard to drown out the voices that told him to stop. Even after a cold shower, he was still dabbing sweat off his forehead.

The man had his back to Max when he opened the door and turned as Max leant against the frame. Smart blue suit, white shirt, no tie and top button undone. Short hair, probably a number two all over. Max put him somewhere in his early forties, but he'd not had too rough a paper round from the few lines on his face.

'Max Brennan?'

'Yes, how can I help you?'

'DI Lumley, Met Police,' he said, flashing an ID badge. 'DI Porter sent me to pick you up. We've got reason to believe the man who attacked you might also be responsible for your father's disappearance.'

'You've caught him?' Max's heart thumped hard against his chest at the prospect.

'Afraid not,' he said with a resigned smile. 'We've reason to believe he might come after you again. The boss asked me to get you somewhere safe in the meantime. Just a precaution, you understand.' He looked past Max, into the house. 'Is your girlfriend here as well?'

Max shook his head. 'She's round at her mother's. Are we meeting Jake at the station, then?'

'Not yet,' said the officer, snapping his attention back to Max. 'The boss told me to take you to one of our off-site locations. Whoever this fella is, he seems to be one step ahead, so we're not taking any chances. The DI will meet us there. If you give me your mother-in-law's address, we can send a car for your other half as well.'

'Sure, OK then,' said Max, reciting the address from memory. 'Come on in a second while I sort myself out.'

He backed into the house, stepped into a pair of Converse, laces still done up, burrowing his toes in, and scooping the backs over his heel with a finger. Keys, phone, wallet. Should he leave a note for Jen? No point, they'd pick her up before she could make it back. The officer was waiting patiently by the door when Max emerged. They both looked down at his phone as it cheeped a message.

'Speak of the devil,' said Max, holding it up for the officer to see. 'Voicemail from Jake.'

The officer cleared his throat. 'That'll just be to tell you to expect me. We'd best get going anyway.' He stepped back to let Max out.

Max let the phone fall back to his side. Jake would probably be driving to meet them now anyway, so no point calling back. He'd see him soon enough.

'Lead the way,' he said, pulling the door closed behind him.

The car he headed to was an unmarked BMW. Older model but looked in good shape. Max looked both ways along the road. Not another soul in sight, so why did he feel like he was being watched, claustrophobic, as if the street was folding in on itself?

Porter's lips were practically touching the letter box as he shouted through.

'Mr Baxter? Mr Baxter, this is DI Porter. Everything alright in there?'

He switched position, put his ear to the opening. Waited

all of two seconds and turned to Styles and the two constables.

'You hear that?'

He saw confusion on their faces, shrugged and turned on his heel. His foot connected with the door just below the lock. It splintered with a crunch like snapping twigs but held. Second time was the charm, and the door cannoned open, shuddering as it slammed into the wall, bouncing back.

Porter turned back to his audience of three, backing into the open doorway as he did. 'Sounds of a struggle, reasonable grounds.' Their expressions were almost identical, somewhere between surprise and disbelief. If he had this wrong, he owed Baxter a new door, and Milburn had yet another reason to throw him to the wolves. He was halfway down the hallway before he heard any footsteps following him.

'This is DI Porter, Met Police. If there's anyone in the building, make yourself known.' He cocked an ear. Nothing except shuffling feet behind him.

'You sure about this, guv?' Styles whispered over his shoulder.

'Yep,' he replied, although he felt anything but.

They moved quickly from room to room, clearing them one at a time. The place was like a show home. Handfuls of magazines on the coffee table, squared into neat piles. Dish rack by the sink screamed singledom. One plate, one cup, knife and fork.

'You reckon he has a cleaner?' said Styles as they moved into the living room. 'This place could pass the white glove test.' He ran a finger along the mantelpiece to prove his point.

'There must be another way out,' Porter said, turning to Williams. No need to come out and say it. That he'd disappeared on their watch.

Williams looked at Waters, and back to Porter, face reddening as if she'd been slapped across the cheeks. 'Sorry, sir, I don't . . . there's a door in the kitchen?'

The four of them migrated through to the rear of the flat and Porter peered through the window, out into the back yard. A trio of bins, bottles poking from under the lid of what must be the recycling one. Nothing else except a bottle-green door, padlock speckled with brown liver spots of rust. Porter tried the door that led out to the yard. Unlocked. It felt like a bricked-up oasis when he stepped outside. Traffic from the main road was little more than a murmur. He walked over to the door, took the padlock between finger and thumb, pulled against it and watched as it swung open.

Waters and Williams were framed in the window, Styles towering above both as he turned to them, gesturing at the lock, giving them a *you had one job* look. They all trooped out to join him. He twisted the padlock enough to let it slip off the catch and opened the door that sounded like it hadn't been oiled since Blair was in Downing Street. A quick glance into the back lane confirmed his suspicions. Same as the front street: only one way out.

'Styles, back out front with me. You two' – he shot a stern look at both constables – 'get out in the lane. We'll knock on a few doors, you check back yards. If he's there, we might flush him out to you.'

They scurried out into the lane, and he strode back through the flat, Styles in tow.

'What's going on, guv?' he asked. 'The place is empty. What did you hear?'

'No time for that now. We need to find him, now.'

That last word came out hard, a command, and Styles knew

better than to waste time asking more questions. Porter took the steps back down to the street two at a time and was halfway to the next door along when his phone rang. He pulled it from his pocket. Max's home number.

'Max? I've been trying to get hold of you.'

'It's me, Jake – Jen. You have to do something. Oh my God, you have to help him.'

CHAPTER TWENTY-FOUR

July 2009

General Patton once said that pressure makes diamonds. When extreme pressure is applied to anything, it either breaks under the strain, or sometimes it can transform into something else, something stronger. It's literally that binary. When it comes to people, if they embrace it, incredible things can be achieved under pressure. Some crumble, others rise to the occasion.

He surprised himself with how methodical he had been. He'd found a pair of gloves under the sink. Both glasses were washed, dried and put away. He examined the one that he'd thrown, amazed to find no damage. Must have made contact plum on the thick base. What else had he touched since he came in? Not much, but better safe than sorry. A rag from the same kitchen cupboard doubled as a duster, and he wiped down every surface he'd been near.

The job ad was folded up, tucked away in a pocket, to be disposed of later. He tried to keep focused but kept glancing over to where Fletcher lay on the floor, expecting to see him stir, hear him moan in pain, but he might as well have been carved from stone. Checked again for a pulse, but this time nothing. Even though he knew that had been a likely outcome, it still hit him like a bucket of ice water dumped over his head. His breathing faster, shallower. He didn't ask to be put in these situations, yet here he was again, victim of other people's choices.

No turning back now. But what to do with the body? He didn't much fancy dragging it outside, arms around it like a scene from *Weekend at Bernie's*. He cocked his head to one side, lost in thought for a few seconds. Five minutes later, the contents of the oversized fridge were in two bin liners, shelves removed and stashed in a cupboard. The sole item now being chilled was Fletcher himself, back flush up against one wall, knees tucked up foetus-like, forehead resting on them. He assumed the cold would delay any decomposition as well as hiding it from anyone who might come looking.

Another idea occurred to him, most likely from one of the many police dramas on TV these days, and he grabbed another bin liner, filling it with anything that looked valuable. He found Fletcher's wallet in a jacket by the door. Phone and laptop went in as well, along with a stack of paperwork and a leather Filofax.

As an afterthought, he went back to the fridge. Even though the contents should be no surprise, it was still surreal to open the door and see him wedged in place. The Breitling on his wrist could be a fake from a Spanish beach for all he knew, but a robber wouldn't leave it behind, so neither could he.

He was breathing heavily now, his back cold and clammy, shirt sticking to it like blotting paper. One last look around. From show home to crime scene and back again. The only sign anything had happened was the cracked coffee table, but he could hardly do much with that. He felt self-conscious as he hefted the bag of Fletcher's possessions over his shoulder. Might as well have 'swag' written on it. He switched to an underarm grip. Much better. Paused as he saw his own reflection in a mirror by the door. His face was a blank canvas, but inside, his guts fizzed like fireworks.

'I did not ask for this,' he heard himself say, but the voice sounded unfamiliar, a dry whisper. 'None of it.'

That may be the case, but it had sought him out, just like the warehouse all those years ago. He was a survivor then, and he'd survive this, whatever it took.

CHAPTER TWENTY-FIVE

Max gazed out of the window as they cruised along the dual carriageway. The flow of traffic growing sluggish as the clock ticked down to the start of rush hour. They had been driving east for around an hour. He'd tried to press DI Lumley for more information, but Lumley had insisted that Porter had a fuller picture to share. He wondered how Jen was taking this; barely back from her own ordeal, then whisked off like this with little or no information. He reached into his pocket, unlocked the screen and tapped to dial Jen's number. From the corner of his eye he saw Lumley's head twitch towards him, then back to the road.

'I'm just going to give my girlfriend a quick call,' he said. 'Don't want her to worry.'

'They shouldn't be far behind us. Might have even picked her up by now,' said Lumley, but Max already had the phone to his ear.

'Hey, Jen, it's me. You still at your mum's?'

'Yeah. Dad's going to drop me off in about an hour. I'm

thinking takeaway tonight? Noodles from the Dragon?'

The Flying Dragon wasn't the closest to their place, but their Singapore chow mein was worth the trip, and Max's mouth watered at the thought.

'I'm all for that. Listen up a sec, though, honey. Nothing's wrong, but I need you to do something for me.'

'Nobody ever starts a sentence with "nothing's wrong" if nothing's actually wrong,' said Jen.

'I'm with one of Jake's guys. They think they know the guy who's behind this. They're tracking him down now, but they're worried he might try something.'

'Oh my God! Who is he? Where is he now?'

'Don't know yet. Hoping Jake might be able to tell me a bit more when I see him. They're taking me to a station near Dartford to meet him, and they're going to send a car to your mum's as well, so stay put till they get there, and don't worry.'

'OK, babe,' she said, a slight tremor in her voice. 'How long before they pick me up?' She sounded so vulnerable, unsure of herself. He moved the phone a few inches away from his ear, tilting his head towards Lumley.

'How long did you say for their car?'

'Half an hour tops,' he said, eyes fixed on the road ahead. 'Tell her to stay inside till the officers get there.'

'Did you catch that?' Max asked, lifting the phone back up, but all he heard was static. 'Jen? Can you hear me? Hello? Think the signal's going.' He was about to end the call and redial when he heard it, a half-choked sob. 'Jen? Everything OK? Can you hear me?'

'His voice,' she said, low enough that she was almost whispering. 'That's . . . his voice . . . it's his voice.'

'Can't understand you, honey,' said Max, sticking a finger in his opposite ear to block out the noise of the car as best he could. 'Say that again.'

'The voice, Max. It's him. I never saw his face, but that voice . . .' She trailed off, two more seconds of silence, then an urgent whisper. 'Run, Max. You have to run!'

'Slow down, Jen. What's happened?'

'It's him, Jake, it's him. He has Max, and I don't know where they are or what to do.' Her words gushed out like water from a burst pipe.

'It's who? Who has Max?'

'It's the same man, the man who took me, who had me . . .' Punctuated by sobs, the last part dissolved into tears.

'Jen!' It came out harsher than he'd intended, but he needed her to cut through her fear. 'Was it Max you spoke to, Jen? What did he say? Think carefully and tell me exactly what was said.'

He thought he'd lost connection for a second, but a loud sniff nearly deafened him, then what sounded like a strong wind blowing in the background. Her breathing hard and heavy against the handset, trying to pull herself together.

'He just said he loved me too. That he'd see me later. That was it. It just went dead after that. Why would he say "love you too" when I hadn't said it first? I mean, I do, obviously, it's just—'

'Shh, Jen, it's OK,' Porter said, even though it felt like the polar opposite. 'We'll trace his phone. We'll find him, I promise.'

He tried to pump confidence in his words, to at least reassure her, even if he couldn't reassure himself.

* * *

253

Time stopped. For the briefest of instances, it actually stopped. He'd swear to that on a stack of Bibles. Jen's words made his breath catch in his chest, throat close up like a collapsed mineshaft. It was as if the world outside was freeze-framed for that single second, and he saw it all so clearly. The red Royal Mail van in the wing mirror. Fine spots of rain, like scratches on the windscreen. Grey clouds hanging above like dirty rags waiting to be wrung out.

Everything inside the car was different. It was more the things that he couldn't see, things that weren't there. A radio, for one. Even unmarked cars had them in, whatever set-up they had to keep in touch with control. Why had that not registered when he'd got in? He'd ignored what was right in front of his face.

His voice. It's him.

Had he reacted when her words hit home? Had he flinched, or stiffened as they dug hooks into his brain? Did Lumley – *no, not Lumley* – did the man in the driver's seat pick up on any of it if he had? No way of knowing, but he had to get off the phone before Jen's voice got any louder. Loud enough for the man to hear.

'OK, love you too, honey,' Max said, forcing a smile. 'Yep, see you in a bit.' He aimed for casual, but it felt awkward, stilted.

'Everything alright?' the man asked.

'Yeah, she's good,' Max said, keeping his gaze fixed ahead, feeling his left leg start to jiggle up and down with nerves. 'Well, I say alright, she's a little bit freaked out, but who wouldn't be. She'll be fine once she's picked up, though.'

His thoughts were like a washer on spin cycle gone mad. What if it wasn't just this one guy? What if an accomplice was headed to pick up Jen right now? Not much he could do while travelling at sixty on the motorway. She wasn't due to be picked up for another thirty minutes. Better to wait until they stopped, he thought, but what if they stopped in the middle of nowhere?

Think, man! Think!

'Hmm, looks like trouble up ahead,' the driver said absent-mindedly.

Max saw the brake lights up ahead, blinking like lights on a Christmas tree. A row of cones began shepherding them all into the left-hand lane. He had no idea how much time he had, where they were going or what to expect when they got there. Not exactly spoilt for choice when it came to options in the meantime.

He turned towards the driver. If this didn't work, he was just going to have to ride it out and see where he was being taken.

Porter sent his phone spinning across the top of the dashboard, slapping a palm against the wheel in frustration.

'What did he say?' asked Styles.

'No grounds for a warrant,' said Porter, puffing up his chest, sounding pompous as he mimicked Milburn. 'How can we assume Baxter knew we even had people watching him, for him to slip past them?'

He didn't tell Styles the rest. That Milburn had ordered him to report back to the station. That kicking down the door would probably have him stuck to a desk for the foreseeable. He knew that claiming he had heard someone calling for help was weak at best, and he wasn't about to ask Styles or the others to stick their necks out for him when he knew damn well there'd been nothing to hear. Nothing except the voice in his head telling him Max was in danger.

'So what now?'

'We can trace Max's phone, but we can't touch the flat,' said Porter, looking wistfully over at the open front door. 'Not enough to say we're dealing with the same man, according to Milburn.'

Heavy emphasis on the last three words. He was about to say something less than flattering about the super when his phone rang, vibrating on the dashboard like an angry insect. Jen.

'Has he called back?' No sense wasting words on pleasantries.

'No, no, but there was something.' She sounded breathless, desperate to force her words out faster. 'Something else he said. He said Dartford. They were driving to somewhere near Dartford.'

'Whereabouts near Dartford?' It was a start, but too vague, and he knew it.

'That's all he said. That's all. Find him for me, Jake. You have to find him.'

Porter ended the call, closed his eyes, pushed hard against his headrest. Milburn had left no room for error. He was to hand over to Styles and report back to the station immediately. Milburn was an arrogant self-serving bastard who would probably sling him under the bus anyway. There was no telling where Max was now, what danger he was in.

He looked over, saw his partner looking at him, waiting for an update, for him to spring into action. He knew exactly what Max would do if roles were reversed. Screw Milburn. He'd never forgive himself if he didn't try, if anything happened. He cracked his door open a foot, shouting back at the two constables to stay put. Pulled it closed again and turned to Styles.

'Sod the flat. Let's go.'

They pulled into a parking space opposite the rows of pumps at a Shell petrol station. Roadworks signs promised disruption for the next five miles, and Max had used that as an excuse to ask for a pit stop. Lumley, or whatever his name was, had said they were only ten miles or so away from their destination, but Max insisted, starting a little shuffle in his seat to emphasise the urgency of the stop.

'Toilets must be inside,' he said, peering out of the window. 'You want anything from the shop? I'm going to grab a coffee.'

'No, I'm good, thanks,' said the man with a polite smile.

Max fought the urge to look back as he walked towards the entrance. What the hell should he do? This was the man who had taken Jen, maybe even assaulted him. Who had posed as his father. In all likelihood, the man who had killed Harold Mayes. What did he want with Max? Did he have a weapon? Max liked to think he could take care of himself, but was getting back in the car even an option? If he didn't there was every chance the guy would get away, assuming that he'd bolt and not come looking for Max, of course. Fight or flight?

Hands curled into fists inside his pockets. Getting back in the car meant no guarantee of his own safety. Wherever the man was taking him, it was hardly going to be for tea and biscuits. The car, plate and hopefully both their faces would be on CCTV now. Would that be enough for Porter to figure out who he was?

He was the only customer in the shop, and the assistant looked up from a magazine as he approached.

'Can you point me in the direction of your toilets, please?'

The bored kid, late teens, with a million places he'd rather be, pointed towards a door in the far corner. Max pushed through it, and into a short corridor, two doors either side. Ladies' and gents' toilets on the left, disabled and a door marked *Staff Only* to the left. He looked from side to side, as if getting ready to cross a road, then spotted the fifth door, straight ahead, at the end of the corridor.

He peered back through into the store, but the assistant was buried back in the pages of his magazine.

The fifth door offered no resistance, and he stepped through into a stockroom. Metal cages were stacked around the edges, full of cardboard boxes and plastic trays. A sign for the exit glowed pale green in the far wall, and he trotted across, pulled it open and looked out into a fenced-off area outside. Beyond that he saw the pumps. Going out that way wasn't an option.

Was that what he was doing? Looking for a way out? He checked his watch. Little over a minute since they'd pulled up. He figured maybe two more minutes, tops, until the man started to get suspicious. He had to let Jen know he was OK. Shit, his phone! Had he left it in the car? He breathed a sigh of relief as fingers closed around it. He bashed out a text to her, fingers feeling like clumsy fat sausages, grumbling at typos.

Am fine will call ASAP.

Half-truth. Little white lie at worst, but the last thing she needed now was any more reason to panic. He dialled Porter's number and it was answered on the first ring.

'I've already spoken to Jen. Where are you? Is he with you?' Right to the point from Porter.

'Thurrock service station, just off the M25. He's in the car. I'm in the gents'. He's driving a dark blue BMW, don't know the reg. Says we're less than ten miles from wherever we're going.'

'OK, that's good, now get somewhere safe and call me back,' said Porter. 'We'll take it from here.'

'I can't let him get away, Jake.' Max hadn't realised he'd made a decision until now. 'I run now and we might never find him again. Who even is he, by the way?'

'Joseph Baxter. Number twelve on our list, and don't be stupid,

258

Max. You know what he's capable of. You need to leave this to me.'

'What if he knows were my dad is?' Max started to raise his voice but checked himself. 'What if he's got him stashed away somewhere like he did with Jen? I can't just walk away, Jake. I can't.'

'Max, you need to trust me, we'll be there—'

'You can trace my phone, right? You can follow me wherever we end up?' He didn't wait for Porter to respond, to try and talk him out of it. 'I've got to go; he'll be getting suspicious.'

Max heard Porter's loud protests as he took the phone away from his ear. Deep breath. And another. Tried his best to look natural as he re-entered the shop, and hoped his best was good enough.

CHAPTER TWENTY-SIX

July 2009

Five nights had passed, and he'd seen the recruiter's face every single one of them. No hot flush of guilt, though, more a feeling of detachment, of drifting. Released from a mooring by action, the polar opposite to his inaction in the warehouse all those years ago, albeit with the same result. Surprising how easily the world still turned. The lack of ripples spreading out from his actions. Almost as if it had never happened.

Except it had. The frayed thread on his suit jacket where a button should be stuck out like an unwelcome weed. He'd unbuttoned it in Fletcher's office. Wore it in the bar that night. Could Fletcher have grabbed it as he fell? Pulled it off, sent it skittering under the sofa?

He half expected to see police tape criss-crossing the doorway when he walked back past the flat, but all he saw were drawn curtains and a ghost of himself keeping time in the dark windows as he walked past. One quick lap of the block and he was back again; still nothing. On the third pass, he walked up to the door, confident, as if he lived there. Let himself in with the spare key he'd found tucked into the back of Fletcher's Filofax.

He stood beside the coffee table, staring at the cracks that ran through it like fault lines. Drank in the silence. Everything was exactly as he'd left it. Closed his eyes, imagined for a second that this was his place, his life.

The button had wedged between two sofa cushions, and he held it up between finger and thumb, appraising it like a rare coin. No bigger than a ten pence piece, but enough to bring it all crashing down around him, to have placed him at the scene, powerful enough to put him behind bars. He checked Fletcher's home phone for messages, but there were none. The handful of calls that had come through to his mobile were from numbers, not names. Could he really be so alone that not one person who mattered enough to be in his contacts had been in touch in almost a week?

The Filofax had been littered with all sorts of information not for prying eyes. Usernames, passwords, PIN numbers. The man must have had a memory like a sieve. Part of him wanted to run, get as far away from this, from London, as possible. As he skimmed through the pages again, strands of an idea started to form, twisting and weaving into a rope that he could cling on to, to help him survive this.

An email, sent from Fletcher's laptop, using his account, to the managing director. Resigning due to ill health. It could be months before anyone came looking. Quick trip to the cashpoint, hood pulled up to avoid any cameras, eyes widening like a kid in a toy shop at the balance, high four figures. He could live off this for months if he was careful. Withdraw in stages, different cashpoints, over a few weeks.

He looked around at the flat one more time. He'd come here for employment. Granted, he'd left without a job, but it had paid off, and handsomely at that. Beat working for a living, that's for sure.

CHAPTER TWENTY-SEVEN

He felt outwardly calm, even if his stomach was sloshing around like a ship in a storm. Stupid to think that Max could look into his eyes, see his intentions, but he'd kept his stare front and centre for as much of the journey as possible. When they'd fought in the kitchen, Max hadn't seen his face, probably couldn't even remember the colour of the eyes behind the ski mask, but it paid to be careful.

The time Max was inside gave him a chance to rehearse what was to come. He had to get the phone away from Max for starters. You didn't need to be Steve Jobs to know how easy they were to trace. Might as well let him fire a flare gun out the window every hundred yards. Nobody should have missed Max yet, but they'd come looking soon enough, and he couldn't get too close to their final stop until he had the phone.

Timing was everything. The where and the when was already decided. He had always been three steps ahead so far, so why should this be any different? He checked his watch. Max had been inside for nearly three minutes. Should he stroll in after four or five minutes, check out what was taking so long?

As he toyed with his options, Max exited the station and headed towards him. Nothing in the way he walked or looked seemed out of place, but something didn't feel quite right. What was it? What was he missing? Max slid into the passenger seat, and it clicked into place.

'Change your mind about the coffee?' he asked as he started the engine.

Max looked blank for a second, stared down at his hands, up at the station, then right at him.

'Oh, yeah, that. I've had five cups already today, to be honest, so probably not a good idea after all.'

It sounded wooden, rehearsed, and he fought back the urge to call out the lie, corners of his mouth twitching with the effort. They rejoined the flow of traffic, crawling past a slow-mo procession of tired, impatient faces, boxed in on all sides. Did Max suspect something? He seemed tense, unnaturally still, staring ahead with his best poker face on. Two can play that game. One thing was for sure, the next hour would bring answers. Just remained to be seen who'd be asking the questions.

Porter took a chance and called the service station. A sleepy voice at the other end snapped to attention when Porter identified himself. It took the 'matter of life and death' card to persuade him to check the CCTV and recite the plate on the BMW. Porter thanked him and promised an officer would be there soon to take a statement.

Next call was to Benayoun back at the station. She ran the plates, but it wasn't what Porter wanted to hear. They belonged to a BMW registered to an address in Kensal Green. He called the service station again to check the plate, but it had been right the first time. Simple case of switching plates, something that most people wouldn't notice for a day, maybe more.

Best they could do now was head in the direction of Thurrock services, and wait for Benayoun to call with a location on Max's phone. Styles's phone was propped up in the cup holder, rattling with every bump in the road. Styles seemed oblivious, but, for Porter, it might as well have been a crash of cymbals. As he reached out to shift it, the first few lines of a text flashed up.

Unless you want to be stuck with Porter indefinitely suggest you get him back to the station asap. 5 p.m. latest.

Porter flicked his eyes from road to phone and back again, phone held in place between finger and thumb. Styles leant forwards, grabbed at it, acting indignant.

'Hey, that could be a saucy message from Emma. A guy's entitled to a little . . . privacy.'

Porter chanced a glance away from the road to watch his partner's expression as he read the message. 'Was it, then?' he asked, seeing Styles finish and look away, out at the traffic.

'Hmm? Uhm, no. I should be so lucky.' Styles's laugh came out a touch high, nervous almost.

Porter let it go for another few seconds, wanting to give him every chance to explain, but Styles said nothing.

'Are you going to make me ask?'

Styles sighed, breathed in deep, opened his mouth to speak but only managed a phlegmy cough, like something was rattling around in his throat. Porter waited it out. Styles took another deep breath before he spoke.

'Milburn. He dragged me to one side last week. Told me I needed to keep an eye, you know, in case you went off it with anyone else, except he spun it to be more a case of doing it for your sake; a favour type thing.'

'And?' Porter said, biting down on his lip. 'How am I doing? You make sure you report back that I took the news well, won't you? You know, having my own people spy on me.'

'Guv, it's not like that. It's just—'

'Just what? Grooming you to take over when he's sidelined me, I take it?' Even as he spoke, he knew he was being too harsh on Styles, but he was here, Milburn wasn't.

'C'mon, that's not fair, you know I would never—'

'Spy on me?'

Styles huffed out a long breath, like a moody teenager. Porter took a deep one of his own. Two more. Felt his temper dropping like mercury in winter.

'Why didn't you say anything?'

'Cos there's nothing to say,' Styles protested. 'It's not like I was going to scurry off and give him a blow by blow account of your day. Sod him. He can do his own dirty work.'

'Look, mate, I'm sorry,' said Porter after a pause. 'Just seems like he's everywhere, throwing enough shit to see what sticks. I know you're not like that, and I shouldn't have doubted you. Just needed to vent a bit, you know?'

Porter felt the atmosphere in the car clearing. They were still at least twenty minutes out from the service station when a final thought landed in Porter's brain, like the last leaf from the tree.

'Stuck with me indefinitely?' he said. 'Where else would you be going?'

Two seconds of silence stretched into ten. He looked over at Styles, saw the slump of his shoulders, fingers picking away at a thumbnail, unable to meet his eye, and knew the elephant had entered the room.

Max guessed they'd covered another five miles since the station by the time they pulled off the motorway. Dozens of questions rested on his lips, but no sense tipping his hand yet. Even seemingly innocent questions could give the game away, so he settled for what he hoped was a comfortable silence.

From the few glances he'd chanced, there was nothing familiar about the man. Nothing out of the ordinary. Average height, average build, average everything. So many times this past week he'd wondered what he'd say if he came face-to-face with this man. Wondered what he would look like. It almost felt like an anti-climax to find it was someone so . . . ordinary.

They peeled off at a roundabout, taking an exit towards Dartford.

'So whereabouts is the place we're heading?'

'Not far now,' replied the driver. 'Ten minutes at most.'

He grinned as he spoke, like they were just best mates having a natter. If Jen hadn't heard his voice, told him who he was riding with, would the smile look harmless enough?

The road was single lane now, bordered by beech trees that looked old enough to have seen the Industrial Revolution. Their green canopies mushroomed out, each barely touching its neighbour, like a string of children holding hands on a school trip. Past the last of the trees were the bones of a half-built housing estate, faded advertising board proclaiming affordable family homes. The green lawn on the picture was a far cry from the dry, brown earth around the sign, pounded into submission by construction traffic. Patches of long wispy grass clung on, Mother Nature's comb-over, hanging on to the last of the topsoil.

They turned into the mouth of the estate and came to a stop by the sign, albeit with the engine still ticking over.

'Do me a favour, there should be some house keys down by your door.'

'Here?' said Max. 'I thought we were going to a station. These aren't even built yet.'

'I just do as I'm told. We use the show home here as a safe house. This place is months away from opening still.'

Max peered out at the row of houses, plastic sheeting spread across a few of them where roof tiles should be. Months? More like a year, and then some. He looked down into the storage pocket on his door. A CD case sat atop a carpet of sweet wrappers, but no sign of any keys, unless they were hidden underneath. He sensed, rather than saw, the movement to his right.

Everything seemed to happen simultaneously. A clicking noise, like a pilot light trying to ignite, but ten times faster. A wave of pain shot through him, from the base of his spine upwards. It felt like somebody had reached inside, grabbed every muscle and nerve ending, and pulled it like a Christmas cracker, and all conscious thought became as scrambled as eggs in a pan.

It felt like it would never end, but eventually it did, dumping him in his seat when it stopped, a puppet with strings cut. His head thudded against the window, vision swimming as if he was looking through a rain-streaked window. A hand cradled the back of his head, almost tender, until it grabbed a handful of hair, propelling him face first towards the dashboard. White hot pain lanced through his head, washing over him, everywhere at once. A lifetime of suffering squashed into a nanosecond, then nothing.

He worked quickly, stowing the stubby stun gun in his jacket pocket, lowering Max back against the headrest and reclining the seat. He grabbed a baseball cap from the rear footwell, tilting the brim down over Max's eyes. Just a sleeping passenger.

Always a chance he could wake up prematurely, of course, but he'd catered for that as well. One pair of cable ties looped over Max's wrists, a second snaked through them and around the hand grip on the door. Flesh puffed up either side as plastic bit tighter, but Max didn't even flinch. He sat back, admiring his work. Only for a few seconds, though. Still so much to do. He reached into Max's pocket and pulled out his phone. It prompted for a password but that had been expected. No matter. More important that he got rid of it. Max would tell him anything he wanted to know soon enough.

He wound down the window, swapped the phone to his right hand and scooted around in his seat, getting ready to throw it out backhand, but caught himself. No point getting sloppy now. Quick wipe with a handkerchief where he'd touched it, then slung it away from the car, watching as it skidded behind a clump of grass so dry it could pass for straw. One last check of Max's restraints, then he spun the car in a wide circle using the flat of his palm against the wheel, like the Karate Kid waxing off. Almost free and clear. Almost.

* * *

'I was going to talk to you about it,' said Styles, legs like spindles fidgeting in the footwell. 'Just never found the right time to say.'

'And since when have I been so delicate that you need to pick your moments?' Porter's anger was back in spades now.

'You've had enough on your plate. I just figured I'd wait till all this blew over. I haven't even decided for sure yet that I even want to transfer,' Styles protested.

'Really? Milburn seems pretty sure you do, and I doubt even he would just make that up on his own.'

'That's not how it happened. I was in his office and he just threw it at me. I hadn't even approached him yet.'

'Exactly, "yet". But you were going to. Look, mate,' Porter said, wrapping that last word in sarcasm, 'you're a big lad. You don't need my permission to skulk off.'

'Oh, come on, that's not fair and you know it. I'd never walk off and drop you in it like this, especially when you're all . . .'

'All what?' Porter's voice was hard, flat, the kind of tone he reserved for a suspect in interviews. Why bother to tone it down? Styles was the last person he'd expect to be making moves behind his back, and this felt like nothing short of betrayal.

Benayoun's voice cut across them both from the airwave handset by the gearstick.

'Guv, it's Benayoun. Trace is up. Signal has him six miles from your current location, and stationary.'

Whether the second part of that was a good or bad thing, Porter didn't like to speculate. He looked to Styles, saw a mix of defiance and frustration. He had some nerve, that one. The only person who had a right to be pissed off was him. Milburn, Styles, Baxter, they could all go to hell. Thinking of Baxter brought him back to Max. The rest of this conversation, however it would play out, would have to wait till they got back to the station. He flipped a switch, watching the traffic part before their blue lights like the Red Sea, keeping Benayoun on the line in case Max started to move again.

'What kind of area is it?' he asked. 'Housing, shops, middle of nowhere?'

'Somewhere in between by the looks of it, guv. On its way to being houses, but Google Maps says it's still pretty much a building site.'

Construction site, away from prying eyes. That didn't sit well with Porter. They left the dual carriageway, and before long spotted the Conniston Homes sign, almost as big as the side of a house itself, welcoming them to the Sycamore Park estate, showing two faceless kids playing on an unnaturally green lawn while their parents watched. You too could be this happy if you lived here. The stark contrast to the reality of the scrubbed brown earth, skeleton houses with their exposed joists and stacks of bricks couldn't be more striking.

A smaller sign fifty feet past caught his eye. A site map, numbered plots hugging both sides of a road that curved back on itself in a semicircle. At the halfway point, another road cut back on itself, and a series of streets filled in the inside of the semicircle with more plots. Looked like a child's drawing of a hat – straight line for the brim, curved top.

Must be at least a hundred plots on there. Where the hell were they supposed to start? It looked, and felt, like an abandoned movie set. Maybe they still had security on site.

'They're not going to shift many at this rate,' said Styles. 'Sign back there said they were due in 2011.'

The further they edged into the estate, the less had been done on each plot. The furthest he could see was just a dent in the ground, dug for foundations that had never been laid.

Porter saw the comment for the peace offering it was. He couldn't let whatever that argument had been turning into put Max in any more danger than he was already. At the same time, he was far from finished with Styles. Another time and place, though.

'The recession,' he said.

'What about it?'

'I heard of a few places like this. Companies threw up one too many estates, ran out of cash, and banks were too twitchy to bail them out, so they mothballed them.'

'Really?' said Styles. 'They'd just walk away from it?'

'Not for ever,' he said, even though the potholes in the road wouldn't be out of place in a war zone.

'Still no movement, guv,' Benayoun's voice squawked over the airwave. 'He's there, give or take a hundred metres.'

'We're going to need some backup. No way we can search this place just the two of us.'

'Roger that, boss. Call you back with an ETA.'

They drove back to the entrance, and Porter parked the car horizontally across the road. There'd been no sign of another vehicle, but if there was one lurking anywhere in there, it made sense to make any escape as difficult as possible.

'Might as well make a start while we wait,' he said, and they both got out of the car, wandering over towards the nearest house. Porter checked his watch – 4.49. Shit, he was due in Sameera Misra's office in a little over ten minutes. Couldn't even manage that with a ride in the police chopper. He hoped she'd understand. Even if she didn't, it wasn't like he was about to turn back and head to the station. Milburn was another matter. He could practically hear the super's fingers drumming against a desk from here.

Porter gave himself a mental slap. Couldn't lose focus, not now.

'OK, we do each house together. One stays on the door, one goes inside. This side first,' he said, pointing to the right. 'You take the doors, I'll do inside.' The unspoken inference: if Max was in any of these, Porter owed it to him to be the one charging in. His mind flashed to what he might find, worst case scenario, but he shook it off, took a deep breath and reached for the first door handle.

'Come on, mate,' Callum said into the handset. 'Pick up.'

He slouched back in the seat of his old Land Rover, right hand holding the phone to his ear, pinned in place by an elbow jammed against the window. Five rings later he heard Max's voice, a cheery 'Hey'. False alarm, just voicemail.

'Mate, it's me. Good news. My guy came through. Your man was at Northridge Industrial Estate, out near Welling. Looks like he connected to their intranet through a mobile hotspot from somewhere in there. I'm heading over to take a look. Give me a shout when you get this, and I'll meet you there.'

The phone was halfway into his pocket when he pulled it back out, dialling Max's home number as an afterthought. He'd rather not disturb Jen if she was resting, but if this didn't qualify as important enough, what did?

'Max, is that you?' A woman's voice, bordering on hysterical.

'Jen, it's me, Callum. I need to speak to Max. Do you know where he is?'

He waited out the noisy sobs and wet sniffling until she started to talk, eyes widening as he listened. To hell with secrecy. He had to speak to Max's pal, the copper. Rather him be pissed at Max than anything bad happen. He had to speak to Porter and tell him what he knew, before it was too late. He finished the call with Jen and started to make his next call when an ugly thought squatted heavy on his chest. What if it was already too late?

CHAPTER TWENTY-EIGHT

July 2009

Fletcher's account was down to pennies, but the charade was still intact. He felt himself drawn back to the flat, almost disappointed each time to see it lying dormant. Even chanced another trip back inside a week later, leaving with a suitcase of clothes to stretch out the story of a man under pressure, needing to get away from it all.

The saddest part wasn't that Fletcher was dead. It was that nobody seemed to care. Michael Fletcher had dropped off the face of the earth, quite literally, and nobody gave a shit. That was a depressing slice of modern life served up right there. So many connections and connectivity in a digital world, but this gregarious City boy had no one, not a single person close enough to know he was gone, let alone mourn him.

He almost felt sorry for Fletcher. Almost, but not quite. He had been everything that was wrong with a city so obsessed with public image, projected persona, that the real essence of a person had to be stashed away, safe from prying eyes that might judge any insecurity.

He sat now, browsing through Fletcher's hard drive. The pictures, music tracks, clients' CVs, emails. His client list ran into the thousands, from people he'd placed in roles, through to those he'd kept on file just in case. He logged on to Fletcher's database, courtesy of his passwords. So many profile pictures practically replicas of the one before, cut from the same cloth, conforming, bland. Not a million miles away from his own headshot.

From such a small observation, an idea was born, began to germinate. Scrambled thoughts clicked into place, like points on a train track, making him do something out of character. He smiled. So much work to be done, and he was eager to get started.

CHAPTER TWENTY-NINE

They had only cleared two houses when Porter heard it. Faint, but unmistakable, and he cocked his head to one side to work out where it came from. Strains of 'Wake Me Up' by Avicii. A ringtone? Hard to get an exact fix, but he was pretty sure it came from outside. The room he was in looked set to be a kitchen, pipes snaking their way up from the floor where a sink would go. Dust carpeted the floor, thick enough that he could see footprints where he'd walked.

Porter tried the handle of a door that looked out onto a flattened square of dirt, weeds popping out from under pieces of rubble and cracked brick. Not quite the garden the signs were advertising. It opened with a loud squeak, possibly for the first time in years, and he stepped outside.

'Styles! Phone. You hear it?' he shouted just as it stopped.

A dozen thumping footsteps on the bare floorboards, and Styles was beside him. 'I heard it too.'

They stood, shoulder to shoulder, nothing moving except a few dandelions, heads bouncing in the breeze. Traffic on the main road was just a low background hum.

'Sod it,' Porter muttered, 'I'm calling him.'

Styles looked at him as the opening bars sounded. Porter whipped his head both ways, walking out to the middle of the back yard. No sign of Max, or anyone else for that matter. Seven rings then voicemail. He hit redial. Did that mean he was unable to answer it? Didn't bode well if that was the case. The phone sang out again, closer this time, like he was playing a game of hot and cold. He walked towards the fence at the far end. Must be around eight feet high sections, overlapping pine panels punctuated by fence posts.

He dialled the number a third time, hopping up onto the lower fence support rail, peering over the top like a meerkat. It backed onto the entrance to the estate, and Porter scanned both ways, hearing Styles walk up behind him. A glow caught his eye and he pushed up, swinging his right leg up and over, letting himself drop over the other side.

Max's phone lay half hidden by a messy clump of grass. Porter took off his tie to pick it up as the music stopped. If they were lucky, there'd be prints other than Max's on there. Couldn't see him throwing his own phone away.

He turned a full three-sixty but saw nothing except a few passing cars back on the main road, and his own where he'd blocked the road with it. He looked at Styles peering over the fence, his partner's expression seeming to mirror his thoughts. This was their only tangible link to Max. He looked back at the phone. Saw the screen start to fade. Wondered if Max's chances were doing the same.

* * *

Callum Carr was on hold. The officer he'd spoken to had gone away with promises of finding a detective almost twenty minutes ago now. He was weighing up his chances of finding Porter through another colleague at the paper who had good police contacts when he saw the sweep of headlights and heard the low grumble of an engine.

He had parked a few hundred yards away from the unit his man had told him about. His Land Rover, enough dings and dints to put a rally car to shame, and permanent coat of everyday grime, shouldn't stand out too much. Times like this, it paid off to neglect your car. Sunset was still a few hours away, but the battleship-grey clouds sitting overhead made it feel much later.

His pulse quickened as the car – BMW, Volvo maybe – pulled up in front of unit 173. He slid further down into the seat, hopefully low enough that he'd border on invisible at this range, and peered over the dashboard. Hard to say for sure but it looked like there were two people in the front. The driver disappeared inside, but the passenger stayed put. He popped open the glovebox and pulled out a pair of binoculars, rolling the fly wheel to bring things into focus just as the driver got back into the car.

Damn it, he thought. *Two seconds earlier, and I'd have seen his face.*

Even from here, the sound carried as the roller door creaked open. Callum switched his attention to the passenger and froze. Their head had lolled against the window, brim of a cap pulled down, but not quite enough to hide the face. Max's eyes looked closed, and he wasn't moving. Didn't even stir when the car started to crawl forwards, and by the time the door rolled back down, Callum's hands were shaking. What the hell was going on? The best he could hope for was that Max was unconscious. Worst case, he was already too late.

The fact that the phone was here meant that Max had been too, but right now that meant very little, like the last breadcrumb in the trail. Three cars, two officers apiece, arrived within a few minutes of the discovery. They'd only been minutes away, so it had seemed pointless calling them off. They could help search the rest of the place, although Porter felt sure that Max and his captor were long gone.

They'd just finished dividing up the rest of the estate when Benayoun came though on the airwave, as excited as she'd been when they'd got the initial trace.

'Got some good news, guv. We've got a fix on your boy.'

'What? Where? How?'

Benayoun relayed the call she'd just taken from Callum Carr. It took Porter a few seconds to put a face to the name. They'd only met a few times, but he remembered Max speaking highly of him. How the hell had he gotten involved?

The journalist hadn't been able to give a description of the driver, or the car, and he'd been rather vague about how he'd come by the location, but he was adamant about the identity of the passenger.

'And he's one hundred per cent sure it was Max?'

'So he says. They're inside the unit now, though, so he can't see a thing.'

'Call him back and tell him we're on our way. He has to sit tight, and under no circumstances does he try and go in. We'll be . . .' Porter did some quick calculations, 'ten minutes. Fifteen tops.'

'Already told him that, boss.'

'Tell him again,' said Porter. 'He's a journalist. They never listen.'

Callum wasn't a hero. He didn't jump in to break up fights, but could he really sit here and do nothing until the cavalry arrived? Max hadn't so much as blinked, let alone moved. God only knows what was happening in there right now, while he sat on his backside in the safety of his car.

The roller-blind-style door was fully shut, and the side door had no window to peer through. Maybe there was a way in around the back?

Jesus, man, get off your arse. What would Max be doing if it was the other way around?

He had a pretty good idea he knew the answer to that one, and it involved getting out of the bloody car and helping his friend. The clock showed six minutes since the officer had called him back to say help was on the way. Probably closer to ten since the car had driven in, maybe a few more.

To hell with it. Every minute he waited was a minute more that Max was in harm's way. He sat up, eyes fixed on the unit ahead, ready to slouch back at the first sign of a door opening, but it was all quiet now. He eased himself out, pushed the door slowly until it clicked, rather than slamming it shut, then scurried across the road. The short dash to the near corner of the building was like crossing no man's land, feeling the itch of unseen eyes as if he was being tracked.

He reached the corner, flattening his back to the wall, peering around to check the front was still clear. His back prickled against the cool concrete, nervous sweat soaking into cotton. He'd studied the buildings while he'd waited in the car. Four units in each row either side of the road. A quick lap of the structure should show him what the options were.

A few seconds' hesitation, then he was away, edging along the line of the wall into the shadows by the rear, listening out for sirens, but all he heard was his own heartbeat. They weren't coming, at least not fast enough. He was the cavalry.

He left Max slumped in the car and went to check on his house guest in the storage room. Exactly where he'd left him, no movement except a soft rise and fall of his chest. He grabbed a battered wooden chair that had resided here longer than he had and set it down next to the car.

Max hadn't budged since the housing estate but it didn't do to take any chances. He moved off to the side, squatted and stared through the window, watching for signs Max was playing possum. Not a flicker. He walked around, leaning in through the driver's side and looped another cable tie around Max's ankles before pulling a pair of scissors from his pocket and snipping the ones that fastened him to the door. Another trip around the car and he opened the door carefully, easing Max forwards so he bent at the waist, slipping him over his shoulder and straightening up into a fireman's lift.

Two minutes of manoeuvring and Max was secured to the chair, facing away from the car, ties looped around wooden legs and armrests. Almost time to wake him up. Just a few things to pop in the car first, for after he was done here. He rummaged in a black rucksack until his fingers closed around the glass bottle he was looking for and walked back towards the storage room with a spring in his step.

* * *

When Max was fifteen, he'd suffered the only knockout of his junior boxing career, and it had stung in more ways than one. His opponent had been big for his age, freakishly quick hands, and the uppercut had been little more than a blur. It caught him flush on his chin, and he'd been out before his head hit the canvas. To this day, he couldn't remember feeling it connect, just the sting of smelling salts as he came around.

He was back there now, the fuzzy face of his coach a smudge of colour. Eyes blinking, trying to jump-start them into focus. Wanting to touch a hand to his jaw, except it wouldn't move. Couldn't move. Colours started to merge, a face forming in front of him. Realisation that he wasn't flat on the canvas but sitting up. Neon lights overhead, bright as a supernova. He winced, eyes watering, tried to blink away the stars hovering in front of him, stench of ammonia in his nostrils.

Blurred lines gave way to an outline, and soon he could make out the face of a man, vaguely familiar, sitting on a chair opposite him. *Sure as hell isn't my boxing coach.* His mind slipped from neutral into first, remembered being in the car. The officer – no, not an officer, Him, driving him somewhere. A housing estate? Remembered the judder of pain that had gripped his body. His face racing towards the dashboard, until it filled his vision, then just black.

'Evening, Max,' the man said. His voice sounded different to what Max remembered from the car. More confident, assured.

Max twisted his head as far around as he could manage, took in his surroundings, saw the restraints pinning him in place. He felt only two things right now: helpless, and for the first time since all this had started, he was afraid.

* * *

The path around the building had been fairly clear, and Callum quickly found himself at the opposite corner, the mirror image of his starting position, and still none the wiser about how to get in unnoticed.

He had scurried past a second roller door at the other side, but that was shut too, and putting his ear to it achieved nothing except getting a dirty smear across his cheek. On the plus side, he had almost tripped over a piece of wood, two-by-four. It was discoloured, like it'd been at the bottom of a pond, but it had a reassuring weightiness and he wasn't likely to find a better weapon anytime soon.

Quick time check. Four minutes since he'd left the car. Ten since he'd been speaking to the police. Where the hell were they? He peeled away from the wall, ready to chance his luck listening at the main door, when he heard the handle turn, saw the door swing open towards him. Whoever was coming out would have their view obscured for a few seconds until it closed again, and Callum used every one of them to flatten himself against the wall.

He bit down on his lip, felt fresh sweat bloom. His ragged breathing sounded like thunder in his own ears. A sound from around the corner. Scraping, scratching, clicking. Cigarette lighter, maybe? Silence, then one long, steady exhale of breath. Curiosity wasn't enough to prise him away from the wall. Fear kept him pinned there like a fly to flypaper, clammy palms pressed against the chilled concrete.

Couldn't have been more than a minute before the handle squeaked again, and before he realised what he was doing, he was edging to the corner, peering around to see the door inching closed. Short, quick steps, up on toes, he managed to grab the handle a half inch shy of the door jamb. Counted to three, wondering if they would come back out, but nobody pushed back against his grip. A five-count next, giving whoever it was time to walk back inside the building, away from the entrance.

Gut check time, fella.

He pulled the handle, carefully peering through the widening gap, seeing the back end of the car. BMW. He'd been right first guess. The door passed the halfway mark, and he stepped through and right into a scene that stopped him dead in his tracks.

'Who are you?' Max asked, dry words croaking through dry throat, as if he'd swallowed a handful of sand.

'I could ask you the same question, Max. You're the fly in my ointment, the uninvited guest,' the man said, leaning back in his chair, arms folded.

'I didn't ask to be your guest, Joseph,' Max spat out, 'or do you prefer Joe?' What he'd give for a drink of water. Every word hurt, scraping their edges along his throat on the way out.

The man gave a short, barking laugh, and slapped a hand against his thigh. 'There you go, Max, you know all the answers already, don't you?'

'I know you won't get away with this . . . whatever this is. Why did you kill Harold Mayes, and where the hell is my father?'

'Is this the part where I take you through my plans for world domination, then leave you in an easily escapable situation like any good villain should?' Baxter rolled his eyes. 'Tut, tut, Max. You've been watching way too many Bond films. No, let me tell you what happens now.' He sat forwards, staring unblinking at Max as though his eyes would bore a hole right through Max's forehead. 'Whether you see your lovely lady again, whether you get to meet your father, very much depends on how you answer a few simple questions I have for you.'

Max held his gaze, slowly pushing against the plastic ties holding him in place, testing for give, finding none. Baxter stood up, walked slowly over to Max and squatted down beside him.

'Don't worry, they're not too tricky. In fact, they're all about you.'

'Me?' said Max. 'Why me, what do—'

'I'm not finished, Max. Don't interrupt me again.' His tone stayed level, but somehow that delivered the command with all the more force. He stood, walked behind Max, placed a hand on either shoulder and leant in, close enough that Max caught a whiff of stale breath.

'It's entirely up to you how this turns out. You give me what I want, we part ways, and you never see me again. You don't . . .' His lips were practically touching Max's ear now. 'Well, that way didn't work out too well for the likes of Harold, did it?'

'Where's my father?' Max tried again but heard the fear in his own voice.

'I'll give you a minute to decide how this plays out,' he said, ignoring Max's question, and headed outside without another word. The door clicked closed behind him, and the sound stung Max into action. He tried pulling against his restraints, but the plastic held firm and cut deep, binding his wrists behind his back. He looked around frantically, heart thudding a desperate rhythm.

Had Porter managed to track him, or was he in this on his own? The guy seemed in no hurry, which suggested the latter. The building looked like a small warehouse, nothing to identify who it belonged to. The car beside him was empty, and there was no sign of anyone else. If he could just get loose, one-on-one, he fancied his chances. He spotted a desk by the far wall, thirty feet or so away, but it wasn't the laptop that caught his eye. Black-handled scissors sat balanced over the edge.

The ties around his legs had maybe half an inch of give in them. Maybe he could push up on tiptoes, totter across to them. He leant forwards as best he could, let his weight transfer to the balls of his feet, but before he could make an attempt, the door clicked open and Baxter stepped inside, tucking a packet of cigarettes into his pocket.

Max let his legs relax, reaching for a plan B and coming up short, when something moved beyond Baxter. The door opened again, slower this time, and Callum Carr peeked through. Max switched his gaze to Baxter, willed himself to not look back to the door. Whatever Callum had planned, he had to give him a chance to do it, not draw attention to him.

Please, God, tell me he has a plan.

Callum was rooted to the spot, fixated on the sight of his friend strapped to a chair, forehead bruised a shade of plum. The hand gripping the piece of wood ached, and he licked dry lips for the hundredth time. He stepped inside, easing the door home, resting it against the frame rather than letting it click shut, like a kid sneaking out of their room at night.

The man walked towards the chair opposite Max and stopped, resting both hands on the back of it.

'So, might as well get started. Hope I made myself clear about both ways this can pan out?'

Callum was less than six feet away now. He switched his grip to a two-handed one, raising the wood slowly over his right shoulder.

Five feet

Four . . .

Three . . . The countdown changed, not measuring distance now, but seconds. The time when he would swing the wood, arcing round, slamming into the back of the man's head.

Two . . .

One . . .

It could have been the defiant look from Max, staring at the man as if he was the only thing that mattered in the world right now. Might have been the absence of something the man was expecting that never came, the missing click of the door closing behind him. Callum tensed his muscles, sucked in a quick breath, held it, ready to let it whoosh out with the effort of the swing. Started to swing the wood over his shoulder and around, baseball-bat-style.

The man turned into a crouch, arms instinctively moving to protect his face before he knew what the danger was. There was never any doubt the blow would connect, but it crashed across forearms instead of his head. The wood felt awkward in Callum's hands, flat edge making it feel more of a paddle than bat. Sweaty fingers slipped as it connected, almost losing their grip. Not quite the knockout blow he'd hoped for, but, combined with the man's own turn, it had enough force and momentum to send him spinning around one-eighty, down to the ground.

Callum adjusted his grip, raising it to strike again, but the brief hesitation cost him. As the two-by-four started its journey from a million miles up, the man moved. Didn't try to get up, or even block with his arms again. Instead, he lifted the arm that had been braced against the floor, letting himself fall back, sweeping a foot towards Callum. It connected with his leading leg, chopping it out from under him, felling him like a tree. Callum's hands opened as he fell, makeshift weapon spinning away as he tried to break his own fall.

Callum landed hard on his backside and tried to push back up to his feet. A hand gripped his shin, another grabbing at his trousers, pulling him across the rough floor. He tried to swat them away, but the man used them like handholds to climb across him. A knee swung either side of Callum, pinning him in place.

He held his hands up in front of his face, hoping to deflect anything heading his way. A fist looped around his defences, crashing into the side of his head, exploding fireworks in his skull and starring his vision with a thousand pinpricks of white light. He was vaguely aware of the other arm, rising high, falling fast, coming to deliver a second blow, and screwed his eyes shut, turning his face away, cheek to the floor.

It never landed. Instead, he felt a jarring impact down by his hips. Heard a voice roar in pain, weight suddenly lifted from him. Callum opened his eyes to see the man lying off to the side, with Max, still strapped to his chair, lying awkwardly on top.

'Get up,' Max roared at Callum, rolling his weight side to side, making it awkward for the man underneath him to get back up. Callum grabbed at the man's hands where he was trying to push Max off himself. The man kept one hand on Max, lashing out at Callum with the other. Callum pushed himself up to a sitting position, grabbing both of the man's wrists, looking around for his piece of wood, but it had skittered out of reach, over by the car.

He felt the strength flowing back into the man's arms, saw his eyes clearing from the impact with Max. Clammy hands started to lose their grip, and the man pulled against him, hard. Callum saw

Max twist his head all the way around to the left, just as the man jerked his wrists free. Max swung his head back towards the man's face like a wrecking ball, side of his forehead colliding with the man's nose, exploding it like a party popper.

Callum saw the man's eyes roll back in his head. He looked at Max, saw him wincing in pain, but conscious.

'Scissors,' said Max, eyes still closed.

'Huh?' What was Max on about? Was he concussed? Callum's own head still rang from the blow he'd taken.

'On the desk. Scissors. Get the bloody scissors.'

Callum's brain popped back into gear, and he realised what Max meant. Cut him free, tip the odds their way, two on one. The man could wake up any second. Callum didn't have the first clue what he would do if that happened, but he was damned if he was going to lie here till it happened and find out.

Even with the blue lights strobing, progress felt painfully slow. Some drivers seemed oblivious until he was literally touching their bumpers. Benayoun had put a call out for all units within a five-mile radius to respond, but Porter owed it to Max to be first there. He'd made a promise to Jen.

Ten minutes out, and the road finally started to clear. Porter called Benayoun back.

'Hey, it's Porter. Get Callum Carr back on the phone and conference me in. I want to know what we're turning up to.'

He stole a glance at Styles as he waited, fighting the urge to pick up what they'd started, squashed it back down into a tight knot in his gut. It'd keep. Benayoun came back to him a minute later.

'He's not answering, guv.'

'Then try him again.' Porter's patience was paper thin.

'Tried him twice, and left a voicemail and text asking him to call ASAP.'

'Just keep ringing till he answers, or we get there.'

The line went dead as she disappeared to do just that. There were plenty of reasons why Carr wasn't answering his phone, but hardly any of them led to a happy ending.

Callum sliced through the cable ties, and Max eyed Baxter warily, massaging the feeling back into his wrists. He touched a hand to his head. Felt the swelling near his temple where his head had connected with Baxter's nose. His fingers came away spotted with red, but he was pretty sure it wasn't his own blood.

Baxter groaned, and Max gestured to Callum for the scissors. He put the flat of the blade against Baxter's neck as he and Callum dragged him to his feet.

'Try anything, and it won't end well for you,' Max said. He felt Baxter shaking. Scratch that – it was his hand holding the scissors, palsied twitching from the adrenaline dump.

'Here, take these,' he said to Callum, nodding towards the scissors. 'Keep an eye on him while I look around.'

'Look for what?' said Callum, switching places with him.

'Something to tie him up with. Anything'll do. More of those plastic ties if he's got them,' he said, rifling through the desk drawers. 'Where do you keep them?'

Baxter's head had been slumped forwards, chin against chest, but he raised it now. His nose was a mess, cranked to one side like he was trying to sniff around a corner. But despite it all, he was grinning. Blood had run into his mouth, red stripes across the white like a barber's pole.

'Well played, gents, well played. I'd give you a round of applause, but you might get a bit twitchy with those things if I moved my hands,' he said, only his eyes moving in the direction of the scissors.

'Cut the bullshit. Where are the ties?' Max snapped at him. His limbs still felt like the energy had been sucked out of them, arms and legs a ton weight.

'Back at the house. Only brought enough with me to do the job.'

'Job?'

Baxter ignored the question. 'Can I move a hand to check my nose? I think it's broken.'

'One hand,' said Max, narrowing his eyes, sceptical of anything and everything at the moment. 'And slowly.'

Baxter slid his right hand up in a slow sweep, took his nose carefully between finger and thumb, and winced as he moved it side to side. He blocked his right nostril with his thumb and blew, hard. Blood sprayed out, speckling his trousers, as well as the floor, a gory join-the-dots. He repeated the process with his other nostril and wiped his hands on his chest.

'You caught me good,' he said, with the slightest of nods. 'Suppose a lift to the hospital is out of the question?'

Max gave a sardonic grin. 'Maybe later. For now, how about you take a moment to think how this could play out,' he said, mimicking Baxter's words from earlier. 'I'm guessing it's pointless asking if you have anything useful we can use to tie you up lying around here?'

'Hmm, if only I'd known,' he said, 'I could have brought a selection.'

Max picked up the chair he'd been tied to and set it opposite

292

Baxter, looking around, taking in the rest of the warehouse properly for the first time. As he leant both hands on the back of the chair, a thought popped into his head.

'How the hell did you even find me?' he asked Callum.

'Quite interested to know that myself, actually,' said Baxter.

'No one's talking to you,' Callum cut in, applying a fraction more pressure so the blade sank into the skin of Baxter's neck. 'Tell you later when this is done,' he said to Max. 'Us journos never reveal our sources. I spoke to your mate as well, Porter. Should be here any minute.'

If this alarmed Baxter, he didn't show it. Max wandered over to the desk, let his eyes drift over the few things on display. He scanned the room next. A row of white units lined part of the far wall. Past the last of them was a door.

'What's that?' he asked Baxter, pointing over at it.

'Nothing.' Baxter shrugged. 'Just storage, see for yourself.'

Max walked over and peered through the glass pane in the door. Barely enough light to see the back of the room, but he could make out rows of gunmetal-grey shelving, bottles of what looked like bleach, cardboard boxes and a mop over in the far corner. A single chair sat in the middle of the room. Max tried the door. Locked.

'Where's the key?'

'I forget,' said Baxter, with a wistful look. 'This blow to the head has made things a bit fuzzy.'

'Where's my father?' Max called across the room.

'Were you two close?'

'Just answer the question.'

'Tell you what, Max. Do you a deal. One for one. You answer one of mine, I'll answer one of yours.'

'I'm not answering a bloody thing,' Max spat back. He was over by the far wall now. The four white containers were stacked along it like building blocks, matching padlocks pinning lids in place.

'What are these? Why are they locked?'

'All these questions, Max. One for one, or I'll wait and take my chances with the police. Can't wait to see their reaction when they storm in and see me, face smashed up, blade to my neck. I might even press charges.'

Max didn't know whether to laugh or swear. 'You're unbelievable! You honestly expect anyone to believe you're the innocent party here?'

When Baxter spoke, he sounded bored, like Max was keeping him from being somewhere far more important. 'You weren't happy at how the police were handling your father's disappearance. You thought I knew something and confronted me at my car. Forced me to drive you here and tried to beat a confession out of me.'

'You listen to me, you lying bastard, no one will believe a word of that. You killed Harold Mayes. You kidnapped me. Kidnapped Jen, and you do know where my dad is.'

'Based on what, Max? What proof have you got that backs up any of that? Even a crap lawyer could throw enough reasonable doubt at that for some to stick. One for one, Max. Offer still stands.'

Max's fists clenched till they ached. The urge to smash them into the already pulped nose was so strong, pulling him towards Baxter like gravity, but he wheeled away, cursing, before anger got the better of him. No way could he be badged as the villain here, reasonable doubt or not. The desire, no, the need, to know what had happened to his father had become all-consuming. If the police came, took Baxter away, boxed him up in a cupboard-sized interview room, he might never get a chance to find out.

In through the nose, out through the mouth. Stay calm.

He turned back to face Baxter. 'We weren't close. He skipped town before I was born. Didn't know I existed for years.'

'And what changed?' Baxter tilted his head, listening, like a friend with an ear to bend.

'Mum hired an investigator. They tracked him down, gave her his address, so I wrote him a letter.'

'A letter?' Baxter chuckled. 'An actual letter, on paper? How quaint. How did he take that?'

'One for one. Where is he?' Max said through gritted teeth, feeling his patience wearing wafer-thin.

Baxter sighed. 'I've not seen him in a little while, but he's closer than you think.'

'What the hell is that supposed to mean?' said Max, walking over to the BMW, peering through the windows again.

Baxter moved past Max's question as if it hadn't been asked. 'Met him a few times at one of those AMT bashes. So, you two have literally just met, then? What are we talking, weeks, months?'

Max shook his head. 'We were due to meet last week, but he never showed.'

'So you've never actually laid eyes on him?' Baxter asked, sounding amused by the idea.

'No, we've never actually met. I've only seen photos of . . .' Max stopped mid sentence. 'Hang on, what happened to one for one?'

Max opened his mouth to ask again where his dad was but stopped as an idea swam to mind. Baxter seemed happy to sit and play games, like he had all the time in the world. Why not give him a taste of his own medicine?

'You can play the victim all you like about how you ended up here, but you're done. You just don't know it yet.'

Baxter looked at Max as if he was a child trying to order the grown-ups around. 'Really? How so?'

'DNA. They've got yours from the crime scene.'

Baxter's expression didn't change. He stared back at Max, unblinking, mocking him with a half smirk, daring him to do his worst.

'The phone you left at the Mayes house had a cracked screen. Someone had swiped it, left skin cells behind. Wasn't Harold. Wasn't my dad. Wasn't anyone they had on file. It'll be interesting when they check it against yours though, eh?'

That got a reaction, the first point scored since Max had been cut free. Baxter's eyes widened, just a fraction, more of a twitch, really, but noticeable all the same. The smirk looked more of a mask now, hiding something else. Uncertainty? Fear? No witty comebacks this time. Max felt things tilting in his favour. Now to press home the advantage.

That bloody phone! Why hadn't he gotten it fixed, or even bought a new one? Max could be bluffing, but how would he know details like that unless the police had told him? This changed everything. If they had that, then they had him bang to rights. Not for everything, but for enough to make sure he'd not be a free man until it was time to draw his pension, at the very least. He could hardly just sit here, wait patiently to be cuffed and led away. What was the saying? You might as well be hung for a sheep as a lamb? You can only serve a life sentence once. Might as well go for broke.

'What's the matter? Cat got your tongue?' Max floated in front of his face, relishing the point scored. 'They've got you nailed for murder, mate. Only a matter of time before they work out whatever else you're hiding.'

His mind riffled through a half-dozen ideas, smart comebacks, taking his chance with the scissors against his neck, settling on one. Risky, but it was either this or sit and wait for the police to come crashing through the door. He took a deep breath, exhaled like a deflating airbed. Nodded as best he could, feeling the blade still held to his neck.

'That they do, Max, that they do. Alright then, Mayes was my work. Not my best, but we all have our off days.'

Max looked stunned at the admission, and Baxter pressed on, filling the silence.

'You can plan all you like, but no matter how hard you try, you can never cover it all. Take you, for example. You weren't supposed to exist.'

Max's expression changed to one of confusion. The pressure against his neck felt an ounce lighter. Was Max's sidekick getting distracted?

'Sorry, I should be more specific. I'm thorough. Very thorough.' He made no attempt to keep the pride from his voice. 'I'm talking full background: work, family, hobbies, inside leg measurement, the works. Gordon had no one, at least no one I could find.'

'What do you . . . I mean why would that . . .'

'I only choose people who won't be missed, Max. If they're all alone, there's nobody to come looking.'

'What do you mean, choose?' Callum cut in. 'Choose for what?'

'You'd be amazed how many there are out there, live to work, not work to live. No family, no friends, well, not real ones anyway. Just another suit sitting in an office, nobody to go home to. You'd be amazed how easy it is, a little creativity with a few bits of ID, some account numbers, a couple of passwords, and Bob's your uncle.'

He could see from Max's face that he had him hooked. As much as the poor fool wanted to interrupt, to bring it back to his dad again, he was worried that butting in would break the spell. Stop the big reveal.

'I mean honestly, the number of people I've seen on Facebook, claiming to have over a thousand friends. Smoke and mirrors. How many of those thousand care where they've gone to? How many do you think come looking for them? I'll tell you. One. You. You're the first.'

'And where have they gone to?' said Max, breaking the spell.

'Think about it, Max. How many of their so-called friends bothered to see how they were after they left their jobs? How many enquired after their health, to see if they recovered?'

'How do you know about . . .'

'About the emails? Who do you think sent them, Max? Come on, I thought you were a smart cookie. You disappoint me. You'll be telling me next you haven't figured out what I've been storing here.'

Baxter tilted his chin up a fraction, looking over Max's shoulder. Max turned, following the gesture. He looked back at Baxter, only for a second, then turned and walked over to the storage boxes. As he got closer, he heard a low hum that hadn't registered before, probably thanks to his head still ringing from the clash with Baxter. He looked down the side, around the back, seeing black cables snaking away behind. The padlock on the nearest looked brand new, as did the units themselves.

'Where's the key?' he asked, without turning around.

'Bottom drawer of the desk, taped underneath.'

Max turned to face him again. 'Did you kill my father?' His words came out flat, as he registered what he'd asked for the first time. No longer just asking where his dad was, but adding in the alternate that he hadn't wanted to admit was possible.

'I'm giving you what you want, Max. All the answers you're looking for are right there in front of you. That's the difference between you and me. You found Harold, so you know how far I'm willing to go to get what I want. How far are you willing to go, Max?'

Max crossed the room for what seemed like the hundredth time, pulling out the bottom drawer, finding the key exactly where Baxter said it would be. He tore away the masking tape holding it in place and strode back across the warehouse. The key slid in smoothly, a knife into butter, and popped the lock at the first twist. He looked back over at his shoulder at Callum. Exchanged the briefest of nods.

He curled his fingers around the handle and pulled the lid up towards him. Fine wisps of vapour rose from the edge, like dry ice. For a split second, it clouded Max's line of sight, but when he saw past it his grip slipped, and he almost let the door fall back into place as he took a half step back.

'What is it?' Callum's voice came from behind him.

Max didn't answer. He leant forwards again, peering inside. The face that stared back at him was dusted with a light frost. Hair and eyebrows had the rigid look of a freshly frozen lawn. The colour had leached from his skin and left him looking more mannequin than man. Not a face he knew. Not his father.

'What is it? What's wrong?' Callum's voice was louder this time.

'Jesus,' Max whispered, turning back to look at Baxter. 'What did you do?'

'Do I have to spell it out for you?' said Baxter, voice as cold as the air from the freezer.

'How could . . . why would you . . . ?'

'Mostly because I could. Because nobody cared enough to try and stop me. Apart from that, there's usually two reasons why people do what I do, Max. Love, or money, and I'm not exactly a poster boy for love. Money makes the world go round, and they have plenty of it. Cash, shares, equity, you name it. Some of them need a little encouragement to tell me where it's stashed. Problem is, once you've stolen someone's identity, you can't just give it back, now, can you?'

'Max.' Callum had a panicked edge to his words now. 'What the hell is he talking about? What's in there?'

'It's a body,' he said. 'A fucking dead body.'

'Two, actually,' said Baxter. 'Think those ones will be Morgan and Fredrickson. Seemed a bit pointless to get one for each of them.'

Max looked at him, stunned at how flippantly Baxter could discuss the practicalities of storing bodies like that, as if they were no more than frozen food. Baxter, on the other hand, looked like he was positively enjoying the conversation, as if they were just two guys in a pub, chatting about football.

'Where is he?' The words felt clunky this time, physical objects forced from his mouth.

Baxter said nothing, just shifted his gaze to Max's left, raising his eyebrows. Max turned, saw the neighbouring unit to the one he'd just opened. Only a few feet away, but it might as well have been a few miles as Max moved towards it with slow steps. The padlock was a twin of the first, and the key slid home just as easily.

Was this lid heavier, or were his arms weaker? Max held his breath as he lifted. The same icy plumes of air escaped as before. His entire world consisted of that one corner of the building. Nothing existed outside of what was right there in front of him.

Max blinked, looked down, and for the first time in thirty-eight years came face-to-face with his father.

CHAPTER THIRTY

Two weeks ago

How many people know with any certainty what they're truly capable of? Not many, he'd wager, but he had yet to find a line he couldn't or wouldn't cross. That could all change, of course. There were no guarantees with what he did. No two jobs alike. That's how he viewed them now: jobs. All you could do was plan ahead. Minimise risk. So far so good. The irony wasn't lost on him that it had taken a recruiter to help him find what he was truly good at.

He parked up a hundred yards or so away, sliding down in his seat, watching Gordon Jackson open his front door and disappear inside. He'd watched him for long enough to know there was nobody waiting to welcome him home, or likely to join him later.

The routine was simple yet effective. He'd carry his pizza box up to the house. Look confused when they said they'd not ordered anything. Ask politely if they'd mind holding the box for a second while he checked the order. With their hands occupied, there was no avoiding the stun gun that dropped them to the floor.

It had been trial and error in the early days, but practice had made perfect, and from there it would progress to an inevitable end. They all gave him what he wanted, although, granted, some needed more encouragement than others. A few had tried giving false account details, but he'd try them out then and there. Dishonesty had consequences, and he never had to ask more than twice.

Thanks to the information in Fletcher's client list, he chose carefully. Few questions were asked, and nobody ever came looking. The most he'd ever had were a few emails wishing a speedy recovery from whatever might be wrong. Most ID could be bought online if you knew where to shop, and long gone were the days when you actually knew your bank manager or had a family solicitor. Nowadays, they all fought like dogs for your business, but forgot your face the moment you paid your fee or invested your savings.

If an Englishman's home was his castle, then modern-day fortresses were built on weak foundations. Mortar too easy to chip away at. Walls dismantled brick by brick. Possessions and the very castles themselves sold off, with barely a second glance at a faked passport or doctored driving licence. Knowledge was power, alright, if you knew it about the right person.

Enough reminiscing. He pulled on his baseball cap, tilted it down an inch. Grabbed a pizza box from the passenger seat, still warm; added authenticity. Quick pat of the pocket to check the stun gun and opened the car door. Off to work.

CHAPTER THIRTY-ONE

Porter braked sharply at the entrance, whipping the wheel to his right, and ploughed on into the industrial estate. Benayoun started calling out directions over the airwave, telling him which turns to take to save him having to stop and read the huge map by the road, like rats being given a guided tour of the maze. No sign of any other police units, but they couldn't be far behind.

'OK, now take the third right, then you're down the far end, right-hand side, number 173.' Benayoun's voice was lost in the revving of the engine as Porter gunned it around the corner.

A couple of the units they tore past had their doors open, interiors lit up and on display. Porter glanced at the numbers above them, counting up; not far now. He saw a flash in his mirror and spotted another set of blue lights back at the last junction. As much as he'd been pissed off at the idea that Callum Carr might have ignored the advice to stay put, he knew if the roles had been switched, he'd have been out of the car in a heartbeat and made a mental note not to be too hard on him.

Anything Callum had been able to do, however small, might have made the difference for Max. For all he knew, he'd pull up and see them safe and sound outside. Or they could both be in trouble, both be hurt, or worse. He hadn't felt this powerless since he was sitting at Holly's hospital bed, and look how that had turned out.

Max stared at his father's face. He'd seen pictures, some from the investigator, some from Google and LinkedIn. He hadn't seen any of himself in those images, and he tried to look for that now. His eyelashes were matted together with tiny ice crystals, like a mountaineer that had keeled over on his way to the summit.

Max's breathing was shallow and fast. He heard voices behind him, but they came from far away, as if somebody was talking into a pillow, muffling the words. His fingers ached from gripping the handle so hard. He stood like that for what felt like a lifetime before the world came rushing back at him, Baxter's voice breaking through the roaring in his head.

'You can't beat a good old family reunion,' he said, sounding on the verge of laughter.

There was something in the casual way he slung out the words that found its way past the last sliver of Max's self-control. Anger boiled up inside him, consumed him, burning him up like a log on the fire.

He let go of the lid, spun around before it fell back into place and strode across the room, hands balling into tight fists. The noise of the freezer door slamming shut barely registered. He was already imagining the feeling of smashing Baxter's nose back across the other side of his face. Hearing bone and cartilage crunch. He didn't know if he'd be able to stop once he started. Didn't know if he'd want to.

Four things happened, links in a chain, each setting off the next event like a trail of dominos. Callum was first. He saw Max charge towards him, felt the scissor handles shift in his sweaty palm. He tensed up as Max rushed in, saw his friend draw back a fist, and flinched, even though it wasn't coming his way. It was the smallest of movements, but it was enough.

Baxter was second. He'd worked patiently, goading, needling at Max, looking for the reaction he wanted. Needed. He wasn't disappointed. As Max drew closer, he felt the blade shift, only by millimetres, but enough to lose contact with skin. In that instant, he leant all his weight to the right, snaking his left arm up and inside the gap between Callum's wrist and his own neck. He turned the arm as it rose, forearm facing outwards. Less chance of anything getting nicked if the scissors slipped. From there, he twisted his hand, grabbing Callum's wrist, swinging him round into Max's path.

Max was third. Baxter's words had shocked him into action, energy cracking through him like he'd been plugged into the mains. As he cocked his fist back, a flash of colour registered off to his right. The bottom edge of the closed roller door flickered blue, like a strip light spluttering to life. He was committed to the punch but couldn't help his eyes flicking away. That cost him. Cost him a fraction of his speed. Cost him time; time to readjust as he saw Baxter move. He tried to angle his attack to the left, tracking Baxter's movement, but it wasn't enough, and he knew it as he closed the gap.

Fourth was a combination of all three men. Instead of landing a punch on Baxter, Max's fist connected with Callum as the journalist spun towards him. He pulled his punch at the last second, but it landed on the side of Callum's head, which in turn kept on coming, propelled by the full weight of his body, crashing into Max's temple with a sickening thud. For the second time today, Max's head swam and darkness swallowed him whole.

Porter moved off to the side of the door as it grumbled upwards. A car engine idled on the other side, only the wheels visible for now. He crouched down, one hand on the ground to steady himself, but the gap kept widening. Three feet now and growing. The top half of a man was visible off to the side, Callum Carr, Max's journalist mate. No sign of Max, though. He glanced back for a second as footsteps scraped behind, and it nearly cost him dearly.

He started to stand as he turned back towards the door, the gap reaching chest height, ducking slightly rather than waiting. Headlights burst into life, blinding him before he could turn away. A second later, the engine roared and Porter threw himself off to the right, away from the door, more out of instinct than choice. He felt rather than saw the car barrel through the door. Heard metal on metal as it scraped down the length of his own car, where he'd left it angled towards the warehouse.

He landed hard on his shoulder, rolling away a half turn. Heard shouting, but it was just noise, words lost in the roar of the engine and screech of rubber. Porter looked up, saw the car, a BMW, its rear end fishtailing at first but quickly coming under control. He felt a hand on his shoulder, looked up and saw Styles.

'You OK, guv?' His partner's gaze whipped from Porter, to the disappearing car, and back again.

'I'm fine,' Porter snapped, scrambling to his feet. He glanced towards the open door, saw Max and Callum both on the floor now that the car wasn't in the way. Callum wasn't moving at all, but he saw Max's head roll a few inches one way, then the other, like he was waking up after a nap. He turned, ran towards his car, shouting back towards Styles as he opened the door.

'Go check on Max.'

He slid into the driver's seat, gunned the engine, looked out and saw Styles torn between doing as he was told and seeing to Max, or jumping in the car with him. Porter spun the wheel around, hitting the accelerator before Styles could protest. The BMW was almost out of sight, heading back the way they had come in, making a break for the main road, no doubt. Porter pressed down hard on the accelerator, feeling the car lurch forwards under him. The BMW had a hundred yard head start on him and he watched as it swung out into the traffic, missing a transit van by the thickness of a coat of paint.

He couldn't afford to be quite so cavalier, and slowed a touch, lights and sirens blaring a warning, helping to create room for him to swing out without stopping. No blue lights in the rear-view. On his own for now.

'Suspect has exited Northridge Estate, turning right. Any air support?' This time of day there was every chance a chopper might be up.

'On it, guv,' replied Benayoun over the airwaves.

Up ahead, the BMW sliced in and out of its lane, chancing it every time there was a gap on the other side of the road. Porter spent the next few frustrating minutes weaving in and out between cars, matching the BMW turn for turn, never quite seeming to close the gap, all the while heading west. Where the hell was Baxter heading? Blackwall Tunnel, maybe. The turn off for that came and went in a blur.

A glance in the rear-view told him he'd lost the trailing patrol car, struggling back in traffic, presumably. He had to wind this up, and quickly, before someone got injured, or worse.

'Where's the bloody chopper?' he muttered to himself, calling out every turn they took, hoping that the cavalry would arrive and help him close this down.

He was gaining ground, an inch here, a foot there, as they tore down Romney Road, past the University of Greenwich, wrought-iron fences blurring to the point of looking like solid sheets. Up ahead, the road forked off in both directions. The BMW drifted across to the left, wheels almost scraping the kerb, then lurched over to the right at the last minute, bumping up on a traffic island, rear wheel clipping a bollard. Porter flinched, tapping on his brakes to make the turn, minus the impact. A group of pedestrians scattered as he approached, already panicked by the near miss.

The road forked again soon after, the BMW making no attempt to disguise bearing left this time, only a few car lengths ahead now. Porter recognised this next stretch, straight as an arrow for half a mile till they got past Deptford Creek. The nearest car heading towards him was at least a hundred yards away, plenty chance for them to see his blues if they hadn't already. As good a chance as any. He dropped it down a gear, floored it, and chopped into the slim advantage the BMW had. It was almost as if it had slowed a notch at the same time he'd hit the gas, but that made no sense. Unless . . .

He saw it too late, level with the passenger door of the BMW now, the glance towards him, hands jerking the wheel, sending the BMW across the front of his car. Porter jerked his wheel to the left, but it was too late. He could only watch as the nose of his car shifted right, cutting across the mercifully empty bus lane, roadside railings rushing to meet him.

He glanced to his left, saw Baxter looking back at him, face set into a mask of anger. His eyes snapped forwards, screwing shut on instinct, bracing himself for the impact. One minute he was looking at the steering wheel, the next it was an airbag, mushrooming out. His face was still angled slightly to the left, cheek slapping against the bag, seatbelt biting into his chest.

Porter groaned, touching a hand to his face, looking at his palm, expecting blood but seeing none. Blurred faces stared at him from the opposite side of the road. He blinked to clear his vision and peered over the deflating bag, expecting to see the BMW wedged into the railings alongside him, but there was nothing.

He opened the door, wincing as he climbed out, a barb of pain shooting through his wrist. Must have bent back in the impact. The bonnet was wedged halfway through the railings, metal concertinaed either side.

'You alright, mate?'

A voice behind him. He turned, saw an old man leaning on a walking stick, peering at him through thick-rimmed glasses.

'I'm fine,' he said, massaging his wrist.

'You'd better hurry up then.'

Porter looked at him, puzzled. 'Hmm?'

'If you want to catch up with him. Looked like he turned into Norway Street up on the right,' he said, using his stick as a pointer. 'That's a dead end, that is.'

It took Porter a few seconds to process, the words fuzzy in ears that still rang from the impact. He stooped into the car, spoke fast into the airwave to give them a location, then took off up the road, suit jacket flapping behind him. He fixed his eyes on the gap further up on the right, expecting to see the BMW come hurtling out any minute. Nothing. He felt rather than heard the slap of his shoes against the pavement, even over the ringing in his ears. Traffic lights up ahead winked from green to red and back again as he neared the corner. Still no car. He was breathing heavily now. So much for being in shape. His chest felt tight, bruised no doubt from the seat belt.

He took the corner wide into Norway Street and slowed to a walk, scanning ahead in the fading light. Deptford Creek was straight ahead. No sign of any car, though. Had the old man been wrong? If Baxter had shot straight over the junction, on towards Deptford, he'd be long gone. Porter sucked in deep breaths, decided to hedge his bets and jog along the side closest to the main road. If what the old man had said was true, there was nowhere to go on the opposite side anyway.

He made it as far as the mid point of the bridge when he saw it. Something in the water across the creek. He squinted, leaning forwards against the railing, staring at the choppy surface, seeing what looked like the corner of a car boot poking a foot or so above the water. His eyes flicked up, taking in the twisted metal railings where it must have ploughed through.

'Shit!' he gasped as he ran back around the edge of the creek. Might be too late. He patted at his jacket as he ran, searching for his phone until he remembered he'd left it in the cupholder of the car. No way of calling it in. No way of telling from here if Baxter was still inside.

Porter's mind raced as he ran. How long since he lost sight of the car? Two minutes? Three? Five? He wasn't even sure how quickly he'd got out of his own vehicle, head still woolly from the collision. He ran as close to the railings as he could, eyes fixed on the corner of the car, scanning for any sign of life, bubbles, anything.

Even before he reached the gap, he had already made his decision. The water level was only a few feet below the path. He pulled off his jacket, kicked off his shoes and socks when he drew level, dropped them by the side and jumped.

Max's head roared with white noise as if it was stuck inside a beehive. He opened his eyes, saw the world was on an angle, blurred shapes, swirling like a kaleidoscope as he tried to move. A wave of nausea crashed over him, driving him back down, cheek pressing against something cool.

He blinked, things slowly swimming back into focus. Callum stood beside him. No, that was wrong; Callum had his back to the floor, and Max realised for the first time that he too was stretched out on concrete. A thin crimson line ran down Callum's face from a cut in his eyebrow, down to his ear, like a plumb line to the floor.

Max heard shouts now, far away but getting closer. He tried a second time to push up from the floor. This time he managed to lift up onto an elbow as two shapes approached him. It wasn't until they were right by his head that he recognised one of them as Porter's partner.

'It's alright, I've got you,' said Styles, putting a hand behind Max's head, lowering him back to the floor. 'No, no, stay down. You're hurt.'

Max tried to smile, but even that felt like too much effort. He looked across at Callum again. Saw another officer next to him, crouching down, checking for a pulse.

'Ambulance is on the way,' said Styles. 'We'll get you checked out.'

'Where is he?' Max whispered, throat feeling like he'd gargled ground glass. 'Did you get him?'

Styles shook his head. 'Not yet, but we will. Baxter opened the door from the inside and drove at us when we tried to come through. Porter's chasing him down now, though. He won't get far.' His face softened. 'Can you tell me what happened here?'

Max tried again to push himself up, making it to a sitting position this time. His head spun like a merry-go-round, stomach churning, a spin cycle gone wrong. He pointed to the containers, hand shaking like an alcoholic gone cold turkey.

'In there.'

He closed his eyes, scrunched them tight shut, touched his free hand to his head. It hurt to touch, but he pushed anyway, as if that would force it back down, bring things back into sharper focus. When he opened them again, Styles was leaning over the nearest freezer, propping the door open, peering inside. He lowered the lid gently, moved on, doing the same with the others.

'What we got, guv?' the officer next to Callum called out.

Styles let the last lid click shut, shoulders slumping forwards as he leant both hands against it. Max felt like the world was running on slow-mo. Seemed hours since he'd woken up here. Days since he'd climbed into the BMW. Styles took an age to turn, expression grim, lips pursed, not wanting to let the words out. Staying silent wouldn't change anything, though. Gordon was still dead. The man responsible was still free.

313

'Max, I'm so sorry,' said Styles, before turning to the other police officers. 'We've got what we've been looking for. It's Gordon. We've found our list.'

There was a brief sensation of weightlessness, that roller-coaster feeling you get in the pit of your stomach, as the car fell. The shock of the cold water hit his central nervous system like a sledgehammer. He inhaled sharply a second later, water pasting trousers to his legs as it poured through the open window.

It was an older model with handles rather than buttons for the windows, and he grabbed at the crank. It snapped off cleanly and his hand flew back into his own chest. He tugged firmly at the seat belt. It might as well be set in concrete for all it moved. Hard to tell if the water in the car was rising, or if the car itself was sinking.

He snapped his head around, left then right, looking quickly over both shoulders. The shoreline was deserted. No sign of the pursuing police cars to save the day, although he could hear their sirens, little more than faint echoes. Not a Good Samaritan in sight. A handful of cars were crossing the bridge up ahead, but the chance of anyone looking out into the river was slim.

His breathing picked up pace, matching his pulse stride for stride, a ragged panting rhythm. He closed his eyes, willed himself to stay calm, stay in control. The dark tide charged in, unabated, rose until it tickled his chin. He took three deep breaths, a swimmer preparing for an underwater length. He used to be able to hold his breath for two minutes in the pool at school. He prayed that would be long enough.

The water was surprisingly cold for this time of year, made worse by his clothes clinging to him like a second skin. Porter pulled himself alongside the car, took three quick, deep breaths, and pulled himself downwards, feeling his way along the car body. He opened his eyes a fraction, but he might as well be blindfolded. The car must have kicked up all sorts from the river bed. He squeezed them shut again, feeling a gritty burn behind his eyelids.

Porter's hand curled around a ridge; the edge of a window, maybe. He reached past it with his free hand, fingertips bumping against something solid. He grabbed a handful; it felt like material. Pulled, but felt no resistance no movement. Chanced another look, but he could only make out the dark shape of the driver. Pulling the door open felt like an impossible task, even though it couldn't be more than ten feet underwater, but it gave eventually. He held himself in place with one hand against the inside of the roof now, fumbling his way across what must be the chest, feeling the seatbelt still in place. He pushed at the button, but nothing happened. Pushed a second time, a third. Nothing. Pressure grew in his chest, swelling, seeping into his head, dark and heavy.

Porter brought his hand out and pushed upwards from the car roof almost before he'd made the conscious decision, self-preservation kicking in. He burst through the surface, blowing hard like a marathon runner, gulping in lungful after lungful, treading water with a hand on the exposed corner. Over on the bridge, blurred figures stood motionless as he rubbed at his gritty eyes.

'Call 999,' he shouted. 'Do it now.' His vision was clear enough now to see one of them jabbing at what he hoped was a phone.

Deep breath in, eyes closed again. Focusing on filling his lungs. A second, then a third. He pushed up as hard as he dared on the boot and let himself plunge back down into the cloudy water.

* * *

The roller-blind door was fully open, and the forecourt was as bright as the Blackpool Illuminations. Max had made it up from the floor and into a chair, ironically the same one he'd been tied to less than an hour ago. A paramedic squatted in front of him, flicking their pen torch past his eyes, like looking down the track at the train he'd already run into. He blinked away the bright smudges it left, and saw Styles watching him from the doorway.

'Go on,' he said, 'help Jake. I'm fine.'

Styles hesitated, but only for a second, turned on his heels to go but didn't quite make it outside. Max saw him lift the airwave to his ear, heard the tinny squawk, but it was as clear as a railway station announcement. Styles's poker face lasted all of five seconds, eyebrows breaking rank, twitching upwards. A tell, but of what he couldn't say. Styles angled his body away, spoke low into the handset so Max couldn't hear. All he could do was watch Styles stand there like a waxwork as seconds trickled past like grains of sand in an hourglass. The jumbled faint words stopped and Styles turned back to face him, but Max still couldn't read the expression.

'What is it?' he asked.

'It's over,' said Styles, sounding almost disappointed. 'We've got him.'

Max felt like a puppet, strings freshly cut, ready to collapse in a heap. It was over, so why did Styles look deflated, like he'd just lost a bet?

'We've got Baxter, but he's dead. Drove his car into the river out by Deptford Creek.'

What little strength Max had left melted like ice in an oven, dropping him back down to the cool concrete, stretched out staring at the strip lights. What was he supposed to feel? Baxter should have been banged up, locked up for the rest of his life for what he'd done, for the lives he'd taken. Instead, this felt too easy, like he'd slipped away scot-free. Either way, Styles was right. It was over. Max felt hollow, insides scooped out like a melon, unsure what was worse. The fact that he'd lost a father he'd never known, and now never would, or the fact that the man responsible would never be punished. Either way, he'd never felt so alone in a room full of people.

Porter saw Jen waiting by the entrance to A&E as he climbed out of the patrol car. His hair was still wet, drips running down his neck and the back of the hoodie he'd borrowed from one of the other officers. She sprang up from the bench like she'd been plugged into the mains. The doors popped open and Max was helped out by one of the paramedics, while Callum Carr waited inside on a stretcher. Porter toyed with getting out but let them have their moment. Jen wrapped her arms around Max's waist, and even from here, Porter saw her shoulders twitching as she sobbed into his chest. Max stroked the back of her head, whispering something Porter couldn't lip-read.

He left them like that until they were ready. Saw them peel apart slowly, an inch at a time. Max looked up as he opened the car door, managed a tight smile before the paramedics ushered him inside. Porter followed them in and sat patiently as a doctor and nurse double-teamed Max, giving him a thorough once-over. He looked down at his phone, at the text from Styles.

Call me when he's settled.

That would have to keep until tomorrow. That, along with the missed calls from Sameera Misra and Milburn. Everyone who wanted a piece of him would just have to wait. He felt like the top half of a Jenga tower; the smallest of nudges in the wrong direction could bring him crashing down. Hard to tell what weighed heaviest. Maybe it was almost losing Max. Could be seeing him and Jen reunited, a happy moment for them but bittersweet for him, reminding him of everything he no longer had. Then there was Styles. How far in Milburn's pocket was he?

In between triage and treatment, Max tried to talk Porter through everything he could remember, but Porter shook his head.

'It can wait.'

'I just thought, you know, while it's fresh in my mind . . .'

'And it'll still be fresh after they've given you the once-over. It's done and dusted, nobody left to chase after.'

Max didn't look convinced but surrendered to the nurse as she came back to take a blood sample, and Porter took his cue to leave. A hug from Jen, surprisingly strong from one so small. A hand on Max's shoulder, quick squeeze, then off out into the corridor. The corridors felt narrower than he remembered them, almost claustrophobic. He double timed it through the maze of corridors, only slowing when he bowled through the exit and out into the car park.

He sucked in a lungful of cool evening air, blew it out once, twice, like a swimmer getting ready for an underwater lap. By rights he should be happy. Max would be alright. Milburn might not agree with the way they'd got here, but it was another closed case that'd look good in amongst his charts and statistics. Porter doubted whether that'd be enough to keep him happy. Maybe he should put in for some time off, get away, clear his head. The thought of having a week away, the first he'd have taken since Holly, both terrified and appealed to him, although he couldn't be sure the proportions of each.

Get tomorrow out of the way, Milburn and Misra double-teaming him, Styles somewhere in the mix, and face up to the IOPC head on. For now, all he could think of was sleep. Maybe Holly would visit him again tonight. Might even be a good one, something happy, enough to remind him what that felt like. One last stop to make first, though, before he could head home.

Styles's face was a picture when he opened the door and saw Porter, like he was expecting a pizza and had just got doorstepped by Jehovah's Witnesses.

'Guv? Everything alright?' He looked past Porter as if expecting to see a squad car or two blocking off the road.

'Ask me on the way out,' said Porter, stepping towards the door.

Styles retreated inside, leaving Porter to pull the door closed behind him. Truth be told, Porter still wasn't sure this was a good idea after the day he'd had. Part of him still said to let things stew until tomorrow, but he knew heading home would make things worse. More chance of things boiling over at the station in the morning; public, messy. Not his style. No point letting fester what you can lance today.

'Emma not about?' Porter asked, having just watched her leave five minutes earlier from the safety of his car.

'Popped round to drop something off at her mum's. Coffee?' Styles said, flicking the kettle on without waiting for a reply.

'Nah, I'm good, thanks.'

A cuppa meant committing to at least a ten-minute stay, and Porter still wasn't sure whether he'd want to hang around that long. Styles rattled a teaspoon of instant coffee into his cup, back to Porter.

'How's Max? They let him home?'

'Uh-uh. Overnighter to be safe.'

Porter waited patiently as Styles picked up the half-boiled kettle, sloshed water in and gave it a noisy stir. Styles looked uneasy as he took a seat opposite him at the kitchen table, like a suspect about to be grilled. There was something else, though – remorse, maybe? Whatever it was, Porter felt himself dial back a notch, set aside the full-frontal approach he'd mapped out on the way over here. Styles was eyes down, staring into his coffee for a second, deciding how to start.

'I love being a copper,' he said, looking up at Porter now. 'S'all I've wanted to do since I was kid, and since I joined Homicide and Serious, it's been . . .' He looked cross at himself, struggling to pick the right words. 'We don't win 'em all, but the ones that we do really feel like they count, you know?'

Porter nodded but stayed silent.

'When Emma told me she was pregnant, I was made up. I mean literally over the moon. You know we've been trying for a while, and when she told me, it felt like I'd won the lottery: job, wife, family.' He counted them off on his fingers.

Porter measured himself against the checklist. One out of three. Saw Styles trying to make his point but struggling.

'Em thinks the world of you, you know that? We both do. It's just . . .' He tailed off, looking around the kitchen for inspiration. 'She worries. About me. The job. I keep telling her it's not like we're across in the States, everyone packing pistols, but she's not been the same since what happened with Locke.'

That had been without a doubt the messiest case Porter had worked on. East End gangster passing himself off as a pillar of the community, all the while knee-deep in everything from drugs to people trafficking. It had ended badly for some. People had died, including Locke, shot twice, and another officer, Andy Palmer, had been gunned down. Could just as easily have been Porter or Styles.

'She's paranoid now. Thinks that's how every day is going to play out for me.'

He looked back down at his coffee. Porter bit back the urge to speak, sensing his partner hadn't quite finished.

'She's asked me for a compromise,' he said finally, lips pursed tight enough to show he wasn't convinced that a compromise is what it would be. 'She doesn't want me to leave the force, but she wants me to go back to my old job. Reckons there's less chance of running into nutters with guns. I love what I do, but I love my wife as well. I just . . . ah, God, I don't know.'

Styles sighed, long and loud. Looked up at Porter like a kid asking their parents' blessing. Porter had come here ready to tear a strip, to tell Styles where to go, but seeing him clearly squashed between the two sides, nowhere to turn, the anger he had left just melted away, changing shape, reforming into something else. Not quite jealous at the fact that his partner had something away from work, something powerful enough to pull at him like this. No, not jealousy. More like acceptance. That this wasn't personal, at least not about him. The fact that Styles hadn't approached Milburn yet, and Porter believed him when he'd said that; it spoke volumes of how hard this had been for him.

Who was he to expect Styles to choose him, the job, over his wife and child? What would he have done if Holly had presented him with the same choice? That decided it for him.

'It's OK,' he said.

Styles didn't react, just stared at the table, lost in his own thoughts still, not back into listen mode yet.

'Hey, it's OK,' Porter said again.

This time Styles heard him. Looked up, confused, clearly expecting something else – an argument, a fight, but not that.

'I don't blame you for not saying anything, and I don't think you're with Milburn. I was out of line saying that. I can tell it's not been an easy decision for you, and that counts for something. That's good enough for me.'

'Look, guv, it's not like—'

Porter held up a hand, getting up from the table. 'Honestly, it's fine. I understand. Anyway, it's been a long day, and I know you can be a bit of a diva if you don't get your beauty sleep, so I'll see you in the morning, yeah?'

Styles looked like he had more to say, but just nodded. They walked to the door in silence, and Porter turned as he stepped outside, hands in pockets.

'Might not feel like it, but this was a good day at the office. We won today. This was one of those ones that count.'

He didn't wait for a response but hadn't heard the door close behind him by the time he got to his car. Styles stood framed in the doorway, hand raised, waving goodbye. Porter returned the gesture, smiled even though he doubted Styles could see it in the fading light, and climbed into his car.

This was a win, he reminded himself as he turned the corner, Styles no more than a glow in the rear-view mirror. Max was safe. Stuart Leyson, the last man standing from the list, was safe. To hell with Milburn, and whatever spin he'd put on this. Probably a good thing that Styles would be moving on. No sense in him getting tarred and feathered as well.

He'd stand and take whatever Milburn threw. That went for the IOPC as well. He didn't need them to tell him they'd won today. He'd stand up in front of all those sanctimonious bastards and stare them down. Alone.

CHAPTER THIRTY-TWO

Porter held out both hands to take the mug from Jen. She retreated back to the sofa, sliding under Max's arm. The pair of them put on a good front, but the effects were still there if you knew where to look. Jen wouldn't meet his gaze for more than a few seconds, eyes constantly flicking to the door and windows. Max drew her in close, some of last week's tension still there in the way he sat, a little too stiff and upright.

Only a week had passed since Baxter had ploughed into the river; it felt more like a month. The story had only just moved to the inside pages of the tabloids, and the clips of Milburn at the press conference had stopped appearing on the news highlight reels. Milburn had been noticeably distant this past week, although Porter guessed it was more for selfish reasons. Wouldn't play well to be the man disciplining an officer who the press was bigging up for bagging two huge cases in the space of a year. Why run the risk when he could just wait and let the IOPC do that for him? A hearing had been scheduled for a week tomorrow, and Porter could practically hear Milburn's hands rubbing together every time he walked through the office.

Sameera Misra was another itch still to be scratched. She'd called in sick the day after they fished Baxter out of the water, but Porter knew he couldn't dodge that bullet for ever. He fully expected the IOPC to mandate it as part of whatever they decided.

In total, nine bodies had been removed from the chest freezers in Baxter's storage unit. Harold Mayes took the tally into double figures, not including Baxter himself. Stuart Leyson had paled with relief to the point of looking anaemic when they told him what had happened, and that he was safe.

The car Baxter had fled the scene in had been pulled from the river, his body still pinned in place by the seatbelt. The irony was that at the time he'd lost control and plunged into the water, the officers in pursuit had actually lost sight of him. He'd been within touching distance of escape before he skidded through the guard rails and into the icy water.

Both front windows had been open, which had meant the water could flood in unchecked. Best guess said it would have flooded in less than a minute. When they pulled him out, his face looked like he'd gone twelve rounds. The airbag had evidently failed to work, and the steering wheel showed signs of impact where his face had struck, more damage to the smashed nose Max had already told them to expect.

'I'll be honest with you and say I don't know how much further we'll get,' said Porter, sipping at his coffee. 'We're following the money trail, but he didn't leave us a hell of a lot to go on.'

He ran them through what they'd managed to uncover so far. All the bodies on ice had been positively identified, as had Baxter himself. Max and Callum's accounts of Baxter's confession, plus the evidence at the storage unit, made for a pretty compelling case that nobody had tried to poke holes in.

Preliminary autopsy results showed that all the men had a significant amount of water in their lungs, suggesting drowning as the likely cause of death. Poetic, then, that Baxter had met the same fate. Taking the lead from Baxter's confession to Max, there was no motive or link to the victims other than money. They had all been successful men in their own right, and Baxter had tricked, tormented and tortured them out of a little over eight and a half million all told. Sold shares, emptied accounts, even sold property. That was what ten lives had been worth when you stripped it back. Saddest part of it all was that nobody had even noticed they had gone.

They hadn't found anything in Baxter's past that should have marked him out as someone capable of anything like this. A plane ticket to Mexico, leaving Heathrow the evening after he'd snatched Max, suggested he hadn't planned to stick around. Whether it was to have been just a break, or maybe him disappearing for good, they'd never know for sure. With the kind of money he had to hand, his options would have been almost limitless, so maybe it was better it had ended this way rather than have risked him getting away entirely.

The money was the piece of the puzzle that still eluded them. Baxter had covered his tracks well. As each man's accounts had been closed, the money had done a hop, skip and jump into a dozen banks across half a dozen countries, any trail evaporating like dew in the morning sun.

'We'll keep trying,' Porter said with a shrug. 'But you want my honest take, it's highly unlikely.'

'That's alright,' said Max, 'I know you're doing everything you can.'

'Goes without saying. Even if they shelve it, I'll keep looking at it whenever I can. He took nigh on three quarters of a million quid from your dad, if you include the house. That's yours if we can find it.'

Max gave a sad smile that Porter read all too easily. Money wouldn't bring him back. The doorbell rang, and Jen went to get up but Max patted her leg.

'I'll get it, sweetheart. It'll be her, right on time.'

'I'd best head, then,' said Porter. He bent over to give Jen a brief hug, and followed Max to the front door, seeing a pair of arms reach around, patting lightly against his back. Max's mum wore a plain back skirt and jacket, hair tied back in a tight bun. Porter had only met her a handful of times over the years but could have sworn the grey streaks to her hair were a new addition. She released her grip on Max and stepped inside, spotting Porter leaning against the wall.

'Jake,' she said, advancing on him, arms out.

'Hey, how you doing?' he said as she hugged him, cringing at how inadequate his own words sounded.

'I'm OK,' she said. 'You're coming with us?'

He nodded, and she turned back to Max, giving him a once up and down. 'You've forgotten your top button,' she said, stepping closer, tutting as she fastened it, sliding the knot of his black tie up an inch, flush against the collar.

'Can't have you keeping your father waiting,' she said, trying to smile at her own joke, but she wore it more like a grimace.

Porter felt like an intruder. Wished he'd made his excuses and met them there. An engine growled softly outside.

'Jen?' Max called out. 'Honey, that's the car. They're here.'

It was time.

Only six other people besides Porter were there to pay their respects, and that included the priest. Two of Gordon's former colleagues had turned up. Max, his mum and Jen. Porter looked around at the empty pews in the church, listened to the priest's voice echo, and it struck him how sad it was that this was the best send-off Gordon Jackson could get.

The service dragged, and the wooden bench was as comfortable as sitting on concrete. *That's the answer*, he thought. *You want more people to come to church, invest in a few cushions.* He stood and sat mechanically when prompted by the priest, and, when it was all over, filed out at the back of a pitifully small line, across the churchyard, and stood at the graveside as the priest said a few final words before the coffin was lowered.

He saw the words carved into granite included 'Father', giving Gordon the title in death that he hadn't realised he had for most of his life. He looked at Max, tried to read the expression, but it kept shifting. Could be grief, might be anger or frustration. Most likely a mix of the lot. One thing he knew Max felt for sure was guilt. He'd said as much when they spoke yesterday. Porter felt an element of responsibility for that. Stupid, he knew, but that was him all over. Blaming himself for other people's shit. He wished he'd never pointed it out all the same.

The fact that Baxter had chosen Gordon, with no family to speak of, because Max had written his letters to Gordon's office. There had been nothing in the house when Baxter had come calling. No emails in the inbox. If Max had written sooner, had met up with his dad sooner, would Baxter have crossed him off the list?

Porter knew the guilt would fade in time. No sense judging yourself on things you had no knowledge of, no idea of what was about to happen. Even as he thought it, he knew he was being a hypocrite. He'd clung on to his own guilt over Holly the way a child hangs on to their comfort blanket. Maybe if Max could let go of his, he could too. Could, or should? Both.

Porter walked in just in time to see Styles coming out of Milburn's office, head down, looking at his phone. Texting Emma, most likely, telling her it was a done deal. He could blame Milburn for many things, but Styles wasn't one of them, even if he had tried to manipulate him into talking behind Porter's back.

Porter went for the head down, look busy approach. He knew in his heart this was the right thing for Styles to do, maybe not career-wise in the short term, but for him, for his family. He heard the chair squeak as his partner dropped into it but kept staring at his screen as he spoke.

'All sorted then?'

'Yep,' said Styles, sounding a little too cheery for Porter's liking. He could at least pretend it was still a tough call. No need to sound bright and breezy just because Porter hadn't been arsy with him this last week.

'So that's it then. Hope you're not expecting too much of a send-off. We'll wait till you're gone to throw the real party.'

'There you go again, making those assumptions of yours. They'll get you into bother one of these days.'

'Assumptions about what?' Porter gave him half a glance.

'About me going. Word is you're too much of a liability to be left on your own.'

That got Porter's attention, his head snapping up. 'What do you mean by that?'

'What do you think I mean? Just told Milburn that rumours of me wanting to leave have been greatly exaggerated.'

Porter shook his head. 'You don't have to do that. Emma will kill you.'

Styles folded his arms, huffed out a loud breath. 'We talked it out. She's OK with it now.'

'How the hell did you change her mind?'

'I told her that I'd struggle to give any kind of lecture about standing up for what you believe in to our son or daughter if I didn't do it myself. That whole mess with Locke was the exception, not the rule. We don't go up against guys like that every day, thank God!' He leant forwards now, elbows on knees. 'And I told her you'd always have my back, so she could take it out on you if anything bad happened.'

What little tension was left between them fell away, like shrugging off heavy wet clothes. They both laughed, and, for the first time in weeks, Porter felt like it wasn't just him against the world. A small victory, but he'd take whatever came his way.

CHAPTER THIRTY-THREE

Porter tried every angle he could think of, but it was like chasing shadows. The money was like smoke on the breeze. Max and Jen were both back at work. Milburn had publicly said they'd keep pursuing the missing funds in his last statement, but, two-faced tosser that he was, had said privately that the case was on the back burner.

Porter sat in the room he and Styles had commandeered as their incident room, staring at the neatly stacked boxes. The storyboard listing all the missing men had to come down today, packed away to gather dust. He wished now that he hadn't sent Styles home early. Could do this in half the time if he was still around, but it didn't hurt to throw him back Emma's way, keep her sweet bearing in mind the concession she'd made.

He worked through a name at a time, popping magnets off the board and stacking the headshots neatly into boxes, as if anyone would care. They'd probably never be opened again until it came time to bin them. The grubby rag just smeared his notes against the whiteboard. It'd need wetting to do the job properly.

Porter was so lost in the tedium of filing, sorting and stacking, he didn't hear the footsteps approaching until they were practically behind him. He looked over his shoulder and saw Benayoun with Max in tow, visitor's pass around his neck and brightly wrapped object in his hand.

'You come to make a confession?' said Porter.

'Found him loitering out by the front, trying to call you, guv,' said Benayoun.

Porter glanced at his phone. 'Ah, it's on silent. Sorry.'

'Just thought I'd swing by and give you a little thank you gift,' Max said, holding out what was clearly a bottle of something wrapped up. 'Jen and I are heading off for a few days. Fresh air, change of scenery and all that jazz.'

Porter took the gift. Turned it end over end. Heard a soft *glug* as he did.

'Is it a football?'

Benayoun rolled her eyes, leaving the two of them alone in the room.

'You nearly done for the day? Time for a quick pint?' said Max.

'Why the hell not. Rest of this can wait till tomorrow.'

Porter picked up the last few sheets on his desk and dropped them into the box marked *David Marsh*. The flipchart was still intact, although the whiteboard only had two pictures left on; Alan Bowles, with his column still scrawled below, and another sitting above a grey swirl of what used to be black marker pen. He looked up, saw Max staring at the faces, moving towards the board and sliding one of the pictures out from under its magnet.

'Just leave 'em, mate. I'll sort everything tomorrow.'

'Just getting them back in the right order for you,' said Max, peeling one from the flipchart and replacing it with the one he held. 'Doesn't help if you've got the guest of honour in the wrong seat.'

Porter gave a confused half-smile. 'What do you mean?'

'Baxter. You had him over there on the other board.'

'Uh-uh, he's already there,' said Porter, pointing at the picture Max had just removed.

'Him?' Max held up the picture in his right hand. 'What you on about? This is him,' he said, dropping one hand and raising the other like a ground controller signalling planes on a runway. 'They're similar, but I won't forget this face in a hurry.' He wafted the picture from the whiteboard like a referee showing the red card. 'I'm telling you, this . . . this is Baxter.'

'Can't be,' said Porter, looking from one picture to the other. 'Makes no sense, can't be.'

'Who's this guy, then, Jake?' Max held up the picture that had been stuck next to Alan Bowles.

Porter walked over, took the pictures from Max and slapped them down on the table.

'We got a positive ID, Max. DNA match against samples we took from his flat. There's no real room for error there.' He stabbed a finger at the picture on the left. 'That's James Bannister. He was another client from AMT. Had the same contact as your dad as well, but he wasn't one of the bodies on ice. He's still missing.'

'And I'm telling you, this is the man who had me tied to a chair.' Max folded his arms, daring Porter to call him out on it again.

'Max, you'd been through the mill that night. Don't forget you took a fairly heavy shot to the head. There's every chance you—'

'Don't go there, Jake. I know what I saw.' Max was animated now, pacing past Porter, stopping only to point at the picture to punctuate his words. 'That's him. His hair was shorter, but that's him. One hundred per cent.'

Porter looked long and hard at the pictures. Two faces cut from the same cloth. Truth be told, Porter hadn't really paid much attention to any of the pictures in the last few weeks, especially Bannister's. It hadn't been on their original list from the laptop recovered at Harold Mayes's house. There hadn't been anything conclusive to even put him in the same boat as the others. He focused on Baxter instead. Only met the man once. The man in the picture was clean shaven, whereas the man on the doorstep had had a chin full of stubble.

He switched to Bannister's picture again. He looked familiar as well. They all had. Another one of the reasons why they'd been picked. He closed his eyes, thinking back to Baxter's doorstep, seeing the face again. He sensed Max by his shoulder, heard his breathing. Stood like that a few seconds more, until it hit him, connecting like a good body shot. That feeling in his stomach like he'd just driven fast over a hump in the road.

His eyes snapped open and he picked up Bannister's picture, staring at the face. Not into the eyes this time, but just above. The eyebrow, a thin but visible scar line running through it. His fingers relaxed their grip and the picture fell edge first to the ground. He turned to face Max, felt his face redden.

'Oh, shit.'

CHAPTER THIRTY-FOUR

One week earlier

He grabbed at the handle. Pulled with all his might until the crank snapped. Wouldn't do to give his passenger a chance to wind the window up, not now the water had started pouring in. Seatbelt next. He tugged at it. Firmly in place, and with the damage he'd done to the catch there was little chance of the driver freeing himself even if he did come round.

Quick check of the shoreline and bridge up ahead. Deserted. No witnesses. No one to play hero and dive in after the car. Perfect. He looked across, stared at Joseph Baxter's body in the driver's seat. Watched as the water rose up his legs. No reaction.

Baxter's nose looked like it had been rotated a full three-sixty, thanks to a pre-river slam into the steering wheel. A necessary piece of improv to match the damage Max had managed to inflict on his own face. Truth be told, it was a small mercy for Baxter. He had been petrified enough being led from the boot after being tossed around during the escape. It was practically doing the guy a favour to let him sleep through these final moments. Once he was sparked out, it had been a simple case of shifting from park into drive, pushing Baxter's foot down on the accelerator and crashing through the old railings.

He took three deep breaths, water creeping up his chest, towards his chin, and he placed a hand over Baxter's. The front of the car tilted downwards, slowly at first, picking up pace until it went under completely. It was almost impossible to see past the dashboard under the surface, and he had to be sure that Baxter was going nowhere. A slow ten count, then he grabbed the sealed bag by his feet and pulled himself through the window and up to the surface.

Quick glance around. No prying eyes. He swam around the bend of the creek and hauled himself out of the water onto an old wooden pier. Five minutes later, wet clothes were stuffed into a bin liner, swapped for a dry set from a waterproof bag he'd dragged out of the car with him. The discarded clothes would end up in a bin a safe distance away. He pulled a cap down low, shading his eyes, and walked calmly down Glaisher Street, and round onto the main road. The first two police cars had pulled up by the river, lights strobing over the water. A figure stood apart from the others, over by the railings, blanket wrapped around his shoulders. He recognised Detective Porter. Took a moment to drink it in, watching the man who had come close to stopping him for good.

He checked his watch. Just over ten minutes since he had clambered onto the bank. No surviving that. They'd have their body; the epilogue to their story. Baxter had had to die in a way that left no room for doubt. The others had mostly met their fate in bathtubs, but Baxter's lungs needed to be full of river water when they sliced him open at autopsy.

336

He had laughed when Max called him by Baxter's name at the storage unit. Even if they managed to strip away the layers, figure it all out, he'd be long gone. He looked down at the pavement as he walked, hiding his broken nose from any passers-by.

Careful. Always careful.

CHAPTER THIRTY-FIVE

One week later

The dealer studied the two men left in the game. The gentleman to his left was marginal chip leader, an honour that had swung back and forth several times in the last half hour. Somewhere in his mid forties. Haircut bordering on military. He was a man of few words, eyes barely leaving the cards. A conservative player, only playing hands where he had something worth fighting for.

His opponent was at least two decades older, with a shock of white hair and a goatee beard Colonel Sanders would have been proud of. The dealer had worked a Texas Hold 'Em table for years, seen thousands of players come and go, and fancied himself as a pretty good judge of character. His money was on the older guy. He'd played his hands to perfection most of the night. Unhurried checks, casual raises.

The younger man had been staring at the neat row of five cards, face up, for over a minute now. Both black sevens, jack of hearts, four of spades and ace of clubs as the river card. The younger man had declined to bet, checking all the way through. The colonel had goaded him into action with a few small raises, but had made his move, pushing half his chip stack in when the ace had appeared.

The dealer sized them both up. His guess was that the colonel had made his full house; sevens and aces, hitting on the last card. Smart move from the young man was to fold.

'All in.'

It was little more than a whisper, and the dealer wasn't certain he'd heard right, but sure enough, the man placed both palms around his stack and pushed them into the centre of the table. The dealer looked at the colonel, saw a twinkle of triumph. He'd called it right. Old age and treachery had won out against youth.

'I'll call,' said the colonel, in a voice rough around the edges from a lifetime of cigars, and toppled his stacks over into the middle.

'On your backs, please, gentlemen,' said the dealer, noticing for the first time a ring of spectators chattering like magpies, gathered to watch what must surely be the final hand.

The colonel was still smiling as he flipped his cards over. Two aces for the full house. The smile morphed into something else when he saw the two red sevens the younger man had been sitting on all along. He had slow played four of a kind, crafty bastard. Only played strong hands all night, then dragged his heels with the best hand of the game.

The colonel shook his head as the young man reached forwards, raking his chips in like pulling earth into a hole. No sign of emotion, though, no punching the air, barely even a smile as he shook hands with the colonel. He was a cold one alright.

* * *

He could tell from the look the dealer gave him, that they all gave him, they thought it was a lucky hand. Might have been a riskier move if he hadn't sussed the older guy's tell an hour ago. Just hadn't seemed worth exploiting until it was all or nothing.

He sniffed again, daren't blow it, though. Still tender to the touch, let alone to risk a full blast into a hankie. The yellow-brown saffron shadows of bruising bordered on jaundiced.

He cashed in his chips, headed up to his room on the tenth floor. Of course, it wasn't booked in his name. Today he was Brian McDermott. Tomorrow, well, he'd just wait and see what that would bring. He helped himself to an overpriced whisky from the minibar, switched the lights off again and stood cloaked in shadow, looking out over the Vegas strip. It looked like someone had vomited neon, bright lights drawing in the punters like moths.

A hundred casinos, thousands of new faces every day, blurring into one teeming mass of people. No one knowing or caring about who they rubbed shoulders with. James Bannister smiled in the darkness. Saw a warped version of it reflected back at him. He'd fit in here just fine.

EPILOGUE

Porter glanced at his watch. Forty minutes until his hearing started. He still had time. Traffic was mercifully light as he drove along Marylebone High Street. One side was swathed in scaffolding like it was getting wrapped up for the winter. The other, still exposed, a row of shops, topped by four storeys of apartments. Million-pound properties within a stone's throw of charity shops. Porter wondered how many of those residents' cast-offs found their way into any of them. Precious few.

He slowed to a crawl as he spotted the blue shop front a hundred yards ahead. Anywhere round here would do, even if he had to make a few trips. A white van pulled out fifty yards ahead. Perfect. He swung into the space and jumped out, opening the rear door carefully. A few of the black bags had fallen against it, and he reached in, pulling them out, stacking a neat pile on the pavement.

Six in total. More in the boot, but he'd come back for them.

He grabbed the nearest two, one in each hand, tops tied like bunny ears twisting around his fingers. Three in each hand and he was good to go. Halfway to the shop he realised he'd left the car unlocked. It'd keep till he went back for the next lot.

The window of Cancer Research was an Aladdin's cave of books and handbags, guarded by a pair of mannequins in last season's jackets. The lad behind the counter reminded him of his school dinner lady. Sixty-something, with flushed face and a neck like a turkey, liable to reach out and pinch both cheeks like a favourite auntie. She gave him a warm smile as he approached the counter, turning sideways to make sure his bags didn't send any clothes rails flying.

'Got some clothes to donate. There's a few more bags in the car.'

She bustled around the counter, taking the bags from him one at a time, muttering thank yous as each one was passed over.

'Having a bit of a clear-out, are we?' she asked.

'They're my wife's. She passed away,' he said, surprised at how calm he felt admitting that to a stranger. It had felt like a taboo subject for so long.

Her face folded into a network of concerned creases, and he wouldn't have been surprised if she'd tried to hug him after she took the last bag. He made the second trip, checking his watch again, although part of him wanted to be late just to stick two fingers up to the bureaucracy of it all. He took another round of sympathies mixed with gratitude and made his excuses, leaving her to sift through the contents of the bags.

He had told himself he could always do this another day, always keep the bags in the car, but now that he'd left them behind, it felt right. It was time. It had been time for longer than he was willing to admit. One last thing before his hearing. A quick WhatsApp tapped out. He could see it was delivered almost instantly, but the two ticks stayed grey. Unread, for now.

He jumped back into his car and took a shortcut along Crawford Street and onto Edgware Road, heading back to the station. What's the worst they could do to him? Kick him out? Doubtful. He hadn't actually harmed Patchett, and he'd seen colleagues get off with slaps on wrists for worse. One thing was for sure: he needed some time to himself after this. These last few years had been tough, and not just because of Holly. The corruption scandal around his previous CO, George Campbell, had cast an unfair shadow on him, and Milburn's political games weren't what he'd signed up to take part in. He had no intention of leaving, more just a case of needing to work out how to deal with this shit on his own terms. Besides, he thought, what else would he do even if he did spit his dummy out?

He managed to make it up to the conference room on the fourth floor without bumping into anyone. Final time check. Two minutes early. Porter walked over to the window, looked out over Edgware Road, at the dozens of people lucky enough to be heading home to loved ones, most of whom would never have to contend with the underbelly of the city. For most, London was a diverse Petri dish where anyone and anything could thrive, given the right conditions. He'd seen the best and worst of it in the last two years, but it was his, warts and all, and he wasn't about to walk away from it any time soon.

The purr of a silenced text message. He pulled the phone out. Two new messages. The first was from Styles, making him smile.

Don't let the bastards grind you down.

The second turned the smile into a full-blown grin. The one he had been waiting for.

Two o'clock is perfect. George Street – Costa? x

The kiss Evie Simmons tagged on the end was probably nothing. Lots of women did these days, according to Styles. Could be nothing. Might be everything.

ACKNOWLEDGEMENTS

There's a big part of me still finding it surreal that I'm a published author, and marvels at the notion that anyone is interested in stuff I basically make up. There's so much more that goes into bringing a book to life than I ever truly appreciated though, and the author lumping together a first draft is just the first step on a long road, so a few thank yous are most definitely in order.

Thanks to my agent, Jo, for all her advice, input and guidance in navigating what are still relatively unchartered waters. Thanks also to Amy for flying the flag in Jo's absence, and to Jessica and Mirette for finding Porter & Styles a home outside of the UK too. To all at A & B – Susie, Daniel, Kelly, Lesley, Christina and Kirsten – the finished product is that much better for having you all on my side to polish it up, and help it magically appear on bookshelves. DCI John Bent of Northumbria Police was kind enough to steer me right on a number of matters of procedure, and make it sound as if I know what I'm talking about. Any mistakes left in there after all of these fine people have contributed are all on me. Shout out to Fiona Sharp in the Durham branch of Waterstones for all her support and welcoming me into the local crime book club, all of whom have made me feel right at home. Thank you to each and every reader who took a chance on an author they'd never heard of with *What Falls Between the Cracks*, and for the reviews, emails and banter on social media. Thank you to Dee Williams for bidding on the right to name a character, and supporting The Book Club on Facebook with their charity fundraiser in the process.

My mam and dad continue to be an incredible source of support in every aspect of my life. Who knew when you piled a steady stream of books in front of me as a kid that I'd end up writing them for a living? My kids – Lucy, Jake and Lily – you're my motivation for persevering long enough to bash out words on those days when the plot feels like it's conspiring against me and the story won't flow. My in-laws, Jude and Malc, and brother-in-law, Michael – thank you for all your support and for not holding me to the foolish promise I made to take all of Nic's hoarded rubbish from your loft into mine.

Saving the best till last, as always, none of this would mean as much, or be as much fun, without the support of my wife, Nic. Partner in crime and proofreader. Everything's just that little bit better because of you.

ROBERT SCRAGG had a random mix of jobs before taking the dive into crime writing; he's been a bookseller, pizza deliverer, Karate instructor and football coach. He lives in Tyne & Wear, is a founding member of the North East Noir crime writers group.

robertscragg.com
@robert_scragg

DID YOU CATCH THE FIRST PORTER & STYLES MYSTERY?

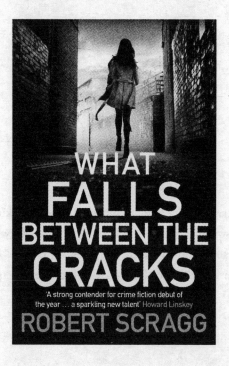

'A strong contender for crime fiction debut of the year ... a sparkling new talent' Howard Linskey

ROBERT SCRAGG

When the severed hand of Natasha Barclay is found in her abandoned London flat, Detective Inspector Jake Porter and his partner Detective Sergeant Nick Styles begin an investigation into her disappearance. Neither can understand why no one has reported her missing.

The pair discover links to another case and uncover a tragic family history that soon takes on a more sinister twist. Hampered by the widespread fear of a loca heavy as well as internal politics, Porter and Styles are scrabbling for answers, but will what they find ever see the light of day?

ALL THAT
IS BURIED

A parent's worst fear is realised when seven-year-old Libby Hallforth goes missing at a funfair; no witnesses, no leads, and no trace. Months later, human remains are found, but they're too old to be Libby. It's the tip of a gruesome iceberg – bodies, buried in pairs, carefully laid to rest in a ritualistic manner. For DI Jake Porter and DS Nick Styles, the trail for Libby is cold, and everyone is a suspect. Nobody can be trusted, including the Hallforth family. Libby's chances of being found alive are fading fast, along with Porter's chances of stopping a killer before they strike again.

To discover more great books and to
place an order visit our website at
allisonandbusby.com

Don't forget to sign up to our free newsletter at
allisonandbusby.com/newsletter
for latest releases, events and exclusive offers

[f] **Allison & Busby Books**
[t] **@AllisonandBusby**

You can also call us on
020 3950 7834
for orders, queries
and reading recommendations